THE PHOTO ALBUM

BRIAN O'SULLIVAN

I spent my college years - all seven of them - in Santa Barbara, so this book is dedicated to all those great nights that I barely remember. Study Hall (yes, it's a bar) and O'Malley's, I'm looking at you...

BOBBY MCGOWAN

I t was a sudden, impulsive move.

I saw a photo album and decided to reach for it. It had been quite a few years since I'd thumbed through some old family pictures. It sounded like an enjoyable way to pass the time as I waited for my father.

The album I'd grabbed was labeled "1999."

I would have been eight years old, and my younger sister Jenny would have been six. My parents celebrated their 10th wedding anniversary that year. I started leafing through the album, looking forward to old memories flooding my brain.

Every plastic sleeve had eight pictures - four on the left and four on the right. They were mostly 4 x 6s, but a few sleeves contained some 3 x 5s that didn't quite fit in the assigned spots.

The first gem I saw was the four of us in Hawaii for our parents' anniversary. We're all wearing Hawaiian-style shirts. Jenny and I have leis around our necks. We're looking up at our parents, unsure what is happening.

I turned another sleeve and started laughing at the next picture I saw. Jenny and I were wearing about the goofiest costumes you could imagine. It was Halloween, and we were both dressed as Prince. We had the requisite afro, purple suit, and a puffy white shirt. I had an unopened beer in my hand, and Jenny had one of those miniature alcohol bottles you'd get on a plane. To complete the costume, we both had a sash that said, "Party like it's 1999!"

It was a wild, hilarious, creative costume. It gave me great joy to see it again.

I leafed through some more pages. Most of them were just pictures around the house. My Dad mowing the lawn. Jenny and I dressed for our first day of school. My mother reading a book by the fire after what I'm sure was a long day looking after us kids.

I tried to move to the next sleeve, but it was stuck together with the page that followed. I attempted to separate them, but it started to rip. I could see some sort of formerly purple liquid binding them together. My guess was that red wine had been the culprit. Possibly grape juice.

I grabbed my keychain and used one of the smaller keys to slide between the two sleeves so as not to rip them. After a good twenty seconds, the sleeves finally separated, and I grabbed a nearby paper towel to set between them so they wouldn't become glued again.

I flipped the page again.

The four pictures on the left weren't all that interesting. There were two pictures of my parents' roof torn apart and two of shingles covering the ground in front of their house.

One of the pictures on the right side of the sleeve caught my attention. It was a picture of my parents with two men in their late twenties. They were standing next to a medium-sized dumpster filled with shingles. I assumed the two guys in the photo were the roofers.

The look on one of the guy's faces is what intrigued me. No, that's not fair. It disgusted me. No, that's not fair either. It had me on edge. That would be most accurate. While the other three were looking straight at the camera, this guy was looking side-eyed at my mother. And not in a flattering way. His piercing eyes were looking at my mother as a piece of meat. Lust was on this guy's mind, that was for sure.

But maybe my mind only went there because my mother had been murdered.

That's right. In 2003, someone broke into our house and strangled her to death. It was the worst day of my life and will remain so for however long I live. It changed our family dynamic forever. My father has been a shell of himself ever since. Once my sister Jenny graduated from high school, she moved back east for college, and she's never been back to Santa Barbara, where we grew up, for more than a week at a time since.

My sister and I butt heads with the best of them, but I love her in spite of it. I think the memory of our mother's death prevented her from ever moving back to Santa Barbara. She is now married and living in Connecticut with two young boys under the age of four. She's never moving back.

I was the opposite. I stayed local. I went to college at UC Santa Barbara and remained close - at least geographically - with my father. Everyone reacts to tragedy differently, and I don't blame my sister for doing what she did, but staying in Santa Barbara was the right decision for me.

So you can see why I might be taken aback when I see a guy giving my mother the side eye. I looked at the photograph again.

There were four people in total.

On the far left was one of the two workers. Second from the left was my father. Second from the right was my mother. And then, on the far right, was the man ogling my mother. Everyone was holding what appeared to be a lemonade. Behind them was the dumpster with the shingles piled up.

The two workers wore matching gray tank tops. My mother wore a yellow, summery dress; my father wore green shorts and a white T-shirt. My father didn't usually wear shorts, so I assumed this picture was taken mid-summer.

I pulled the photo out of the album. I looked on the back to see if there was a description written as my mother had been prone to do. Nothing.

I slid the photo back into the sleeve.

"Going through old photo albums?"

I was startled. I hadn't heard my father coming, and I jumped ever so slightly when he spoke.

"I am. Do you know who these people are, Dad?"

I pointed to the picture in question, and he grabbed the album and moved it to within a few inches of his face. My father was only sixty, but his eyesight resembled someone twenty years his senior. His whole body did, really. He'd recently had a hip replacement, two years after having a knee replacement as well. He had arthritis in just about every place you could imagine. It's safe to say that my father was no longer moving around like he did when we were children.

"I sure do," he said. "They were our roofers. Our shingles were quite old and at a serious fire risk, so we installed a new roof."

"I vaguely remember that."

3

"Do you know who took that picture?" my father asked.

"Me?"

"You sure did. That was their last day on the job, I believe. Your mother made them lemonade. It was a hot day. It had been hot every day they were up on that roof. I think it was mid-August if memory serves. An ice-cold lemonade was the least we could do."

The picture held even more intrigue, knowing I'd taken it.

"Do you remember the names of the roofers?"

My father took his time thinking about it. While his body was falling apart, his mind was still sharp as a tack. As I said, he'd never fully recovered from our mother's death, but it hadn't affected his cognitive ability. Those may not seem related, but I did a lot of studying on families whose loved one was murdered, and frequently, the spouse's mental acuity suffers significantly in the months and years that follow.

"Sorry, I don't remember their names, but I do remember how we came around to hiring them."

"How?"

"Your crazy uncle Rick."

Rick had earned his nickname. The guy was a wild man like no one I'd ever met. He was my mother's older brother and, some might say, the black sheep of the family. My mother loved him, but she'd tense up whenever he said he was coming over. Even at a young age, I noticed things like that.

"How is Rick?" I asked.

We hadn't mentioned him in a few years. After my mother was killed, we kept in touch with my mother's brother and sister (her parents were dead), but that had slowed in recent years. I hadn't seen Rick or Yvonne - her sister - in probably two or three years.

"I don't know how Rick is. Maybe he's calmed down by now."

"I doubt it," I said.

My father laughed, which wasn't always the easiest feat to accomplish.

"Yeah, probably not," he admitted.

"What were the roofers like?" I asked.

"They were fine from what I remember. Good at their job. I've still got their shingles over my head twenty-something years later."

My father had never moved. Our mother was killed in the house he still lived in. Some people found it odd, but my father saw no reason to move. He felt if he moved, it would be like killing my mother twice. He'd often say he felt his wife's presence in this home, which would be gone forever if he ever moved.

I think there was some truth to that.

As for me, I did move out of the house when I went to college. Yes, I attended college locally at UCSB but chose to live in the dorms. My sex life would have been nonexistent if the girls knew my father lived in the room next door. I'd conceded to stay close to home, but I wasn't going to sacrifice my entire social life.

"I mean, what were the roofers like personality-wise?" I asked.

"Nothing stood out. Where is this all coming from, Bobby?"

That's me. Bobby McGowan.

Actually, my full name is Robert Francis McGowan III, but everyone has called me Bobby since I was a kid. And I do mean everyone. Friends, family, teachers, even the butcher at our favorite supermarket or the waiters at our most visited restaurants.

There was an obvious reason why. I was the third in a line of Robert Francis McGowan's, and my father still went by Robert. Calling me Bobby helped differentiate between the two of us. Bobby was also more of a kid's name than Robert, so it fit when I was growing up. It just happened to have stuck, and now, even at thirty-two years of age, everyone still calls me Bobby.

I'm 6'1", 190 pounds, with dark brown hair, and no, this isn't my bio for a dating app.

"Do you see the way that guy is looking at Mom?" I asked.

"Stop, Bobby."

"What?" I protested, although I knew what was coming next. My father has been saying the same thing for years.

"You've been doing this ever since your mother was killed. Every time someone was arrested in Santa Barbara, you thought they'd killed your Mom. If a serial killer was caught five states away, you figured it was him. And now you think it's a roofer because of how he's looking at her? Just stop it. Your mother was a beautiful woman. If you suspected every man who ever looked at her funny, you'd have a list of ten thousand people. And by the way, this photo album is from 1999. Your mother died in 2003. You think the roofer returned four years later to come back and kill her?"

Every word he said was accurate. Anyone who made the paper for untoward reasons immediately jumped to #1 on my suspect list. And my mother was a beautiful woman who had undoubtedly been gawked at thousands of times over the years. What made this random roofer any different? And the fact she'd been killed four years later was problematic to my "theory."

I knew there was no way I would win my father over. Better to let sleeping dogs lie.

"Alright, I'll let it go," I said.

I returned to the album and showed him the picture of me and Jenny on Halloween 1999. He laughed his ass off. I couldn't remember the last time I'd seen him so happy.

"That was your mother's idea," he said. "She loved Prince, and it was 1999, so that costume almost made itself."

"Did anybody complain?"

"What could they possibly complain about?"

"About an eight-year-old and a six-year-old carrying around a beer and a miniature bottle of alcohol?"

"Oh, no one cared. People had senses of humor back then."

I could have said, '*So did you*,' but he had laughed twice in the last ten minutes, so I gave him the benefit of the doubt.

"I put some coffee on while I was in the kitchen," my father said. "You want a cup?"

"Sure. Thanks, Dad."

As my father headed back toward the kitchen, I leafed back through the photo album until I found the photograph I'd been fixated on. My father was convinced it was nothing—just another in a long line of people that I suspected of my mother's murder.

Maybe that was true, but hey, a leopard can't change his spots.

I took the photo from its sleeve and put it in my pocket.

2

The last I'd heard, Uncle Rick lived in Santa Maria, a city an hour north of Santa Barbara. Then again, the last I'd heard, Uncle Rick was still alive, and knowing his lifestyle, that was no foregone conclusion.

I asked myself, if Rick had died, would we have been notified?

We kept in touch with my mother's sister, Yvonne, until a few years ago. So, I assumed she would have let us know if Rick had passed. But then again, what if Yvonne had passed?

My head hurt.

I'd always liked my mother's family. I regretted that we hadn't kept in touch as we should have. It wasn't even a falling out. It was more of a slow drifting apart.

I was pretty sure Rick was not the cell phone type; I'm not sure he'd ever owned one.

So, to get to Rick, Yvonne would be my best bet.

"BOBBY, THIS IS TWICE IN TWO DAYS."

I was back at my father's house.

"Can't a son come to see his father?"

"I'll let you get by with it this time, but if I see you again tomorrow, I will know something is up."

I managed a smile.

"So, what are you here for?" he asked.

"Do we have any sort of Rolodex of old phone numbers and addresses?"

My father eyed me suspiciously.

"Does this have to do with the photo album?"

My father had always been very intuitive. That hadn't changed over the years. There was no need for me to lie.

"Yes. I'm doing a little investigating."

"You know I think this is going nowhere, but I guess you have some free time right now."

I could have assumed that was a shot at me, but I knew my father didn't mean it that way. I'd been let go from my job as social media manager for a bar/restaurant syndicate based out of Santa Barbara. They owned six bars/restaurants, and I was in charge of promoting their brand. I'd post on social media, accentuating deals at the bars or glowing reviews for the restaurants.

'O'Malley's has a two-for-one Happy Hour from 4-8 p.m. on Friday!'

'Sammy's has the best Pepper Steak in town!'

It was more than just that. I also helped build the websites, contacted neighboring businesses, and set up sponsorships and things of that nature. But to be honest, it wasn't much more than that. Any well-trained primate could have done my job just as well as I did.

Unfortunately, three of the six businesses had closed in the last nine months, and they no longer needed a social media manager. I'd been fired two weeks ago.

"Yes, I have a little free time," I admitted. "But this would interest me no matter what."

"Maybe you can start a blog about your mother," my father said.

I wasn't sure whether he was serious or not, but it struck a chord with me.

"That's not the worst idea."

"I was joking."

"I'm not."

"Do we really need to bring the spotlight back on our family about a murder that occurred twenty years ago?"

It would be precisely twenty years in October, a few short months away.

"What if it helped our chances of catching Mom's killer?"

My father bowed his head.

"Then I guess I'd be in favor of it."

"So, do we have that Rolodex?"

"Mom had an old address book if that's what you mean."

"That's perfect. You still have it?"

"It's around here somewhere. If you head to the family room, I'll come get you when I find it."

"Thanks."

❦

I WALKED INTO MY FATHER'S FAMILY ROOM FOR THE SECOND TIME IN two days. I looked over at the photo albums I'd reached for only twenty-four hours previously. I was afraid to go and look at them again. What if I saw another guy looking at my mother longingly? Would he then replace the roofer as my suspect-du-jour? Would it prove that my father was right and I suspected way too many people of my mother's murder?

Instead, I turned on the TV and selected an old Law & Order episode. Sure, the show was ridiculous - I mean, how many times can people be interrogated without their lawyer present? - but it was entertaining and passed the time.

This episode was from the 90s, and at the beginning of the episode, Jack McCoy, Claire Kincade, Lenny Briscoe, and Ray Curtis watched someone receive the death penalty, which I found ironic since New York hadn't executed an inmate since 1963. Oh well, like I said, it passes the time.

My father walked in a few minutes later.

"Here you go," he said.

The address book looked like it was straight from the 1950s, not the 90s and early 2000s.

"This thing is a relic," I said.

"Yeah, it's seen better days, but haven't we all?"

I wouldn't have felt the need to add the last part, but that was part of the "charm" of my father.

"Did you keep this updated?" I asked.

"No. It hasn't been touched since your Mom died."

"Are there cell phone numbers in it?"

"Your mother kept this current while she was alive, so it goes to 2003. There are probably some cells in there."

"I'm mostly looking for Aunt Yvonne's or Uncle Rick's if you have either."

"Don't you have their numbers?"

"Rick never had a cell phone, and I tried Yvonne's this morning, but the one I had was disconnected."

"And you think one from a 2003 address book will work?"

"I'm thinking about going by her house."

My father nodded.

"Gotcha. Last I heard, she was still living in the same place- in Ventura, I believe."

Yvonne had lived in Ventura since we were kids.

"That's why I wanted to get the address. I'm not sure I'd remember exactly how to get there. It's been years since I've been to her house."

"If the address is all you were looking for, you could have just called."

"And miss out on seeing you?"

My father managed another smile.

"These unexpected house calls are for the birds," he said. "You need to get back to work right away."

I laughed.

He looked at the address book.

"Yvonne's address is here. And you're right, only a house phone for Rick. I can almost guarantee that one isn't active. I know he's moved several times since 2003."

"I'll find him," I said. "Assuming he's still alive."

My father handed over the address book.

"Are you sure about all of this, Bobby?"

"I'll probably investigate for a week, find nothing, and then get back to applying for a new job."

He looked at me wearily.

"You know you can do both at the same time?"

"You're right. I'll keep applying to jobs while I investigate the creepy guy in the photo."

"What if I told you I don't think he looks all that creepy?"

"I'd tell you you're getting old, and I trust my judgment over yours."

I said it tongue-in-cheek, and my father took it that way.

"Oh, Bobby. Always the flatterer," he said and laughed.

"See, my recent visits are already bringing us more laughs than usual."

My father looked at me with regret. He knew I was right, and our lives, especially his, had become a bit melancholy over the years.

"Could an investigation into the worst day of my life lead to some happiness in my older years?" my father asked.

It was as open as my father had been in years. It could have saddened me, but there was a sense of possibility behind it. I chose to look on the bright side.

"It can and it will," I said.

"Your sister probably isn't going to love this idea."

"She'll come around to it."

"You know she has always looked up to you."

"I know."

"She used to tell all her friends how great you were."

"I know."

"She didn't leave because of you. It's because of me and my morosity."

"I know."

"You don't have to reply with the same thing every time."

"I know," I deadpanned.

And that's when my father lost it. He started laughing uncontrollably.

The investigation into my mother's murder would likely go nowhere, but the sound of my father laughing had already made it worthwhile.

"I gotta run, Dad. I'll come see you in a few days."

He gave me a big hug as I left.

⚜

YVONNE FIELDS HAD NEVER MARRIED.

I heard she used to date many guys back in the day but apparently never found the right one. Unlike some older women who rued never getting married, Yvonne took pride in it.

No man is going to tie me down.

I can do whatever I want, whenever I want.

She said things like that all the time when I was growing up. It's safe to say that I'd always liked Aunt Yvonne. The Event, as she liked to call the murder of my mother, changed everything, but I still had a soft spot in my heart for her.

With no way to reach her by phone, I drove down to her house in

Ventura. It was thirty minutes south of Santa Barbara and a pleasant ride, hugging Highway 101 and the Pacific Ocean for most of the drive.

She lived in a modest but pleasant home in the suburbs that she'd owned for probably thirty years. I can't imagine many single, never-married women living in the burbs alone.

She opened the door, and I was pleased to see that she still lived there.

"Hello," she said, a quizzical look on her face.

"You don't recognize me, Yvonne?"

She realized who I was before I'd finished my sentence.

"My favorite nephew!" she said. "Bobby, what a pleasant surprise. Come on in!"

She escorted me inside and had us sit across from each other at a small four-seat dining room table.

"Your only nephew," I said.

"You got me there. You would have been my favorite anyway, Bobby. You were always such a great kid. What are you now, forty?"

"You trying to age me? I'm still a young buck of thirty-two."

"Shit, even forty would have sounded young to me. Or fifty. Shit, I'm getting old."

Yvonne saying shit twice in a matter of seconds was no surprise. She'd always had a very colorful vocabulary. She and her brother had that in common.

My mother was thirty-six when she died, so she'd have been fifty-six if she were still alive. Yvonne was her older sister by two or three years, so she was approaching sixty, which meant Rick had already passed his 60th by a year or two.

"But you're young at heart, Yvonne, and always have been."

"Thanks. I try."

There was a pause. She had to be wondering why I was reaching out to her after so long, which got me thinking. Why had I waited so long? We had always gotten along so well. Yes, The Event changed everything, but that shouldn't mean you no longer talk to family. We had talked frequently in the years that followed her death. What had changed in the last several years? No matter what happened going forward, I told myself not to lose touch with Yvonne again.

"Can I get you a coffee?" she asked.

"How about just a water?"

"That's easy."

She returned a few seconds later with a bottled water.

"You're probably wondering why I've come to visit after so long," I said.

"It did cross my mind."

I told her about the photo in the family album, her brother having referred the roofers, and my suspicions of the one guy.

"Looks like you've got that roofer dead to rights," she said, and I smiled.

Her sarcasm was obvious.

"Open and shut case," I replied.

"Signed, sealed, delivered. Given the amount of evidence you have, they'll probably call off the trial and go straight to the death penalty. An expression in a long-ago photo? I mean, it doesn't get any more concrete than that."

"I'm starting to remember how thick you can lay it on."

"Hey, if we don't joke about it, we have to think about The Event instead."

She had a point.

"True. So, despite the jokes, what do you think of my idea?"

"What idea exactly?"

"Looking back into my mother's murder."

"How is your father with it?"

"He's on the fence, but I did get him laughing the last few days."

"Nothing like the murder of a spouse to get the old funny bone going."

I tried my hardest not to smile but I wasn't strong enough.

"I've missed you, Yvonne."

"Me and this acid tongue of mine?"

"Exactly."

"So it sounds like your father is at least partly on board with this?"

"Not sure he loves it, but he's not going to stop me."

"How about that sister of yours?"

Yvonne had never been as close to Jenny as she had been with me. I never really knew why. My guess was that Jenny couldn't handle her sarcasm as well as I could.

"I haven't told her yet."

"Don't tell her you told me first. She was never my biggest fan."

"That's probably some good advice," I said, responding to the first sentence and leaving the second one be.

"Well, I'm happy you're doing this," Yvonne said.

"Glad to hear it. So I'm assuming Rick is still alive?"

"Ah yes, I should have said that off the bat. He is, although he's not doing all that great. Rick is sixty-two now but looks more like he's eighty-two. He's lived a hard-charging life."

"I heard all about it."

"You should have seen the guy in his twenties and thirties."

"My mother told me stories. I remember hearing about four people on a motorcycle or something."

"Which lasted all of five seconds. Rick tried to put three women behind him on his motorcycle. Within twenty feet of driving off, the two girls at the back fell off and hit their heads. Luckily, both were wearing helmets. The helmets were one of the few good ideas that Rick ever had. There weren't many others."

"Is he all there?"

"Yeah, his brain is surprisingly good. When he's not drunk and slurring his words, obviously. It's just his body that's giving out on him."

"It sounds a little bit like my father. His mind is great, but his knees and joints and all that fun stuff are fucked."

"My guess is Rick is worse off. Your father didn't resort to drinking when your mother died. At least, not that I know of."

"No, he didn't."

"Good."

"Are you and Rick still close?" I asked.

"I go and see him about twice a month, so yeah, I'd say so."

"Do you guys bring up my mother?"

"We bring up our childhood. We never talk about The Event or how our family suffered since."

"It had always sounded like my mother had an idyllic childhood."

"She sure did. The prettiest girl in three counties. That's what all the boys would say."

"I never heard that."

"Your mom was too modest to tell you something like that."

"I meant from you."

Yvonne laughed.

"Did you expect loudmouth Yvonne to tell you everything?"

"That's not what I meant."

"I know, Bobby. Just busting your balls."

"So, the prettiest girl in three counties?"

"Your mother was beloved, and not just because of her looks. She was nice to everyone, even the dorks and the nerds. A lot of girls who are as pretty and popular as your mother go the other way and become nasty."

"She couldn't have been that perfect."

I instantly regretted saying it. I didn't want to hear any dirt on my mother.

"She was pretty great, but don't think I'm calling her perfect. She used her All-American girl persona to her advantage."

Now, I was curious.

"In what way?"

"She'd tell our parents that she was going to some bake sale or some crap like that and then head off to some party. She was the golden child compared to me and Rick, so our parents let her get away with whatever she wanted."

My mother's parents had died within months of each other, about two years before her murder. It was probably for the best. No parent should ever have to go through the murder of a child.

"I liked Grandma and Grandpa."

"They were great parents, just a little gullible. Especially when it came to Heather."

It was odd to hear my mother called by her given name. She was always Mom to me, and I rarely thought of her as a Heather. But a Heather she was. Heather Fields at birth and Heather McGowan after marrying my father.

"Did you ever suspect anyone in her murder?" I asked abruptly.

"Jeez, Bobby. Thought we were having fun with the childhood recollections."

"How about this? I'll come visit you soon, and all we'll talk about is the Fields' kids growing up together."

"I'd like that. More to see you than to rehash old memories."

"I'll swing by next week. Now, as to my question?"

"I can't say I ever had a definitive suspect, but I'd always despised Roy Cooper. He was one of Heather's few serious judgment errors."

Roy Cooper was an ex-boyfriend of my mother's who had remained fixated on her even fifteen years after they'd broken up. He'd call and leave messages, pretending to be an old friend, but we all knew what he really wanted. My father confronted him a few times and even considered getting the police involved but he never did.

Since they'd grown up together, Roy had some of the same friends as my mother, so when there were weddings or funerals in Santa Barbara, they'd often be in the same room. I can remember my parents arguing before events like that, and it always had to do with the looming presence of Roy Cooper.

"I always hated him," I said. "Not cause I knew him, but because I knew how much distress he caused my mother."

"He was handsome and charismatic, so I understand why your mother first fell for him. The problem was that he was also a sociopath."

"Do you know what happened to him?"

"Roy's still alive. Living in Portland, I believe. Despite his sociopathic tendencies, he had a lot of friends in this town as a young man."

"He had an alibi, though, right?" I asked.

I was only twelve when my mother was murdered, and I'd forgotten some of the details over the years.

"He said he was with two friends at a little dive bar that day. Let me tell you, they weren't the most trustworthy friends."

I was one day into looking at my mother's murder, and I was already tempted to look in a different direction. Maybe the roofer from the photo album had nothing to do with my mother's murder and had just served as the impetus to get me back into the case.

"Maybe I'll do a deep dive into Roy Cooper as well," I said.

"It couldn't hurt. But check out your photo album guy first. Hey, that's what led to you ending up here."

I took the first sip of my water.

"I have to head out soon," I said. "Before we go, can I get Rick's number? And I promise to come visit you next week."

"It's 805-555-3492. It's a landline, so you may have to call a few times to get ahold of him. And just a warning. His place is a shithole."

"I don't care."

She smiled.

"I've enjoyed this, Bobby. Can't wait to see you again, you old man of thirty-two."

"Don't ever change, Yvonne."

"Too old to change. That ship has sailed."

"Well, you were on the *Titanic*, weren't you?"

"It was the *Lusitania*. Get it straight."

I laughed.

"You're too much."

"Goodbye, Bobby."

3

My conversation with Rick would go less swimmingly.

He answered my initial call and agreed to meet with me, so we got off to a relatively good start. His quasi-retirement community was on the outskirts of Santa Maria, an hour north of Santa Barbara. Santa Maria was an ever-improving city, but Rick's community hadn't got the memo. Rick had never been all that successful, but even this "community" was beneath him.

All the paint had peeled on the tiny homes. Garbage was spread everywhere. And worst of all, there was animal dung all over. Who was in charge of cleaning this darn place?

Rick was living in room B-12. I couldn't remember precisely what Vitamin B-12 did for your body, but I found it ironic that a man who had aged prematurely was staying in an apartment number synonymous with a vitamin.

I knocked on the door, and a man in a red robe and long, straggly hair answered. He looked like Nick Nolte crossed with Gary Busey if neither had slept for a week.

"Who are you?" Rick snarled as he opened the door.

Yvonne had told me his brain was alright, and I'd just called him the previous day to tell him I was coming. He knew who I was.

"It's Bobby, Rick. Your nephew."

"I only have one nephew and haven't seen him in years."

"Well, you're seeing him now."

"That wasn't my choice."

Rick could be a bully if you let him, so I decided to play back at him.

"Actually, it was. We talked yesterday, and you said I could come up and talk to you."

He let out a sound that I had never quite heard before. It was a grumble crossed with a grunt with a hint of a growl—all the G's.

"Then I guess you better come in, Robert."

He'd intentionally called me by my given name. That much was obvious.

I tapped him on the shoulder.

"See, you do know me."

⬧

I WALKED INTO A HOUSE AS DISHEVELED AS THE MAN LIVING THERE.

There were newspapers spread all over the floor - hey, at least he was reading - and a smell that wasn't going away anytime soon. It wasn't feces or puke or anything you could clean up. It's like the walls were infected with the smell. I felt terrible for Uncle Rick.

"How long have you lived here?" I asked.

"Too fucking long," he answered. "Do you want to take a seat?"

I realized that the newspaper could come in handy, and I grabbed one and put it below me.

The couch I sat on looked like it had survived the Lincoln administration. Uncle Rick also sat down; there would be no newspaper below him.

"I had a nice talk with your sister yesterday," I said.

"You communicating with the dead?"

"I hope that's not a joke about my mother," I said.

He looked at me and realized he might have gone too far.

"Oh, you meant Yvonne."

"You know who I meant. I told you on the phone yesterday."

"Then why repeat it today?"

He hadn't lost the qualities that had made him the "black sheep" of the family.

"I was trying to break the ice," I said.

"Speaking of ice, I'm going to pour myself a drink. Would you like one?"

"No thanks."

He went to the minuscule kitchen contiguous to the living room and poured himself some bourbon. If he put a mixer in it, I must have missed it. I'd guess more cocktails were being poured than meals cooked in Rick's kitchen.

"So what brings you here, Robert?"

"You do know that everyone has always called me Bobby, right? Even you did back in the day."

"Well, back in the day, you were a kid, and Bobby was cute at that age. It doesn't translate well to an adult's name, so I'm going to call you Robert instead."

I'd be lying if I said that didn't hurt. Yes, the source was a drunken madman, but it still hit home.

"Okay, Richard," I said, but my retort fell flat. There's not much difference between Richard and Rick. I then realized I should have used Dick instead, but the time had passed.

He took a big sip of his drink, finishing half in one fell swoop. Then he looked back at me with a somewhat subdued expression. That quick infusion of booze had calmed him a bit.

"Bobby is a fine name. I'm just being an asshole. We had some nice times when you were a kid, didn't we?"

"We did. I think my mother might have limited our visits, so you were like the rowdy uncle we always looked forward to spending time with."

"Your mother wasn't wrong to do that. Shit, I'm a wild man now, imagine me twenty, thirty, forty years ago."

"I've heard some stories," I said, leaving it at that. I didn't feel a need to bring up the motorcycle story twice in two days. And I'm sure that was one of the tamer ones.

"I've lived a hard life, that's for sure," he said. "And your mother probably resented me for being a pain in the ass growing up."

Whenever someone mentioned my mother, I always wanted to hear more. Losing a parent at twelve years old will do that to you.

"In what way?"

"In every way, but especially with her boyfriends. I'd always intimidate them and tell them I was going to beat their ass if they came around again. Heather lost quite a few boyfriends because of me."

"Were you looking after her or just being a jerk?"

"A little of the former and a lot of the latter."

Rick had always been well-spoken and was introspective on his good days. Sadly, his vices had led him to a dump like this.

"She never badmouthed you to us," I said.

"Never?"

"Well, she'd say you were a wildcard but never specifically said to be wary of you."

He looked momentarily happy.

"Heather was a great woman. Pretty as a button, too. You probably get why I had to scare off all those gentlemen callers."

I loved hearing just about everything about my mother, but her love life as a young woman was not one of them.

"Were you and Yvonne close?" I asked, changing the subject.

"Closer than Heather and me. Yvonne and I were in high school together. Heather was quite a bit younger, and it wasn't the same."

"Yvonne told me she still comes and visits you."

"She does. And the fireworks usually start once I pour myself the first of these," he said, twirling the drink in his hand.

I almost said, '*Can you blame her?*' but held my tongue.

"Do you wonder if you and my mother would have gotten closer as you aged?"

"She would have kept me in the loop, even if I fucked up. And it's because of you and that sister of yours. She'd want you to know your uncle."

I felt sad. If that were true, then my mother was somewhere looking down at me, disappointed I hadn't kept in better touch with my aunt and uncle.

"Maybe we'll start making up for lost time," I said.

"Sure. Road trip, me and you. Go see Skynyrd if they are still touring."

I laughed.

"How about something a little easier? I could drive you to a grocery store, and you could stock up on a few things."

I'd meant food as opposed to liquor. I'm not sure if he'd taken the hint.

"That would be nice. Let's do it next time you visit so I have something to look forward to."

"It's a deal," I said.

"So what are you really here for? It can't just be to catch up on old times."

It was time. I grabbed the photo from my wallet. I realized then that I'd done nothing to preserve the photo. I took out my phone, took a picture of it, and told myself to print up a few copies when I got home..

"Do you remember these guys?" I asked, handing him the photo.

"I sure do," he said without missing a beat. "They installed the roof on your parents' house."

Shingles were in the background, so this was hardly rocket science, but I was still glad to hear Rick say he recognized them.

"Do you remember their names?"

He paused, hoping it would come to him.

"I don't, but I do know who they worked for."

"Who was that?"

He handed the photo back.

"A guy named Jim Broadhurst. He owned a roofing company back then."

"Do you know if he's still alive?"

"I don't, but he was a pretty young guy, so I'd assume so."

I took out my phone and Googled 'Jim Broadhurst Roofing.' Sure enough, he owned a roofing company, which was still in business.

"So you didn't know these two?" I asked, showing him the photo again.

"I knew Jim. I had a few nights out with those two guys after they worked at your parent's house, but I can't say I knew them well. Nor do I remember their names."

"Can you tell me anything about them? Were they good people? Jerks?"

"Let me see that again."

I handed it back to him.

"This guy was a piece of work. I remember that."

He was pointing at the guy who was glaring at my mother.

"In what way?"

"He got us kicked out of a bar one night. Yelled at the bartender and knocked out the bouncer. He was a tough dude."

"Did you warn my mother?"

"No. This was after they'd finished the roof. I probably met them while they were installing it."

"How did he treat women?"

"Shit, I don't remember. Wait, you don't suspect this guy of..." Rick said, stopping himself before he went further.

"I don't know what I suspect. I just decided to start asking a few questions about my mother's murder."

He grabbed the photo for the third time.

"Look at this asshole. He's peering at your mother like he wants to fu...."

"You don't need to say it," I interrupted.

"You're right. I'm sorry."

"Nothing more you can tell me about the guys?"

"There isn't. Maybe Jim Broadhurst will know more."

I decided to ask Rick the same thing I'd asked his sister.

"Did you ever hone in on one suspect?"

"No, I just suspected every Tom, Dick, and Harry who lived in a hundred-mile radius."

Sounded like me.

"Did you ever think Roy Cooper could have done it?"

"He was an all-time asshole. One of your mother's boyfriends I couldn't scare off. And he had a temper, that's for sure. He had an alibi, though."

"Yvonne said she doesn't trust the two guys who gave Roy his alibi."

"Neither did I, so I confronted one of them, and he swore on his kids' lives that Roy was at that bar with them."

"And that convinced you?"

"He knew I would give him a beating if he lied to me, so yes."

I believed Rick's story but still wasn't ready to eliminate Roy as a suspect.

"Anything else you can tell me?"

"I'm sure I'll think of something by the next time you visit, and then we can hit up that grocery store."

"My word is my bond. How about next week?"

I rose from the couch as the newspaper stayed glued to the couch.

"That will work. Thanks for coming, Bobby."

He'd closed with Bobby, not Robert. It said a lot.

Rick gave me a handshake as I turned to go. I don't think he was much of a hugger.

As I left, the door shut very slowly, and I could see Rick already back in the kitchen and pouring himself another.

❧　4　☙

"I know that fucking jerk," Jim Broadhurst said.

He was younger than I'd expected. I figured someone who owned a business for twenty-four-plus years would be getting up there in age. That was not the case with Broadhurst. He looked to be around fifty - possibly younger - meaning he'd owned his business from a very young age.

I was now in Lompoc, a city about fifty miles northwest of Santa Barbara. I was always told that it had seen better days, but to be honest, Lompoc had been a dump since I was a kid. Maybe I was missing something.

Uncle Rick's community would have been right at home in Lompoc.

Broadhurst's shop was on a dirt road beside a used car lot. I wondered if there was any crossover: *Buy a car, and you'll get 25% off your new roof!*

I'd talked with Broadhurst for about five minutes before pulling out the picture that had started this all. I had specifically not mentioned Rick, fearing it might skewer his reaction one way or the other.

"Which one is the fucking jerk?" I asked.

"The one on the right staring at that woman."

"That's my mother," I said, hoping to preempt him from mentioning her beauty.

"Pretty lady. She still around?"

Jim Broadhurst wasn't the most cerebral guy on the planet.

"No, she was killed a few years after this picture was taken."

"You don't think one of my employees did away with her, do you?"

I hated the phrase *'did away with,'* but I guess there wasn't any expression that could adequately summarize a family member's death.

"I don't know. I'm just trying to find out more about this picture."

"The guy on the left was a hard worker. His name was Vance, something or other. He passed about five years ago, I heard. Cancer of the ass, I think."

Broadhurst certainly had a way with words.

"How about the other guy?"

"You won't be seeing him around these parts. Around fifteen years ago, I gave him what turned out to be his last job. He got in a fight with the people who owned the house. He attacked the man and beat him to a pulp. He was charged with aggravated assault and was given a few months in the county jail. When he got out, he returned and asked me for another job. I told him he must be crazy. I'd never hire him again. He'd put my whole business at risk. I thought he was going to attack me when I told him that. He was one crazy motherfucker."

"What years did he work for you?"

"I'd be guessing, but probably like 1999 to 2008. Just don't quote me on that."

"Do you remember his name?"

"Oh, what was it? Let me think. Ty or Kyle, something like that. Wait. Lyle. That was it. Lyle Taft. We called him Lyle Lovett, and he hated it. *'I hate that queer singer,'* he'd say. We'd remind him that Lovett had been married to Julia Roberts and wasn't gay, but it didn't matter to him. Lyle sounds like a pretty mellow name, right? Well, they misnamed this one. Lyle Taft was the furthest thing from mellow."

"Why did you employ him?"

"He was good at his job, and finding roofers is not always easy. I had no idea he was such a hothead when I hired him. I had a feeling that a screw was loose, but he'd never attacked a client of mine. Like I said, once I heard about that, I was done with him forever."

"Do you know that happened to Lyle?"

An employee walked through the door. He exchanged pleasantries with Broadhurst and then headed to the back part of the office.

"I don't, but I have a few older employees who were friendly with him. They might know. As you can guess, we have a blue-collar crew here. One fight wouldn't turn these guys off of Lyle forever."

"Hey, I'm not here to judge. Can I get the numbers of those employees?"

"Sure."

"You said they have been working here for a while?"

"Yes. Most roofers aren't rocket scientists," Broadhurst said. "It's not like they can quit and become doctors or lawyers."

Broadhurst was upfront and didn't pull any punches. He was repulsive yet kind of endearing at the same time.

"Got to be tough on your body, though," I said.

"True that. True that."

Just when I thought our conversation was ending, Broadhurst surprised me.

"Wait, let me see that picture again."

I gave it to him.

"Did your mother have a brother named Rick?"

"Yes."

"Oh shit, I remember now. I knew I recognized that face. Just terrible what happened to her."

"Thanks. It was."

"And you think that Lyle might have been involved?"

"I'm not sure what I think. I'm just trying to bring some new eyes to the case."

"I hear that. Rick and I had some good times when we were younger men."

"I think you're a lot younger than Rick."

"Well, I'm about to be fifty-two, and I think your uncle had like a decade on me. Shit, maybe more. Not that any of that crap matters. We had fun hanging out. What the fuck is age anyway? Just a number if you ask me."

Broadhurst continued to drop swear words like he was Richard Pryor.

"I saw Rick yesterday."

"How's he doing?"

There was no need to sugarcoat it.

"Still kicking," I said.

"Probably still drinking, too. Am I right?"

He tapped me on the shoulder and laughed as if someone drinking their life away was the funniest thing in the world.

"Yes, he is. Would you like to see him? He could use a few visitors."

"Before you go, leave his address. Maybe I'll swing by."

I could tell Jim Broadhurst was never going to swing by. He didn't strike me as being the sentimental type. I couldn't imagine him driving to Santa Maria and talking about old times with Rick.

"Did Lyle have to leave any sort of next of kin or someone to contact?"

"Shit, he probably did. Been a long time, though."

"Do you still have it?"

"I did them all by hand in the late 90s and early 2000s."

"And did you save the copies of those papers?"

"I save them all for at least a few years after the employee leaves. After that, I usually get rid of them at some point. I'll tell you what. When you get out of here, I'll take a look and see if I somehow kept any of Lyle's info. It's pretty unlikely, though. Are you thinking a family member is more likely to know his whereabouts than one of his old friends?"

Jim Broadhurst was a sharp one.

"Yes."

"I reckon I agree with you."

He handed me a business card.

"All this information is free, but if you decide to reroof your house and don't choose me, I'll be disappointed."

"You guys still do work in Santa Barbara?"

"Of course. Do you think these poor bastards down in Lompoc can afford new roofs? Shit, you must be crazy."

I imagined Jim and Rick had some wild times back in the day. They were two peas in a pod. Obnoxious, profanity-laced, and yet oddly engaging.

"When I buy a house and need roofing, I'll call you," I said.

"I'm holding you to that."

I took out my business card from the company that had fired me.

"My number is on here. Call me if you have any information on Lyle Taft."

"You got it. I'm sorry about your mother. Hope you catch the motherfucker who did it."

He'd used motherfucker to start our conversation when talking about Lyle Taft. And now he'd used it to describe my mother's killer.

Were they one and the same?

Time would tell.

5

Over the next few days, I built a website dedicated to the murder of my mother.

It wasn't likely to win any awards, but it did the trick.

There were links to old articles I found online. I summarized my mother's final few days as well as I could remember. I also added a brief biography of our three remaining family members. I'm sure my sister would have a few words with me about that.

I named it helpfindheatherskiller.com. Something like *'find Mrs. McGowan's killer'* didn't have the same ring to it, so I used her first name.

I wasn't sure what to do with the picture of Lyle, Vance, and my parents. I couldn't just accuse him of murder on the website. I'd be sued, and I'd deserve it.

Still, I was growing more suspicious of the picture and the man himself. I couldn't leave the photo off entirely. It had spearheaded this whole thing.

I decided to have a *'PHOTOS'* section on the website and put that picture at the top of the webpage. I even included his name below the picture. If anyone had dirt on Lyle Taft and saw this picture, I was hoping they'd contact me, which they could find in the *'CONTACT'* section. I'd set up a new email, which was just the website's name at gmail.

I was proud of what I'd built.

I went to sleep that night with heightened expectations.

❦

A WEEK PASSED, AND NOTHING HAD HAPPENED.

Jim Broadhurst had gotten back to me and said he couldn't find any paperwork from twenty-plus years ago. No surprise there. He put me in touch with two of Lyle Taft's former co-workers, but they basically just confirmed what Broadhurst had said. Lyle was a wild card and someone you didn't want to cross. Neither man had kept in touch with him after he'd been fired, nor did they know where he was now.

I tried Googling him but found nothing on the Lyle Taft in question. A Lyle Taft in Colorado specialized in underwater rolls while kayaking. He sounded interesting but certainly wasn't my guy. There was a Lyle Taft in Alabama who'd just turned 100 and a thirty-six-year-old Lyle Taft in Maine who'd climbed Everest.

And several other Lyle Tafts who weren't my guy.

I hadn't expected to find much. Taft sounded like a guy who lived on the fringes of society. A Facebook or Instagram page with a smiling profile picture wouldn't fit my impression of him.

I needed to check with the DMV or some similar agency and see what I could come up with.

That could wait.

I had a more pressing idea.

❦

THE *SANTA BARBARA NEWS-PRESS* (KNOWN MERELY AS THE *NEWS-PRESS* by locals) has been the predominant paper in Santa Barbara since well before I was born.

They published their first edition back on May 30th of '68. Not 1968. 1868. It was called the *Santa Barbara Post* back then, but it eventually morphed into the *Santa Barbara News-Press*.

It's the longest-running newspaper in Southern California, even over those big, bad Los Angeles papers.

They had recently moved their offices from Santa Barbara to Goleta, a town just north of it and also the location of my alma mater, UCSB.

I walked into their offices on a warm August day. It had been ninety degrees for a third straight day, something relatively uncommon for the Santa Barbara area. We had great weather, partly because it usually hovered somewhere in the 80s and never got too hot. This summer was proving a little different.

An older female receptionist greeted me.

"How can I help you?" she asked me.

"If I have an idea for an article, who would I contact?"

"Usually, you would submit an email online."

"Well, since I came all this way, what would you suggest?"

She looked a bit annoyed.

"Hold on," she said.

She picked up the phone.

"Is Mrs. Crabtree in?"

Pause.

"Can I send someone back?"

Pause.

"Okay, thanks. Mrs. Crabtree will see you."

"Which office is hers?"

"Take a right and stay along that wall; you'll see her name on one of the office doors about twenty-five yards down."

"Thanks."

"Next time, go through protocol."

I couldn't resist.

"Proto what?"

She winced as I walked away.

I ARRIVED AT KIM CRABTREE'S OFFICE.

She looked to be only a few years older than me.

I shook her hand and said, "I'm Bobby. Thanks for meeting with me."

"What can I do for you, Bobby?"

She didn't extend an offer to sit down. I think she was hoping this meeting would be over in a matter of seconds.

"My name is Bobby McGowan, and my mother's name was Heather. Does that mean anything to you?"

It did, and her expression bore that out.

"Why don't you have a seat?" she asked.

I obliged.

"I was a sophomore at Dos Pueblos High School the year that

happened," she said. "I remember it well. What a horrible tragedy. I'm sorry for your loss."

The two leading high schools in Santa Barbara are huge rivals: the Santa Barbara High School Dons and the Dos Pueblos Chargers. I went to SB High, so I was facing the "enemy" across from me.

"Thank you," I said.

"Is there some new information? I haven't heard about the case in years."

"I've decided to start investigating it myself."

"I see. Have you found anything?"

I'd debated on my drive over whether to mention the photo. I'd decided against it. At the very least, she'd think I was presumptuous. She might think I was downright bonkers.

I still didn't have much to connect Lyle Taft to my mother's murder. Instead, I had a suspicious photograph, knowledge that the man had a temper, and knew that he lived in the Santa Barbara area in 2003. It wasn't nothing, but it wasn't a whole lot, either.

I was hoping to get the *News-Press* to mention my website, and that's how I'd get the photo of Taft into the public sphere.

"Nothing specific, no," I said. "But I'd love it if you guys would consider publishing an article on the case. The twentieth anniversary is coming in a few months, and I'm sure people would still be interested. I've also built a website that contains information on the case and asks people for any leads they might have."

Kim Crabtree's face lit up. I think she saw some higher-than-usual newspaper sales in her future. The most famous murder in Santa Barbara's recent history had a 20th anniversary around the corner. A front-page spread on the anniversary would surely get many people to buy that day's newspaper. Shit, maybe they'd make it a three or four-parter and get increased sales for days. That's what Mrs. Crabtree was thinking; I was sure of it.

"I think the public would eat up a 20th-anniversary article," she said, immediately realizing her mistake. "I sounded way too eager. I apologize."

"No problem," I said.

I was using them to get my mother's name back out there and bring attention to my website, just as they'd be using me for increased sales. There was no need for hard feelings.

"What is the actual date of the anniversary?" she asked.

"October 28th, 2003, was the day she was killed."

"What if we talked in the coming weeks and set up something for that date? It could be a long article on everything you and the police know. Or suspect."

"I'd be fine with that, but that's two months away. Could we put something out there in the coming days? It could be a short article, but I'd like it to mention my website."

"I'm sure we could do something, Bobby," she said, using my name for the first time.

"Great."

She handed me a business card.

"This is my cell phone number. Why don't you call me tomorrow and we'll schedule another meeting. I can introduce you to a few of our writers, and you can tell them what you want to include in the article. I'll bet we could get one written up in a day or two."

"Sounds good. I'll call you tomorrow."

Kim Crabtree walked me to the front door and even followed me fifty feet down the street, talking the whole time. She saw the 20th anniversary of the worst day of my life as a chance to sell a few papers.

I didn't begrudge her that.

⚜

I STARTED TO DRIVE BACK TO MY PLACE WHEN ANOTHER THOUGHT CAME to mind. We were in the year 2023. Newspapers were old school. Why not get the news out there via television as well?

I stopped by the offices of KEYT, Channel 3 in Santa Barbara. I talked my way into a meeting just as I had at the *News-Press* and pitched the man on the idea of interviewing me for the 20th anniversary.

Much like Kim Crabtree, Mr. Jenkins (the general manager of KEYT) seemed eager to do something for the anniversary. He also broached the idea of me doing a quick two-minute interview for that evening's news. I looked down at my white henley shirt and navy blue chino shorts. I was hardly dressed for an interview, but that's not what mattered. Getting my mother's name back out there and hopefully bringing attention to my website are what really mattered.

"Sure," I said, although I had no idea if I was making the right decision.

And just like that - three days into my investigation - I was about to be on television.

❦

FIFTEEN MINUTES LATER, AS I WALKED OUT OF THEIR OFFICES, I KNEW I'd made a terrible mistake.

It wasn't their fault. They hadn't exactly blindsided me. They'd asked me if I wanted to be interviewed, and I'd said yes.

The problem occurred when they asked if I had a picture of my mother. I pulled out the one I'd been carrying around, and they asked me who else was in the photo. That's when I should have shut up or dodged the question.

But I didn't.

I told them it was my father and two roofers, Lyle Taft and a guy named Vance.

I could have cut my losses at that point by shutting up.

But I still didn't.

The reporter asked me why my only picture of my mother had roofers in it, and I panicked.

It all happened so fast that I'm not sure exactly what I said, but it was something along the lines of, "I'm not positive he's involved, but if anyone has information on Lyle Taft, you can email me through the website helpfindheatherskiller.com."

As I continued digging my own grave, I used my finger to point out which one Lyle Taft was.

The interview ended seconds later.

I should have asked them then and there not to run the interview, but I was in a daze and just wanted to get out of there.

A few minutes later, I realized I'd fucked up. Bad.

If Lyle Taft were still alive, I'd be hearing from his attorney.

6

CONRAD

I looked in my fridge and realized I was out of eggs.

I didn't throw a fit. I was merely disappointed.

I'd had my mind set on eggs all morning. I still hadn't decided if I was going to fry them or make a scramble, but eggs were on the freaking menu.

The store was only five minutes away.

Fuck it, I was making eggs this morning.

And just like that, I was in my car and headed toward the local grocery store.

I PICKED UP A FEW OTHER THINGS WHILE I WAS THERE.

Bacon. Hot sauce. Milk. Butter.

"How are you today, sir?" the bespectacled young woman asked me when I reached the front of the check-out line.

"Fine."

I was a man of few words. I'd been that way for most of my life.

As she started running my groceries across the scanner, a man in his fifties came to replace the young woman.

"You're on a break in two minutes, Kelsey."

"Okay, thanks."

"You grew up in Santa Barbara, right?" he asked her.

"I did."

"Are you old enough to remember the murder of Heather McGowan?"

My ears perked up.

"No, it doesn't ring a bell. I'm only twenty-two, though. When did it happen?"

"When you were two," the man said.

"Sorry, I don't remember."

"I guess you don't need to remember the murder to enjoy the interview."

"What interview?" Kelsey asked.

She ignored my groceries, but I didn't care. I needed to hear the end of their conversation.

"Go to KEYT and check out one of last night's interviews on the eight o'clock news. The son of the woman who was murdered makes an ass of himself. He basically starts accusing some random roofer in one of his family photos of being involved in his mother's death. It was a real shit show. That son never should have agreed to that interview."

He then laughed.

"You've got a weird sense of humor," Kelsey said, never mentioning the man by name.

She looked back over at me.

"I'm so sorry," she said, running my last two items past the reader. "That will be twenty dollars and six cents."

I gave her exact change and left the store.

As soon as I arrived home, I grabbed my laptop and went to keyt.com

Bobby McGowan gave a rambling interview, talking about how it was approaching the 20th anniversary of his mother's murder, saying he'd built some website and was taking any tips from the public. Finally, he almost accused some roofer named Lyle Taft of being involved in his mother's murder.

It was just as the grocery store employee had described.

I set my laptop back down and started smiling.

A normal person's reaction probably would have been to worry, but I wasn't normal.

CHAPTER 6

I found it amusing.

Bobby McGowan had to be in his early thirties at this point, but he still looked like a Boy Scout. He was in way over his head. This interview proved it.

What did I have to fear anyway?

Bobby thought some random roofer murdered his mother.

Let him destroy that guy's life.

Meanwhile, I'd be watching from afar. If Bobby ever started getting closer, I'd take more of an interest in him. Not yet.

Plus, I had other things on my mind.

Another murder, to be precise.

Heather McGowan may have been the first murder I'd ever committed, but it was far from my last.

7

BOBBY

"You could be sued for libel!" my sister yelled at me.

I was sitting in my apartment, having a peaceful morning, when she called. I knew that was about to change.

She had either seen or heard about my appearance on KEYT the night before. She wasn't happy.

"What the fuck were you thinking?" she asked, although she sure didn't seem to be phrasing it as a question.

"I went there hoping to set up some sort of interview for the 20th anniversary of Mom's passing. Two minutes later, they were asking me to record an interview for that night's show. It had been three long days, and this Lyle Taft guy had never left my mind. When I showed the picture of Mom, they asked me who that guy was, and I panicked and mentioned his name on air. What do you want me to do about it now, Jen?"

"What I've always wanted you to do with this case. Drop it. You're never going to catch the guy. Shit, he's probably dead. And I can tell you one thing with 100% certainty. It's not going to bring Mom back. And what is this 20th-anniversary crap? We won't be celebrating the 20th anniversary of the worst day of our lives. This isn't some sports team celebrating a championship from twenty years ago. This is the death of our mother. Stop with this anniversary nonsense."

My sister was already pretty high-strung, and the intensity increased whenever we talked about our mother.

"I hate thinking that the guy might still be out there, Jen."

"You don't think I feel the same, Bobby?"

"It's different for you."

"Why?"

"Because you're 3,000 miles away. You're not in the same city where she died. You don't see some creep ball at a grocery store and wonder if that's the guy. It eats at me in a way that it can't if you live back east."

"Even if I grant you that, nothing will come of this wild goose chase. All you're going to do is make Dad sadder and me madder."

"What if it led me to catch Mom's killer?"

"Have you discovered anything that would lead you to believe you're making progress? And don't give me the same crap you gave KEYT last night. You're trying to get some info on a roofer in a Polaroid picture from God knows how long ago? I mean, are you freaking kidding me? Why do you need to find this guy?"

"I'll text you a screenshot of the photo. You should see the way he's looking at Mom."

"Is this a joke? A horny roofer from decades ago is staring at a hot woman? Shit, why stop at KEYT? I think the BBC and PBS would want to jump on this."

I wanted to yell at my sister. The thing was, she wasn't wrong. Yvonne and my father had voiced the same concerns. I was jumping to a Grand-Canyon-sized conclusion regarding Lyle Taft.

"Those are my next two stops. And then CNN and FOX on Thursday."

Jen knew I was joking, but I couldn't tell how she would take it.

"No Al Jazeera? How about a live Q and A session on Twitter?"

She'd taken the bait.

"That's the Jen I know and love."

I heard her exhale.

"You know I love you too, Bobby. This is ridiculous, though. You plucked some random roofer out of an old photo album."

"The guy beat up a client, and everyone I've talked to said he was a menace to society. And he was still working around SB when Mom died."

"Was he ever charged with crimes against women?"

"I don't know. I haven't gotten that far."

"If the answer to that question is yes, then I'll be more responsive."

"I'll keep you posted."

BOBBY

"If I were you, I'd hope this Lyle guy is dead. If not, you might be hearing from his attorney."

I wasn't going to tell her I'd thought the same.

"It's not like I said he was the murderer. I just said I'd like to find him and ask him a few questions."

"You singled him out and asked for information on him. Don't give me that shit. Everyone knows what you meant. I'd be furious if I were him."

"It sounds like Lyle Taft was always furious," I said.

She didn't take the bait this time.

"I know why this all started," Jen said.

"It's because I randomly reached for a photo album."

"That's not what I'm talking about. Dad told me about you being laid off."

"I wasn't laid off."

"Dad was mistaken?"

"I was fired."

"Oh. Even better."

"I'm still looking for other jobs. It's not like this thing with Mom has taken over my life."

"Not yet, but I know how this ends."

At times in my life, I'd had what you'd call an addictive personality. I'd become consumed with things. That's what my sister was trying to not-so-subtly refer to.

"It ends with me catching the guy who killed our mother."

"Like your investigation, this discussion is going nowhere. You're as stubborn and hard-headed as ever."

"And you're a bouquet of roses," I said.

She didn't react to my attempt at humor.

"I'm coming back to SB in the middle of September. You ready to see your nephew and niece?"

She had changed the course of the conversation, and I was grateful for it.

"I sure am. Face Timing them just isn't the same. Are we still on for tomorrow night, by the way?"

"Yup. Same bat time, same bat channel."

"Are you going to tell your husband about this?"

"We had turned a corner, Bobby. We were talking about fun things, like my pending visit and my mini-me's. Why you gotta swing it back?"

Jen's husband, Justin Ridgely, and I had never seen eye-to-eye. Some might argue that I would never see eye-to-eye with whoever my sister ended up marrying. Maybe that's true, but I particularly didn't like Justin. He was as WASPy as they come, and while I don't have a problem with that per se, he pretended to be above other people, and I hated that.

Then again, he made good money and was helping support a family of four as a dermatologist. Meanwhile, I was a recently fired social media manager who went on television and made an ass of himself. Who the hell was I to criticize anyone else?

"I'm not swinging it back. I'm just asking if you are going to tell him?"

"About this thing with Mom or about you being fired?"

I'd meant about my interview on KEYT, but now I thought that him knowing I was unemployed would be even worse. That's when his holier-than-thou attitude would rear its ugly head.

"I was talking about Mom, but you can leave that other part out too."

"Grow up, Bobby. Justin doesn't care about your employment situation."

"Is he going to be joining you on your trip?"

"Yes. He's my husband and the kids' father."

"I can't wait to see him and talk about his stock options and the sport of Polo."

"You're an asshole."

"I love you, sis."

"I love you too, but you're still an asshole. Stop accusing people of murder on live television."

This was us at our best. Jen calling me an asshole, but me knowing it was meant out of love.

"It wasn't live. I recorded it like an hour before it aired."

"You know what I mean."

"And by the way, I didn't accuse him of a damn thing."

"You keep saying that, but that wasn't my impression. Walk down State Street and ask anyone who watched the interview whether they thought you were accusing him of being involved in Mom's murder?"

"That sounds like a lot of fun. I'll get right on that," I said sarcastically.

"You're impossible," she said. "I'll see you in a few weeks."

"Bye, Jen."

And that was the end of the phone call. It summed up our relationship. You could find the love, but only if you looked past a series of daggers and biting comments.

❧ 8 ☙

BOBBY

Mark Patchett was the lead investigator for my mother's murder.

He was a fresh-faced thirty-year-old who had just been thrown his first big case back then. We met with him in the days following the murder, and my father thought he came off as confident and proficient, two characteristics crucial to being a good homicide detective.

I was only twelve, but my impression was similar to my father's.

While Patchett's confidence never wavered, my belief in his competence waned as the weeks and months rolled by.

They interviewed neighbors, family members, and an old boyfriend or two, but it didn't go anywhere. No one was arrested, and no one was even officially labeled a suspect. They didn't have any DNA, eyewitnesses, or surveillance cameras, which are so prevalent nowadays.

The case was seemingly going nowhere. And I mean nowhere.

After about a year, even Patchett's confidence started to fade. We'd still meet with him every few weeks, but new information was becoming harder to come by.

Many detectives took a crack at my mother's case in the years that followed, but when I wanted to find out where it stood, I'd still return to Patchett. He hadn't gotten us what we wanted, but he had been honest with us and had certainly put in the time. This was killing him as much as anyone outside of our immediate family.

40

I'd seen Patchett a handful of times over the past several years. He was no longer a young, cocky thirty-year-old. He was now fifty or fast approaching it, and his hair had all turned gray. He looked like a man ten years his senior.

It was time I paid him a visit.

"How are you, Bobby?"

Mark Patchett had agreed to meet me, so I drove to the Santa Barbara Police Department's head precinct on East Figueroa Street. Patchett heard me talking to the clerk at the front and walked out to greet me. He looked even worse than when I'd last seen him.

"Hello, Detective Patchett."

We had known each other long enough that I could have called him Mark, but I usually addressed him as Detective or, sometimes, just Patchett.

"Follow me," he said.

We walked the twenty yards to his office, and both took a seat in the cramped office.

"I saw your interview on KEYT the other night."

"Sounds like the whole city did," I said.

"Isn't that what you wanted?"

"Do I want the attention on my mother's case? Yes. Do I wish I could take back a few things I'd said? Also, yes."

Detective Patchett slyly smiled.

"Have you heard from Lyle Taft's attorney yet?"

"No, but thanks for being the fifth person to make that joke over the last few days."

"Sorry. I had to."

"Did he ever come up on your radar during the investigation?"

"No. From what I've been able to gather since your interview, Lyle installed your parents' roof four years prior to your mother's murder. And you found him through an old family photo album. No offense, Bobby, but how the hell was I supposed to know about him? Not that it matters. You're just as likely to find the killer by pointing at some random person walking the streets of Santa Barbara right now."

"So you don't think it's him?"

"He's guilty of taking a bad picture. And maybe of having impure thoughts about your mother. Neither of those is a crime."

I'd recently started to consider if, subconsciously, I knew this from the beginning, and the picture had just been the driving force to begin my investigation. There was likely some truth to that. The photograph did give me the heebie jeebies, however. The dude was a creep. It wasn't just a bad picture.

"Well, like you said, at least it's got people talking about her murder again," I said.

"Yeah, I guess that's a good thing," Patchett said, but I'm not sure he truly felt that way. My guess was that he thought the killer was gone. Either dead or vanished into thin air, but regardless, never to be seen (or found) again.

"Are you still the lead investigator?" I asked.

"Technically, I've never been replaced, even though twenty other detectives have taken their crack at it over the years."

"So it's still an open case?"

"You know it is, Bobby."

"Yeah, I guess I did. Has there been anything new since I last saw you?"

"What was that, six months ago? No, nothing new. If anything in the case changed, you and your father would be the first to know. Your sister, too, but she never wanted to get as involved as you."

"That hasn't changed. She chastised me over the phone after my interview."

Mark Patchett laughed.

"She was a tough cookie," he said.

"Still is."

"Probably smart of her to get out of town and distance herself from all this. Have you ever thought about doing the same?"

"Yeah."

"And?"

"And I've always decided to stay."

"I'd ask that brain of yours for a second opinion."

"Story of my life."

Patchett moved around in his seat. They were uncomfortable as hell. I couldn't imagine having to sit in them day after day, year after year. And I had a feeling Patchett was sitting in his office a lot more now than he was in his younger days. I wouldn't call him a desk jockey, but he always seemed to be at the office when I dropped by. Fifty is still a relatively young age, but not for police officers. You were a lot closer to your way out than your way in.

"So, what brings you here today, Bobby?"

"You've already answered what brought me here. I wanted to know if there was anything new on the case and if Lyle Taft had ever come on your radar."

"Sadly, the answer to both is no. Is that really it?"

"Since there's nothing new, yeah, that's it."

I almost got up but decided to throw one last thing out there.

"Did you know that Lyle Taft beat up someone whose roof he was working on?"

"I found that out yesterday. I did a quick little dive into your purported suspect."

"That doesn't give you a second's pause?"

"Sorry, Bobby, but it doesn't. I really wish it did."

"You're never going to be done with this case, are you?" I asked.

"No. Detectives always talk about the one case that sticks with them forever. Your mother's case is that one for me. The only way that will change is if it gets solved or if I pass away."

"Let's hope it's the former," I said.

He gave a resigned smile.

"I fear it's going to be the latter."

With that, he stood up, signifying the meeting was ending.

"But I'm not giving up," he added. "And who knows, maybe this stunt you pulled with KEYT will be the break we needed."

Patchett had gone from downtrodden to optimistic in world record time.

"That's better," I said.

We shook hands, and I turned to go.

"Let's meet again before the 20th anniversary," Patchett said. "Maybe I can help get the word back out."

Detective Patchett was slightly reinvigorated. I took that as a victory.

"One last thing," I said.

"Sure."

"Can I get a copy of the initial police report? I haven't read it in years."

"Yeah, come with me. I'll print one up for you."

❦ 9 ❦

BOBBY

October 28th, 2003.

It felt both like yesterday and like fifty years had passed.

I was twelve years old, and Jen was ten. My my mother was thirty-six, and my father had recently turned forty. They'd been married for fourteen years. It should have been the prime of my mother's life. Still youthful, a happy marriage, and two (hopefully tolerable) children.

My father worked as a civil engineer, and we lived in the house they'd bought five years previous. It was nothing to write home about, but it was perfect for two young kids, with a little backyard where we could run amok.

It wasn't one of the multi-million dollar houses that were so common-place in Santa Barbara. Instead, it was a modest home for a hard-working father and an equally hard-working (arguably more so) stay-at-home Mom.

It was the same house that my father remained in to this day.

I remember that morning well. My parents got into one of their rare arguments before we went to school. I'm sure it still eats at him to this day. They were arguing over something stupid. My father had cooked us bacon and eggs for breakfast, and my mother thought we should eat healthier. My father said something like, "I try to help with breakfast, and this is what I get," and my mother responded, "Making cereal or cutting up some fruit would still be helping."

It was a tiny fight in the grand scheme of things, but it was enough to leave an impression on me. I remember telling the cops about it when they interviewed me later that day. I hope that didn't give the Santa Barbara Police Department a moment's pause to consider if my father was involved. Not that it mattered either way. They always suspect the spouse at first, don't they?

My father left for work after making us breakfast. I think my parents kissed and made up before I left, but I can't be sure. Maybe that's just wishful thinking on my part. My mother drove us to school. Jenny and I went to the same school; I was in 6th grade, and she was in 4th. The following year, I'd start at a different school.

My mother seemed fine when she dropped us off. She had no idea of what was to come. How could she?

School was school. I remember having to make a short speech in history class and being a little nervous about it. However, I ended up nailing it, and I couldn't wait to tell my parents. They took great pride in me and my sister's schoolwork. A good education was essential to them, as they'd told me approximately 5,361 times.

My mother had graduated from Santa Barbara City College but then met my father, and they were married within two years. She never returned to school. Life may have gotten in the way of continuing her education, but she wouldn't let that be the case with us. We were fully expected to attend a four-year university. Even as a twelve-year-old runt, I knew that.

Our first inclination that something might be wrong was when our mother wasn't there to pick us up after school. It could have been twenty different things - had to get gas, a minor accident, a maintenance guy still at the house - and I don't remember being alarmed at that point.

I'd been given my first cell phone six months before. My parents had made it clear that it was only for emergencies. There was no internet, and it was an old-school Motorola flip phone. I only used it to call my parents and an occasional friend. I'd say about one-third of twelve-year-olds had a cell phone in 2003. I was one of the lucky ones.

I used it to call my mother's cell phone, which kept ringing. That was very much unlike her. I next called our home phone, but there was no answer there, either.

There had to be some rational explanation. No one assumes the worst that early on.

Next, I called my father, who answered. I told him Mom was late and I couldn't reach her. He said he'd get back to me.

Jenny was holding my arm tight and kept asking where Mom was. Looking back on it, it's heartbreaking, but I thought she was overreacting in the moment.

My father called me back five minutes later and said he would come pick us up. That was when I began to get a little worried. He rarely picked us up from school. He had to work until almost six every night.

I started to entertain the possibility that something had happened to my mother, but I never could have guessed the tragedy that awaited us.

❧

MY FATHER TOOK US HOME AND PARKED IN THE GARAGE.

"Stay in the car, you two."

I remember him saying those exact words.

My heart was beginning to race. Jenny was sitting in the back, but she leaned forward and grabbed my wrist.

She looked up at me, and I could tell she was on the verge of tears.

I was still hoping there was some logical explanation.

About thirty seconds after my father entered the house, we heard an ear-piercing scream. I'll never forget the sound of that scream.

Our father came back out to the car.

He looked and talked to me. I was the older brother and would be in charge of Jenny.

"Bobby, I want you to walk Jenny to the Engelbrechts."

"What happened to Mom?" I asked.

"Do as I say. I'll be over there as soon as I can."

"What happened to Mom, Dad?"

My father rarely raised his voice, but he did on this occasion.

"Bobby, no more questions. I need you to take your sister across the street. Right now!"

I did as he requested, holding Jenny's arm as we crossed the street. She'd started crying, and a few seconds later, so did I.

The Engelbrechts mother was home and must have been shocked to see the two of us crying. She asked what had happened, and through tears, I tried to tell her about my mother not showing up at school. That our father had picked us up, and then we heard him scream when he went inside our house. And then he sent us over to her house.

As I finished talking, the first cop car appeared. Less than a minute later, an ambulance showed up.

I tried to open the door and run over to our house, but Mrs. Engelbrecht wouldn't let me.

"Stay here, Bobby."

I was sobbing at this point.

"Is my mother dead?"

"I don't know," she said.

TEN MINUTES LATER, MY FATHER WAS WALKING ACROSS THE STREET, tears streaming down his cheeks. I knew in that moment that our nightmare was just beginning.

How was this possible? I'd seen my mother that morning; she was as alive as any human could be. She was being a great mother, as she always was. How could she have been taken from us? What had happened?

Mrs. Engelbrecht talked to my father outside for a few seconds and then let him in.

"Is Mom dead?" I asked.

My father's eyes were red, and he was trying - unsuccessfully - to wipe the tears from his face.

He hugged me and my sister for what felt like five minutes. We were all crying uncontrollably.

"Your mother is gone," he said.

"Does that mean she's dead?" Jenny asked.

"Yes," my father said, and then he let go of us. "I need to sit down somewhere."

He looked like he was going to pass out. Mrs. Engelbrecht led him to a couch where my father buried his head into his hands. Jenny and I went and sat next to him. For that brief moment, we'd become the adults, consoling our sobbing father.

After a minute, he raised his head and wiped the tears off.

"I'm sorry, you two."

"It's okay, Dad," I said.

We saw someone approaching the Engelbrecht's house. It was a police officer.

My father stood up.

"You and your sister have to stay here a little longer," he said and walked with the police officer back over to our house.

A house where our mother now lay dead.

BOBBY

By the time the next police officer came to the Engelbrechts, there were seven police cars, an ambulance, and a big van with the ominous name "Medical Examiner" out in front of our house.

There were also 20-30 people from the neighborhood milling around the street. Yellow tape extended all around our driveway, leaving the neighbors to stand on the street.

The officers came over with my father and asked if they could ask me and Jenny some questions. I looked to my father, who nodded.

"Yes," I said, my face swollen from crying.

The officers interviewed me and my sister right then and there. I remember wondering why I'd been remanded to a neighbor's house. My father told me later that he wanted to wait until after my mother's body had been taken from the house. He thought it would be too much for me and Jenny to see her removed on a gurney, even though she'd be covered in a sheet of some sort. He wanted us to remember her as the full-of-life person she was.

As I answered all the police officer's questions, I heard people talking and a few shrieks from across the street. I also noticed that my father had moved to stand between me and the window that looked across the street. Later on, I found out that's when they were taking my mother's body to the medical examiner's van.

After we finished with the police officer, my father thanked Mrs. Engelbrecht profusely, and we walked back across the street. I can't imagine what my father was thinking at that moment.

His wife was dead. His kids were traumatized beyond belief. He certainly couldn't sleep in his house tonight. And somewhere, probably far down on the list, he knew a killer was walking the streets of Santa Barbara at that moment.

As we approached our house, I looked out at the gathered neighbors. Half of them were crying. They gave my father room, and he escorted us to the front of the house.

He talked to another officer for about thirty seconds.

"Okay, kids. You're going to wait right here. I will run in and grab some of your clothes, and we'll drive to Aunt Yvonne's house. Does that sound good?"

Obviously, it sounded far from good, but my father didn't know what else to say. Who would know what to say in a situation like that?

48

A few minutes later, my father emerged from the house. He talked to yet another officer, who started moving a few police cars from the driveway and asking my neighbors to move out of the way.

My father packed us up in the car and drove us to Yvonne's. An officer had to hold up the yellow police tape to allow us to leave.

Yvonne greeted us with a smile that was forged through red eyes and puffy cheeks. She had been crying as well. Her younger sister was dead. This was a tragedy for everyone.

She took us inside and put our bags in the guest room. Then she and my father went outside, and I could hear them talking, crying, and hugging at least three times.

My father came back in and addressed me and my sister.

"I have to go back and talk to the police for a little longer. I will return and get you tonight, and we'll go to a hotel. We can rent a movie, get an ice cream, or do whatever you like."

"I'm not a kid, Dad," I said, even though that's exactly what I was. "I don't need an ice cream. I want to know how Mom died."

Jenny looked on. There was only a two-year age gap, but there was a big difference between ten and twelve. I'm not sure she realized everything that was going on.

"Alright, Bobby. We'll discuss what happened to your mother when I return here tonight."

He came over and gave us another multi-minute hug.

"I love you guys very much," I said. "And so did your mother."

Just hearing her talked about in the past tense was jarring.

"Is Mommy in heaven looking down on us?" Jenny asked.

"She sure is," my father said as the waterworks started again.

Yvonne was also crying about ten feet away from us.

It was undoubtedly the worst day of my life, and this was the most harrowing moment of all.

"I'll be back in a few hours, guys. Bobby, I want you to look after your little sister, okay?"

"Okay, Dad."

"I love you two very much and will see you soon."

My father hugged Yvonne as he walked out of the house.

WE SPENT THE FIRST TWO NIGHTS IN A HOTEL.

On the second night, Jenny said, "I want to go home."

My father looked at me. He'd booked a hotel for all the right reasons, but it was just making things worse.

"So do I," I said.

So, the following morning, we went home to a house that would never be the same.

THE DAY WE RETURNED HOME WAS DREADFUL.

People had heard we'd returned to the house and kept stopping by to express their condolences. Most brought food, and they all wanted to talk. I was twelve years old and had just lost my mother. The last thing I wanted to do was talk to some neighbor I barely knew who lived two blocks down the street. All I wanted was for my mother to walk back through the front door. Which, even at twelve, I knew was never going to happen.

My father looked like he'd been hit by a truck. I remember wondering if he was ever going to be the same again.

It turned out he wouldn't be.

THE FUNERAL HAD TAKEN PLACE FOUR DAYS AFTER HER MURDER.

Several people spoke, and I remember crying through most of it and just wanting it to end so I could go home with my father and sister.

THE WEEKS THAT FOLLOWED WERE NO BETTER.

There were no arrests. No serious suspects.

The cause of death was strangulation, but there was no DNA left behind. She had not been sexually assaulted. That's something I found out later on. No one wanted to bring up those specifics to a twelve-year-old.

Over the following weeks, my mind often wandered, and I started to suspect different people. If a neighbor acted a little weird, I'd tell my father. He pretended to take me seriously the first two or three times, but after the fifth or sixth time, I became the boy who cried wolf.

"This isn't healthy, Bobby. You can't just accuse every person you see of being the killer. More than likely, it's someone none of us has ever met."

I stopped telling him about my suspicions, but that doesn't mean they suddenly ended. I continued to suspect way too many people. I even made a little journal where I listed the reasons why.

"*Dick Hoyt. He lives three blocks away, but I didn't see him at Mom's funeral. His family didn't bring any food either. I saw him get mad at his son once. Has a temper.*"

It probably would have been considered cute if it weren't under such horrific circumstances.

AND THEN, ONE DAY, A YEAR HAD PASSED.

We still had nothing. The murder had been the biggest story in Santa Barbara for months and months. It had even gotten some national airplay, but it was no longer the hot story during the latter stages of 2004.

At one point, and I think it was also around a year after, my father had a long conversation with Jen and me at dinner, telling us we needed to move on with our lives. He said that Jenny and I had our whole lives ahead of us, and our mother would have wanted us to concentrate on ourselves. He was dialed into the speech, showing emotions other than just grief. It was as vibrant as I'd seen him since her death.

"If you want to make your mother happy, make something of your-selves!" he said in closing.

It was a great speech, and it still sticks with me to this day.

From then on, our father tried to mention our mother less and less. Obviously, she still came up, but my father made it a point to tell us not to spend every waking moment thinking about her.

It was the right thing for him to do.

OVER THE NEXT SEVERAL YEARS, WE ACCLIMATED TO OUR NEW NORMAL.

Our father drove us to school when he could. On the mornings he couldn't, we'd get rides home from various parents of our friends, and then we'd be at the house alone from about three p.m. until our father got back at six.

We were old enough that we could look after ourselves.

My father had insisted we do daycare for the first six months after our mother's murder. After all, there was still a killer out there. My father feared maybe he was targeting the family.

I confronted my father one day. I told him that Jenny and I hated daycare and were too old for it. He allowed us to go home after that.

⚜

ME AND JENNY BOTH HAD MANY FRIENDS. WE WERE NORMAL KIDS, with the obvious exception being that our mother was never there.

We did the best we could. That included all three of us. I'd said my father was never quite the same - and certainly, part of his light had been extinguished - but he didn't let it affect his parenting. He loved us and did everything he could to give us a relatively normal childhood.

And for the most part, he succeeded.

⚜

I STAYED LOCAL FOR COLLEGE, AND JENNY MOVED BACK EAST TWO YEARS later when she graduated high school.

She thrived at Dartmouth and got a great job on Wall Street, where she met her husband and was now married with the two young kids. Austin was five, and Avery was three. She'd returned to work when Avery turned one. Jenny liked working in the stock market and decided that daycare was the way to go for them.

I wasn't surprised. I never saw Jenny as the stay-at-home Mom that our mother had been.

Meanwhile, after finishing at UCSB, I got jobs in various social media positions. They paid the rent in an expensive city, but you'd hardly say I was crushing it. I'd had a few girlfriends over the years, including a three-year relationship with Ivy Harrington that had recently ended in heart-break (for me) but had never been engaged or married. I lived a decent life and wasn't complaining, but *The New Yorker* wasn't exactly banging down my door to write a featured article titled 'The Fascinating Life of Bobby McGowan."

If you compared me to my sister, you'd inevitably say she'd accomplished more. Maybe I should have left Santa Barbara as well. Perhaps the burden of my mother's death would never leave me if I didn't get out of this city. Or, maybe I just wasn't as driven as my sister. That was probably the more likely answer.

OUR FATHER HAD KEPT WORKING THROUGH ALL OF IT.

If he'd stayed at home or quit working for a protracted period, it would have been torture for him. He had to keep moving. That doesn't mean he ever fully got over his wife's murder - he didn't - but at least he stayed busy.

In 2015, twelve years after my mother's death, our father remarried. Her name was Angie. Jenny and I thought it was the best thing for him. She was always kind to us and never tried to replace our mother. Jenny and I were in our twenties by that point anyway, so there wasn't much Angie had to do except look after our father. We liked her a lot.

They divorced in 2020 after five years together. It was because my father could never fully let our mother go. He said he and Angie grew apart, but I knew better.

Angie still lived in Santa Barbara and hadn't remarried herself. I always kind of hoped they'd get back together at some point.

AS FOR ME, I'D FOUND A CAUSE.

At least, for the foreseeable future.

Catching my mother's killer.

Was it Lyle Taft?

Maybe not. No, probably not. Shit, let's be honest; there was almost no chance.

But seeing his picture inspired me to dive back into my mother's murder.

It's like my life had meaning again after my breakup with Ivy and getting laid off from work.

It was all I thought about.

Morning. Noon. Night.

My tendency to be consumed by something was about to be on full display again.

If it wasn't already.

❧ 10 ❧

BOBBY

It was tough rehashing all those terrible memories.

I read the police report twice, and even though I'd probably read it five other times over the years, a few things stuck out this time.

One is that my mother was still alive at 2:00. I'd forgotten that she'd talked on the phone with Barbara Palatino, the mother of one of our classmates.

That information always hurt because she was only an hour from picking us up. If she'd set off to run a few errands before picking us up, maybe none of this ever would have happened.

The second thing that struck me, and this was quite obvious, is that she'd been killed during the day. It's very brazen for a killer to murder a woman during the day. There are so many minefields you have to avoid. Murdering at night seems like it would be far more manageable.

Unless the killer knew my mother was going to be home alone.

I REREAD THE STATEMENTS OF MY MOTHER'S TWO EX-BOYFRIENDS, whom they interviewed extensively. One was Roy Cooper, who no one seemed to have a positive impression of. And the other was a man by the name of Victor Tribe.

He'd dated my mother for four months and was my mother's last boyfriend before meeting my father. She'd dated Roy at eighteen and Tribe at nineteen before meeting my father at twenty and getting married two years later at the ripe old age of twenty-two. It was a different time.

Victor Tribe still lived in Santa Barbara when my mother was killed, and I have to imagine that was the main reason he was interviewed. It had been seventeen years since they had dated, and I'd literally never heard his name mentioned once in our household, unlike Roy Cooper, who came up quite often.

I read the transcript of the interview with Tribe, and I felt bad for the guy. He was a father of five and claimed that he had run into my mother twice in the last ten years. They exchanged brief pleasantries, and that was it. And yet, he was being interrogated about her murder.

That interview held very little interest to me. Victor Tribe had nothing to do with my mother's murder.

On the other hand, Roy Cooper hadn't been ruled out by the SBPD despite having an alibi. He'd been interviewed on three occasions, and I read each one. I also read the statements of Ty Brownstone and Ethan Drury, the two people he was supposedly having drinks with on the day of the murder.

Nothing else really jumped out. I had forgotten my mother was murdered on a Wednesday. From noon to four p.m. on a Wednesday didn't seem the most common time to be out drinking with the guys, but from what I'd heard about Roy Cooper, no time was off limits.

Yvonne had told me she didn't trust Cooper's friends one iota, but Uncle Rick told me he interrogated one of them and he guaranteed the guy was telling the truth. I tended to believe Rick.

Amazingly, there were no other suspects. At least none that the police seemed to focus on. Several of my neighbors were interviewed in the days and weeks after the disappearance, but none of them ever approached the status of being a suspect. Our cable guy, our PG & E guy, and a few other people who'd been around the house in the weeks before had been interviewed as well. As with the neighbors, none of them ever seemed to be on the SBPD's radar.

I'd become addicted to true crime in the years that followed my mother's death, and I never remember hearing of a case with as few suspects as hers. They interviewed my father several times, but it was just to get information about his wife. He was with five co-workers between 1:00 and 3:00 p.m., when the crime occurred.

And I know that the spouse is always the number one suspect, but anyone who'd ever met my father knew that he worshiped the ground my mother walked on. Still, it was better he had an alibi so the police could use their resources elsewhere.

❧

FINALLY, AFTER SPENDING THE MAJORITY OF TWO DAYS READING ABOUT my mother's murder, I decided that the key to solving it wasn't in the police reports.

I had to get out there and investigate it myself. Knock on a few doors; maybe piss a few people off.

It had been nineteen years and ten months, but I was convinced somebody knew something. Maybe they didn't even realize they had pertinent information.

It was going to be up to me to jog their memories.

❧ 11 ❧

CONRAD

A s someone who'd studied up on serial killers more than most - okay, more than 99.999% of the world - I'd separated them into two categories.

The first group was the ones who did all they could to keep their crimes on the front page—the ones who enjoyed conversing with the police and the media, sometimes even the families themselves. The most famous of these include the Zodiac Killer, Jack the Ripper, and Dennis Rader, also known as the BTK killer. Ted Bundy stayed in the public eye because of his two escapes, but he never alerted the media to his murders while a free man.

The second group was the ones who went about their business and let their crimes do the talking. They refused to add any fuel to their fire. This constituted the majority of serial killers, and they figured they'd be increasing their chances of getting caught if they took unnecessary risks.

❧❧❧

UNTIL RECENTLY, I'D FIRMLY PLANTED MYSELF IN THE SECOND GROUP of serial killers: The ones who shut their mouths. I never contacted or bragged to the police. I have never called one of the deceased's relatives, and I never wrote a letter to the media.

But something started to change a few years back.

I was watching a documentary on serial killers, and they featured ones who had no business getting any adoration. They hadn't accomplished a sliver of what I had.

And I hate to admit it, but I was a little jealous. These fucking assholes hadn't done shit, and they were getting documentaries made about them.

Wait till they found out the things I'd done.

Fuck documentaries, they'd be making movies about me.

You see, there's never been a serial killer like me.

I've committed nine murders, which may not in itself seem all that impressive, but I've managed to frame five of my enemies in the process—five innocent people.

That's right, four men are currently serving life in prison for murders that I committed. The fifth is serving twenty-five to life.

Name me any other serial killer in history who has accomplished that.

I'll wait.

My murders are also more meticulous, more ingenious, more unique, and more unreproducible than any other serial killer in history.

Name another serial killer who killed with their left hand, all because he was framing someone left-handed. I'll wait.

Name another serial killer who collects someone's hair when they go to the barber and leaves them at the crime scene, sealing his fate. I'll wait.

Name another serial killer who waits years before enacting his revenge so as never to get caught. I'll wait.

Fuck Van Gough. Fuck Picasso. Fuck Michaelangelo.

I was the one producing unparalleled pieces of art.

No one had ever done the things I've done.

No fucking one!

CHAPTER 11

AND BECAUSE I WAS THE MOST INVENTIVE SERIAL KILLER EVER - AND knew I'd never get caught - I decided to throw Bobby McGowan a crumb.

❧ 12 ❧

BOBBY

It had been a week since I'd appeared on KEYT, and much to my dismay, the investigation hadn't proceeded as I'd hoped.

I'd received a total of two messages on my website. One said they hoped I was able to catch the killer. They'd been following the case since it began. It was as vanilla as that. The second message was from a woman who'd gone to school with my mother and mentioned how great a person she was. That message meant a lot personally, but it meant nothing to the investigation itself.

Two messages in a week. I was hardly striking gold with my new website.

And nothing on Lyle Taft despite my shenanigans on KEYT.

So I was surprised when I logged in on a Sunday night and saw that I'd received another message. It was only seven words, but I was shaken by what I read.

"You're looking at the wrong photo album."

I clicked to see who had sent the email.

youstillwontcatchme@gmail.com

I almost dropped my laptop when I read the email address.

Was it the killer who'd sent me this?

There were a lot of kooks out there. During my extensive time reading up on true crime, I'd found scores of examples of people who had nothing to do with a case trying to involve themselves in one way or another.

This could easily be some crackpot who wanted some attention.

On the other hand, there were also numerous examples of killers throwing themselves in the mix.

Shit.

I THOUGHT LONG AND HARD ABOUT WHAT TO DO NEXT.

The logical thing to do would have been to notify the police. They'd likely go to my father's house and confiscate our family albums as evidence. That's if they took this email seriously.

And if they did take the albums, where would that leave me? On the outside looking in, that's where.

This had been my idea. I'm the one who'd set up the website. I'm the one who KEYT had interviewed. It was my mother who had been murdered.

And most importantly, the SBPD hadn't accomplished shit while investigating this case.

No, I wasn't going to the cops. At least, not yet.

I was going to go through those photo albums with a fine-toothed comb. If I found something or someone I found overly suspicious, I'd go to the police, but not before then. They'd had twenty years on the case. I'd been on it for less than two weeks and was already getting somewhere.

My father would be alarmed if I came over and grabbed twenty photo albums to take home with me.

And while he'd given a tepid thumbs-up to me investigating my mother's murder, he hadn't been all that enthusiastic about it. I didn't want to alarm him any more than I already had.

So, I would visit him and "borrow" a few albums each time. When he was away from the family room, I could just grab them and rush them out to the car, and no one would be the wiser.

I ARRIVED AT MY FATHER'S HOUSE THE NEXT DAY AND WAS GREETED with a hug.

We walked to the kitchen, and he poured me some water.

"It's been a week this time," he said. "After last week, I was half-expecting I'd see you every other day."

"I figured you could use a break from me."

"I don't need a break from you, Bobby. I do need a break from talking about your mother, however."

"I won't bring up my investigation."

"Good," he said, but I knew he was curious. "Anything new? That's my only question."

"No, not really," I lied.

"So you're just here to hang out with dear old Dad?"

"Yup. And to tell you that Jen is coming into town next month."

"Old news. Jenny called me last week and told me."

Whether we called my sister Jen or Jenny seemed to change with the seasons. She didn't seem to have a preference, so we were free to call her either.

When I was mad at her, I'd often use Jenny, like a parent who includes a middle name when flustered with their child, but besides that, there was no rhyme or reason.

"Are you going to be happy to see her?"

"Of course. I get to see my two grandkids."

"And your only daughter."

My father stared at me. He and Jen were very close growing up - closer than me and him had been - but that ended when Jen moved back east for college. He'd never outright said it, but I'd always thought my father felt abandoned by Jen.

It wasn't fair on his part. Jen had her own life to live and had chosen to escape the tragedy in Santa Barbara. I didn't begrudge Jen her decision one bit.

In fact, our father had told us many times over the years to go and live our lives, which is precisely what Jen had done.

"Yes, it will be great to see Jenny as well," he said, most likely just to appease me.

"She loves you very much," I said.

"I know what you're trying to do, Bobby. And I know your sister loves me. And I love her. But let's be honest, you butt heads with her too. So don't try to make this some father vs. daughter battle."

"I'm not."

"Oh, but you are."

Was I? Maybe a little bit. Not because I wanted an argument but because I wanted to hear my father say he loved my sister. Which, in my heart, and despite his misgivings, I knew he did. Just like me.

"Let's plan something big for the kids," I said.

"Like what?"

"How about a trip to the Zoo?"

I thought my father would protest. I was wrong.

"That would be nice."

"You're getting soft as you approach your sixtieth year on the planet," I said.

He didn't acknowledge that his birthday was in a few days. Maybe he didn't remember.

"Sure seems that way. What happened to me this last week?"

"By me bringing up Mom, you've started thinking more about your family," I said, somewhat surprised it came out of my mouth.

"This is too much for me right now, Bobby. Baby steps for me."

"Okay. You catch that Giants-Dodgers game?"

He smiled, knowing I was changing the subject for his benefit.

I stayed for ten more minutes, and we didn't mention my mother or sister again. At one point, he had to use the restroom, and I ran into the family room, grabbed three photo albums, and put them in my car.

Before I left, I told my father I was taking him out to dinner on Friday. He asked why.

"Because it's your birthday, you big dope."

"Oh yeah, that."

"And it's a big, round number," I said.

"Don't remind me."

I laughed.

"I'll pick you up at seven."

"Don't I get a choice?"

"Only in the restaurant."

"In that case, let's go to The Palace."

⚜

I SPENT THE NEXT TEN HOURS LOOKING OVER THE THREE PHOTO albums.

I'd been in a rush to grab them, so they were just three random years. I probably should have gone chronologically, but I didn't have time to look at the years on each one. I ended up with 1990, 1994, and 1997.

One of these (1990) had taken place before I was even born, and it was thirteen years before my mother's murder. I doubted I'd find anything important in it.

Even the 1994 and 1997 albums were nine and six years before the murder, and I wasn't confident I'd find anything in them either.

But that didn't stop me.

I looked at the photos, looked at them a second time, turned them over to see if my mother had written anything on them, and then turned them back over to look at them a third time. I was nothing if not meticulous.

I felt like I was trying to find a needle in a haystack. There were probably fifty different random men in the three albums. Most appeared to be neighbors. Would my father even remember them? Did I even want to bring my father into this?

And that was only three albums. How many hundreds more were scattered throughout the other albums?

I hated to admit it, but I might have bitten off more than I could chew.

❧ 13 ☙

BOBBY

The Palace Restaurant had been my mother's favorite restaurant. It was something straight out of New Orleans. They even had a zydeco player who'd patrol the sidewalk and play the music of the Bayou.

Every night on the hour, they'd have their waitstaff grab a flute of champagne (I don't know if they drank it). They'd cheer the customers around the room, usually to Louis Armstrong's "What a Wonderful World" but occasionally to Dean Martin's "That's Amore."

It was a festive environment, and the food was top-notch as well.

I picked my father up at seven and drove him to The Palace. We used to eat there every year or so but hadn't been there in a few years.

We got a table, and my father ordered a vodka gimlet. I got a beer.

We discussed some memorable visits there, including my mother's thirty-fifth birthday. She was so full of joy that night. It was inconceivable to me that she'd be dead a little over a year later.

We ordered the cajun popcorn shrimp as an appetizer, as we had every other time we went there. The dipping sauce was out of this world.

As an entree, my father ordered the gumbo, and I ordered the stuffed blackened filet mignon, which came with crawfish tails and was topped with a Hollandaise sauce. I probably put on five pounds as I devoured it, but it was worth every bite.

For the coup de grace, I had the waiter bring a Louisiana Bread

Pudding Souffle with the requisite candles. All the waiters came to our table and sang "Happy Birthday," and some neighboring tables joined in.

No, there weren't sixty candles - there were five - but my father played along.

Several tables clapped as my father blew out the final candle.

"Guess my oxygen levels are alright, blowing out sixty candles like that," he said.

I laughed.

"Five. Sixty. What's the difference?"

"I know, right? Thanks, Bobby," he said.

"You're welcome, Dad."

"You've made this very special."

I just smiled. I was delighted he'd had a great time, but I knew the coming days might be challenging. Jenny's visits always raised his anxiety levels, and if I asked for his help looking over the photo albums, that would only add to his unease.

The waiter brought our check over after we finished the meal - despite being unemployed, I insisted on paying - and we had one drink at the bar next door before I took him home.

He'd had a great night and told me so when I dropped him off. He wasn't married, and his other child lived back east, so I hoped I'd done enough.

He would have been made if I'd invited some random work colleagues so I resisted.

I was tempted to call his second wife, Angela, and tell her to make a house call, but I resisted.

⚜

I DROVE HOME AND TURNED ON MY COMPUTER WHEN SOMETHING hit me.

I'd never responded to the message I'd received.

Even if there was a 99% chance the person wouldn't respond, I wasn't doing my "job" if I didn't try to engage him.

I decided to exaggerate the number of photo albums to elicit a response.

I emailed the following to youstillwontcatchme@gmail.com.

"My mother has something like sixty photo albums. Around what year should I

be checking? If not, I have zero chance of finding a clue. At least put me in the game and give me a chance."

I decided to call him out at the end of the message. While it was still overwhelmingly likely this was just some crackpot, if by chance this was the killer, maybe this would entice him to say more.

I pressed send on the message and waited.

After an hour, I hadn't received a return message and decided to go to sleep.

❊

I WOKE UP AT 7:00 A.M., WENT STRAIGHT TO MY COMPUTER, AND WAS shocked to see an email alerting me I'd received a message.

I clicked on the link.

"You should be checking photo albums where you weren't even born yet."

I was born in 1991.

He was telling me that he had known my mother since before then.

Or, if he didn't know her, he had somehow appeared in a McGowan family photo album. Why, I had no idea.

I looked at the time stamp on the email. It was sent at 3:55 a.m.

I stocked that information away.

Was the guy a night owl or an early riser?

With a time like that, it could be either.

Any information I could gather might prove useful in the long run. Nothing was too unimportant.

❊

TRUSTING SOMEONE YOU DON'T KNOW ON THE INTERNET - ESPECIALLY one who might be a killer - certainly isn't advisable.

On the other hand, if I didn't follow his suggestion (I continued to believe it was a male), I had thirty or so photo albums to look through, each containing approximately 80-100 photos. We were talking about 2,400-3,000 photographs, and while maybe half of them were just members of our immediate family, we were still looking at well over 1,000 photos to weed through. It was way too much for me. And no, I wasn't ready to involve the police.

So, I decided to take the word of a stranger on the internet. One that was likely a crackpot, and if he wasn't that, he might have killed my mother. What the hell was I thinking? Who knows?

I returned to my father's and secured all of the photo albums that pre-dated my birth. There were six more. I already had 1990 at my place, so seven total.

This was becoming surreal.

What had started on a whim had now become a full-blown inves-tigation.

14

CONRAD

I'd managed to remain a serial killer for a long time.

And the one character trait that was more important than any other was my ability to think things through. Being patient is a more concise way to put it. I was never in a rush. If I didn't like an option, I'd mull it over a second and third time. I'd then look at it a fourth time from a different angle. And if I still had any lingering doubts, I'd scrap it altogether.

My interaction with Bobby McGowan was no different. I'd thought this through; I wasn't just conversing with him for no reason.

I was going to make Bobby - I chose to think of him by his first name - look like a madman. Someone who had utterly lost it. Someone that the police wouldn't want to have a cup of coffee with. Someone people wouldn't want to touch with a ten-foot pole. Someone whose Santa Barbara friends would turn on and start considering him a crackpot. Someone who couldn't be taken seriously.

And, most importantly, someone who would no longer get attention when he screamed about his mother's murder.

It was going to be glorious.

I just had to bide my time.

❧ 15 ❧

BOBBY

I was getting a sandwich at Tino's Italian Grocery when I ran into Ivy Harrington, my ex-girlfriend of a few years.

She broke up with me about four months ago. Despite her mother not being my biggest fan, I thought we'd had a pretty good relationship. I guess not.

Ivy had never given me a great reason; she just said she wanted to spend time apart. She didn't say she'd fallen out of love with me. That would have been easier to accept.

When I pressed her on it, she'd just say it was nothing I had done. She just needed her space.

The underlying reason was still a mystery to me.

❧

WE'D ORDERED SANDWICHES TOGETHER AT TINO'S MANY TIMES DURING our relationship. They had the best in town. I'd always gone for the Italian Sub with the works, while Ivy had usually opted for a Turkey sandwich with extra sprouts. She'd always been the healthier eater among the two of us.

"Bobby, what are you doing here?" Ivy asked.

Her sandwich was being made, and I'd just stepped in line behind her.

It's almost like she felt my presence because she swiveled around and saw me before I noticed her.

"I'm getting a sandwich at the place I introduced you to," I said.

It came off as more snooty than I'd planned.

"Italian Sub?" she asked.

"I'm nothing if not consistent."

Ivy was wearing a white tennis skirt and an orange tank top. Her light brown hair was up in a bun. I was sure she'd just come from a tennis match, something she'd been doing twice a week for years. Her legs were tanned, and she looked great, but then again, she always had.

People had often told me I'd outkicked my coverage when I'd landed Ivy. They weren't wrong.

"Turkey sandwich for you?"

She smiled.

"You know it."

Neither of us said anything for a few seconds.

"I saw you on the news the other day," Ivy said. "You're investigating your mother's murder?"

She didn't mention that I'd come off looking like a clown. Thank God.

"I am. I got laid off and figured that's what I'd do with my free time."

She moved to the check-out line as they started making my sandwich, but we were still only a few feet from each other.

"Have you made any progress?" she asked.

Ivy had always been fascinated by my mother's murder despite having never met her. She always asked me questions; it wasn't just a girlfriend trying to feign interest. She genuinely wanted to learn everything about it. That didn't mean I would be telling her about the email I'd received from the potential killer. Not a chance.

"Not much," I said.

They finished making my sandwich, and Ivy waited as I paid for it. We both walked outside.

"You look good," she said.

I'd love to have interpreted it as her still having feelings for me, but I feared it was more of her just looking for something to say.

"Thanks. So do you," I said.

Unlike her, I meant every word of it. She looked spectacular.

"Well, I guess I'll see you around," Ivy said.

"My sister is coming out in a month. I'm sure she'll probably try to hit you up."

Jen and Ivy had always gotten along during the times Jen had visited. I used to tell Ivy that it was only because Jen lived far away, and she was much more difficult if you had to see her every day.

"Maybe I could see your father as well."

I was starting to get my hopes up.

"You know my family always liked you," I said.

"I know. It wasn't them."

That was like a dagger to my heart.

"I'm sorry," she said. "I didn't mean it like that. I was trying to compliment them."

She looked genuinely sorry, so I gave her the benefit of the doubt.

"Are you dating again?" I asked.

"Couple casual first dates, but that's it. You?"

"It's been quiet on that front, but I am staying busy."

"That's good. Especially if you're not working."

"I'll probably be working harder on this investigation than I did at work."

Ivy laughed.

"Well, it matters more to you. Not sure you ever loved being a social media managing web designer."

"That's a mouthful, " I said. " And yeah, my job bored the shit out of me. Was I becoming boring myself? Is that why we broke up? Shit, we used to be animals when we first met. We couldn't keep our hands off of each other."

Ivy blushed.

A few people walked by us to get into Tino's.

"C'mon, Bobby. This isn't the time or the place."

"Then why don't you come over to my place sometime soon? I'm going to dedicate part of my living room wall to the investigation."

"Sounds interesting, but I'm not sure I'm ready yet."

She wasn't ruling it out, which I took as a good sign.

"The offer is out there. It can just be as friends."

She knew I wanted more, but I wouldn't come out and say it.

"Maybe," she said. "Look, I have to be somewhere soon, but it was nice to see you."

"You too, Ivy. I hope to hear from you."

She smiled, but it was tame, as if she was trying to appease me.

She leaned in and hugged me, and I kissed her on the cheek.

"Nice to see you, Ivy."

"You too, Bobby."

With that, we walked to our respective cars.

I SPENT THE NEXT TWO DAYS BARELY LEAVING MY APARTMENT.

I ate the Italian sub, and then Door Dashed Chinese food that night, which lasted me through the following day.

Really healthy, I know.

I was working on two things simultaneously. I was trying to learn more about what happened to Lyle Taft and, at the same time, sorting through all the photos in the albums that pre-dated my birth.

I grabbed every photo containing someone other than my mother or father, including relatives. I checked the back to see if my mother had written anything on them, and then I logged them into a ledger I'd started. I wrote down what year the picture was taken, who was in it (if my mother had written down a name), and either what was going on in the photograph or what occasion it was for.

I included pictures that had women I didn't know. While I was all but convinced the killer was a male, I wouldn't be doing a proper investigation if I didn't look at every possible angle. And maybe it was a male perpetrator with a female accomplice. Who knew? Anything was possible.

After reviewing the seventh and final album, I looked down at my ledger. I'd "narrowed" it down to 109 pictures.

Yes, it was a high number, but it seemed doable.

I looked down at all the pictures on the table in front of me, and that's when I remembered what I'd told Ivy. I was going to put everything up on my living room wall.

I would buy some cork bulletin boards and hang them on the wall. I would then pin each picture to the board. With 109 photos, I would need two or three boards.

It would be in my line of sight and wouldn't be the chaotic mess that they were on the table.

It also made my investigation feel more official, almost like I was a real detective looking over actual evidence. Which, in a way, I was.

BOBBY

I BOUGHT THREE HUGE CORK BOARDS THE FOLLOWING MORNING AND
hung them on my wall.

I pinned each photo to the first two boards. Pinning them might not
have been the best choice, but it worked for me. Plus, that would make
them easy to remove once I decided an individual photo had nothing to
do with my mother's murder.

The third cork board would be for theories, connections between
people, phone numbers, news articles, and anything else that tickled my
fancy.

❦

AFTER REVIEWING ALL OF THE PHOTOS FOR A SECOND AND THIRD TIME,
five jumped out. I decided to start my investigation with them.

They were as follows:

(1) A picture of my mother, father, and several next-door neighbors at
their apartment complex. The year was 1989. It was before my birth and
well before they'd moved into their home. There were probably ten people
in the picture in total. I found it possible that an old neighbor might have
harbored an unhealthy fascination with my mother.

(2) A picture of my mother, Roy Cooper, two other friends their age,
and two young neighborhood kids. This photo was from 1986; my mother
was a senior in high school. It was well before my parents ever met. It was
also before my mother started dating Roy, which didn't happen until my
Mom was in junior college, but he was still the primary reason I'd selected
this photograph.

(3) This one was a long shot, but it was my mother with five women
that she used to play racketball with. The year was 1990. I was born a year
later. I only included it because I'd completely disregarded the idea that it
was a woman. Maybe one of them was crushing on my father, and things
got out of control. No, I didn't think this was likely, but I included it so as
not to rule out women altogether.

(4 and 5) The final two pictures belonged in the same category. The
years were 1984 and 1985. They were pictures of the annual block party on
the street my mother grew up on. There were approximately fifty people
in each picture. While I don't remember my mother mentioning any
creepy childhood neighbors, a wolf in sheep's clothing could easily be
hiding out in one of those photos.

I HAD TO DECIDE WHICH PHOTO TO TAKE ON FIRST.

The next-door neighbors at the apartment complex seemed like too big an undertaking. It was a bunch of twenty-somethings living in an apartment complex. The odds were basically nil that any of them still lived there. Shit, the complex might well be gone. Would my father even remember any of them? Had they kept in touch in an era before cell phones or Facebook? Unlikely. I'd return to that picture but wouldn't start there.

The racketball photo could also wait.

At least with Roy Cooper or the annual block party, I had people still in town I could talk to. Find out if there were any rumors that people would be willing to divulge. Santa Barbara wasn't a small town, but it had that small-town feel. Everyone seemed to know each other, and they weren't against a bit of gossip, which, hopefully, I could use to my advantage.

Roy Cooper would have been the obvious one to look at first, but I still believed Uncle Rick when he said he had questioned/threatened one of the other two people at the bar on the day in question. And they swore that Roy was with them. That was enough for me.

I decided I'd go with the block party pictures first. I could go back and find out who still lived on that street all these years later. Maybe someone could identify the creep of the block or, at least, someone who might have had an unhealthy obsession with my mother.

After that, I'd double back and do a little more investigating on Roy Cooper. The picture at the apartment complex would follow that. Then, the one with the women playing racketball.

And then I'd be left with "only" 104 more pictures.

What the hell had I got myself into?

❦ 16 ❦

BOBBY

"Lyle Taft is dead."

Jim Broadhurst, the roofing company's owner, was on the other end of the phone.

"How do you know?" I asked.

"Remember when I told you that a few of my current employees worked for him back then?"

"I do."

"One of those old employees took it upon himself to discover what had happened to Lyle. It was after that *interesting* interview you had with KEYT."

He accentuated the word interesting for obvious reasons.

"And..." I said.

"And my guy talked to a friend of a friend of a friend who remembered Lyle. He claims Lyle moved to Alaska when he could no longer get employment as a roofer in and around the Central Valley. I wasn't the only one who wouldn't hire the guy. Word had gotten around."

"And this friend of a friend claims that Taft is dead?"

"Friend of a friend of a friend. He doesn't just claim it. He was there when it happened."

Broadhurst didn't talk again for several seconds. He was enjoying holding out the information that I so clearly wanted.

"When what happened, exactly?" I finally asked.

CHAPTER 16

"Lyle got work on one of those fishing boats in Alaska. I know on the T.V. shows they always say it's one of the most dangerous jobs in the world, but I never believed them. Well, I guess it was for old Lyle. His friend said he went overboard one day and never came back up, if you know what I mean."

The king of subtlety was back at it. I remember thinking Jim Broadhurst had been slightly endearing the first time I'd met him. Now, he was just annoying.

"Do you have anything besides just a guy's word?" I asked.

I was almost certain Broadhurst was telling the truth, but I just wanted to dot my i's and cross my t's.

"I used the Google machine and proved it myself," he said.

"A few weeks back, I'd tried Googling Lyle Taft's obituary, and nothing came up."

"That's my fault, I guess. I should have told you that he went by Lyle, but his real name was Everett. I looked back at some old paychecks."

"I thought you didn't keep old stuff."

"I didn't keep his initial signing papers where he might have mentioned some relative or something. I did find an old paycheck, though."

"And it said, Everett Taft?"

"Even better. It said Everett Lyle Taft and the obituary for the fisherman said Everett L. Taft. It's your guy."

I was being more combative than necessary. Maybe I didn't want to believe that Lyle Taft was dead. The reason wasn't hard to surmise. He had been the impetus for me starting this investigation. Knowing he was dead and my reason for beginning this investigation was bogus didn't sit well with me.

Not that it mattered all that much. I was on to new things and hadn't thought much about Lyle Taft over the last several days.

"I believe you, Mr. Broadhurst," I said.

As I continued talking to him, I Googled '*Everett L. Taft obituary*'; sure enough, one came up. The one-paragraph obit did not include a picture or mention of working in Santa Barbara, but the age range looked about right. Despite being a contrarian with Broadhurst, I'm sure it was the right guy.

"I could give you the number of my employee if you need to find out how he went from friend to friend to friend to discover Lyle's demise."

It couldn't hurt.

"Sure. Thank you."

He gave me the number.

"And remember, if you get your roof redone, you best be calling me," he said.

"I will. Thanks for your help, Mr. Broadhurst."

I didn't bother mentioning that I rented an apartment and wouldn't be buying a new roof anytime soon.

❦

SEVERAL MINUTES LATER, I TALKED TO THE ROOFER, AND IT BECAME apparent this was the same Lyle Taft. He spoke of Taft's not being able to find work after his altercation with a client, how he fled to Alaska, and how he met his demise on a fishing boat.

He said the guy he'd talked to sent him a picture of Taft on the boat, and it was the same guy he'd worked with.

I thanked him for his time.

The photo that had started all this had turned into a dead end.

Or had it?

Just because Lyle Taft was dead doesn't mean he couldn't have killed my mother.

This would be the worst-case scenario. I could spend months on this investigation without ever having a chance to catch the guy because he was already dead.

Then again, the alternative was that the killer was still alive.

I certainly shouldn't prefer that.

My brain was tired again.

I had too much going on.

I looked back at the wall and the scores of pictures I'd tacked to the giant corkboards.

Maybe it was a good thing I was single at the moment. I'm sure any girlfriend would take issue with the look of my apartment.

I glanced at the picture that had started this all.

Was I sure that Lyle Taft hadn't killed my mother?

No, but he was dead, so that part of my investigation was over.

Maybe it was just ceremonial, but I went to the cork board on the far left of the wall, removed the photo of Lyle Taft, and put it back in the photo album it came from.

One down, 108 to go.

17

BOBBY

Calle Rosales was a street in the heart of Santa Barbara in a neighborhood called San Roque.

It's northwest of downtown and is much more residential than the famous Santa Barbara streets like State, Chapala, or Anacapa. Those consist mainly of bars, restaurants, and shops. San Roque has a little of that but is more suburban, a place for raising families.

And it's where my mother grew up.

It's a tree-laden section of the city and an idyllic place to raise a family. No, that's not coming from the Santa Barbara Transportation Board but from my mother herself. She'd always mention the trees and how "idyllic" it was. I used to get tired of hearing that word.

"You raised me in Santa Barbara as well," I'd tell her. "Is it not idyllic for me?"

"It is," she'd say. "It's just different. Growing up in this town during the 1970s was a lot more innocent."

It's probably a conversation that a million parents and kids had.

Things were different in my day. We didn't have cell phones. We traversed the city on our bikes and didn't have to worry about crime.

"As if there were no abductions back in the 70s and 80s," I'd say.

And now I get a knot in my stomach every time I remember saying that.

MY MOTHER WAS THE YOUNGEST, WITH YVONNE THE MIDDLE CHILD and Rick the oldest.

Their parents - my grandparents - were both strict and loose at the same time, if that's possible. My mother said that until the sun went down, they were free to do whatever they liked. They had to attend school first, but it was free game after that. They could ride their bikes. Go to friends' houses. Go to the beach—anything within reason.

However, once the sun went down, they became strict parents and made sure that all three kids told their parents about their day. And every last piece of homework had to be done before they could turn the T.V. on.

As for dating, my mother thought there was a double standard. Rick could go out with whoever the hell he wanted. On the other hand, my mother's boyfriends had to be approved by her parents, and that was only acquired after the guy did a sit-down before they went on their first date.

While drunk one day, I remember my mother telling me that Roy tried to date her several times in high school, but her parents weren't having it.

Ironically, the reason she was drunk on the day in question was that Roy had left another voicemail on the house phone, which had led to an argument between my parents. As I usually did, I comforted my mother after they fought. And honestly, it's what my father preferred. He made sure we were always protective of her.

Luckily, I didn't have to choose sides that often. My parents had a great relationship, and most of their fights were minor in nature.

As Yvonne and Rick had told me a thousand times, my mother was attractive and popular growing up. However, she would never have said that to me, as she was too modest.

She was a good, but not great, student and decided to attend a junior college before finding a four-year college to transfer to. She had so many good friends in Santa Barbara that she wanted to remain in town and decided to attend Santa Barbara City College (SBCC), one of the better JCs in the country.

Her father said she could go to SBCC if she moved out, got a job, and paid rent. That was the strict part of her upbringing. Her father didn't want his daughter staying at his house until she was nineteen, twenty, or - God forbid! - twenty-one.

My mother was okay with that. She loved her parents but was tired of them looking over her shoulder with every guy she went on a date with. Rick was bad enough by himself.

She moved in with two good friends and lived in a desirable section of Santa Barbara called the Mesa, right next to the city college. This was in the mid-80s when rent was much more affordable in Santa Barbara. I could barely afford the Mesa now as a thirty-two-year-old man- sure, an unemployed thirty-two-year-old man, but you get my point.

It was during this time that my mother started dating Roy Cooper. They didn't last long, I think only six months or so, but the ripples would be felt for a long time. Two years later, right after graduating from SBCC, she met my father.

She told me many times that she was ready to leave Santa Barbara at that point. She had just turned twenty-one and had never lived anywhere else. She'd been accepted into several universities and was leaning toward attending the University of Washington. However, she was in love with my father and didn't want to leave town and potentially lose him.

My mother said it was the most challenging decision of her life. After much thought, she decided to remain in Santa Barbara and see where her relationship with Robert Francis McGowan II would go.

Maybe if my mother had left town, she would still be alive today. Then again, Robert Francis McGowan III - me - never would have been born.

Thinking of things in those terms had always troubled me.

֍

As for the house on Calle Rosales, my grandparents stayed there until they passed away in 2001, and Yvonne, Rick, and my mother decided to sell it.

I'd had many great memories at the house. My mother loved showing Jen and me off to her parents, and our grandparents loved showing us off to their neighbors.

It was a great place to visit.

֍

As I pulled up to the house, I started to get a little choked up.

I hadn't driven by it in years, and when I started imagining my mother as a happy, carefree young kid, it got the best of me.

My mother should still be alive! Thirty-six years old is way too young to be taken!

I parked and walked towards the familiar home. Shit, I almost felt like I'd grown up there. We went to our grandparents' house probably 2-3 times a month. With my father's parents on the East Coast, it was only natural that Jen and I would become closer to our maternal grandparents.

The house looked vastly different from the last time I'd visited. There was a new paint job, and it looked like they'd added a new section to the side of the house. I guess I shouldn't have been surprised. It had been years. Probably five years. Possibly longer.

As I approached the door, I tried to remember who last lived in the house. *The Rusks? The Rucks?* Something like that.

I knocked, and the door was answered by a man about the same age as me. This was definitely only the Rusk/Rucks if this was their son.

"Can I help you?" he asked.

"My name is Bobby McGowan, and my mother, Heather, grew up here many moons ago."

He looked at me, and I could tell he knew who I was. I'm sure it was either by reputation because of my mother's fate or possibly because he'd seen my meltdown on KEYT.

"I'm Griffin. Yeah, I think I remember hearing the name," he said.

I didn't bother telling him that it would have been Heather Fields back then, not Heather McGowan.

"Nice to meet you, Griffin. How long have you lived here?" I asked.

"Almost four years. My wife and I bought it just as Covid was starting. Nice timing, right?"

"Hey, at least you had a nice house you never got to leave," I said.

He laughed.

"That's true. What can I help you with, Bobby? Did you want to come and see what the house looks like now?"

"I might take you up on that later, but for now, I was wondering if you knew who on this block has lived here since the 1970s or 80s."

"Whew. I don't know. We know most of our neighbors, but I'm unsure who's been here the longest. Two elderly families live on the block. I'm not positive they've been here that long, but I'd probably start with them."

"Is one of them the Ruskin's?"

"You know them?"

"Yeah. I spent a lot of my childhood here. Great to hear they are still alive."

"I should have been clearer when I said families. She is still alive, but Mr. Ruskin died in the last year or so."

"Oh, I'm sorry."

"Don't be sorry for me. It sounds like you knew him better than I ever did," Griffin said.

"He used to always have candy at his house."

He looked at me oddly.

"Not in a creepy way," I said. "They were about the nicest couple you'd ever meet. They just liked giving away candy to the neighborhood kids. Every day was Halloween at the Ruskin house."

"I'm not sure that's any better," he said.

I laughed.

"Good point," I said. "Who was the other elderly family you mentioned?"

"Oh, I always forget their damn name. It's the last house on the left."

I tried to remember who lived in that house but was drawing a blank.

"No problem. I'll knock on their door after talking to Mrs. Ruskin."

"Sounds good. Don't be shy if you want a tour of your mother's old place. Just stop back by. My wife should be home any minute, and she can show you all the changes she's made."

"Thanks. I may do that. Although, I think you're now the 3rd or 4th family who has owned it since."

"We bought it from the Englerts."

It was the Englerts. How the hell had I gotten the Rusks?

"Okay, they had brought it from my grandparents. So I guess you're only the 2nd family to own it since then."

"Nice. What do we win?"

"You win the prize of showing a complete stranger around your house."

"Swing by later. My wife knows what changes we've made. I just get handed the bill."

I laughed.

"Will do. Thanks for your help."

I WALKED THE SIXTY OR SO YARDS TO THE RUSKIN HOME.

I remembered the house well but couldn't remember their first names. I was sad to hear that the husband had passed. My mother had always felt at home at the Ruskin's.

I knocked on the door, and a young Asian woman answered.

"Hi," I said, a bit surprised. "I was looking for Mrs. Ruskin."

"I'm her caretaker, Nina. I don't think she was expecting visitors today."

"This was out of the blue. I used to play around at this house when I was a kid."

"Oh, you grew up on this block?"

"My mother did, but she brought us here when we were kids."

"Maybe seeing some old friends would be good for Mrs. Ruskin. Jar her memory a little bit."

This didn't bode well for our upcoming conversation.

"Is her mind all there?" I asked.

"For being eighty-eight years old, she's pretty darn good. She has her senior moments, but for the most part, her memory is intact."

"That's nice to hear."

"Let me go make sure she's up for a conversation," she said.

"Great. Thanks, Nina."

She returned two minutes later.

"Mrs. Ruskin would love to see you."

Nina led me to the living room area. Mrs. Ruskin was in the right corner of the room. She had multiple tubes going in and out of her, and it looked like she should have been in a hospital.

I looked at Nina, who nodded. My interpretation of that was that she didn't have much time to live. I was starting to wonder if there was more of a hospice-type situation.

I approached and put my hand out to Mrs. Ruskin, and she took it immediately. Her handshake was almost non-existent. Even a mere hand-shake took a lot of effort on her end.

"How are you, my son?" she asked.

I hope she didn't think I was her son. I tried to remember back. If memory serves, the Ruskin's had two sons and a daughter.

"I'm alright. Thanks for asking. My name is Bobby McGowan. Do you remember me?"

A blank expression came upon her face.

"I don't think so."

"My mother was Heather Fields."

"Oh, sure. I remember Heather."

I thought she was going to ask how she was.

"Such a tragedy with what happened to her."

Mrs. Ruskin had a better memory than Nina had let on.

I should have had more tact than to ask my next question, but if the woman was in and out of mental clarity, I had to strike while the iron was hot.

"Did you ever have any idea about who might have wanted my mother dead?"

"Oh no, my son. That wasn't my place. I just grieved her loss. She was such a cute child and then a pretty young woman."

I half-expected her to say, *'The cutest in three counties,'* but mercifully, she didn't.

"Do you remember anything that might help?"

"Help what?"

"I've started investigating my mother's death again."

That's when Nina grabbed me by the arm.

"Can we talk?" she said.

We walked to the front door, and I knew what was coming.

"You didn't tell me this was what you would ask about."

"Would you have let me in if I had?"

"No."

"See. I had to."

She looked at me. Her expression was part anger and part sympathy over what she'd just overheard. The latter won out, at least for a little while.

"I'll give you a few more minutes, but that's it. And try to make it the least stressful you can. Phrase it around your mother and not her death."

Jeez. Nina was a pro at this.

"That's good advice," I said.

She pointed back toward the living room.

I walked back.

"Did you say you're investigating Heather's murder?"

I could feel Nina staring at me.

"I'm just trying to get some recollections of my mother. Do you have any?"

"Oh, I just remember her as a baby, coming over to our house a few times a week. She was a few years younger than our youngest."

"Do you remember anything when she was a little bit older? Maybe like when she was a teenager."

"I didn't see her as much as she got older. Didn't she go to Kansas to go to college?"

"No, she stayed local and went to Santa Barbara City College."

"Are you sure she didn't go to Kansas to play basketball?"

It was the first time Mrs. Ruskin had shown her age.

"No, I'm pretty sure she stayed in Santa Barbara."

"The Kansas Jayhawks. Yeah, that's where she went."

I feared this was trending downhill.

"I just have two more questions."

"Okay," she said.

"Did you know a guy named Roy Cooper?"

"What did you say his name was?"

"Roy Cooper."

"Was he a jerk?"

"Yeah, some people thought so."

"Neighborhood bully, right?"

"Right."

"Yeah, I remember the name but don't remember what he looked like. I think he went to Kansas for college. They are called the Jayhawks."

I started feeling bad. It was time to cut my losses.

"I have one last question, Mrs. Ruskin, and thanks so much for your time."

"You're welcome, my son."

"Do you know anyone who might have wanted to harm my mother?"

I could feel Nina's stare, but I didn't care. I was ready to leave.

"No, of course not. Your mother was perfect. Must have been some deranged animal."

I extended my hand again, and Mrs. Ruskin took it.

"Thanks so much for talking with me," I said.

"Come again any time," she said. "It gets pretty lonely here."

"Maybe I will," I said.

Nina walked me to the door.

"How much time does she have?" I asked.

"A month tops."

"Do any of her kids live locally?"

"One. Freddy, the youngest. There are two other kids. One lives in New York, and one lives in Europe. They always call Freddy for updates, but obviously, they can't be here themselves."

Mrs. Ruskin said Freddy was only a few years older than my mother. Assuming she had got that one right.

I took out a business card from the company I no longer worked for.

"Can you please give this to Freddy the next time he comes over? I'd love to talk to him."

Nina eyed me skeptically, but I knew she'd give it to him. I'd managed to win her over.

"Yeah, I'll give it to him."

"Thanks, Nina."

"You're welcome. I hope you catch your mother's killer."

I surprised myself by leaning in for a hug.

"Thanks."

I left seconds later.

❧ 18 ❧

BOBBY

I was surprised to receive a phone call from Freddy Ruskin later that night. The fact that he called me wasn't that surprising; I just didn't expect it the same day I'd visited his mother.

It was nine p.m., and I was looking at one of the photos on the cork boards. This was starting to feel like a 16-hour-a-day job.

"Hello," I answered.

"This is Freddy Ruskin. I think you came and visited my mother this morning."

"I did. Thanks for calling me back."

"I heard what you were there for," he said, then slightly paused. I thought he was about to admonish me. "Was my mother lucid? I hope she was helpful."

I could have mentioned the Kansas Jayhawks, but what was the point? It's better to tell a little white lie sometimes.

"She was very accommodating. Thanks. And I appreciated the conversation."

"I knew your sister," Freddy said.

"Your mother said you were just a few years older than her."

"Yeah. I'm Yvonne's age."

"Were you and Yvonne close?"

"In proximity because we lived so close but were never great friends.

88

It's not that I didn't like her. It's just that when you are a kid, how many girls do you have as friends?"

"I get it. How about in high school?"

"Kind of ran in different circles. We were always cordial, though."

"And my mother?"

"She was a freshman or sophomore when I was a senior. So, we didn't overlap all that much in high school. The thing was, I was kind of a dork, and as I'm sure you know, your mother was part of the cool crowd."

"I was told she was nice to everyone."

"She was. That wasn't a judgment against her. I'm just saying that we didn't have a huge crossover regarding friends."

"Did you know anybody who wished her ill will? Especially someone who might have lived on the block?"

"I guess, like most streets in America, Calle Rosales had mostly great people intermixed with a few weirdos."

"I'm more interested in the weirdos."

"I'll give you their names, but keep in mind that I graduated high school forty years ago. For all I know, these guys might be rocket scientists at this point."

"Point taken, and I'll never mention your name. I probably won't find them anyway. They might be rocket scientists in Finland, for all I know."

I heard Freddy laugh slightly on the other end.

"Does Finland even build rockets?"

"Good point," I said. "Probably not."

"Anyway, there was a set of twins who I always thought were a little off. I remember them thinking your mother was hot, which, let's be honest, everyone did. It's just that they would always knock on your mother's door and ask her to come out and play. And this is when we were like twelve and thirteen. It was odd. Their last name was Maker, and I remember one of the twin's names was Bill. We'd say he was a Bill Maker, like he printed money. Hey, we were young kids. We found it funny."

"I probably would have, too," I said. "Do you remember his brother's name?"

"For the life of me, I don't. I could ask my mother. Sometimes, she surprises me and remembers things that I don't."

"You don't have to bother her. I'm sure I can find out the other brother's name."

"Wait," Freddy said. "Never mind. I just remembered the twins moved to Australia in their late twenties. They wouldn't have been around when your mother was killed."

"False alarm, I guess," I said, sounding deflated.

"There was one other guy who came to mind."

"Who?"

"Roy Cooper. He was always coming by our block, trying to chat up Heather. He was an asshole. I moved away after high school, so I'm not sure what happened with him."

"I hate to admit it, but he and my mother dated briefly after high school."

"She was way too good for him. He was scum."

"So I've heard."

"And I hate to ask, but was he ever considered a suspect? I moved to Chicago after high school and only returned five months ago once my mother got sick, so I don't know much about the case."

Life is weird.

This was an extremely tough time for Freddy Ruskin as his mother lay in hospice. And yet, part of me was jealous of him. He was getting time with his mother in her later years that I would never get with my own. His mother was eighty-eight. Mine had been taken at thirty-six.

"He had an alibi," I said, leaving it at that.

"I'd double-check it. That guy was no good."

I could have told Freddy I would double-check it, but I saw no need to go further down the Roy Cooper rabbit hole with him.

"Last question for you, Freddy. Of anyone who lived on Calle Rosales, who would you say knew my sister best?"

"Mott Larsen, I guess. I'm surprised I'm going with a guy, but his family lived directly across the street from Heather. And I think they were the same grade as well."

"Okay, thanks. I told your mother I would stop by again. Is that alright? I won't bring up my mother's murder."

"That would be fine. Any visitor is good for her. And yes, please keep it upbeat. Maybe mention how much your mother liked going to her house."

"She did. I liked going there too. They always had candy."

Freddy Ruskin let out a big laugh.

"They sure did. I guess nothing changed even after all of us kids left."

"I'll tell her I had fifty Reese's Peanut Butter Cups there over the years."

"She'd love to hear that."

"Consider it done."

And then he uttered what was becoming a commonplace goodbye in my conversations.

"Good luck with your investigation."

❧

I FELT LIKE ROY COOPER WAS HOVERING OVER EVERYTHING.

Every person I talked to seemed to mention him. He was the number one suspect for many, even Freddy Ruskin, who'd left for Chicago when my mother was still in high school. Cooper certainly left an impression, and it was never a good one.

So, while I wanted to talk to Mott Larsen, I decided to make an executive decision and jump to the Roy Cooper photo next.

❧

I SHOWED UP UNANNOUNCED AT THE SBPD PRECINCT AND ASKED TO see Detective Patchett. They sent me back to his office.

"Twice in a week, Bobby?"

"As I'm sure you know, an investigation never sleeps."

He laughed.

"Spoken like a true cop...only you're not."

"Is it too late to become one?"

"I assume you're joking, but I'll take the bait. How old are you?"

"Thirty-two."

"There's no maximum, but let's just say if you were north of forty, you probably wouldn't get the job. Thirty-two? We would give you a look."

"I was joking, but nice to know I have a job to fall back on now."

Patchett smiled.

"So, what brings you here?"

"I wanted to talk about Roy Cooper."

"Everyone's favorite suspect, right?"

"That's the name I keep hearing over and over."

"Jealous ex. Had a temper. He checked a lot of boxes."

"But his alibi was believable, right?"

"An alibi has to be more than believable, Bobby. We need to know with certainty that there was no chance he could have been at your mother's house. An alibi has to be verified."

"And his was?"

"From the information we have, yes."

"From the information we have? What does that mean?"

"We have sworn statements from Ty Brownstone and Ethan Drury that they were at Archer's Bar that day. A bartender, who I'll admit isn't the most reputable, swore that the three of them were there from noon to five p.m."

"Why wasn't the bartender reputable?"

"He was known to imbibe on the job. And I'm not talking about a random beer here and there."

"He'd get hammered behind the bar?"

"At times, yes."

"How about the two friends? Do you believe them?"

"I do, Bobby. I interviewed Roy the day after the murder, and then I interviewed Ty and Ethan hours later. I know everyone else thought Roy was the killer, but I never did. Roy Cooper might be an all-time jerk, but I believe he was at the bar that day."

"No cameras at the bar?"

"Have you ever been to Archer's?"

It was a hole in the wall. It was also twenty years ago when video cameras were far less prevalent.

"I get your point," I said.

"And by the way, you don't have to ask me if a place had cameras. Did you think I would have overlooked something that simple?"

"No," I admitted.

Patchett nodded, but I could tell he was slightly perturbed at me.

"Could Roy Cooper have paid someone else to do it?" I asked.

"Anything is possible. But we never found one shred of evidence to lead our investigation in that direction."

I decided to switch topics.

"Has your opinion on anything changed over the years?"

"That's kind of a random question."

"I know."

"Yeah, I guess a few have."

"Like what?"

"Well, when I initially started on the case - and I'm talking the first few days - I just assumed it was someone close to her. A neighbor who secretly stalked her. A guy from the grocery store who started having a crush on her. Something like that."

"You don't feel that way any longer?"

"It's hard to explain, but I now feel this was more impersonal than I originally thought."

"Why do you say that?"

"Also, hard to explain. More gut feeling than anything else. But the guy didn't rape her. He didn't even take her panties or bra off."

Detective Patchett paused.

"You don't mind me talking about these things?" he asked.

"I hate it, but I understand it's unavoidable if we're going to talk about the case seriously. I've read the police report and been asking myself the same questions for years, so you don't have to hold anything back."

"I guess my point is that this didn't seem personal to me."

"Isn't choking someone to death personal?"

"It's up close and personal if that's what you mean. But no, I don't think that's personal. Stabbing someone twenty times or beating someone to a pulp so they are unrecognizable. Those are personal. Raping someone or leaving her body in a vulnerable position would be personal also. I don't think choking is. That said, I'm sure many cops would disagree with me."

"What you say makes sense."

"Thanks a lot, Bobby."

"You're welcome."

It was weird, the detective thanking me. This case had obviously beaten him down, and he'd take an affirmation from anyone, even someone who had never been a cop or a detective.

"Why all the questions about Roy Cooper?"

"A childhood neighbor of my mother's mentioned him."

"Why are you interrogating people in her childhood neighborhood? She hadn't lived there in almost twenty years."

I'd already decided it was too early to tell Patchett about the email. One day, but not yet. So I couldn't mention the photos of block parties and why I'd ended up on Calle Rosales.

"Just wondering if it could have been someone from her childhood, and Roy fits that bill."

"Not that I'm telling you to do this, but if you're going to be out there investigating anyway, you should be talking to the neighbors of the house where your father still lives. The house where your mother was murdered. That's where someone might have seen something. I'd always hoped someone had seen a suspicious car pull up that day, but no neighbor ever reported anything. And I interviewed them all multiple times."

Twenty years later, two couples still lived on my father's block. I'm sure it hadn't been easy on them either. They had been close to my mother, so they had to grieve her death. Plus, they had to worry that a killer was on the loose in their neighborhood.

Three families moved within that first year. I couldn't blame them. I always wondered if they found it odd that my father stayed. Probably. If anyone should have moved, it would have been him. But he insisted that he still felt our mother's spirit in that house, and if he moved, part of her would be gone forever. I understood his rationale for staying even if most others didn't.

"I'll interview some people on my father's block next," I said, even though I knew I wouldn't. If the remaining families had seen anything, they would have told my father years ago. "By the way, is law enforcement mad I'm out there doing things on my own?"

"If this case had occurred recently, we wouldn't look kindly on it. Since it's been twenty years, and let's be honest, it's not exactly a high-priority case right now, I don't think you'll catch any flak."

"Nice to know it's not a high priority," I said.

"C'mon, Bobby, it's been two decades."

"I know. I was kidding."

"A joke about your mother's investigation? Are you sure you're okay?"

"I'm interviewing people daily and asking the same darn questions to each one. I could use a little levity. You should see my apartment. It looks like an episode of some crime drama. I've got framed cork boards with photos tacked to them."

"Sounds like you're taking this pretty seriously."

"I wouldn't have started this if it was going to be half-assed."

"No, I don't think you would have."

"I have another favor to ask," I said.

"What is it?"

"It wasn't in the initial police report you gave me. Can I get the statements of the two guys who gave Cooper his alibi?"

"Three guys."

"I thought there were two."

"You're forgetting the disreputable bartender I told you about."

"Ah. I was only referring to the two friends."

"I'll see what I can dig up and call you tomorrow."

"Thanks for your help, Detective Patchett."

I got up to go.

"I'll tell you one thing, Bobby. I wouldn't be as liberal with these police reports if it hadn't been twenty years."

"You know what, Detective Patchett? I think you want this case solved almost as much as I do."

"It would help ease twenty years of pain."

"I'm looking for the same thing. And it will only ease it. She was my mother. The pain is never going to go away fully."

Patchett nodded.

"Good luck out there, Bobby."

❧ 19 ❧

BOBBY

We were now in early September.

I had to do a double-take when I looked at my phone. The days were starting to run together. The months, too.

After a few calls, I secured Mott Larsen's phone number. I was ready to see if he was as close to my mother as Freddy Ruskin believed. I'd call him in a few hours.

I had some other things on my mind as well.

My sister was coming to Santa Barbara next week, and I had to prepare myself. Not as in keeping my apartment clean, although she'd hate that I'd turned my part of my living room into an investigative wall. No, I mean I had to prepare myself mentally. She could be a drain on me at times, and her husband was no picnic either.

The fact that she knew I was investigating our mother's murder wouldn't make it any easier. I'm sure she was loading some mental quivers with the sole intention of shooting them at me.

Yes, I loved my sister. But it's also true that sometimes I preferred loving her from 3,000 miles away. When she visited Santa Barbara, our differences inevitably reared their ugly head.

I hoped to make the next several days productive ones. I knew I'd be busy once she arrived.

"Hello."

An older voice answered my call.

"Is this Mott Larsen?"

"It is. Who am I speaking to?"

"My name is Bobby McGowan."

"That doesn't ring a bell."

"My mother was Heather Fields."

"Oh, jeez. I know who you are. I'm sorry."

No one ever had to say why they were sorry. It was understood.

"Do you mind if I ask you a few questions?"

"Of course not. I always liked your sister, but not in a romantic way. That's not what I was saying. As friends. Yeah, as friends."

It was funny to hear a man in his mid-fifties fumbling around with his words.

"I was told you guys were pretty close."

"Who told you that?"

"Freddy Ruskin."

"Freddy Ruskin. I haven't heard that name in decades. How is he?"

"Just moved back to Santa Barbara. His mother is dying."

"Oh, that's too bad. Their house was always open for us neighborhood kids. They had a pool, which didn't hurt. I spent many summer days over there."

"My mother took me there as well," I said. "They always had candy.

Mott laughed.

"They sure did," he said

"I plan on going and seeing Mrs. Ruskin again. I'll tell her you said hi."

"I'd be grateful. I'm in Ohio, or I'd see her myself. I'll be curious to see if she remembers me."

"Her mind seems to have its ups and downs, but maybe she would."

No one said anything for a few moments.

"What did you want to know about your mother?" Mott finally asked.

"I guess we'll work backward. Were you still friendly with my mother when she was murdered?"

"Yes and no. I returned to Santa Barbara about once or twice a year, and we'd try to meet up then. Get a few of the old friends together for a beer. Now, that wasn't always possible. She was raising you and your sister, so she couldn't always make time. And we didn't talk on the phone very much at all. I left Santa Barbara and went to college at Ohio State and have remained in Ohio ever since. And I'll tell you what. During a ten-degree day in January, I'm still jealous of those who stayed in SB. I miss that weather. So, anyway, to answer your question. We were friendly when we saw each other. It just wasn't very often."

"Had it been that way since you left for college?"

"Yeah, pretty much. You know how it is. You go away to college, and it's hard to keep in touch with everyone. Especially back then. We didn't have cell phones or Facebook or any of that."

"It was a different world," I said.

"You can say that again. Your generation has no idea what it's like to use a map or a pay phone."

I was thirty-two and hardly a child, but I almost felt like I was being treated like one. Not in a malicious way, but it was still a bit condescending.

"Maybe I'll buy a map to locate the closest pay phone," I said.

"Ahh, the good old days."

"Can I ask you a few questions about the people who lived in and around Calle Rosales in the old days?"

"No problem."

"Do you know who Roy Cooper is?"

"Yeah, I knew Roy. I was a year older than Heather, but she and Roy were in the same class. He didn't have a good reputation."

"So I've heard. Did you like him?"

"No, not particularly."

"I heard he often knocked on my grandparents' door, looking for Heather."

"Yes, he did. Most of us tried to dissuade him, but Roy Cooper was not the dissuading type."

"Did you know Ty Brownstone or Ethan Drury?"

"Yeah, I knew those guys, too. They were also a year younger but grew up in SB, so I'd known them longer. I think Roy transferred in during high school at some point."

"He did."

"I thought so. As you know, Santa Barbara can be a small town."

"For sure. What did you think of Ty and Ethan?"

"Not my favorite people. They were basically punk skaters. I played basketball and football, and they tended to hate the jocks. They would loiter around downtown till ten at night or later. Always up to no good if you ask me. Where their parents were, I had no idea."

"When you say up to no good, what do you mean?"

"Smoking weed. Probably drinking from a young age. Harassing young girls. Probably stealing from the local 7-11s they'd loiter around. Listen, it wasn't the end of the world. They weren't the devil reincarnate or anything. Just rubbed me the wrong way."

"Do you know if they lived near Calle Rosales or San Roque in general?"

"I think they were Eastside kids, if memory serves."

"Was there a rivalry between the two back then? I know what it's like for my age group, but how about in the 70s and 80s?"

"Eastside kids would say that we looked down on them."

Before I could ask another question, he added, "They were probably right about that."

"I'd say that part hasn't changed much."

"The whole Westside-Eastside thing was just fun banter. It was a great city to grow up in. And I lied earlier. I don't just miss it during cold Midwest winters. I miss it all the time."

"Thought about moving back?"

"I work for the Ohio State athletic program, so it's probably unlikely."

"That would make it difficult."

"You said your name was Bobby, correct?"

"Yes."

"Can I ask why all these questions now? I mean, your mother has been gone a long time."

"The truth is I got laid off and had some free time, so I decided to start investigating her murder on my own."

"I respect that," Mott said. "As I've told you a few times, I was long gone by the time she died, but I still had a lot of friends in town, and I know how much her murder shook everyone up. You'd probably be a local hero if you solved it."

"That's not why I'm doing this."

"I know this hits way closer to home for you."

"I just want to catch the motherfucker."

"Maybe he's already dead."

I got off the couch and walked to my storyboard, cell phone still in hand.

What if the email I had received was a hoax?

What if the killer was already dead, and I was doing this for nothing? It was certainly possible. It had been twenty years.

Or what if the killer was in jail on another charge? What if I had no chance of ever catching or locating this guy, and this was all just a fool's errand?

I chose not to believe that. My gut told me the message I'd received was legitimate.

"I've got a feeling he's still alive," I said.

"Maybe he is. Maybe he is."

"Did any of your friends who stayed in SB ever voice a suspect to you?"

"Roy Cooper was mentioned, but only because there were rumors he was still stalking her. Nothing concrete and certainly no evidence."

"How about back in the day when you guys grew up? Did anyone who attended those annual block parties have the wrong type of crush on my mother?"

"No offense, Bobby, but everyone had a crush on your mother. You never heard what they said about her?"

"If you're talking about the three-county thing, I have."

"That was it. So if you're asking whether some of the teens from Calle Rosales ogled your mother, the answer is yes."

It made me think of Lyle Taft and how foolish I was to jump to a conclusion based on a single glance.

"How about acting inappropriately?"

"Nothing that I remember. A lot of the kids were scared of Rick so they wouldn't get too close to your sister. Kind of just gaze from afar."

"I heard he was a tough older brother."

"He was, but he was also just tough in general."

"No one fucked with Rick?"

"You had a serious set of balls if you did, especially if his sister was involved."

I was proud that Rick defended my mother like that. I felt sad about the squalor he was currently living in. I had promised him a trip to the grocery store and hadn't followed up. It was time I visited him again.

"Is there anything else you can tell me, Mr. Larsen?"

"I'm sorry, but no."

"Okay. Thanks for your time."

❧ 20 ❧

BOBBY

When I pulled up to Rick's place in Santa Maria, he was smoking a cigarette outside.

"What's up, nephew?" he said. "Fashionably late?"

I was an hour late.

"I'm sorry. I've been swamped."

"So I've heard."

"Who told you?"

"You think just because I'm living in this dump, I'm unaware of what is happening in Santa Barbara?"

I kind of did, but I didn't tell him that.

"I assume you're referring to my investigation."

"I sure am. Have you gotten anywhere? Any idea who killed my baby sis?"

"No, not really. I eliminated Lyle Taft. He's dead."

"Just because someone is dead doesn't mean he didn't do it."

"True, but everyone told me I was crazy for suspecting him based on a look."

"They were probably right. So, who have you been out there talking to?"

"Anyone who will talk to me. And I'll tell you whose name keeps popping up."

"Who?"

"Roy Cooper."

"Don't you remember what I told you?"

We were still standing on his minuscule front deck. I assumed his place was still a mess, and that's why he didn't want to invite me in.

"I remember. And you're positive his two cohorts didn't lie to you?"

"I'm positive. Roy Cooper might have been able to stand up to me, but not Ty or Ethan. They were more scared of me than they were of Roy. I will tell you a second time. I'm positive that Roy was at the bar that day."

"Okay, " I said. "I believe you."

"What else have you learned? You're putting too many eggs in the Roy Cooper basket."

Rick had been borderline eloquent with his speech. And there was no drink in his hand. Had he turned over a new leaf?

"Okay. What if I told you I thought it was somebody from one of your sister's photo albums?"

"I thought you said Lyle Taft was dead."

"I'm talking about somebody else."

"Who exactly?"

"I don't know. I just think it's someone from one of the albums."

"How could you possibly know that?" Rick logically asked.

"I don't know. It's just a gut feeling I have. If you grant me that it's true, and let's say the photo had to be from before I was born, who would you begin to suspect?"

"Sounds like a bullshit game to me, but if I'm playing by your rules, I'd have to see some of those old albums. I can't just conjure some name out of thin air."

The Rick I had met with two weeks ago never would have used the word "conjure." At least, not correctly. My curiosity got the best of me.

"You're looking a lot better this time, Rick. What's different?"

"Been sober for ten days."

"Good for you."

"The fog is beginning to lift. I know it's going to take a lot longer than that after almost fifty years of boozing."

"You're trying to quit for good?"

"That's the plan at this moment. Of course, that's been the plan several times over the years."

"I've got a feeling it will stick this time."

"Got any good reason to believe that, or is this one of your photo album theories?"

I couldn't help but laugh.

"Even sober, you're a ball-buster, Uncle Rick."

"That ain't going away any time soon."

"Good. Listen, I'll bring the photo albums next time, but do you still want to hit the grocery store today?"

"Why do you think I was waiting on my front deck?"

"Let's get out of here," I said.

FORTY-FIVE MINUTES LATER, I'D DROPPED RICK OFF WITH TWO BAGS OF groceries. I had enough money to last me six months, give or take, plus my apartment was twenty times more livable than his pig sty. I felt guilty and didn't mind picking up the tab for the groceries.

I promised Rick I'd be back within a week.

I ARRIVED HOME AND REALIZED I HELD TWO CONFLICTING VIEWPOINTS.

I believed Rick when he said that Roy Cooper wasn't involved, but I also understood why some people considered him their number one suspect.

I hoped Rick's sister could help me out.

"Hello."

"Hey, Yvonne, this is Bobby."

"Sounds like you've been pretty busy since I saw you last."

"You must be talking about my KEYT interview."

"Yes, that's part of it. A lot of people are starting to talk around town. I've heard at least three people mention that you were out there investigating your mother's case."

"Are you talking about Ventura?"

"No, I'm talking about my friends in Santa Barbara."

Three people in a town of 88,000 hardly constituted "a lot of people talking," but I wasn't surprised that word was getting around. I'd interviewed a lot of people at this point. That, along with my disastrous interview, meant it was spreading.

"That's a good thing, right?"

I meant it rhetorically, but Yvonne didn't get the memo.

"For you catching the killer, maybe. The problem is that it opens up old wounds for this city, and I'm not just talking about me, Rick, and your family. The cops, the neighbors, and Heather's friends probably don't love being asked about it again twenty years later."

"If my family can deal with it, they can deal with it," I said.

"That's fair."

"You haven't turned against me on this, have you?"

"Not at all. I'm just trying to warn you that not everyone will be as eager to discuss it. It's a black eye for our great city, and some people would prefer it not become a talking point again."

"Screw them," I said.

"That's the attitude. By the way, Rick called me twenty minutes ago. I heard you went and saw him. He sounds great."

"He looked great, too. No booze and a command of the English language that I'm not sure I knew he had. He was dropping Thesaurus-level words on me."

Yvonne laughed on the other end.

"Being a drunk and being loquacious are not mutually exclusive."

"Certainly not," I said. "Some of the all-time great writers were drunks."

"Indeed. I just hope Rick keeps it up. Whenever he's been on the wagon over the years, it's inevitably hit a pothole."

I laughed at the visual my mind conjured up. Rick, on a wagon with a drink in hand, hitting a pothole and being thrown from said wagon.

"I'll be rooting for him, that's for sure," I said, not bringing up my wild visual.

"Thanks. Me too. So, is there a specific reason for your call, or is it just to catch up?"

"Well, you will be getting these catch-up calls more often now that we're talking again, but yes, I had something specific this time."

"What is it?"

"I'm trying to get the phone numbers or addresses of Roy Cooper, Ty Brownstone, or Ethan Drury. I was also wondering if you knew if they still lived locally."

"Roy Cooper has moved away, and Ethan Drury lives locally. I have no idea what happened to Ty Brownstone."

My main line of inquiry was Roy Cooper's alibi on the day my mother was killed. I'd rather talk to Brownstone or Drury than Cooper about that, so I was glad to hear that Ethan Drury still lived in Santa Barbara. I was hoping to meet with him to eliminate Roy as a suspect. I trusted Uncle

Rick, but I had to do this. I couldn't take anyone's words for things—even relatives.

"Could you find me Drury's phone number or address?" I asked.

"It will take a few calls, but I'm sure I could."

"Thanks so much, Yvonne. Can you call me back once you have it?"

"Of course."

"And one other thing. My sister is coming into town next week. Would you like to see Heather's grandchildren if I can talk Jen into it? I'm not sure exactly what you call their relation to you. I've never been good at that."

"They are my grand niece and nephew; I'd love to see them. I once met the boy, but I've never met the girl."

"Hopefully, we can change that. I'll reach out to Jen and see what I can do."

"Thanks. And I'll reach out to my friends about Ethan's address."

"Great. Talk soon," I said.

WHILE I WAITED FOR YVONNE'S CALL BACK, I TEXTED JEN:

"Hey, Jen. Is there any chance Yvonne can meet her grand niece and nephew while you're in town? She has only met Austin once and has never met Avery."

I didn't bother mentioning Rick. I figured that would be a non-starter.

A minute later, I got a text back from Jen.

"We'll see."

All things considered, I'd take it. My sister not saying no straight away gave me hope I could make this happen.

YVONNE CALLED ME BACK FORTY-FIVE MINUTES LATER WITH A PHONE number and an address for Ethan Drury. I decided not to call him. I'd just go to his house and surprise him. Give him less time to prepare.

✾ 21 ✾

BOBBY

Ethan Drury didn't technically live in Santa Barbara, but it was close enough.

He lived in Summerland, a small town of only 1,500 people, about five miles south of Santa Barbara.

Despite its catchy name, you won't find many people visiting Summerland during the summer months. It's nice, and there's nothing wrong with it, but there's only a few shops and a restaurant or two. It's nothing like its big, bad neighbor to the north.

Ethan lived in a tiny house at the end of a small gravel street. I parked my car on the road and walked toward his front door. It was 1:30 p.m., and I'm not sure why I'd decided to come at this time. He was likely at work. I should have called ahead instead of hoping to go with the stupid "element of surprise."

I rang the doorbell once, twice, and then a third time. No one came to the door. I decided to call him using the number Yvonne gave me. Maybe he was home and hadn't heard me.

Just as I grabbed my phone, I heard a voice coming from the side of the house.

"Who's there?"

I then saw a man appear and start walking in my direction. He was of average height and very skinny.

"I'm looking for Ethan Drury," I said.

"That's me. What do you want?"

He didn't appear to be the most hospitable man. Then again, a stranger was standing outside his house. What was he supposed to do, throw me a ticker-tape parade?

His jeans looked like they might fall down at any time. He couldn't have weighed more than 130 pounds. And why was he wearing jeans in the first place? It was eighty-something degrees out.

Despite being skinny, Ethan Drury looked like a tough guy. Wiry strong is how I'd describe him.

"My name is Bobby McGowan, and I wanted to ask you a few questions."

I could see in real-time that my name registered with him.

"You related to that woman who got killed?"

"She was my mother."

"Fuck. I'm going to be eighty years old, and they'll still be asking me about this damn case."

"Has someone talked to you lately?"

"No, not lately. But I just thought after thirty years, maybe people would get over the damn thing."

"It's been twenty years, and I'm sorry, but my mother was killed. I can't just get over the damn thing."

He spit some chewing tobacco on the ground and looked to be sizing me up.

"You right," he said. "My bad."

"So, is it okay if I ask you a few things?"

"Why the hell not? I had nothing to do with it."

He crossed his arms over his chest, and I could tell our conversation would occur outside. I was reminded of my recent talk with Rick that took place exclusively on his minuscule front deck. At least that was shaded.

"I know you had nothing to do with it," I said, trying to appease him.

"Then why you's here?"

Ethan Drury didn't have the best command of the English language. He hadn't put the great schools of Santa Barbara to good use.

"Because you and your friend Ty Brownstone gave Roy Cooper his alibi."

He sized me up a second time. I knew he didn't like me being there; I just hoped he wouldn't bum-rush me. Ethan Drury seemed unpredictable.

"We didn't give him no alibi," he said as I ignored the double-negative.

"We just told the truth. Roy didn't kill that woman. Or, at least, he didn't do it himself. He was with me and Ty for like four or five hours that day."

"Were you guys drinking a lot?"

"No more than usual."

Ethan spat out some more tobacco juice.

"What were you guys talking about?" I asked.

I didn't want him to abort our talk, but I also was trying to get him on edge. Make it more likely he'd make a mistake if there was even a mistake to be made.

"Shit, I don't fucking remember. But let's go with cars, women, and booze. That's what the three of us usually talked about."

"Were you interviewed by the cops that night?"

"No, the next day."

"What did they ask you?"

"The same things you asking me right now. If Roy was with us. Things like that. Those cops knew me and Ty had nothing against Heather. They were convinced it was Roy, even though I told them fifty damn times he was at the bar with me."

"Why do you think they suspected Roy?"

"Don't you know this shit already? He used to date your mother, and I don't think he was the best boyfriend."

"He wasn't so great after they broke up, either."

"Sounds par for the course for Roy."

"It begs the question of why you were friends with the guy."

"Begs the what? Who's begging?"

I decided to rephrase it.

"Why were you friends with Roy if he was such a jerk."

"Looking back, I probably shouldn't have been. He was a total bully to everyone. All the kids around town. Even to my little brother. And I did nothing to stop it. Truth was, Roy was popular, and Ty and I became somewhat popular because we hung out with him. We was in high school, man. I didn't know no better."

"That may be true, but you were in your mid-thirties on the day my mother was killed. Out drinking with Roy. You were no longer a naive teenager."

He eyed me suspiciously for a third time.

"Are you a fucking teacher? I didn't know I would have to do math today."

His statement was so absurd it was almost humorous. As if someone wouldn't know the difference between being a teenager and being in their mid-thirties.

I didn't want to lose him just yet, so I didn't bring that up.

"When did you and Roy start going your separate ways?"

"Soon after your mother got killed."

"And why was that?"

"Cops were bringing me in to answer questions. People started asking if I was involved. Shit like that. Just realized he was more trouble than he was worth. Plus, Roy moved six months later, so we lost touch. There was no cell phones back then."

A few thoughts came to mind. First, cell phones existed in 2003, but the last thing I wanted to do was bring up numbers and math to Ethan Drury again. Second, despite his big talk of realizing Roy was more trouble than he was worth, I'd bet Ethan would still be friends with him today if Roy still lived here. Roy's move was the real reason they were no longer friends.

"When was the last time you talked to him?"

"Shit, probably seven or eight years. We had our twentieth high school reunion, and I saw him then."

For a third time, Ethan's math was way off. If they had a reunion seven or eight years ago, it would have been their 30th.

"Do you know where he's living?"

"Last I heard was Portland, but who knows?"

"And you swear that Roy was with you that day from noon till four or five p.m."

"You're starting to piss me off, buddy. Yes, I was with freaking Roy that whole afternoon. Like I already told ya. And like I told the cops back then."

Despite being mathematically challenged, even Ethan Drury would have remembered the time in question when he was interrogated by the police a day later.

There wasn't much more I could learn from him.

"Okay, thanks for your time," I said.

Ethan just grunted.

I turned to go and swiveled back around.

"One last thing. Did you ever suspect anyone of my mother's murder?"

"I figured it was just some neighbor who got the hots for your Mom."

That was a possibility, but I still hated hearing it from the mouth of Ethan Drury. And more so, I hated the way he phrased it.

"Goodbye," I said and walked back to my car.

❧ 22 ❧

BOBBY

My sister's visit was two days away.

The anxiety that came with her visits increased as the day approached. The fact that I was also investigating our mother's murder, something Jen was adamantly against, meant the anxiety would ratchet up a little.

I had a few things to do before she arrived, one of which was to visit Rick again.

The 20th anniversary of my mother's death was also fast approaching, and I wanted to follow up with KEYT and the *Santa Barbara News-Press* to make sure they were both still on board as far as publishing articles/segments on her murder. Hopefully, my interview hadn't deterred them. I doubted it. It probably made them eager to interview me. *What will Bobby say next?*

The general public might prove my best source for a new lead. That's why getting coverage in the local newspaper and TV station was so important.

I decided to visit Rick, KEYT, and the News-Press the following day, killing three birds with one stone.

Then I'd be ready for my sister's visit.

BOBBY

I woke up the following morning and made myself a French Press.

As had become customary every morning, I walked over to the wall of photos. I looked over the 100-plus photos I had remaining. I'd put the images of the block parties back in their sleeves. That didn't mean it couldn't have been anyone pictured in them, but it did mean I'd looked into them enough for now. I'd talked to Freddy Ruskin, his mother, and Mott Larsen. I couldn't focus on any photo - or set of photos - for too long.

The next photo to go back in the album would be the one with Roy Cooper, Ty Brownstone, Ethan Drury, and the two younger kids. I hadn't put it back in the sleeve just yet because I had one last question to ask Rick about them.

I considered several photos and settled on two to look into next. There was a picture of my mother with a few Santa Barbara Police Officers at the annual Fiesta Parade, the biggest party in Santa Barbara. The year was 1988.

Fiesta went from Wednesday to Sunday and was always the first week of August. It brought tens of thousands of visitors to Santa Barbara, and the bars and restaurants were more crowded than any other time of the year.

During the late 90s and early 2000s, Michael Jordan bartended on State Street during Fiesta. Yes, that Michael Jordan. He held his annual Flight School basketball camp in Santa Barbara every year during Fiesta. Apparently, he was in O'Malley's - a famous bar on State Street - when people started pestering him for his autograph. Colin, the bartender working, told Jordan he could come behind the bar so the public couldn't hassle him. Somehow, it stuck, and Jordan would bartend at O'Malley's for one or two days every year at Fiesta.

I was a young kid and a long time away from getting into bars, but I'd heard the lines were out of control. It was Michael damn Jordan bartending. There better have been some long lines.

As for the picture with the police officers, it's not that I necessarily suspected a cop of being involved, but I couldn't exactly rule it out, either. It would help explain why the killer seemed to be a step ahead of the investigation over the years.

The second photo I snagged from the wall was one from Las Vegas. It was my parents and three other couples. The year was also 1988. I'd ask my father about these other couples, and if they were a toss-out, so be it. I'd chosen it because I wanted to remind myself to ask my father about old friends who might have had a crush on my mother. Maybe something that went deeper. Someone who became infatuated with her.

I knew it wouldn't be an enjoyable conversation with my father, but I had to have it.

❧

I REALIZED I HADN'T HEARD FROM THE MYSTERIOUS EMAILER IN A FEW weeks.

Had I put too much stock in his email? Almost certainly. I'd followed the advice of a random person on the internet. Most likely a kook. But, what if it was the actual killer? Would he really tell me the truth about being in one of the photo albums? It seemed unlikely.

What if it was meant as a diversion, one he knew would lead to nothing? If so, I might spend an untold amount of weeks looking into a dead end.

And yet, I still believed he was telling me the truth. People would probably think I was crazy, but I had to go with my gut. This was my investigation now. What was the point of all this if I didn't go with my gut?

After I chose the two photos, I set them down on the table below the storyboard and took a cell phone picture of both. I also took a few photos of the entire storyboard.

If I ever solved this crime, people would be fascinated by my process, and these pictures would be sought after.

Or, I might never solve it, and I would look back at these pictures lamenting the time I spent trying to find a ghost.

23

BOBBY

"Three times in a month and twice in a week. My nephew is making up for lost time."

Rick wasn't wrong.

"You sure seem to be keeping track."

"I'm not complaining."

"Maybe I feel guilty about all the time we missed."

"Do you have a good reason as to why we stopped talking? I never knew the reason why."

It was evident that Rick was, once again, sober. I was happy to see it. He was standing on his deck just as last time. Maybe I'd even get an invite into the house on this visit.

"I don't have an answer, either. There would be no good reason anyway. Time happened. That's the real explanation."

"That time is a son-of-a-gun," Rick said.

"It sure is."

"Would you rather sit inside, Bobby?"

"Thought you'd never ask."

He smiled and escorted me into a clean apartment. It looked markedly better than the first time I'd been there. This complex - if you could call it that - was still a dump, but Rick was doing his part to class his place up a little bit.

We sat on the couch, which was still one of the worst in the history of man. No more newspaper was on the ground, so I just plopped on the couch, risking life and limb.

"So, what's the latest?" he asked.

"I went and saw Ethan Drury. You were right. I think Roy Cooper was at that bar all day."

"What have I been telling you?"

"You were right, but I have to do this investigation on my own. I can't just rely on others telling me, '*Oh, that lead has been checked*' or '*That person had been talked to.*'"

"That's the right approach. Look at it with new eyes. Don't listen to no one, and that includes me."

"That's the idea."

"How was Ethan Drury?"

"He was eighty percent sheepish and twenty percent menacing. I know those seem like opposites, but that would be my description. I couldn't tell if he was afraid of his own shadow or whether he wanted to kick my ass."

"That makes sense, I guess. He was never much without Roy by his side."

"Ethan kind of subtly referred to himself as a pushover. He said that Roy bullied his brother, and he wouldn't even stand up to Roy over that. And that's family we're talking about."

"Not many people stood up to Roy."

"You did."

"I sure did. But wouldn't you know it? Heather still ended up dating him."

"Why do you think that was? I keep hearing how my mother was such a good person and rarely made mistakes. Why did she with Roy?"

"Because she was eighteen and had just moved out of the house for the first time. Everyone makes mistakes at that age. She was still a teenager, for Christ's sake. Shit, I bet Mother Theresa was balling guys at that age. Plus, Roy was like the forbidden fruit. Our parents didn't like him coming around the house, and I'd certainly made it clear that I didn't like the guy. And then your mother moves into an apartment with two other girls. She probably dated Roy partly in response to me and our parents hating him so much."

"It's understandable when you phrase it like that."

"Try not to hold it against your mother. They dated for about six months, and then she realized her mistake. Fuck, I've been making mistakes for fifty-plus years. At least it only took Heather six months to know she'd done wrong."

"I'm not holding it against her."

"Your mother has been dead twenty years. All you should be thinking are good thoughts."

"I think good thoughts about her all the time. It's everyone else that I'm suspicious of."

"That's the attitude. Hey, I was thinking about something."

"Let's hear it."

"Would your father be against me coming down to visit him?"

My father always found Rick entertaining. While my mother dreaded his visits, my father thought he was an eccentric drunk. Rick never did anything wrong to us kids or to him or his wife, and nothing else mattered to my father.

"I'm sure he'd love to see you," I said. "Why don't I talk to him, and I'll get back to you."

"Awesome."

Rick looked like a little kid who'd just gotten approval from his parents, which was not an expression you often saw on a hardened man in his sixties.

"Maybe we could bring Yvonne as well," I said.

I knew it would probably have to wait until after Jen's visit.

"Get the band back together and tell great stories about your mother," Rick said.

"I'd like that a lot," I said, my eyes starting to water ever so slightly.

"So, what brought you over today, Bobby?"

I didn't want to tell him it was because my sister was coming into town, and I probably wouldn't make my way up here for the next week.

"I've got a few more photos I'd like you to look at."

"Hit me with them."

I pulled out the two pictures I'd taken from the wall that morning.

"Do you know any of the people in these pictures?"

I'd ask my father about the pictures next, but I figured I'd give Rick a go first. He pointed at one of the pictures.

"I know that guy. I think he might be your father."

"Smartass."

Rick looked at the photos a second time.

"I don't know the couples. The cops look familiar. Shit, I probably had a few run-ins with them."

I laughed.

"I should have guessed you'd know the cops."

"What can I say? I've lived a wild life."

"And now you're living the sober life. You look good again today."

"Thanks. One day at a time."

"If you don't mind me asking, why did you pick now to try and stop? Did me coming here have something to do with it?"

"Yes and no. I'd been thinking about giving up the booze for a while. Fuck, I've been thinking about it my whole life, but I mean, I've been seriously thinking about it for the last several months. And then you came over, and we started talking about my sister. I imagined her up in Heaven looking down at my shit-hole community and shit-hole apartment. That helped push me in the right direction."

Even if I never caught my mother's killer, something good had come of this.

"Well, I hope you keep it up, Rick," I said.

"Thanks, Bobby."

We shot the shit for another fifteen minutes before I got up to go. I told him I'd talk to my father and Yvonne and get back to him soon.

"Thanks. Looking forward to seeing your pops."

"Great."

"And one more thing. Do you have Ethan's number?"

"Sure. You going to visit him?"

"Not him, actually. I was somewhat friendly with his little brother that you mentioned. He used to work for Amtrak, and I'd always ride it. Thought I'd reach out to him."

"That's the one who got bullied?"

"Yeah, he got it rough."

"What was his name? I'm not sure Ethan told me."

"It's Conrad."

𝕾 24 𝕾

CONRAD DRURY

Everyone always wants to get into the head of serial killers.

It's obvious why. We are society's outcasts, the '*How the fuck did they end up like this?*' of our country. And the world.

I won't go blow-by-blow through my childhood, but I'll highlight some key points. And then I'll explain how I've never been caught after all these years. I find that immensely more interesting than my upbringing.

I grew up in Santa Barbara, the younger of two brothers. Due to a delay - my father being in jail for five years - there was quite an age difference between me and my brother. He was already seven when I was born.

You'd think having an older brother to show you the ropes might be advantageous. Teach you how to play sports, talk to women, and defend yourself—shit like that.

The problem was that my brother Ethan was an asshole. Well, that's not exactly fair. His friends were assholes, and he sat idly by, which may have been worse.

Before you start feeling sorry for me and thinking I was bullied my whole childhood, and that's why I ended up this way, you may want to hear what I did to pets first.

And yes, I know it's a stereotype for killers - it just happened to be true with me.

I'd torture those little suckers every chance I got. I started with our family's goldfish at age five or six. I used to love to see that little thing flop back and forth while out of the water, knowing I controlled its destiny. I'd then return it to the bowl before my parents or brother saw what I'd done. It was a little secret between Goldie and me, my nickname for that stupid little thing.

I slowly graduated to other animals like mice and birds. I once put an injured House Finch out of its misery after I tortured it for a while first. Hahaha.

I didn't get to kill my first cat until I was about eleven. I'd been scared I'd be caught. Even at a young age, I knew I was different and had to be careful, so I bided my time until I knew I could get away with something.

And then I showed Bella - our neighbor's cat - a good time. Well, at least it was for me.

I was too young to get away with killing a human, so I had to make do with killing pets. Notice that I didn't say I couldn't kill a human. I'd already thought of many ways to accomplish that. I said I couldn't get away with killing a human. There's a huge difference.

I knew I would be in this for the long haul. No 'One and Done' for me. I was going to be sure I got away with my first murder.

❀❀❀

So, while I did get picked on throughout my childhood, I was already a sociopath before that—Tally one up for nature over nurture.

I first met Roy Cooper when I was ten. He was seventeen, had just moved to Santa Barbara, and quickly became friends with my brother, Ethan. Roy was the popular kid, and my brother wanted to be friends with him. My worthless, spineless brother. And, might I add, stupid? My brother has the vocabulary of Goldie the goldfish. I was given the brains in our family.

Usually, the popular kids are not transfer students, but Roy was the exception. Everyone wanted to hang out with him when he arrived in Santa Barbara. The guys wanted to be friends with him, and the girls wanted to date him.

Roy didn't have any redeeming qualities; he was just popular. Being a bully increased the amount of his friends. People were scared of him, and so they joined his side. Stupid, but true.

My brother was one of them. So was Ty Brownstone. Those three became inseparable. Roy, Ethan, and Ty. With Roy being the undisputed leader.

I won't bore you with details, but Roy treated me like shit. Bullied me. Yelled at me. Hit me. Sometimes pulled my pants down to "pants" me. Sometimes pulled my pants up to "wedgie" me. He was an equal-opportunity bully.

Meanwhile, my brother Ethan would continue to do nothing. He was way too intimidated by Roy. Part of me thinks he had a man crush on the guy. Not me. I wanted to put Roy's head in a vice, but I was too young and weak to do a thing about his aggression.

YEARS PASSED. ROY MELLOWED EVER SO SLIGHTLY IN HIS TWENTIES AND early thirties, but not enough for me to give him a pass. I never forgot how he treated me. I'd always known I was going to get back at him. I considered removing the brakes on his car, leaving rattlesnakes at his apartment, and other things I quickly tossed out as infantile.

I wanted something more substantial.

When Roy was about thirty-five (and I was twenty-seven), I decided what to do. It was an evil, wicked, absurd plan, but one I thought I could pull off.

I'd always wanted to kill a human. Lord knows I'd killed enough animals, but I also wanted Roy Cooper to suffer for a lifetime. Sometimes, a quick death is an easy way out. I wanted worse for Roy.

That's what led me to my plan.

Needless to say, I held grudges with the best of them. Very few people in history could hold a grudge like yours truly. If you wronged me in any way, you were immediately and forever on my radar. I'd stand there, maybe even give you a fake smile, but I was just thinking about ways of getting back at you.

Roy Cooper was the first person I felt this way about. There'd be dozens more in the decades that followed.

THE PLAN I'VE BEEN REFERENCING FIRST CAME TO ME ONE DAY WHEN I had lunch with my brother Ethan. He told me that Heather McGowan and her husband were getting sick of Roy. Roy kept calling them, leaving messages, and then "randomly" running into them at events around town. Inevitably, Roy would approach Heather, and things would get awkward.

The word was starting to spread around Santa Barbara. Roy was infatuated with Heather.

They'd dated years previously, but it was apparent Roy had never gotten over it. People around town were beginning to turn on him. He was now the creepy guy who stalked ex-girlfriends. He'd always been a jerk and a bully, but you can get away with that when you're a teenager. It's frowned upon when you're a grown man and stalking a married woman.

As my brother told me this, my mind went to some pretty dark places.

Could I kill Heather McGowan and frame Roy Cooper for her death?

It was like a bomb went off in my head. I'd never heard of a serial killer who framed other people. I could be a one of one.

🐍

I STARTED TO TAKE AN INTEREST IN HEATHER. I'D KNOWN HER BY reputation my whole life. The prettiest girl in three counties, everyone would say. And maybe they were right. She was a hot piece of ass.

I'd only met her in passing, but I was told she was a very nice, polite woman. Not that information like that would derail my plan. I didn't - and still don't - care one fucking iota about other people. The fact that Heather McGowan was a good person meant nothing to me. If I could kill her while framing Roy Cooper for her murder, then I was going to proceed. That's all there was to it.

As the months progressed, I kept tabs on both Roy and Heather. I asked my brother about the former and stalked the latter. I followed her to grocery stores and watched from afar as she dropped her kids off at school. I was getting her schedule down pat so nothing would surprise me when I decided the time was right.

I'd already read probably twenty books on serial killers despite not having committed a single murder yet. They fascinated me to no end, and I knew that when I committed a murder, I was going to do it right.

It's like I was writing my thesis on serial killers. Which, basically, I was. Only I wasn't trying to alert society to their atrocities. I was trying to join their fraternity.

I worked for Amtrak, and I used to put a fake cover over the books I read, which were almost exclusively on serial killers. I remember one time I had some Danielle Steel cover over a biography of John Wayne Gacy. I found the dichotomy of the two to be humorous.

One of my co-workers looked over my shoulder and saw a picture of John Wayne Gacy.

"Why is a picture of that creep in a Danielle Steel novel?" he asked.

His name was Marcus Young. He was a thirty-ish black guy who took tickets and roamed the train, doing more talking than working if you asked me.

"I'm taking a class on serial killers, but I don't want to scare off our customers."

I wasn't taking any classes, but Marcus bought it. Lying came easily to me. It's a trait I share with every other serial killer.

"Okay, that makes sense," he said. "Still, it's a bit odd."

I stared at Marcus, who got the idea and meandered down the train. I had a few more incidents with Marcus. He was very close to making my list but transferred to the Midwest.

He got lucky.

Many others didn't.

BACK TO HEATHER MCGOWAN. MY BROTHER TOLD ME SHE AND HER husband were considering getting a restraining order against Roy. Things looked to be escalating.

I knew if I could pull off this murder, Roy would be one of the prime suspects. But I wanted more than that. I wanted him to be convicted of her murder. This was as much about getting Roy as it was about committing my first murder.

So, I concocted my first murder plan. And my first "framing someone for murder" plan.

And before you think I only go after scumbags like Roy, as if I'm some real-life Dexter Morgan, you better think again. I've framed some of the nicest people you'd ever meet. One I remember all too well. Dale Collier.

That was some of my best work.

More on him later.

IN THE WEEKS LEADING UP TO HEATHER MCGOWAN'S MURDER, I'D created a checklist of nine things. Every single one of them had to be a Yes before I'd go through with her murder.

Some were obvious:

It had to be a time when Heather would be home alone.

It couldn't be within thirty minutes of her going to pick up her kids from school.

It had to be a time when Roy had no alibi.

Things like that.

ROY WAS UNEMPLOYED AT THE TIME AND WOULD MOSTLY JUST PLAY video games alone at his house. I just had to make sure it wasn't one of his drinking nights with my brother.

I had lunch with my brother on Tuesday, October 27th, 2003. I was ready to proceed with my plan the following day, but I had to make sure Roy would be at home alone.

My brother would never suspect me of anything. He was too dumb.

Still, I didn't want to be the one asking questions about Roy if I could avoid it.

Luckily, he volunteered the information.

"Let's go do something tomorrow night, Conrad. Maybe see a movie," Ethan said. "I'm laying low during the day. Roy said he's just going to play his stupid video games all day long, and Ty only wants to come out if Roy does. So I'll be free." Ethan said.

"Cool. I'll call you tomorrow," I said.

SO, ON THE MORNING OF WEDNESDAY, OCTOBER 28TH, 2003, I WOKE up and could finally check all nine boxes. It was time.

Unbeknownst to me, plans would change, and Roy, Ethan, and Ty would go drinking on the day in question.

My life as a serial killer was about to get off to a rocky start.

❧ 25 ❧

BOBBY

My sister and her family arrived at 5:45 p.m. on a Wednesday. They had to fly through O'Hare Airport in Chicago since it flew directly into Santa Barbara, which doesn't have the biggest airport.

I was there to greet them. Jen ran over and gave me a big hug. We were off to a good start.

I then shook her husband's hand.

"Nice to see you, Justin," I lied.

"You too, Bobby," he said.

I ran up and hugged my nephew and niece. They only saw me about twice a year, so I wondered how much they remembered me.

"Can you say hi to Uncle Bobby?"

"Hi, Uncle Bobby," Aaron said quietly.

Avery was just sucking her thumb.

"So everything is going great in Santa Barbara?" Justin asked.

"I'm single, unemployed, and investigating my mother's murder. What's not to love?"

"You're hilarious," Jen said.

Justin had managed to smile, but I couldn't tell if his amusement was at my joke or my standing in life.

"Jen told me," he said.

"About me being fired or investigating the murder?"

Justin looked at Jen. Meanwhile, Jen was giving me an evil glare.

"What you're doing in regards to your mother's death," Justin said, trying to tiptoe around using the word murder.

Jen continued to stare at me with hate in her eyes.

I realized I was being an asshole.

"Honestly, Justin, everyone knows at this point. I had a terrible interview locally, so it's not like I can hide from it."

"You're a smart guy. If anyone is going to make inroads on your mother's murder, it will probably be you."

It was probably the kindest thing he'd ever said to me. I felt even worse about being such a jerk.

I patted him on the shoulder.

"Thanks."

Jen quickly nodded as if to say, *"Finally."*

WE WALKED OVER TO THE BAGGAGE CLAIM AND WAITED FOR THEIR luggage. The Santa Barbara airport was tiny, and the carousel was only a few hundred feet from their gate.

I turned toward Aaron.

"What do you want to do while you're in Santa Barbara?" I asked.

"I want to go in the ocean!" he exclaimed.

"Wawa," Avery said, her way of saying water.

"Maybe we can get you out on a boat," I said.

"Did you hear that, Mom?"

"I did. Uncle Bobby is going to take you out on a boat," Jen said.

"Since you guys are waiting on the luggage, I'll head to the rental car place and fill out that paperwork," Justin said.

They had a rental car reserved since they had two kids who still required car seats. Being childless, I'd never had to consider the ins and outs of traveling with young kids.

The first bag was spit out onto the carousel a few minutes later.

"Let me know which bags are yours. I'll grab them," I said.

"Thanks. They're easy. They are all green."

"Sowing our Irish roots?"

Jen managed to smile.

"I guess so. Also, it makes it easier when the kids' bags are the same color."

"Justin is being nice," I said.

"That makes one of you."

I couldn't deny it.

"You're right, Jen. I was being a jerk."

"Don't make me regret this trip," Jen said.

I leaned in and hugged her.

"I'm sorry. I'll be better."

She hugged me back.

A few seconds later, I saw a green Samsonite - I was way off! - hardshell suitcase.

"Is that one of yours?" I asked.

"If you see a green tag on it as well, it's ours."

There was a green tag, and I picked it off the carousel.

The other three green Samsonite suitcases with green tags rapidly followed. I pulled each one off, and I'd never seen two young kids so excited for inanimate objects.

A few minutes later, Justin came over and joined us.

"You get the car?" Jen asked.

"I got the key and the paperwork."

"And the two car seats?"

Justin smiled.

"Nah, I told them I'd hold the kids on my lap as I drove."

"You're hilarious," Jen said and kissed him.

He pointed to the car seats a few feet away from us.

I hated to admit it, but this version of them was borderline cute.

"Lead the way, Bobby," Justin said. "The car is in section A-6."

I'd been in and out of this airport dozens of times and knew my way around it.

I led them to their car, and Justin started setting up the car seats in the back.

Jen and I were by ourselves on the passenger side.

"Thanks," she said.

"For what?"

"For meeting us at the airport. And for stopping being an asshole. At least for the moment."

I smiled.

"I'll try not to revert back."

"We're all set," Justin said.

"So I'll see you at Dad's tonight?" Jen asked.

"Of course."

"Tell me again why we are going to his place and not The Palace?"

"Because I took Dad there a week ago for his 60th."

"That's right, I forgot that's where you guys went. I'd originally hoped to make it out for that, but Justin's work schedule wouldn't allow it."

My asshole self of five minutes ago might have said something like, '*You could have come alone,*' but instead, I behaved and said, "Well, I'm just glad you're all here now."

I said goodbye to the kids and told everyone I'd see them in a few hours.

❦

I SPENT THE NEXT NINETY MINUTES AT HOME, LOOKING OVER THE photos for the umpteenth time.

I looked down at my watch and realized I was running late. I took a two-minute shower and threw on some khakis and a button-down white T-shirt.

❦

I SAW TWO UNEXPECTED FACES AS I PULLED UP TO MY FATHER'S HOUSE. Yvonne and Rick. I'd talked to both about potentially meeting up, but I hadn't nailed anything down yet. It must have been my father's doing.

Rick had a grin the size of Texas.

I walked out of my car and approached the house. Yvonne rushed over and gave me a big hug. I thought saying, '*Who invited you?' would be rude,* so I let her talk.

"Boy, did I get a great call this morning," she said. "From an unlikely source."

Could it have been my sister?

"Who?" I asked.

"Robert called me and invited me to dinner."

I always found it odd when I heard people say Robert. One, because I shared the same name with my father, and two, he was always just Dad to me.

Rick took a step in our direction. He remained smiling.

"And my sister was nice enough to ask if I could tag along."

"Your father said yes to that as well," Yvonne said.

"Then why are you guys standing out here?" I asked.

"We knocked on the door but didn't hear an answer.

"My Dad is going deaf," I said. "We'll just have to barge in."

"With all due respect, I'll let you do the barging in," Rick said.

It was funny seeing Rick so passive. My guess was that he knew he was a late invite and didn't want to rock the boat.

"Follow me," I said.

I hadn't seen my sister's rental car, so Rick and Yvonne must have been the first to arrive.

I grabbed the door handle and twisted it. As I expected, it opened right up.

"Dad," I yelled.

"Bobby, is that you?"

"It is. You've got guests who have been waiting outside."

Yvonne and Rick were still standing at the door. My father walked around the corner.

"Well, come on in, you two. I'm not going to be serving dinner by the door jam."

Yvonne and Rick laughed and then simultaneously approached my father to hug him. Rick backed off, and Yvonne gave my father a twenty-second hug. To my surprise, they were both in tears.

"Why did we ever wait this long to get back together?" Yvonne said.

"I don't know," my father said.

"You guys were scared I'd show up drunk," Rick said.

My father laughed as if it was the funniest thing ever said.

"Get over here, Rick," he said, and they hugged almost as long as he and Yvonne had.

"Thanks for including me, Robert."

"Of course, Rick. Wouldn't be the same without you."

With the front door still open, I saw my sister and her family pulling up. As they got out and approached, I closely watched my sister's face. I was curious about her reaction upon seeing Aunt Yvonne and Uncle Rick.

She had a smile, and it looked pretty authentic to me.

She came and gave Yvonne a huge hug.

"What a fantastic, unbelievable surprise," Jen said.

She was laying it on a little thick, but she did seem genuinely happy to see them. Next, she hugged Rick.

"Crazy Uncle Rick! How are you?"

I would have omitted the first word, but Rick seemed to soak in it. He probably took it as a badge of honor.

Jenny then introduced Rick and Yvonne to Justin and their kids. I know Yvonne had met Aaron. I was unsure if Rick had met Justin or the kids.

"One big happy family," my father said, and for the moment, we were.

I looked around, and everyone had a smile on their face.

"Let's all go inside," my father said.

As Aaron passed by my father, he said, "Hi, Grandpa."

My father's eyes teared up for the second time in five minutes. That had to be a record for him. I'm not sure I'd seen him cry since the months that followed my mother's death. I'd kind of always assumed he'd dried up all his tear ducts on her, for good reason.

Nope, the old man of sixty could still be brought to tears.

"Have a seat at the table," my father said. "Who wants wine?"

We made our way to the dining room, where my father had gone all out. Setting a table was not in his wheelhouse, but it looked beautiful.

If there was any issue, it was that the table was only meant to fit six comfortably. We were a little cramped with the six adults and the two kids. Not that anyone was going to complain. We were just happy to have everyone together.

Everyone but Rick and the two kids said yes to the wine.

"No drinking for me," Rick said.

"Well, this is a pleasant surprise," Jen said.

It almost sounded like a backhanded compliment, but Rick took it in stride.

"It's been almost a month," Rick said. "And your brother gets credit."

"I didn't do anything," I said.

"Yeah, you did. When you came over and asked questions about your mother, I imagined her sitting in heaven, looking down at me. And she wouldn't have been pleased with what she saw."

"You deserve the credit, not my brother," Jen said.

"She's right," I added.

My father brought white and red wine bottles and asked what we'd like.

"What are we having for dinner, Richard?" Yvonne asked. "It helps me decide what type of wine I'm going to have."

"It's a roast cooked with vegetables, red wine, and beef broth."

"I think you just answered my question," she said.

My father smiled.

"Red it is."

We all ended up choosing to go with the red.

"It's great to see everyone," Jen said. "But let's get something out of the way early. Since Rick brought up my mother, I wanted to know how you all feel about Bobby investigating her murder."

Uh oh.

Yvonne spoke up first.

"I'm all for it. It's been almost twenty damn years, and some asshole might still be out there, running around. If your brother ever caught the guy, I'd sleep better at night."

"I agree with my sister," Rick said.

Jen looked around. I don't think she was expecting those two responses.

"Dad?" she asked.

"I was on the fence, to begin with, but Bobby has talked me into it. At least, I think he has. As long as I don't have to get involved, I'm all for letting him do his thing."

And then a surprising ally jumped to my defense.

"Shit, even I'm for it," Justin said. "Let's see what he can find out."

He saw Aaron looking up at him.

"Only Daddy can swear," Justin said, and everyone at the table got a nice laugh out of it.

"Well, I don't want to be considered a party pooper, so I guess I'm for it also," Jen said.

"Thanks, sis," I said.

"Like I said, one big happy family!" my father exclaimed.

And we were for dinner that night.

And for the next three days of my sister's visit.

And then the last day came.

✤ 26 ✤

BOBBY

It was Sunday and the last full day of my sister's visit. They were flying back at five a.m. the following morning.

I woke up early and went to look at the investigative wall, as I'd started calling it. I always did this first thing in the morning. Before I showered, before I shaved, and even before I went to the bathroom. I considered it a ritual.

I looked out at the 100+ pictures left.

Did one of you murder my mother?

I stayed there for ten minutes and tried to focus on some photos I hadn't spent as much time looking at.

My mother, with five other women, all holding their young children.

My mother, with the owner of a local restaurant.

My mother, with our old neighbor, Gus Wilkinson.

My mother, at a Halloween party, surrounded by people in costumes.

EVERY TIME I LOOKED AT ALL THE PHOTOS, IT REGISTERED JUST HOW monumental my task was. What if the killer was in the 62nd picture I ever researched? Would I even make it that long, or would I have given up far before then?

I grew mentally exhausted and walked away. I used the bathroom and then sat on my couch, turning on my laptop a minute later.

I'd shower later.

I checked my email first.

A few SPAM emails made it into my regular Inbox. One told me I could make $25,000 weekly by reviewing products online. The other told me I could increase the size of my penis by forty inches. I think there might have been a typo on that one.

The final email in my inbox got my attention. I'd received a new message at helpfindheeatherskiller.com.

I quickly clicked on the message, which took me to the site.

The message popped up.

Keep your phone handy today. If you keep your mouth shut, you might discover who I am. If you talk to anyone, I'll know. That includes the cops.

I unnecessarily read it a second time. I already knew what it said.

I started tapping my foot on the Ottoman in front of me. I didn't realize how hard I was doing it until I accidentally pushed it five feet away.

"Fuck," I yelled. "What should I do?"

As if someone was going to appear from the walls of my apartment, divulging sound logic.

I knew I wasn't going to tell a soul. I'd been through this before. I'd accomplished more in a month than the police had accomplished in two decades.

Was this just some jackass looking to pull me along for the ride?

I'd put the odds at eighty percent.

But that meant there was a twenty percent chance of the unthinkable.

And I wasn't going to risk screwing that up.

THE PLAN WAS TO EXPLORE STATE STREET WITH THE FAMILY.

My father committed to three hours, which, all things considered, was fairly generous of him. With his arthritis, bad knees, etc., he usually limits his walking to an hour or so. The fact that he was willing to join Jen and the kids for three hours showed me that he was having a really good time on their visit.

I was delighted.

It had been a rollicking several days, starting with the surprise of seeing Yvonne and Rick on that first night, and my father loved hearing the word "grandfather" from his grandkids' mouths.

I'd been getting along famously - do people still say that? - with Jen and Justin, who asked me to visit them back east sometime this fall.

We agreed to pick a week once they returned home.

It was the best family "vacation" we'd had in a long time.

❦

WE AGREED TO MEET FOR LUNCH AT LONGBOARD'S GRILL, EVEN though my sister, father, and I knew the food wasn't very good.

It made up for what it lacked in culinary delight with spectacular views. It was located on Stearns Wharf and had views of the ocean that we knew Aaron and Avery would love.

We were supposed to meet at 12:30, but I was running a little late. I'd volunteered to pick my father up, and he was still getting ready when I arrived.

We finally arrived at Longboard's at 12:49. Jen and her family were all smiles as we set eyes on them.

"We figured you might be a few minutes late, so we walked the kids down to the end of the wharf," Jen said.

"Did they like it?"

"They loved it. As much as we love our home back East, there's not quite the views that Santa Barbara offers."

"You can always move home," my father said.

This is when my sister would have jumped on him in the past, and a day-long fight would have ensued. Not on this trip and not today.

"Never say never," she said. "It's been extra nice being home this time."

For what felt like the 5th time this trip, it looked like my father might start crying.

"You about to get emotional again?" I asked.

My father laughed and then took his shirt to wipe his eyes.

"So many onions being cut this weekend," he said.

All of the humans above five years old laughed.

"I'm hungry," Aaron said.

My father patted him on the shoulder.

"Way to change the subject, grandson. Get these people off my back."

Aaron looked at him as if he was speaking Greek. My father laughed.

We approached the hostess at Longboard's.

"McGowan, Party of six," I said.

"Follow me," the young server said, leading us right back outside from where we'd entered. I'd made the reservation and requested outdoor seating.

"Good," Aaron said. "I want to see the water and the fishies."

Avery had been quiet and was just looking around in awe.

"Wawa," she said, confirming that she enjoyed the water as much as her brother.

I got the clam chowder, which I'd found to be the best item on the Longboard's menu. As a general rule, I found it hard for restaurants to screw up anything that contained a lot of whipping cream.

Jen and Justin went with a fish and chips to split, and my father ordered the Lobster roll.

"Will you have a few bites, Bobby?"

"Sure," I said.

Usually, I'd have ordered more than a large soup for lunch, but we were having dinner at six, and I'd make up for it then.

"Wawa," Avery said again.

"Do you want to go to the beach in a few hours?" Jen asked.

"Yes!" Aaron exclaimed.

Avery nodded feverishly.

I'm not even sure she knew what the beach meant.

✺

WE FINISHED LUNCH FORTY-FIVE MINUTES LATER.

It was one of the better times I'd had at Longboard's.

I'd made fun of my father for getting emotional in his old age, but maybe I also felt it. The fact that we were all getting along so well and laughing at all the right times made me happy.

It even made the food taste better.

✺

WE HIT STATE STREET NEXT, CATCHING IT WHERE IT STARTED - ON Cabrillo and only feet from Stearns Wharf.

We stopped at a few stores and window-shopped at several more. While not as famous as 5th Avenue or Rodeo Drive, I'd put State Street among the most underrated streets if you just wanted to browse.

There were scores of bars and restaurants if shopping wasn't your thing. We passed O'Malleys, one of the bars I used to work for, saying hello to several of my old coworkers.

They asked if I wanted a drink, but I told them I was hanging out with the family.

We ventured another block up, and that's when Aaron started complaining.

"I'm tired of walking," he said.

He was too big for a stroller and was stuck being a big boy, something he resented at that moment.

"My feet hurt."

I was always in awe of how much patience parents had. I'm not sure I could do it.

I looked down at my phone. I'd received an email to helpfindheatherskiller.com

I quickly clicked the link on the email, which took me to the website.

I knew who it was going to be from: youstillwontcatchme@gmail.com

My heart rate accelerated as I read it.

Do you want to be a hero and save some lives? The SBPD is currently having a little giveaway outside of the courthouse on Figueroa. A bunch of kids are there waiting to get their hands on some free sweets. I've randomly poisoned five of the cupcakes and cookies. I can't wait to see what little kids are going to die today. They'll be sprawled all over the sidewalk, unable to breathe. It will make your mother's death look like a goddamn picnic.

Holy fucking shit!

Sure, this email might be bullshit. It probably freaking was.

But what if it wasn't? Could I really take that chance?

No, I had to act.

"We have to go to the courthouse," I yelled.

"What are you talking about, Bobby?" Jen asked. "It's a Sunday. Why the hell do you have to go to the courthouse?"

I couldn't get caught up in conversation; every second mattered.

"Meet me there."

And with that, I took off running.

THE COURTHOUSE WAS ONLY A FEW BLOCKS AWAY, AND I ARRIVED within two minutes.

Approximately fifteen police officers were standing by the steps outside of the courthouse. I didn't see any children.

What I did see was Detective Patchett standing off to the side. And that's when I saw the treats. There were about five pink boxes full of cupcakes and cookies.

I ran up to Patchett.

"When do the kids get here?" I asked.

"Nice to see you too, Bobby."

"Just answer my question, please."

"We start in five minutes, so any moment, I imagine. Hey, there's the first one now," he said.

I turned around and saw a child around Aaron's age approaching the officers. He was holding his mother's hand and had a big smile on his face.

I hated the position I was in. Maybe the message from youstillwontcatchme@gmail.com was bullshit. Honestly, it probably was, but I couldn't just do nothing.

If I ended up looking like an idiot, then so be it. That was infinitely better than having some dead kids on my conscience for the rest of my life, even if the odds were 100-1 against it.

Maybe I could talk Patchett down before I had to resort to making an ass of myself.

"You can't serve these cupcakes to those kids," I said.

"What are you talking about, Bobby?"

"Please, just believe me. You can't."

"And why is that?"

"Because they are poisoned."

Patchett laughed.

"I picked these up from Annie's Baked Goods about ten minutes ago. Annie is a sixty-year-old sweetheart. You think she's trying to poison kids?"

He stared at me as if I was a moron.

"Please, Mark. You can't serve these to the kids."

It was one of the first times I called him by his first name, but it didn't help.

"Stop, Bobby. You're going to make me mad if you ask again."

I heard a voice from behind me.

"The line starts here."

It was a police officer who'd just started forming a line a few feet from the pink boxes loaded with goodies. Four kids were now waiting in line, and I saw several more approaching.

The top of the pink boxes were all lifted up, exposing the cupcakes and cookies. It would only take a second or two for one of the kids to get from the front of the line to the boxes.

"What's your name, little guy?"

The officer asked the young boy at the front of the line.

"Steven," he said enthusiastically.

"Well, Steven, you get to eat the first cupcake today."

I looked at Patchett and knew he wasn't going to do anything.

I was about to look like a crazed lunatic, but I had no choice.

Not acting was much worse.

I ran over to the first set of cupcakes and flipped the box over, emptying the contents to the ground. I grabbed the second box and did the same.

"What the fuck are you doing, Bobby?" Patchett yelled.

The other police officers looked in my direction, not quite sure what the hell was going on. I could see some parents and a few kids also looking in my direction. Their faces were in shock.

Two officers quickly approached me, and I knew I wouldn't have the chance to flip each box over individually. So I took my hand and side-swiped the remaining three or four boxes to the ground.

The next thing on the ground was me. The two officers tackled me at the same time.

"The cupcakes are poisoned!" I yelled.

I couldn't risk the kids grabbing the sweets off the ground, or this was all for naught.

"The cupcakes are poisoned!" I yelled again.

The officers were not impressed.

One of them was pushing my head into the ground. The other officer put my hands behind my back and attached some handcuffs.

"Big fucking mistake, my friend," one of them said.

My head was still being pushed to the ground, but I allowed my eyes to look up toward the gathered crowd.

Staring back at me was none other than my father, my sister, and her family. They must have just arrived. To say they had disapproving expressions would be the biggest understatement of all time.

The officers stood me on my feet.

"What is Uncle Bobby doing?" Aaron said.

With the biggest scowl I'd ever seen, my sister said, "Your uncle is going to jail."

❦ 27 ❧

BOBBY

Forty-five minutes later, I'd been processed into the Santa Barbara County Jail.

Before they sent me to my cell, they put me in an interrogation room, and none other than Mark Patchett walked in.

"What the ever-loving fuck, Bobby?"

"I can explain."

"This better be good," he said.

I told him about my website and the messages I'd received.

"If this is true, you should have contacted me weeks ago, but that can wait until we finish this."

"Can I show you the emails?"

"I'll have to get your phone. I'll be back in a few minutes."

He returned ten minutes later with my phone.

"Show me," he said.

I went to the link and clicked on it.

I held up the phone and saw Detective Patchett's face turn white as a ghost.

"You're in a lot of trouble, Bobby."

"What are you talking about?"

"If you wanted people to believe this shit, you probably should have left that last sentence off."

I had no idea what he meant.

"Can I see my phone?" I asked.

He didn't give it back but held it up for me to see.

I couldn't believe what I was reading.

"DO YOU WANT TO BE A HERO AND SAVE SOME LIVES? THE SBPD IS currently having a little giveaway outside of the courthouse on Figueroa. There's a bunch of kids there, waiting to get their hands on some free sweets. I've randomly poisoned five of the cupcakes and cookies. Can't wait to see what little kids are going to die today. They'll be sprawled all over the sidewalk, unable to breathe. It will make your mother's death look like a goddamn picnic."

AT THE BOTTOM OF THE EMAIL WAS THE FOLLOWING:

Note to self: This should work. It sounds believable enough. Send this one to yourself.

"I DON'T KNOW WHERE THAT BOTTOM PART CAME FROM!" I YELLED.

"Sure, Bobby. It magically appeared after you were arrested. That's believable."

"What the fuck is going on?"

"You're going downhill. That's what the fuck is going on. You're pretending the killer is out there conversing with you, all to bring attention to your mother's murder. That's despicable."

"I would never do that."

"This email says differently."

I had no idea what to say. Or do.

"I swear to God, Detective."

Patchett shook his head.

"I don't believe you."

"Can I show you something on my phone?" I asked.

"This is now evidence, Bobby. How do I know you won't erase something?"

It was my turn to shake my head.

"Have I ever lied to you?"

"Not until today."

"You won't let me see my phone?"

"Tell me what to do," he said.

CHAPTER 27

"Are you still on my website?"

"Yes."

"Click on messages in the upper right-hand corner."

"Okay. What next?"

"What's the oldest message?"

"The title is 'I Knew Your Mom in High School.'"

"It's not that one. What's next?"

"No title, but it says it's from youstillwontcatchme@gmail.com."

"Click on that one," I said, a little too excitedly.

Patchett clicked on it and, after a few seconds, gave me a steely glaze.

"What?" I said.

"If I had to give you some advice, Bobby, I'd tell you that now is the time to shut the fuck up."

"What does the message say?"

Patchett turned the phone toward me.

"YOU'RE LOOKING AT THE WRONG PHOTO ALBUM."

AND AT THE BOTTOM OF THE EMAIL:

Note to self: This makes it sound like the killer is following the case. Also, makes me sound pathetic looking through old photo albums. The media will eat this up. Get some sympathy building for my Mom. And me."

"THAT WASN'T ME!!" I YELLED.

"Like I said, Bobby. I'd shut the fuck up now."

And so I did.

I WAS RELEASED FROM JAIL AT 9:00 P.M. THAT NIGHT.

I had a court date in two weeks for disturbing the peace. Patchett notified me that there might be some added charges coming.

I ordered an UBER and had them drive me to my car, which was still on State Street. Then I drove home.

As I lay in bed, I wondered how the fuck the killer - I believed it was him now - was able to attach things to his email/messages that I previously couldn't see. He had some sort of program that could manipulate my website.

Meanwhile, I had corkboards with tacks holding up old photos.

I was so freaking overmatched.

❧ 28 ❧

BOBBY

I woke up the following day and texted my sister.

"Can I come see you guys before you fly back today?"

"Is this a joke?"

"No, I want to say goodbye."

"I think we're going to pass on that."

"Why? We were having such a nice visit."

"Exactly. We were. That changed when you were arrested in front of your niece and nephew. I think we've seen enough of you for one trip."

"I'm being set up, Jen. You have to believe me."

"Knocking cupcakes over that were meant for kids? What the fuck were you thinking?"

"You have to believe me, Jenny," I repeated.

"We'll talk once I get home."

"I can't come see you guys?"

"For the last time, I think we've seen enough of you for one trip."

I set my phone down and felt like I could cry.

I wanted to call my father but decided to give him some time to cool off.

That was going to be another interesting talk.

Fuck.

BOBBY

NEXT, I CALLED MY MOST TECHNOLOGICALLY PROFICIENT FRIEND AND told him about my website and what had happened. I didn't go into specifics about my arrest.

"It can be done," he said. "They probably sent the bad part with the initial message, but it's somehow blacked out or invisible. Then, the program retroactively adds the deleted part whenever he wants. Did you know they had poker websites fifteen years ago where the programmers allowed themselves to see their opponents' hole cards? What your guy did is child's play compared to that. Anyway, long story short, yes, it's possible, and I'm sorry it happened to you. "

"Thanks," I said and hung up abruptly.

I asked myself a question.

Did it really matter that he'd added the Note to Self at the bottom of the emails?

Even if Detective Patchett only saw the original email, he could have assumed I'd made up the email address youstillwontcatchme@gmail.com and sent it to my website.

Sure, it looked worse that I was leaving myself "Notes," but either way, I could have been behind it all.

I was fucked either way.

THE WEEK THAT FOLLOWED MY ARREST WAS ALMOST AS BAD AS THE arrest itself.

Twice, I was recognized out on the town, and both times I was mocked.

One guy said, "Stealing cupcakes from kids is an underrated side hustle."

And another said, "If you're so desperate for a sugar high, grab a Snickers."

Apparently, there was a video on YouTube with me knocking over the pink boxes, yelling, '*The cupcakes are poisoned!*' and then getting arrested.

I could only imagine what they were saying about me.

Do you know who Bobby McGowan is? The kid whose mother was killed. Well, he has fallen off the deep end. He's gone full-on bonkers.

CHAPTER 28

MY FATHER WAS EXTREMELY DISAPPOINTED WITH ME AND TOLD ME TO drop the investigation into my mother's death. He also asked me to wait a few days until I visited him. That hurt more.

Detective Patchett called to tell me that none of the cupcakes were poisoned and that they'd added a charge of criminal mischief, whatever the fuck that was.

And it didn't end there.

I called the *Santa Barbara News-Press* and KEYT, asking them if they were still interested in doing something for the 20th anniversary of my mother's death, which was now only a little over a month away.

The paper and the TV station suddenly balked at the idea they'd originally been interested in. They tried to let me down gently, but it was easy to read between the lines. My arrest had made me persona non grata in print or on T.V.

I felt like a pariah in my own town.

❦ 29 ❦

CONRAD

My sense of humor was basically nonexistent, but I was literally laughing out loud while watching the local news that night:

"This is Angela Diaz, reporting with KEYT. We had an interesting event in front of the courthouse today. The police were giving away cupcakes to Santa Barbara's youth today when this happened."

The video showed Bobby McGowan pushing several boxes of cupcakes to the ground and then screaming, "The cupcakes are poisoned!" after he was tackled to the ground. The video concludes with him getting arrested.

Even in my wildest dreams, I couldn't have imagined it going as well as it had—pure perfection.

Monumentally embarrassing the son of a woman you'd murdered twenty years earlier? Name me another serial killer who has done that. I'll wait.

I ADMIT WHEN I MAKE MISTAKES.

And I had in the murder of Heather McGowan. Roy Cooper should have been convicted, but I made some rookie mistakes, making it impossible. Namely, I didn't double-check to ensure he was staying in on the day in question. My brother had given me that information the day before, but that wasn't good enough.

I also didn't think to leave any of Roy's DNA at the crime scene. That was something I started implementing during my second murder. It was a game-changer and a colossal reason so many of my enemies had been convicted of my crimes.

Looking back, I was probably lucky I didn't leave any of Roy's DNA at the scene. The police surely would have wondered how Heather McGowan had Roy's DNA under her fingernails when people confirmed that Roy had been at a bar.

It might have looked like a botched framing job.

And I couldn't have that idea floating around Central Coast police departments. Not with what I had planned.

I guess, all things considered, my first murder had gone better than I could have hoped. No, Roy Cooper wasn't convicted, but he was long considered a suspect, and I had no doubt it made his life miserable for a few years. Good.

And I learned a few lessons. (1) Make 1,000 percent sure the person I'm trying to frame doesn't have an alibi. And (2) Convicting someone on circumstantial evidence is much more challenging. DNA was king.

From then on, I vowed to get DNA samples of the people I was trying to frame and leave it at the crime scene.

It's tough to explain DNA away.

And, if the prosecution had a suspect's DNA, they tend to overlook other things. I found that as my career progressed.

Three of the people I framed argued that their phone was in their home (where they were) on the day they allegedly committed murder. In each case, the prosecution argued that the defendants intentionally left their phones at home, so they had a built-in alibi.

And that's all because the prosecution had their DNA. It led them to assume guilt..

MY DEMONS HAVE RETURNED RECENTLY.

That's what I tell myself when I start getting the urge to kill again.

I "blame" it on the demons, knowing full well that demon is me.

⚜

IT'S BEEN ALMOST FOURTEEN MONTHS SINCE MY LAST MURDER. THAT may seem like a long time, but as I've said many times, I'm painstakingly meticulous.

The time, the victim, and the circumstances all have to be perfect to ensure I never got caught.

I felt that scenario was fast approaching, which meant victim #10 was in my sights.

Her name was Victoria Bosco.

And she had a month left on earth.

Maybe less.

30

BOBBY

"Hello?"

"Is this Bobby McGowan?"

A number I'd never seen had popped up on my cell phone. Since starting my investigation, I'd begun answering these types of phone calls, something I'd never done in the past.

"It is. Who is calling?"

"It's Roy Cooper."

I couldn't have been more shocked.

"What can I help you with, Mr. Cooper?"

"I'm going to be in Santa Barbara in a few days. Could we talk?"

His voice was less combative than I would have guessed. I told myself to be careful. At the very least, he stalked my mother while she was alive. At worst, he was involved in her murder.

"What did you want to talk about?"

"I'm hoping to convince you that I had nothing to do with your mother's murder. I've heard you're asking a lot of questions around town, and it's causing me a great deal of distress. People are starting to talk about me again, and I had nothing at all to do with her murder. I may not have been a great guy, but I genuinely liked your mother. I never would have killed her."

He sounded convincing. I had to give him that.

"It's probably better to do the rest of this in person. When do you arrive?" I asked.

"On Thursday," he said.

"Want to meet up on Friday morning?"

"Sure. Where?"

"How about a coffee shop?"

"I'd like something more private. We'll probably talk about things I'd rather no one else overhear."

I looked up at the investigative wall.

"How about we meet at my apartment?" I suggested.

"Sure. What's the address?"

I gave it to him. We picked a time, and I hung up.

Roy Cooper had known my mother as long as almost anyone. Maybe he could offer an opinion on some of these photos,

Assuming he wasn't just coming over to kill me.

I MET WITH ROY COOPER ON FRIDAY MORNING AS WE'D SET UP.

I greeted him outside of my apartment complex and led him in.

He graduated from high school the same year as my mother, so I knew he was around fifty-six or fifty-seven. He looked healthy for his age, which surprised me. I'd repeatedly heard how hard-living a guy he was, so I expected to meet a weathered man. That wasn't the case.

"Thanks for agreeing to meet with me," he said. "I'm sorry for what I did to your family. I never should have kept calling your mother after she'd gotten married. I was an idiot. I'm sure you think ill of me, but I hope to change that opinion."

I could have lied and told him I thought he was fine and dandy, but I didn't want to start our conversation with a lie. His apology did carry some weight, however. It seemed authentic.

"I'm here with an open mind," I said, and that was the truth.

We were hovering in the kitchen, so I told him to sit on the couch. The monstrous cork boards would be facing him. There was no way he could avoid it.

"Would you like something to drink?" I asked.

"What have you got?"

"Water, coffee, orange juice. Or I've got a beer if you'd prefer."

It was early in the morning, but with his reputation, I extended him the offer. Plus, people were likelier to talk too much when they had a drink or two.

"I quit drinking," he said.

First Uncle Rick and now Roy Cooper.

"I'll just take a water," he added.

"Sure."

I grabbed him a water and then sat next to him on the couch.

"That's quite the wall you've got there," he said. "Is it what I think it is?"

"Yes. It's everything I know when it comes to my mother's murder."

"What's with all the photographs?"

"I have reason to believe that whoever murdered her is in one of those photos."

I stared at him, hoping to see a reaction, but nothing stood out.

"Why do you think that?" he asked.

"I'll tell you when I know you better."

He laughed, and it wasn't just a courtesy laugh.

"You're not what I expected," I said.

"I'm not the same man I was five years ago. And certainly, not the same man I was when I knew your mother."

"You stopped drinking five years ago?"

"Yeah"

"You know my Uncle Rick, right?"

"Heather's brother?"

"Yes."

"Sure, I know Rick."

"He just quit drinking about a month ago."

"Good for him. We were similar in a lot of ways. People were intimidated by us, especially when we drank."

"Were you intimidated by him?"

"Maybe a little bit. Mainly because he was Heather's older brother and was trying to prevent me from dating her."

"You guys did date in college."

"I'm talking about high school when Heather lived at home. Rick lived around town but always seemed to be back home when I showed up. It's like he had a sixth sense."

I smiled. You have to love Uncle Rick.

Roy continued.

"I felt like he and his parents badmouthed me to Heather so she wouldn't date me."

"Sounds like they had reason to. You didn't exactly have a sterling reputation."

"How about this? I'll grant you that I used to be an asshole if you stop bringing it up."

He was quiet serious. I'd seen the first glimpse of Roy Cooper's intimidating side.

"Deal," I said.

He took a sip of his water.

"So, what specifically brought you here today?" I asked.

"It's just like I said on the phone. People called me and said you've been asking about me. I've been a good person since I got sober, but these calls are testing my sobriety."

"I'm just trying to get to the bottom of my mother's murder. It's nothing personal; it's just where the investigation led me."

"It led you to me?"

"No offense, but you have been the lone suspect for years."

"I have an alibi."

"I know. I talked to one of the two guys you were drinking with."

"Which one?"

"Ethan Drury."

"And what did he say?"

"He said he was at the bar with you that afternoon."

"Ethan is telling you the truth," Roy said.

"I want to believe you," I said.

"That's all I'm asking for."

We both stayed quiet for a few seconds as if that part of the conversation was now over.

"Who do you think killed my mother?" I blurted out.

"I have no idea."

"You must have thought about it over the years."

"To be honest, I was too busy defending myself. If I'd had any inkling who'd done it, I'd have told the police. I'd have loved to get them to look anywhere besides at me. I never had an idea who it was, though. Honestly."

"What vibe did you get about who killed her?"

"What do you mean?"

"Did you think it was a stranger? Someone who knew her? What type of overall vibes did you get about the case?"

"I guess I always assumed it was someone who knew her. Maybe someone who lusted after her. I don't know. I mean, how often does someone just break into a random person's house and kill them? I've watched enough *Dateline TV* shows. It's much more likely to be...someone they knew over some random serial killer."

He paused before saying 'someone they knew.' I think he was going to say "husband" or "loved one," but knew those would hit too close to home for me.

"How did you find out?" I asked.

"That she was murdered?"

"Yes."

"It was early the next morning. I'd passed out pretty early after drinking most of the previous day."

"Who told you?"

"Ty called me and told me. I'm not sure how he'd heard before me. And then, within minutes of Ty calling, the cops called, and I was answering questions about Heather later that morning at the police station."

"And that's when you told them you'd been at the bar."

"Of course. It was the freaking truth."

It was the second time he'd shown his darker side. He seemed genuinely upset.

"Calm down," I said. "I'm just trying to get the full story."

I could tell he didn't like my '*calm down*' comment. Good, I wanted to see the real Roy Cooper—or, at least, the Roy Cooper from thirty years ago.

"I'm trying to answer these honestly," he said.

"The police released you that same day?"

"Yes. If memory serves, I was only in there a few hours. I'm sure they verified my alibi, and that's when they let me go."

"And yet you remained a suspect. Why do you think that is?"

"I think people probably figured I'd put Ethan and Ty up to it. They looked up to me, so people assumed they were lying for me. That wasn't the case, but you can't stop people from gossiping."

If Roy Cooper was telling the truth - and I tended to think he was - he'd also had his life turned upside down. Nothing approaching what our family had been through, obviously, but being accused of a crime you didn't commit is no picnic either.

"Did you lose friends over it?" I asked.

"Yeah. Most everyone started distancing themselves from me."

"Is that why you moved ?"

"Yes. I would have moved sooner, but I thought people would then be even more suspicious of me. Including the police."

I'd read the police reports so many times I knew most of the answers to the questions I was asking.

We could have done this question-and-answer thing anywhere, but I'd invited him to my apartment for a reason.

"Would you mind looking at some old pictures for me?" I asked.

He stood up before answering, walking to the wall in question.

"What am I looking for exactly?" he asked.

"Anything that jumps out. Did any of these people have a crush on my mother? Did any of them harbor grudges against our family? Did any of them have well-known tempers or spend time in jail? Did any of them have problems with women in general?"

Roy nodded and stared at the wall. He didn't move or say anything for about three minutes.

"I see a lot of old faces I recognize. I even remember some of their names. But no one jumps out as a suspect. I'm sorry."

"Nothing jumps out?"

"No. I'm sorry. I'd love to help. I want this case solved as much as anyone."

I stared at him.

"I'm sorry," he said. "Besides your family, of course."

I nodded, ostensibly accepting his apology.

"What happened to the guy you accused on KEYT?" he asked.

I could have told Roy Cooper that I hadn't accused Lyle Taft, but what was the point?

"I found out he's dead. So he's no longer on the wall. I've been taking photos off the wall once I no longer suspect them."

"Am I on the wall?"

"Yes, for now."

"Where is it?"

I grabbed the photo with him and handed it over.

Roy Cooper smiled.

"Wow, we were just kids. Me, Ethan, and Ty were probably seniors in high school. And look at their little rugrat brothers. They can't be a day over eleven or twelve."

Although he had smiled, there was a sadness in his eyes as well. I'm sure he was thinking about all the time that had passed and how he was now very much on the back nine of his life. Maybe he even regretted how he'd treated people as a younger man.

"I heard you were pretty rough on Ethan and Ty's younger brothers."

"That's true, but then again, I was rough on everyone. Especially the younger kids around town."

He handed me the photo, and I returned it to the wall.

"Let me know when you finally take that photo down," he said and smiled.

Coming into this meeting, I wanted to hate Roy Cooper. And I assuredly would have had I met him as a younger man. But this version of him was different. He still had an edge, but it was hard for me to hate him.

"What made you quit drinking?" I asked.

Roy was back looking at the photos. He was now reading one of the news articles I'd posted to the wall.

"I lost visitation rights to my children," he said. "That was the final straw."

"Can you see them now?"

"Yes, but for two years, I couldn't, and I'll never get that time back. I don't blame my ex-wife, though. It was the right thing to file for sole custody. I was a drunk and an asshole."

He was still reading the article when he turned around to face me.

"I can't imagine how tough that day was for your family. I hope you find peace even if you don't catch Heather's killer."

"Thanks," I said..

"I'm sorry," he said. "I used to call your mother when she was a married woman. I'd attend events around Santa Barbara in hopes of running into her. I was a jerk of the highest order, and I apologize. Heather never even gave me the time of day. She wanted nothing to do with me. She loved your father and was always faithful to him."

I'd always known that, but it was still nice to hear.

Roy looked at the faces in the photos again, almost mesmerized by them.

"Santa Barbara was such a safe town back then. These people you have on your wall? They were good people. Maybe I was wrong, and it was a random serial killer. Did your investigation ever lead in that direction?"

"No, I guess it hasn't. I've spent more time looking at her friends and people who lived close by, things like that."

What if the killer was a random serial killer and had emailed helpfind-heatherskiller.com just to throw me off his scent? He tells me it's someone from a photo album when he knows it's not.

I'd been way too willing to believe his messages, culminating in me flipping over the cupcakes. If this were indeed a random serial killer, he'd accomplished his goal. I'd wasted several weeks looking through old photo albums and limiting my suspects to people my mother knew.

"Listen, I'm not here to tell you how to investigate your mother's death," Roy said. "But maybe start looking at other murders around Santa Barbara. Or close cities. Maybe there's a pattern."

I'd invited Roy Cooper to my apartment in hopes that he'd be able to point me in the direction of a suspect. Instead, he was telling me that maybe the entire wall I'd built was a waste of time and my mother had been murdered by some random person no one would ever suspect.

"I'll consider it," I said.

He turned around and faced me.

"So, where do we stand?" he asked.

"I don't think I'll mention your name around town anymore. I'm sorry if my actions caused you grief."

"And I'm sorry for causing your family grief. Tell your father I apologize."

"I will."

Roy Cooper turned to go.

31

BOBBY

I didn't take down all my photos but did heed Roy Cooper's suggestion.

It was time to consider a second possibility: that my mother was murdered by a random person, possibly a serial killer.

This didn't mean I would stop looking at people she knew. It just meant my investigation was now going to be two-pronged.

⚜

"I'M HERE TO SEE DETECTIVE FRICK," I SAID.

"And your name is?"

"Bobby McGowan."

I'd called the Ventura police department and asked if they had any detectives working there since 2003. They said to talk to Frederick Frick. I asked if I could set up a meeting with him, and they obliged, so I drove down to Ventura the same day.

My goal was to find out any information on murders similar to my mother's. I planned on hitting Ventura and Oxnard before making my way to Santa Maria, Lompoc, Pismo Beach, San Luis Obispo, and a few other cities north of Santa Barbara.

I'd decided to ignore Los Angeles for the time being. It was just too sprawling, and they'd inevitably have innumerable murders around the

157

time of my mother's death. LA was just too daunting, plus it was ninety minutes from Santa Barbara. I was hoping to find murders that were closer to home and, thus, more likely to have been committed by the same guy. Assuming there was even a serial killer out there.

"Wait here. I'll go get Detective Frick."

Frederick Frick appeared a few minutes later. He looked like a detective out of the 1930s. He was sporting an old-school fedora and a weathered suit. Think Humphrey Bogart as Sam Spade. Shit, even the name Frederick Frick sounded like someone from a bygone era.

He led me down to a surprisingly spacious office. I wasn't used to seeing them in police stations. They were usually claustrophobic.

I knew I'd be asking for something that most detectives wouldn't want to give me: information on cases they'd been unable to solve.

So, while I originally hadn't planned on playing the victim card and name-dropping my mother, I decided it was probably the best way to get what I wanted—a clear case of the ends justifying the means.

"Nice to meet you, Mr. McGowan," Frick said.

"You as well. Thanks for meeting with me."

"What can I help you with? You said you wanted to talk about some murders that happened twenty years ago."

"That's right."

"So, where do you want to start?"

Why wait, I told myself.

"I guess we'll start with me," I said. "My mother's name was Heather McGowan."

I would have been surprised if it didn't register. Ventura was a half hour south of Santa Barbara, but my mother's case had gotten so much attention that most people within a hundred-mile radius had likely heard of it.

Especially if you were a detective who had been working at the time.

"I know your mother's case well. I'm a good friend of Mark Patchett's."

I'd have taken that as a good sign as recently as two weeks ago. With what happened outside of the Santa Barbara Courthouse, it was likely that friends of Patchett's now looked at me as a loose cannon. Maybe I'd dodged a bullet, and Frick hadn't heard about it.

"Detective Patchett has been very upfront with our family, even though he never did come up with a suspect."

I gave Patchett both a compliment and a putdown. It seemed fair.

"We all have one case that eats us up at night. I'd bet your mother's is that for Mark."

"He told me as much," I said.

"I figured."

"In fact, that's kind of why I'm here. I've decided to do a little investigating on my own. I've spent about six weeks looking into my mother's death. That may not sound like much time, but I've dedicated fourteen hours a day to it. Seven days a week."

"Don't let it overwhelm you," he said as his fedora fell slightly to the right.

"Too late for that."

I couldn't get over this guy's outfit. I didn't know whether to laugh or bow down in deference.

"So, how can I help?" Frick said.

"I've come to a bit of a standstill. I've been investigating people from in and around Santa Barbara. People she knew. People she grew up with. I've started considering the possibility it was someone she didn't know. And that led me to contemplate the outside chance it was a serial killer."

"And you want to see if some similar murders took place down here in Ventura?"

"Exactly."

"You're not a police officer, are you?"

"No."

"A private investigator?"

"No."

"Just a concerned citizen?"

"No offense, but I'm more than just that. My mother was murdered, and the killer is still out there."

"If he's still alive."

I wanted to say 'Obviously' but held my tongue.

"Yes."

"So what exactly do you want from me? Case files? I can't do that."

"What can you do for me? I know I'm just an amateur, but who knows, maybe I'll find something relevant to one of your cold cases."

I wasn't sure if cops actually called them cold cases, but I'd heard it enough on TV to roll with it.

Frederick Frick looked me over.

"Like I said, I can't give you the case files."

He wanted to help me in some way, though. I could tell.

"But…" I said, leading him in what I hoped was the right direction.

"But I guess it wouldn't hurt to give you the names of the victims in our unsolved homicides."

"Thank you. Could I also get the name of a loved one?"

Before he could answer, I said, "I'll tell them that I also lost a loved one to murder. I won't bring you up. I promise."

He started to mull it over. I was not expecting what he said next.

"I heard about your little skirmish with the SBPD a few weeks back."

SHIT!!

"And I kind of felt bad for you," he added. "An investigation can cause people to go a little crazy. I can't imagine it being my own mother and the investigation having stretched on for twenty years."

I wanted to tell him I wasn't crazy and had received those messages, but he was about to give me something, so I had to play it cool.

"It hasn't been easy," I said instead.

"Alright, here's what I'm going to do for you. I will contact the loved ones myself and ask them if they mind if you reach out to them. If they say yes, I'll give you their contact info. I feel more comfortable doing that than just giving you their number straightaway."

"I appreciate it very much, Mr. Frick."

"And if by some miracle you find a connection to any of my unsolved Ventura cases, I will be the first one you contact. Right?"

"Of course."

"You know what," Detective Frick said. "If I deem a few of our solved cases to be almost identical to your mother's, I'll include those too. Maybe this asshole is rotting in jail."

I hadn't given that possibility nearly enough consideration. There was at least a decent chance this asshole was in jail for another crime. I'd probably avoided that scenario because if it were true, I was spending all this time for naught.

"Thanks. I'd appreciate that," I said.

"Alright. I'll call you in two days or so and let you know which - if any - of the next of kin want to talk to you."

"Thank you."

"Can I share one piece of advice before you go?" Frick asked.

"Sure."

"If you don't catch your mother's killer in the next few months, let it go. If not, it's going to eat you alive for the rest of your life."

It was good advice, even though it had already been eating me alive for twenty years.

"I appreciate that," I said.

With that, we shook hands, and he promised to call back in two days.

◈

AFTER LEAVING VENTURA, I DROVE DOWN TO OXNARD AND TALKED with another detective.

He seemed more reluctant than Frederick Frick, but after I told him what Frick had done for me, he agreed to do the same. They knew each other, and he probably figured if Frick did it, he could also.

I planned on using that strategy for the other cities as well; if it ain't broke, don't fix it.

❧ 32 ❧

CONRAD

Angie Billows. Jill Venable. Greta Smith. Lily Spector. Bobbie Sax. Jessica Moore. Mary Jane Cushing. Patricia Patterson. Ginny Towers.

The nine women I'd murdered.

Derek Tice. Zed Billings. Dale Collier. Rog Thurl. Cameron Edding.

The five men who'd been convicted of murder.

There have been very few men in history who have framed five innocent men for murder unless you're talking about corrupt prosecuting attorneys.

Certainly, no other serial killer. That's for sure.

I HAD THE LAST FEW DAYS OFF FROM WORK.

I spent most of that time writing in my journal, focusing on the early stages of what will eventually be the murder of Victoria Bosco.

And the more I write, the more I want this journal released during my lifetime.

I read back through my early murders like this is some sort of greatest hits album.

And I want to share it with the world.

I want to be mentioned on creepy Reddit threads. I want to be acknowledged among the all-time great serial killers. I want to accentuate why I'm different from any of the others.

To sum it up, I want my fifteen minutes of fame.

There is one significant drawback, however. And no, it's not that the police will then know who I am and arrest me. Don't worry; I've got that all taken care of. I will not be spending my elder years in any jail cell. And no, I won't be committing suicide, either. I'll be living my days out on a five-acre ranch, happy as a clam.

The drawback I'm referring to is that Tice, Billings, Collier, Thurl, and Edding will eventually be released from jail. My journal describes in detail how I committed the murder they were convicted of. They can't just leave them in jail.

Which is too bad because I want those fuckers to rot in jail for the rest of their lives.

So I have to make a choice.

Never get any recognition during my lifetime, but they remain in jail for life. Or, I get the attention I now desire, but they get released from jail.

For most of my life, I would have chosen the former, but I now was leaning toward the latter.

And there was one added bonus to them getting out of jail.

They would know that I, Conrad Drury, was the one who took their freedom for all those years.

It was me who had killed their wife or ex-girlfriend.

That's something I'd revel in.

The way I looked at it, either way I won.

Either they wasted away in jail for the rest of their lives or had to come to grips with the fact that I had ruined their lives.

Both outcomes were beautiful.

Fuck, I am genuinely deranged.

But I know it, so I'm not crazy.

Evil? Yes. Crazy? No.

❧ 33 ❧

BOBBY

Detective Frick had been the first detective to call me back. It was two days after I'd visited him, just as he'd promised.

He told me he'd used the time frame of 1998 to 2008. That would help include all the murders that occurred five years before or after my mother's. There were six murders in Ventura during that time that Frick felt had at least a few similarities.

He gave me the name and number of someone to contact for each of the six murders.

I thanked him profusely.

❧

OVER THE NEXT FOUR DAYS, I RECEIVED BETWEEN THREE AND EIGHT names from the six police departments I'd approached. In total, I had thirty murders that, in at least some small way, bore a resemblance to my mother's.

As with the photo albums, I didn't know where to start, so I just went with the first cases sent to me, which meant I started with Ventura and the names Frederick Frick had sent.

In each case, I did quite a bit of research online. I found at least one article on each of the murders. Some had twenty articles. And one case, the murder of a twenty-six-year-old pregnant woman, had garnered national attention.

After I'd done my proper research, I reached out to the loved one. Of the six Ventura cases, four of the people I talked to were the deceased's spouse or significant other. One was the brother of the murdered woman, and the last one had been the mother; that was probably the most difficult of all.

ALL OF THE CASES INTRIGUED ME, AND YET NONE STOOD OUT. THERE wasn't one that screamed, 'THIS IS WAY TOO SIMILAR TO BE A COINCIDENCE!'

Tears were shed on a few Ventura calls, but everyone seemed to admire what I was doing.

My immediate goal was to find a correlation to my mother's murder, but if I found some information that might help break the other cases, I was all for it.

And that was just the unsolved cases. There were also six cases where someone had been sentenced for the crime, but the detectives felt it was close enough to my mother's to include.

Those intrigued me more than I thought they would.

Was the scumbag who murdered my mother already in jail?

SANTA MARIA HAD BEEN THE NEXT TO GET BACK TO ME, EVEN THOUGH I'd gone to Oxnard a day earlier.

Oxnard was next, followed by Pismo Beach, San Luis Obispo, and Lompoc.

My modus operandi stayed the same. I'd do some research online before reaching out to the loved one.

I spent four days immersed in the new set of crimes.

It was heartbreaking.

For each case, I had to read about a new woman who'd lost her life in a brutal matter. On top of that, I had to talk to loved ones whose lives were changed forever. They were all still grieving in one way or another, and more tears were shed.

It was overwhelming.

❦ 34 ❦

BOBBY

I'd decided to put the right side of my living room wall to good use.

I went and bought three more cork boards and started dedicating that side of the wall to the thirty murder victims. I wrote down the details of their murders, the salient points of my interviews with their loved ones, and included a photo when I'd been able to find one online.

A busy police precinct had nothing on my living room wall.

As with the photos, I had to determine which murders to look into first. I narrowed it down to three.

Sissy Trafalgar had been killed in 2006 at the age of thirty-seven. The murder took place in San Luis Obispo three years after my mother's death. There were several similarities. She had been home alone and was the mother of two young kids, just like my mother had been. The murder had occurred during the day, and she had not been sexually assaulted. So far, it was exactly like my mother's. However, there was one significant difference: Sissy had been shot. A murderer can change his mode of killing, but it isn't common. Her assailant was never caught.

Brynn Markinson was killed in Santa Maria in 2001. She was also a young mother who was murdered while home alone. However, she'd also been shot, and her murder had occurred at night. It was still close enough to my mother's to look into, but to me, it more closely resembled Sissy Trafalgar's death, with the lone difference being that Brynn had been killed at night. Still, not all murders are going to be identical, and except for them being killed by gun, Sissy and Brynn's were close enough to my mother's case for me to take an interest in them. Brynn's killer was also never caught.

The third murder I planned on looking into was the most similar to my mother's, but it came with a caveat. A huge caveat. Mary Jane Cushing had been murdered in Pismo Beach in 2005, two years after my mother. She had been strangled while home alone. Mary Jane was thirty-two and had no children. She even looked quite a bit like my mother. Mary Jane wasn't married and had no kids, but that didn't seem that important to me. I never thought my mother had been killed because she was married and had kids. The huge caveat was that someone had been convicted of Mary Jane's murder. His name was Derek Tice.

You'd think that would end my interest in the case, but there was more. A lot more.

I'd reached out to Mary Jane Cushing's mother, Evelyn. She was in her late seventies but lucid as any forty-year-old. She told me that Derek Tice had been her daughter's boyfriend, but they'd broken up a year or so before her murder.

Evelyn said that she got along well with Derek Tice from the start. He treated Mary Jane respectfully, and her daughter seemed to love him. Evelyn had been hoping for wedding bells, so she was surprised when they broke up. Mary Jane told her mother that she still loved Derek and that there was a chance they would get back together.

Mary Jane was killed before that could ever happen.

And Evelyn was shocked when Derek Tice was charged with, and eventually convicted of, her murder.

THERE WAS MORE.

Evelyn told me that a year ago, an attorney called her and said she worked for a law firm called Lawyers for the Wrongfully Accused. The attorney informed Evelyn that she was going to take the case of Derek Tice, whom she believed to be innocent of Mary Jane's murder.

Evelyn told me she was conflicted. On the one hand, she'd at least gained some closure when Tice was convicted. She assumed she was mistaken about Derek, and the legal system had gotten it right. After all, Derek had no alibi, and they found his DNA on Mary Jane. It wasn't just a stray hair. Mary Jane had a good bit of Derek's DNA on her.

"How can you explain that away?" Evelyn had rhetorically asked me.

On the other hand, Evelyn still felt in her heart that Derek couldn't have killed Mary Jane.

And when the attorney called, Evelyn's doubts resurfaced.

I asked her what her current thoughts were.

"I just don't know," she said. "I really don't."

Before we got off the phone, I asked her for the number of the lawyer defending Derek Tice.

"Her name is Rachel Tatum. Just a heads up, she's got quite the personality. I bet she'd be pretty damn convincing in court."

"What's the latest? Has she procured a new court date for Derek Tice?"

"Not yet. Trying to get a new trial can take a long time."

I thanked Evelyn for her time and got off the phone.

⚜

IF I WERE BEING LOGICAL, I WOULD HAVE CHOSEN ONE OF THE FIRST two murders to follow up on. After all, the killers had never been caught, and they were similar enough to my mother's murder to arouse my suspicions.

Newsflash: I wasn't always logical.

The murder of Mary Jane Cushing fascinated me more. As with my mother, Mary Jane had been strangled, whereas Sissy Trafalgar and Brynn Markinson had been shot. The fact that a potentially innocent man had been convicted of her murder only added to the intrigue.

I'd love to talk to Derek Tice and find out who he thought killed Mary Jane Cushing.

⚜

I LOOKED UP AT THE THREE CORK BOARDS ON THE LEFT OF MY WALL, which contained the photos from our family albums.

Was I making another poor decision?

I'd followed enough true crime to know that it was almost always someone close to the victim. Serial killers - while fascinating - were exceedingly rare. And yet, I'd abandoned the photo albums to start investigating seemingly unrelated murders in the hopes of potentially finding a serial killer. Had I lost my mind?

I LOOKED DOWN AT MY LAPTOP. IN THE DAYS FOLLOWING MY ARREST, I tried a few times to contact *you stillwontfindme@gmail.com*. I'd received no response. Maybe it was time to try again.

I constructed the following message.

"Are you done interacting? You do the cupcakes prank and then go into hiding? I guess you never really wanted to have a fair contest anyway. Never really wanted to give me a shot. You just wanted to hide behind your computer. You're nothing but a keyboard warrior."

And I pressed send.

It was a Hail Mary, calling him a keyboard warrior. Let's see if he took offense to it.

AS THE DAY WENT ON, I COULDN'T STOP THINKING ABOUT THE MURDER of Mary Jane Cushing.

I went online and found the phone number for the attorney representing Derek Tice. I called the number.

"Hello, this is Rachel Tatum."

I realized that Evelyn had given me Rachel's cell phone number. I'd assumed it was going to be her law office.

"Hi, my name is Bobby McGowan."

"Make this quick, Mr. McGowan. I'm going into court in thirty seconds."

I had no time to waste.

"My mother was killed in a very similar fashion to Mary Jane Cushing."

"McGowan...McGowan...McGowan...," she said as if tossing the name around in her head. "Was your mother's name Heather?"

"Yes."

"Your name was on my potential list of people to contact. The problem is I'm currently working on three of these cases, and I'm pretty swamped."

"Could we meet and talk? You could just give me ten minutes."

"Sure, I could do that. I really am going into court right now; that wasn't just a line. Call my secretary and set up a meeting."

With that, she hung up on her end.

I WENT ONLINE AND FOUND THE NUMBER TO HER LAW FIRM.

It was actually named "Rachel Tatum for the Wrongfully Convicted."

Her secretary answered, and I asked to set up a meeting.

Rachel Tatum was booked tomorrow and didn't take appointments on the weekend. I was able to set up a meeting for 8:00 a.m. on Monday.

The secretary informed me that Ms. Tatum had court at nine that morning so we'd be ending at 8:30, regardless. I told her thirty minutes would be ample.

My investigation was about to enter it's craziest phase yet.

❧ 35 ❧

CONRAD

Victoria Bosco was a bit of an outlier.

I wasn't trying to frame anyone. I was going to kill her out of pure, unadulterated spite. You know how they say Hollywood stars will do one movie for the studio and then one for themselves? Well, this murder was for me.

She wasn't the first woman I was killing with no intention of framing someone. There had been three in total. Maybe she wasn't an outlier, but this was still rare.

Victoria and I met on a dating app about four years ago and agreed to go for dinner on State Street. We ordered a drink, and the small talk was going well. Or, so I thought.

Before we could order our entree, she said she had to use the ladies' room. She never returned.

There was no reason for her to have left. I hadn't done anything wrong.

Well, there was one small thing.

It was nothing, but women always overreact to the most insignificant things.

I told her that if we started dating for real, I'd want her to work less and stay home more often. She was a bartender, and I told her I didn't like the idea of guys staring at her all day and night.

She said, "This is a first date. Who the hell do you think you are?"

I guess she had a slight point, but it's not fucking enough to leave a dinner. Jesus. What happened to women? I would have preferred them in the 40s and 50s.

About thirty seconds later, she told me she had to use the restroom. And then I sat there for fifteen minutes looking like a goddamn fool as she never returned. Fuck that bitch.

It got worse.

After paying the waiter for the drinks and saying I wouldn't be ordering dinner, I started walking down State Street. I was furious and wanted to get drunk as all hell. The first bar was about half a block down, and I peered in to see the vibe. To my shock, I saw Victoria Bosco sitting at the bar talking to some guy.

I was seething. She'd gone to the closest bar and cozied up to the first man she saw.

Luckily, I was a deliberate man, or I'd have shot her right then and there. Let her new man see her brains splayed out in front of him. Maybe I'd shoot him too.

But I was smarter than that.

So, instead of blowing her brains out, she made it on my list.

It was that simple.

She'd embarrassed me. And no one embarrasses Conrad Drury.

She was going to find out the hard way.

⚜

WHEN I WENT HOME THAT NIGHT, I IMMEDIATELY DELETED THE dating app I had used.

I also deleted the email address associated with it. If I was going to kill Victoria Bosco, it wouldn't be for several years, but even then, I knew not to leave a trace.

I never gave my real name on the dating apps. EWheneverI set up a new profile, I used an unknown email address, which I'd delete when I was removed from the dating app. That happened quite often, usually after a girl complained about me after our date. Quite a few of them said I made them feel nervous. Fucking cunts.

Sadly, I couldn't kill them all.

Victoria Bosco had hit a nerve, though.

Ghosting me at dinner? You'd think nothing could be more humiliating, but you'd be wrong. Seeing her rub up against a different guy a half hour later sealed her fate.

I knew at that moment that, in response to her wickedness, I would enact my revenge, even if it took me years.

As they say, "Revenge is a dish best served cold."

And I was getting close to serving that dish.

⚜

VICTORIA BOSCO STILL LIVED IN SANTA BARBARA.

I had subtly stalked her several times in the years that followed our date. I'd follow her from her work - she remained a bartender - to her home, always keeping my distance. My name may have been Archie on the dating app, but she'd seen my face. And even though we only spent ten minutes together five years ago, there was a chance she'd still recognize me. So I wore a hat and some sunglasses and stalked from afar.

Back then, it was still too early to enact my revenge. I usually waited at least a year or two. In one case, I'd waited seven years until exacting my revenge. I had to scratch that Seven Year Itch. Hahaha.

⚜

ABOUT THREE MONTHS AGO, BEFORE BOBBY MCGOWAN ENTERED MY life, I decided that I'd waited long enough. Nothing tied me and Victoria Bosco together anymore.

I escalated how often I stalked her. I discovered she was still single and bartending. Victoria often brought guys home with her. What a slut. She brings guys home twice a week but can't have dinner with me?

She lived in the bottom left apartment of a four-unit complex. There were two apartments on the bottom - including hers - and two on top of them.

It wouldn't be easy, but I could make it happen. It would have to be a nighttime murder. I'd committed a few daytime murders over the years. Heather McGowan and Jessica Moore came to mind, but murders at night were the safer way to go.

Victoria worked many night shifts at the bar, including ones that ended at two a.m., so this would be easy enough. I could break in at midnight or one a.m. and bide my time until she arrived.

That would be no problem.

CONRAD

I'd always been good at waiting.

❧ 36 ❧

BOBBY

After a long weekend continuing to look into the new murders, I headed down to Ventura early on Monday morning.

It seemed like an odd city to have a law firm dedicated to the wrongfully accused. Los Angeles made a lot more sense. I'm sure Rachel Tatum had her reasons.

Her office was on East Santa Clara Street, and I was able to find parking about fifty feet from her office. I'd always thought downtown Ventura was a little underrated. I didn't make it down here much, but I always enjoyed my time.

For a case that revolved around Santa Barbara, I'd now made two visits to Ventura. First to see Frederick Frick, and now Rachel Tatum.

I walked toward the law offices, which read, "Rachel Tatum For the Wrongfully Convicted."

Which got me thinking.

How did they decide what cases to take?

I'm sure there were thousands - if not tens of thousands - of mothers, fathers, husbands, wives, or siblings of convicted murderers who thought their loved one had been wrongfully convicted. How did Rachel Tatum narrow down her prospective client base?

I opened the door. It was a smaller office than I expected. Three chairs were to my right, and directly in front of me, a middle-aged woman sat at a desk behind a plastic barricade. I approached her.

"I'm Bobby McGowan, and I'm here to see Rachel Tatum," I said.

"Ms. Tatum will be ready for you in just a minute. Do you mind sitting?"

"Sure. Thanks."

I sat down, and sure enough, less than a minute later, Rachel Tatum appeared from the back. She was younger than I'd expected. Probably only around thirty. I'd seen her picture online, but it was a professional shot, which sometimes can make people look older than they are.

She was attractive but also looked to be no-nonsense. She certainly wasn't wearing an outfit that accentuated her body. Maybe being attractive in her field was looked down upon as if she'd climbed the ranks based on her looks. I'm sure that wasn't the case with Rachel Tatum; I'm just saying that stigma was likely out there for women.

Her long hair was in a bun, and she wore a black pantsuit. Her glasses were light purple and drew my attention.

I rose from my chair, and she extended her hand.

"I'm Rachel Tatum," she said.

"Bobby McGowan. Thanks for meeting with me."

"Of course. Follow me."

She was direct and to the point.

I followed her. We walked through the door by the secretary's desk, which led us toward the rear of the office. It was more spacious than I'd realized. There appeared to be two or three offices, and we also passed a conference room packed with scores of legal books.

We entered her office, and she had me sit on a couch that faced her desk. I was so used to small, rickety chairs that the couch was a welcomed change of pace.

"Nice office," I said.

"We try. Now, how can I help you, Mr. McGowan?"

"Please, call me Bobby."

I often said those exact words, but for some reason, it made me sound like I was hitting on her.

"You can call me Rachel then," she said, with much less aplomb.

"Okay."

"How can I help you, Bobby?"

She wasn't here for small talk; that much was certain.

I spent the next ten minutes describing my mother's murder and then another five minutes talking about meeting with the detectives along the central coast, which led me to Mary Jane Cushing's mother, Evelyn.

"Evelyn is a tough old woman," Rachel Tatum said. "She's been through a lot. All of the significant others and parents of these murdered women have suffered greatly."

"So have their children," I said.

She instantly realized her mistake.

"Of course. I'm sorry, I should have included the children."

"So, do you think my mother's case resembles Mary Jane Cushing's?"

"Without question. A young, attractive woman who was strangled to death. Do you mind if I ask a question that may be painful?"

"Go ahead."

"Was your father ever a suspect?"

"No. He was at work with plenty of witnesses."

"Sometimes the police will consider the possibility they hired someone to kill their spouse."

"My father was never a suspect," I said firmly.

"I'm not trying to press your buttons," she said. "I ask because Daniel Tice thinks that someone tried to frame him. I wondered if your father ever thought someone was trying to frame him."

"No, he never thought that. He was always going to be at work that day. You'd be doing a pretty shitty job of framing someone if they had a built-in alibi."

"Fair point, Mr. McGowan. Excuse me. Bobby. So, who did the police suspect?"

"Her ex-boyfriend Roy Cooper was probably the #1 suspect. The only one, really."

"Hmmm."

I wasn't sure exactly where Rachel Tatum was going with this.

"Could someone have been framing him?" she asked.

I felt like I was missing out on something.

"Why are you so convinced that someone tried to frame Derek Tice?" I asked.

"His DNA - via some hair - was found under Mary Jane Cushing's fingernails, and he swears on his life that he didn't kill her. If we assume he's telling the truth, someone put several of his hairs under his girlfriend's fingernails."

"It couldn't have been residual hair from when they'd dated?"

Rachel shook her head.

"No way. They'd been broken up far too long."

Ms. Tatum continued to be straight and to the point.

"So you think someone put Derek Tice's hair under Mary Jane's fingernails in order to frame him?"

"Yes."

"Even if I take that as the truth, which is a big stretch, it doesn't mean some guy is going around framing people. It could just be an isolated incident."

"You'd think so, wouldn't you?"

She had more to say on this.

"I'm listening," I said.

"I've discovered two other cases that are quite similar.."

I saw Rachel Tatum look down at her watch, so I quickly looked at mine. It was already 8:28. I'd spent too much time talking at the start, and now our time was almost up.

"Can you give me the names of those two cases?" I asked.

Rachel looked me over.

This felt like my conversations with the detectives, who didn't want to divulge any information.

I continued: "You said you were extremely busy right now. Give me one of the two names, and I'll do a little research on that case. I'll let you know if I find anything out."

She looked at her watch again.

"I have to head to court, Bobby."

"Give me one name, and we'll meet again soon."

"Do you still live in Santa Barbara?" Rachel asked.

"Yes. Why?"

"I have to be down there on Friday. Let's meet up and talk more about your mother's case."

"Okay, sure, but how about throwing me a bone on one of the other cases?"

She grabbed some papers from the edge of her desk and walked outside her office.

"Stay here," she said.

She returned a minute later with three or four pages of papers stapled together.

"Follow me," she said.

She headed back through her office. We walked outside into what was now a bright sun. I found myself squinting. She pressed a fob on her keychain, and I saw a sleek BMW come to life. She then handed me the stapled papers.

"Her name was Jill Venable. We'll talk about it more on Friday."

"Okay. Thanks for this."

"Be subtle," she said. "I've had this feeling that I'm being watched. Don't draw any undue attention to yourself."

I could tell by her expression that she wasn't kidding.

"I won't. Thanks for this, and I'll see you Friday."

She opened her car door quickly and was speeding off a few seconds later.

✵ 37 ✵

BOBBY

The Jill Venable case had very few similarities with my mother's. Jill was single, older, and had been stabbed to death. From what I was able to gather, it happened late at night. And most importantly, they'd caught the man responsible for it: Dale Collier.

Rachel Tatum didn't think so. She thought Dale was being railroaded. I told myself to take everything Rachel said with a grain of salt. Her law firm was dedicated to freeing the wrongly convicted. Of course, she was going to have a bias toward believing people were innocent.

That didn't mean she was wrong.

Jill had been a life coach and public speaker. Nowadays, those are a dime a dozen, but back in 2007 when she was killed, they weren't nearly as ubiquitous. She specialized in helping people get back into the workforce after getting out of jail or quitting a nasty alcohol or drug habit.

On the night of January 28th, 2007, someone broke into her house and stabbed her to death. Jill wasn't found for three days. A relative had called for a welfare check, and that's when the police found her body. She'd been stabbed over thirty times.

No, I wasn't a cop, but usually, when someone is stabbed that many times, law enforcement tends to believe it to be a crime of passion.

Which is likely what led them to Dale Collier.

Dale and Jill had dated for ten years before breaking it off slightly over a year before she died.

They met when they were both in their mid-forties, and both had grown children from previous relationships. That probably explained why they'd dated so long without getting married.

The breakup wasn't a good one, which didn't bode well for Dale once Jill was stabbed thirty times.

❧

THE PISMO BEACH POLICE BROUGHT HIM IN FOR AN INTERVIEW THE DAY they found her body. Two days later, he was placed under arrest and charged with her murder.

His trial started five months later, and after a short six-day trial, Dale Collier was convicted and sentenced to life in prison for the murder of Jill Venable.

All of the case was circumstantial, except for one piece of evidence: Dale Collier's hair was stuck in Jill Venable's fingernails. And that proved to be the difference.

Had I stumbled into a story more significant than I could have imagined? Namely, that someone was framing people for murder.

Possibly, but it was unlikely my mother's murder was part of it.

There was no loved one convicted in my mother's death. My father was at work. And no hair was found under my mother's nails.

I didn't think my mother's murder was related.

❧

IT HAD BEEN THREE WEEKS SINCE THE "CUPCAKES HEARD AROUND Santa Barbara," and I'd only seen my father two times.

I'm not sure if it was embarrassment on my part or whether I was just subconsciously giving him a break from yours truly, but twice wasn't nearly enough. We lived three miles apart; more importantly, he was my father.

I called him and told him I was coming by that afternoon. He initially resisted, but I was persistent, and he finally relented.

"You'll never guess who I just ran into," he said.

My father was waiting for me outside his home as I pulled up. He seemed excited.

"I have no idea. Who?"

"Ivy."

Ivy Harrington, my ex-girlfriend. No wonder my Dad was so happy.

He'd always loved us as a couple and was pretty distraught when we broke up.

"Where at?"

"At Tino's."

"I should have guessed. The last time I ran into her was also at Tino's."

"She likes the sandwiches there."

We were standing outside, and my father showed no inclination to go inside.

"I turned her on to those sandwiches," I said.

"So, what's your point, Bobby? That she can't enjoy Tino's after you guys break up?"

"That's not what I'm saying."

"Then what are you saying? You sound like a pissed-off ex-boyfriend who doesn't want your ex-girlfriend to enjoy a great sandwich."

"Jeez. I sure am glad I decided to come over today."

My father laughed.

"Sorry. You just know how much I liked Ivy. I was happy to see her. It was the first time since you two broke up."

"Do you want to go inside, Dad?"

"Nope. Let's stay out here. The local weather guy said we'll likely have some nasty weather in a few weeks, so let's enjoy this great Santa Barbara weather while we can."

"Okay, but let's sit down," I said.

"Alright."

We chose to sit on a wooden bench that had been around since my mother was still alive. It needed a paint job or two.

"So, how did Ivy seem?" I asked.

I hated talking about my ex-girlfriend with my father, but curiosity got the best of me.

"She asked about you a lot."

"Really?"

I sounded too excited.

"Yeah. She asked how you're doing after what happened with the cops."

"Oh...that."

"Don't worry. She wasn't mocking you. She genuinely seemed interested in how you were doing.""What did you tell her?"

"I said you're trucking along."

"Hardly a glowing review. What else did you say, Dad?"

"I told her that you were currently unemployed and that you'd stopped investigating your mother's murder after what happened with the SBPD."

I hadn't kept my father in the loop about Roy Cooper or the other murders I was currently investigating, but I hadn't told him I'd stopped entirely either.

"I never told you I'd definitively quit."

"Well, you haven't given me any updates, so I figured you'd just let it go."

I didn't say anything, so he tapped me on the shoulder. He always knew how to read me.

"Am I wrong?"

"I'm still investigating it. In fact, I met with someone important to the case."

"Who?"

"You may not approve."

"Just tell me," my father said sternly.

"I met with Roy Cooper several days ago."

"Why would you want to meet with that jerk?"

"He called me and said I was causing him trouble by mentioning his name all around town."

"Did you tell him that he caused trouble to our family by repeatedly calling and stalking your mother?"

"Yes, I did bring it up."

"And what did he say?"

"He admitted he was an asshole back then."

"You didn't forgive the idiot, did you?"

"I'm not sure if I used those exact words, but we were cordial by time our meeting ended."

"You're the one getting soft, Bobby. Screw that guy."

"He apologized several times. The guy quit drinking a few years ago and says he's a new man and seemed to want to repent for old sins."

"You know some cops still think he did it."

He didn't have to say what 'did it' meant.

"He didn't do it, Dad. I'm sure of it."

"He may not be guilty of murder, but he is guilty of being an asshole. I'll never forgive him."

"I understand. He did say to apologize to you directly."

"Why didn't you tell me that earlier?"

"Because then you'd know I was back investigating, and I didn't think you'd like it."

"Have you discovered anything new?"

"I'm looking in a new direction."

"What does that mean?"

"I've been so focused on people that Mom knew. I'm now considering the possibility that it could have been a random occurrence, possibly even a..."

I couldn't get it out.

"A serial killer?" my father asked.

"Yes," I said.

"Is that what you think?"

"I'm not sure yet, but I'm following some interesting leads."

"Shit, you're even starting to sound like a detective."

I smiled.

"Should that be my next job?" I asked jokingly.

"It's better than being unemployed."

"Ouch."

"Have you applied to any jobs recently?"

"No," I answered honestly. "Finding Mom's killer is my job right now."

"Until when?"

"Until my money runs out."

"Which is when? You can't have that much saved up."

"I'd say I've got about five months until I start worrying."

"Then you better wrap up this murder investigation pretty quick."

"I'm trying."

"And it doesn't mean you can't look for jobs in the meantime. Come on, Bobby. You know the only thing worse than not catching your mother's killer?"

"What's that?"

"Not catching the guy and going broke at the same time."

He then leaned over and hugged me.

"Sorry if I'm coming off as a jerk."

"It's okay," I said. "Sometimes I need a kick in the ass."

"And I forgot to tell you the best thing."

"The best thing about what?"

"About Ivy. She said she would call you soon and wanted to have dinner with you."

"Dad, we broke up."

"But you still like her, don't you?"

My silence confirmed his suspicions.

"Let's talk about something else," I suggested.

"What, Roy Cooper? No, I'd rather talk about Ivy Harrington."

I smiled.

"Maybe you should date her, Dad."

"If I was your age, there's no way I would have let her go."

"It's complicated."

"Tell me about it."

"I'm going to pass on that. As much as I love you, talking about the ins and outs of my relationship with Ivy is a bridge too far."

"Fair enough. Just don't rule out a reconciliation. That's all I'm saying."

"Speaking of reconciliations, why don't you reach out to Angela?"

"There is a lot we'd have to unpack there."

"Kind of sounds like 'it's complicated.'"

It was my father's turn to laugh.

"You got me there. I'll tell you what. If you and Ivy get back together, I'll bring Angela to dinner with you guys."

"Double dating with my Dad. Have I sunk that far?"

My father smiled.

"Fine, I'll take Angela out on our own date," he said.

"Now you're talking. It would be good for you."

"You know what, you were right. We should talk about something else."

He grabbed my shoulder, and we rose from the bench.

"Alright, let's go inside. I'm now going to give you shit about not calling your sister enough."

"Oh, great. Like I said, sure am glad I came over today."

He laughed as we headed toward the house.

38

BOBBY

Detective Patchett called me out of the blue the following day.

"Hello, Detective."

"I've got some good news for you."

I allowed my mind to wander. Had they found a new clue? Had someone come forward claiming to know who'd murdered my mother? Had all my hard work finally come to fruition?

"What is it?" I asked excitedly.

"We've decided to drop the charges against you."

Oh, that. It was still excellent news, and I was happy. It just wasn't the first place my mind went.

"That's great to hear. Not to look a gift horse in the mouth, but may I ask why?"

"We've always liked you here at the SBPD. You've always been fair with us and haven't pressured us even when we weren't making much progress in your mother's murder. Furthermore, we know how much pressure you've probably been under out there investigating it yourself. Those are all my reasons. And there's one more from the hierarchy above."

"What's that?"

"They think it's a bad look to prosecute the son of a murdered woman whose killer we never caught."

"I could see how that wouldn't be a great PR move," I said.

186

"The SBPD agrees with you. So, on our recommendation, the DA has decided to drop the case."

"Tell everyone involved thanks."

"I will. And by the way, I heard you met with my friend Frederick Frick a week ago."

"I did."

"Was he helpful?"

"Yes, he was."

"If I ask you something, can you give me an honest answer?"

"I've always been honest with you, detective."

He made a noise that sounded something like "Mmm hmm."

"I used to think that. Okay, my question is this. Were you lying about the messages that were sent to your website?"

"No, I wasn't lying."

"Someone told you that those cupcakes were poisoned?"

"Yes."

"Really?"

"How many different ways can I say yes, detective? I'm not lying."

"I'm starting to believe you."

I believed Roy Cooper was telling the truth, and now Detective Pathcett was conceding that I might be too. This case was being thrown on its head.

"Why now?" I asked.

"In the moment, it just sounded so crazy. Poisoning little kids? And then the 'Notes to Self' section of the messages? It still sounds a little nuts. I then thought back to the twenty years I'd known you, and you'd never once seemed off-kilter. That's when I started considering that maybe you didn't make it up."

"I didn't."

"Okay. Now what?"

"Would you be willing to meet with me?" I asked.

"Sure. What would you like to discuss?"

"There's a few things I might have kept from you."

"Don't make me write you off again," he said, but in a joking manner.

"I met with Roy Cooper recently."

"Really? What the hell did he want?"

"Why don't we wait until we meet in person?"

"Alright. When and where?"

Should I do it?

If I invited Roy Cooper over to look at the investigative wall, I could do the same for someone who has been on the case for twenty years.

The more people who saw them, the better. Something might eventually stand out.

"Would you be willing to come to my place? There's something concerning the investigation that I'd like to show you."

"Sure."

"How about tomorrow at nine a.m.?"

"I'll be there. What's the address?"

I gave it to him and got off the phone.

❧ 39 ❧

CONRAD

I'm not a one-trick pony.

I don't just leave someone's DNA at a crime scene in hopes that's enough to convict them.

There's so much more to it. There are several other subtle little things that I have incorporated into my bag of tricks.

Let's talk about one of those.

One of the ideas I'm most proud of involves the shoes I wear to each crime scene. That's right: shoes.

Every time I've ever framed someone for murder - since Roy Cooper - I've worn the same shoe size as the man I'm trying to frame.

Just as I stalk the woman in the days leading up to the murder, I also stalk the man. I need to know when he's going to be alone. If he's not going to be alone, then I can't frame him. There have been men who have made my list over the years, but if they go from work to home every day, I've had to scrap the plans.

As I stalk them, I'm not just trying to find out when they will be alone. I'm also doing my damndest to discover any pertinent information I can, and shoe size is one of the big ones.

How I find it out has varied over the years. I've had to break into their house or apartment several times and look at a shoe.

Once, I followed my target to a bowling alley and was in earshot when he checked out and asked for his size ten shoe back. Another time, my target's family went to a water park, and I watched him put his shoes in a little cubby hole. Once they left, I took a peek.

Another time, I was following a guy, and he walked into a shoe store. That was easy enough.

So yes, I always wear the same shoe size as the man I'm trying to frame, but it goes even further. As I follow him, I notice what type of shoes he wears. Brand new Hokas? Old school Stan Smith Adidas? Black and Red Jordan 1s? Whatever brand and model they are, I buy a pair of those exact shoes in his shoe size. Right down to the same color.

One guy I framed had a size thirteen shoe. As a man who wears a size 10, I probably looked like the proverbial clown with the oversized shoe. His name was Cameron Edding, and I murdered his girlfriend, Lily Spector.

Several years earlier, he'd embarrassed me in a movie theater. I was in San Luis Obispo for the night. Our Amtrak train had an issue, and we wouldn't be able to go back to Santa Barbara until the following day, so I had to get a hotel for the night. I was bored and decided to catch a movie at one of their local theaters.

I got my ticket and started walking down a row when I saw a beautiful woman sitting alone. This turned out to be Lily Spector. I sat directly next to her in an uncrowded theater. Some might say that's weird, but she was alone and maybe wanted some company.

Only she wasn't alone. Some guy - whose name I later found out to be Cameron Edding - was getting food for both of them. He came back and asked who the fuck I was and why I'd sat right next to his girlfriend when there were plenty of open seats.

"I thought she was alone," I said.

"I don't care if she was," Edding yelled. "That's creepy as fuck, you psycho."

"Yeah, you creep," Lily added.

The other people in the movie theater started looking at what was happening. They all seemed to side with him. I wanted to smash Edding's face into a thousand pieces, but everyone was watching us, so I backed off and sat in a different row.

I was seething throughout the entire movie, already enacting my revenge in the deep recesses of my mind.

I left a few minutes before the movie was due to end. I no longer cared how it ended.

This movie theater had a contiguous parking garage, and I assumed everyone just parked there. I had. I got to my car and scrunched down so nobody could see me. I'd occasionally peek my head up and see if I saw the two of them.

Cameron and Lily entered the parking garage several minutes later, and I saw them walking toward their car. I started my car up and slowly followed from behind. I didn't want them to see me, that's for sure. I just wanted to get his license plate number, which I did seconds later as they got into a gray Lexus. I wrote the license plate down, ducked my head, and drove out of the parking garage.

Finding out his name was easy after that. Several years later, I got my revenge against Cameron and Lily.

You'd be correct if you said I took grudges to the next level.

If you wrong me or embarrass me in any way, I want you dead.

It's that simple.

Now, I can't always follow through with my desires, but if I have the opportunity, you're damn right I'll take it.

ALRIGHT, BACK TO THE SHOES.

Now, not only is the man's DNA at the scene, but experts will testify about the shoe imprints left at the scene. And sure enough, the shoe size will match. The prosecution will dig deeper and ask the expert what type of shoe has that exact imprint. And wouldn't you know it, the defendant has that identical shoe and has been seen wearing them lately.

Try explaining that away!

And the shoes have come up at every trial. I should know; I've been there.

Yes, that's right. I've sat in on each and every trial, some for several days and some for only a day or two. I've always worn a disguise - usually, cheesy facial hair and a hat. Sometimes, I'd wear several layers of clothing and a puffer jacket to look fat. And I'd always enter after court had started, sit in the back, and make sure that I sat behind someone.

The defendant faces the judge and rarely turns around, so maybe I was going to extremes, but as I'm sure you've realized by now, I take no chances.

In most cases, these defendants haven't seen me in years and probably wouldn't even recognize me. The fact that their back is to me, and I'm in disguise in the back of the courtroom, means there's no chance any of the defendants even knew I was there.

My favorite day, the one I tried never to miss, was when they'd reached a verdict.

"*We, the jury, find the defendant guilty!*"

It's great seeing their shoulders sag and hearing their family members shriek.

God, I love that part.

I know that I've won our little battle. A battle they are almost assuredly unaware they were even involved in. Take Cameron Edding. Do you think he remembers some forgettable argument in a movie theater that happened five years before Lily Spector's murder? The odds are miniscule.

Not that I fucking care. These people pissed me off at some point in their lives, and they were now paying for it. They would be spending the rest of their life in prison in a tiny cell.

Whenever I'd walk out of the courtroom after a guilty verdict, I'd have the biggest smile. It made everything all worthwhile. All the planning. All the stalking. The murder itself. Whenever I heard the jury's foreman say, "*Guilty,*" I was like a kid in a candy store.

I'd won.

They never should have fucked with Conrad Drury.

40

BOBBY

Detective Patchett was set to arrive in a few minutes when I heard the alert for an incoming call.

I assumed he was calling to say he'd be a little late. Nope. The call was coming from Ivy Harrington.

"Hey, Ivy."

"Hey, Bobby. How are you?"

"I'm good. You?"

"I'm doing alright. I saw your father the other day."

"He told me. I think you made his week."

Ivy laughed on the other end. God, I loved that laugh.

"I was happy to see him too. You know we always got along well."

"Ironic, don't you think?"

"Because your mother hates me," I said.

"Does she like me?"

"Like is a strong word."

I laughed.

"Thanks for making my point. Anyway, I told my father that maybe he should have dated you."

"No, that would be awkward considering I like his son," Ivy said.

"Still?"

"I'll always like you, Bobby. The question is whether we can make it as a couple."

"Are you trying to say you're willing to give it a second chance?"

"I've been thinking about our relationship a lot lately, and for the life of me, I can't remember exactly why we broke up."

"Really? It was only four months ago."

"I had a lot going on when we broke up. Remind me exactly what I said."

"You said you wanted to spend some time apart. I think you used the term malaise."

"That's right. I do remember using that word. Was I wrong, though? Don't you think we were kind of at a crossroads?"

"A crossroads of what?"

"About whether we were going to go all-in with our relationship?"

"Are you talking about marriage?" I asked.

"No, Bobby, I'm not talking about marriage. But you hardly ever broached the subject of moving in together. I felt like I was stuck in quicksand."

"I brought up moving in together."

"No, I did. And then you'd inevitably change the subject."

I thought about it for a moment.

"That's probably true. So, you wanted to move in together?"

"I wouldn't have brought it up if not."

"Okay, so let's move in together now," I said, 62 percent joking.

"Nice try. You'll be lucky if you get a lunch date out of this call."

I laughed.

"So, you're saying there's a chance," I said, quoting one of our favorite movies, *Dumb and Dumber*.

Ivy laughed.

"A very small chance," she said.

Right then, there was a knock on my door.

"Fuck," I said.

"What is it?" Ivy asked.

"It's not you, Ivy. I forgot that I have a meeting with Detective Patchett this morning."

"And you have to head to the police station?"

"No, he's at my apartment right now."

"SB's finest are making house calls now?"

"Can I call you tonight? I'll explain then."

"Sure."

I HUNG UP THE PHONE AND HEADED TO MY FRONT DOOR.

Detective Patchett was standing there, wearing civilian clothes.

"Thanks for coming over," I said.

"This is a one-time thing. I don't make many house calls."

I laughed, reminded of Ivy's "house call" reference from a minute ago.

"Something funny?"

"It's nothing," I said. "Here, follow me."

I led him into the living room, and he immediately saw the investigative wall. Not that there's any way he could have missed it.

"Now I know why you invited me here."

He approached the wall and tried to take it all in.

"This is impressive work, Bobby."

"Thanks. Let's hope it amounts to something."

He spent a solid five minutes looking it all over.

"So, the boards on the left are dedicated to people she knew, and the right is dedicated to women who died in a similar fashion to your mother?"

"Exactly."

"What's with all the Polaroids on the left?"

It was time to come clean.

"The guy who contacted me on the website, who told me the cupcakes were poisoned, also claimed that the killer was in an old photo album of my mother's."

"Did he say he was the killer?"

"I'm not sure he ever used those exact words, but he definitely inferred it."

"So you think the guy who lied about the cupcakes is now telling the truth?"

"I put all these photos up well before that went down."

I was so sick and tired of talking about that incident.

Patchett kept looking at the photos before gradually moving to his right, where the other murders were emphasized.

"Did you ever think it might be a serial killer?" I asked.

"We never ruled out any possibility."

"That's not what I asked."

He turned around to face me.

"I never thought it was likely. She was killed in the middle of the day in a nice neighborhood. That doesn't give off the vibe of a serial killer."

"What vibe do they give off?"

"I don't know. Someone who probably strikes at night."

"There are tons of examples of serial killers who met and/or killed their victims during the day."

"I don't know. Maybe it just seemed more personal. The thought of a serial killer parading through Santa Barbara just seemed unlikely. There weren't enough unsolved murders to think there was a serial killer out there."

"What if it wasn't just Santa Barbara, and they were killing up and down the Central Coast?"

He had turned back to look at the boards, but his head swiveled around toward me.

"Do you have some evidence of that?"

"Not exactly, but some of these cases are pretty darn similar to my mother's."

I spent the next five minutes explaining a few of the other murders, mainly Mary Jane Cushing and Jill Venable.

At different points, Detective Patchett looked both interested and dismissive.

While I described the deaths in detail, I didn't mention Rachel Tatum or her opinion that there might be a killer out there framing people. It sounded so outlandish, and Patchett was already on the fence about my mental state, so I decided not to bring it up.

"Had you ever heard of any of these women?" I asked.

"Honestly, no. In my defense, the Central Coast is a big area, and I can't investigate every unsolved murder."

"Some of these murders have been solved. Have you ever thought my mother's killer might already be in jail?"

"Yes, it's certainly a possibility."

"Would you concede that the Central Coast is generally a pretty safe place?" I asked.

"We're not perfect, but overall, it's a pretty safe place to live."

"Then don't you find it surprising that this many women were killed in the years right before and right after my mother's murder?"

"How many do you have up here on the wall?"

"Thirty."

He took his hand and ran it through his thinning hair, a subconscious gesture signifying he was deep in thought.

"Yes, that does sound like a lot. But surely you don't think a serial killer killed thirty women along the Central Coast."

"No, I don't, but what if, and this is all just a crazy theory, twenty-five of these murders were independent of each other."

"Meaning the same person did five?"

"Yes."

"I'd be more willing to buy five than thirty. How exactly would you know which ones were connected?"

"Well, that's what I'm trying to find out. And the reason I've ruined my living room wall," I said, pointing to all the cork boards.

Detective Patchett smiled.

"What does your girlfriend think of it?"

"I'm currently single," I said, instinctively thinking of Ivy.

"Probably for the best right now."

He meant it as a joke.

"Yeah, I don't think this decor is going to catch on."

Patchett smiled.

"Have you told Frederick Frick about all of this?" he asked.

"I haven't got back to him yet. I'm still trying to conure up something more than just a theory."

"What about Roy Cooper? You said he came here."

"I put up the boards on the right side of the wall after his visit. It was his idea, actually."

"His idea?"

"He saw how much time I'd spent on the left side of the wall, with the 100-plus pictures from the photo albums. All people that my mother knew or had met at some time in her life. So Roy asked, '*What if it was someone she'd never met?*' That's when I started considering the possibility it might be a random killer or - God forbid - a serial killer."

"You do know that a huge percentage of women are killed by someone they know?"

"Don't go all *Dateline NBC* on me," I said.

He laughed.

"Fair point."

"So what do you think?" I asked.

"Of what?"

"Of my current theory?"

"I'm intrigued, but my money would still be on the fact that she knew the guy."

He was probably right, but I still thought he was being dismissive of other possibilities. I didn't feel like arguing with him, so I gave a vanilla response.

"That's what the percentages say," I said.

"Regardless, this is impressive stuff, Bobby. It almost looks like a police precinct."

"My father told me I sounded like a cop the other day."

"God help us," Patchett said.

He left a few minutes later.

I'm not sure his visit had accomplished much.

I CALLED IVY BACK THAT NIGHT, AND WE AGREED TO MEET FOR LUNCH on Friday.

She had a break from work from noon to one, so we agreed to meet at Joe's Cafe, a place we knew well. Joe's served their food reasonably quickly, and I knew she could get back to work by one.

I also had my meeting with Rachel Tatum on Friday morning.

Looks like it was going to be a busy one.

❧ 41 ❧

BOBBY

I got a call at 9:00 p.m. on Thursday.

"Hello."

"Bobby, this is Rachel Tatum."

"Are we still on for tomorrow morning?"

"I'm sorry, but my court date got delayed by a week. I was going to call you earlier today, but I got swamped and forgot about it."

"No problem," I said.

"My appearance is now on for next Friday at one p.m., so can we meet that morning?"

"I'm trying to learn more about the cases you're working on. Sooner rather than later."

"I understand. I'm just really busy at the moment."

"How about sometime next week? I could drive down to Ventura and meet you at your office."

I didn't hear back from her for a good twenty seconds. I heard her rustling some papers.

"I'm free Monday morning at eleven a.m."

"I can make that work. Your office at eleven on Monday?"

"Yes."

"I'll see you then," I said, and Rachel hung up.

She continued to be a woman on the move.

THERE WAS NO CANCELLATION FROM IVY, AND I MET HER ON FRIDAY AT Joe's Cafe on State Street. Joe's was famous for pouring the most potent drinks in Santa Barbara, but their food was also solid. The food had become underrated because all anyone wanted to discuss was their stiff drinks.

Each table had one of those old-school, red-and-white Italian-style placemats. And while they did have some great Italian food, they also specialized in all things American. Big, juicy steaks, pulled pork sandwiches, fried chicken. You get the idea.

I arrived mere seconds before Ivy and was waiting at the bar when she walked in.

She was wearing tan slacks and a white blouse. The last time I'd seen her, she was showing off her killer legs, having just come from tennis, but today, she was dressed like the businesswoman she was.

Ivy worked for Charles Schwab as a financial advisor. When I was a kid, I'd have referred to it as a stockbroker, but on many occasions, Ivy let me know that she deals with a lot more than stocks.

IRAs. Bonds. Mutual funds. Retirement plans. And a few others I couldn't currently think of.

She'd probably wince if she saw my dwindling checking account balance.

Sure, I had some in savings, but I wasn't exactly killing it for the former boyfriend of a financial advisor.

Which got me thinking. Was I going to get a job soon?

I still had enough money to get by, but I couldn't exactly make a career out of trying to find my mother's killer. I was going to have to put myself back out there relatively soon.

I was a web designer with five years of operating social media accounts. I didn't think I'd be unemployed for long.

Ivy saw me and approached the bar. I was wearing jeans and a lightweight white hoodie. The weather had started cooling down, and fall had officially arrived a few days ago.

And in less than a week, it would be the 20th anniversary of my mother's murder. I know my sister Jen was saying it's not something you celebrate, but no matter how you looked at it, it was a monumental anniversary. It's not like I could just dismiss or ignore it.

I got up and hugged Ivy.

"You look nice," I said.

"Thanks. Let's see if I can avoid getting food on this white blouse."

"I see a big bowl of spaghetti in your future. Extra marinara sauce."

Ivy smiled.

The bartender approached.

"Would you like a drink?" he asked us.

"We're just here to eat," I said.

"No problem. Pick any table you want."

There were tables in the middle of the room and booths against the walls. We chose a booth, which gave us a little more privacy.

We'd eaten at Joe's probably ten times over the years. We'd still had more sandwiches at Tino's, but we'd probably been to Joe's for a sit-down restaurant more than any other.

We both unnecessarily scanned the menu.

"What am I doing?" I asked. "I know this menu by heart."

"I already know what you're getting, anyway," Ivy said mischievously.

"Oh, yeah? What's that?"

"Well, if it were dinner, you'd get the New York Steak or the Prime Rib, but since it's noon and you probably don't want to be stuffed all day, you're going to go with a sandwich."

"Not bad. Now, which sandwich?"

"Either the Philly Cheese or the Grilled Chicken Breast with Tomato and Mozzarella."

I couldn't help but laugh.

"You're right so far."

"And..." Ivy said and paused. "I think you'll go with the Grilled Chicken Breast sandwich."

I laughed again.

"Impressive. You nailed it."

"And you know why?"

"No, why?"

"You'd usually get the Philly Cheese Steak sandwich, but that's messy, and you'd be licking your fingers and going back and forth to your napkins."

"What's wrong with that?"

"You're trying to impress me today and put on a presentable front, so you'll go with the generic, clean, safe chicken breast sandwich."

"You are crazy," I said.

Ivy laughed.

"Now you do me," she said.

If we were still dating, I would have had a sexually-inspired comeback, but I decided to play it cool. Maybe Ivy was right, and I was trying to appease her todays.

"You're also going to go with something light," I said. "You've got to go back to work. And you probably don't want some greasy sandwich, considering your outfit."

"So far so good."

"I'm going to guess the Chicken Caesar Salad."

"Oh, so close," Ivy said. "I'm getting the Salmon Salad with Feta."

"You should have gone with my choice," I said.

"Oh yeah, why is that?"

"Because you don't want to return to work smelling like salmon."

"You are too much, Bobby. Don't worry. I'll be fine."

"It's not you I'm worried about. You'll put Danny from HR to sleep when he smells your breath."

Ivy laughed quite loudly.

"You crack me up," she said.

I grabbed her hand.

"It's good to see you."

"You too," she said.

We were having a moment, but it was quickly tempered as the waiter came over and took our order.

"I'll get the Grilled Chicken Breast Sandwich, and she'll have the Chicken Caesar..."

Ivy interrupted.

"I'll take the Salmon Salad," she said.

As the waiter walked away, Ivy threw her napkin at me.

"You are being a twerp today," she said, smiling the whole time.

"I prefer to think of it as being frisky."

"Got some pent-up aggression? Sounds like someone needs a roll in the hay," Ivy said.

"Ouch," I said. "You volunteering?"

"Stop," she said, but I could tell she was enjoying this back and forth.

"Can we have dinner next time? Give me a better chance of talking you into coming home with me."

"In that case, let's do breakfast."

It was my turn to laugh.

"Breakfast in bed?"

"You wish," Ivy said.

We both sat there and smiled at each other. I didn't know if we would get back together, but this lunch had gotten off to a great start.

Our friend Joey - no, Joe's wasn't named after him - who was the general manager of the place, came by and said hello. If he was surprised to see us back together, he didn't say anything.

◈

Fifteen minutes later, the waiter delivered my sandwich and her salad.

We thanked him, and both took our first bite. At this point in our conversation, the flirting had been replaced by talking about our respective families. Ivy had two brothers I'd gotten along well with. One lived locally, and one lived in Texas. Her parents were divorced and lived in different parts of Los Angeles.

Her mother had not liked me from the beginning. I'm sure that hasn't changed.

As for my side of the family, Ivy had gotten along well with both my father and my sister.

After finishing about half of our lunch, Ivy grabbed me by the wrist.

"It's time we talked about the elephant in the room," she said.

"What are you talking about?"

"Your mother's death. What was with that interview with KEYT? And what the hell happened with that whole cupcake thing? And now, you're having Detective Patchett make a house call? Is there something new I should know about?"

Ivy had taken a keen interest in my mother's murder from the moment I'd told her about it. She'd come along with me a few times when I'd met with Detective Patchett and knew who some of the main characters were. She'd have been shocked I'd agreed to meet with Roy Cooper.

"There's a lot of new things," I said. "You should see my apartment. I turned the living room wall into a shrine dedicated to my investigation."

A skeptic might assume I was thinking with my little head when I invited her over, but that wasn't the case. I truly wanted her to see it.

"Really?" Ivy said, genuinely interested. "What does it look like?"

"There are five cork boards, 100 plus Polaroids, and thirty summaries of murders similar to my mother's."

"Jeez, Bobby."

"I know, I went all out. Do you want to see it?"

I had a feeling Ivy wanted to say, '*Is this a ploy to get me over?*' but this was my mother we were talking about, so she thought better of it.

"I'm out of town this weekend but I'd love to see it. Can it be next weekend?"

I didn't want to wait that long to see her again, but I didn't want to seem needy. We'd had a fun lunch and flirted a lot — no need to end on a sour note.

"Next weekend would be great."

"I'll hit you up next Friday, and we'll figure out a time."

WE FINISHED OUR RESPECTIVE LUNCHES A FEW MINUTES LATER.

It was already 12:45, and she had to head back to work.

I offered to pay, but Ivy said splitting this time was better.

I wasn't sure if it was because she knew I was unemployed or because we were no longer a couple. I tended to think it was the latter.

As we got up to go, I saw her put two mints in her mouth.

"Danny from HR will thank you," I said.

She laughed, we hugged, and then went our separate ways.

❧ 42 ❧

BOBBY

Monday arrived, and it was time for my meeting with Rachel Tatum.

I'd done a lot of reading over the weekend, hoping to find that one piece of information that changed everything. It wasn't there. Or, if it was, I read it, and it didn't register.

I spent most of my time on the cases of Jill Venable and Mary Jane Cushing. I wanted to be prepared for my meeting with Rachel.

I PULLED UP TO HER NOW FAMILIAR OFFICE AT 10:55.

I was able to park directly out front this time. I entered the office, checked in with the secretary, and took a seat.

A minute later, Rachel Tatum appeared.

"Hello, Bobby. Follow me back."

We didn't go to her office but instead into the conference room. It was surrounded by massive bookcases filled with legal books. They all looked the damn same. And I bet a lot were.

'Go to Part II of Subset A of Batch C of Subdivision E to find out what California's Drunk Driving laws looked like in 1982.'

No, thanks. I don't think I was cut out to be an attorney.

"Daydream much?" Rachel asked.

"Sorry. I was looking at all the legal books and just imagining how overwhelming they all must be."

"You should have seen me when I was studying for the bar. I was immersed in those books for months on end."

"I don't think I could handle it," I said.

"It has its moments."

"Like keeping innocent people out of jail."

"Of course, but in my case, it's getting innocent people out of jail."

"That's why we're here, right?"

"That's why I'm here. You don't seem convinced your mother's case might be connected."

"I'm not ruling it out. You'll have to convince me, however."

"I'm not here to convince you of anything, Bobby. In fact, I find your mother's case to be quite different from Jill Venable's case, just like you do."

"If my mother's case is connected to any of your cases, my bet would be on Mary Jane Cushing," I said.

"Yes, that has more similarities."

"How many '*wrongfully convicted*' cases are you working on?"

"Three."

' "I should have asked this earlier, but is the court appearance you made in Santa Barbara the third case?"

"No, that's just a DUI case."

"I didn't realize you did DUI cases."

"She's my cousin. It's just a favor I'm doing."

"Gotcha."

"If any of the cases had occurred in Santa Barbara, I'd have told you that by now."

"Of course," I said, feeling stupid. "You said there are currently three. What is the third case besides Jill Venable and Mary Jane Cushing?"

"The man's name is Norm Unger, and he's accused of killing a woman named Grace Goodall."

"And is the MO the same? Was Mr. Unger an ex-boyfriend of Ms. Goodall?"

"He was an ex-boyfriend, but his case is a little different. Give me a second."

She left the conference room and returned with some pages stapled together.

"It's the case I'm the least acquainted with," she said. "I've only had one meeting with Norm's family."

"What brought it to your attention?"

"Eleanor Cushing. Now, this is pretty odd, so stay with me. Eleanor joined a support group after the murder of her daughter, but Pismo Beach isn't a big city, and there's rarely a murder there. Following so far?"

"Yes."

"So anyway, this support group extended to other neighboring cities. I think it extended as far north as San Luis Obispo and as far south as Ventura. Maybe even L.A., I'm not quite sure about that."

Rachel cleared her throat and then continued.

"Once I started talking to Eleanor, she told me about Jill Venable's mother and how they became close. Jill's mother had confided to Eleanor that she never thought that Dale Collier could have murdered her daughter, and Eleanor passed that information on to me."

She paused, so I said, "Got it so far."

"That was six months ago," Rachel said. "And I've been working on those two cases since then. Then Eleanor called me about a month ago, almost as if in a panic. She said that she'd completely forgotten about it, but there had been a woman about ten years ago who'd also been suspicious that they might have convicted the wrong man in her daughter's death. The woman didn't stay in the support group for long, and it took Evelyn several minutes to remember the woman's name. It finally came to her. Her name was Janet, and her murdered daughter was named Grace Goodall. I reached out to Janet. I asked her if she thought Norm Unger was innocent of her daughter's murder. She said she didn't know up from down anymore but said I should reach out to Norm's family, which I did. I told them I'd be willing to look into his case but explained that because of the timing, the other two cases would take precedent."

Rachel paused for a breath.

"Any questions so far? We're almost at the end."

"I'm following."

"Now, on to the murder itself," Rachel said as she quickly skimmed the papers she'd brought in. "Just need a quick refresher course. Sorry, I've got so much on my mind these days."

"Tell me about it. I've got thirty murders I've been reading up on."

"Any that might interest me?"

"The majority of them. The suspects pretty much all claimed they were innocent at trial."

"Most do."

"Then how do you know which cases to take?"

"You feel it right here," she said, pointing to her gut. "Also, there are several 'Project Innocence' type programs around. They will do the vetting themselves. If they contact me, it's, at the very least, a case worth looking at."

"Is that how Evelyn Cushing originally came to your attention?"

"Not exactly. Hers is such a weird scenario. She's not a loved one of the person in jail; quite the opposite. She's the mother of the woman Derek Tice is accused of killing. And yet, she's done more shouting from the rooftops than his family has ever done."

"Did Derek Tice's family excommunicate him?"

"He hardly has any family. He didn't have any kids, and his parents had passed by the time he was convicted. He had one brother who lives back east, but I reached out to him, and he seemed completely disinterested when I told him that his brother might be wrongfully convicted."

"That's terrible."

Rachel nodded.

"So, anyway, once Evelyn contacted me, I reached out to a local 'Project Innocence' branch, and they said there were some inconsistencies in the conviction of Derek Tice. That was enough to get me interested."

"Inconsistencies?"

"Yeah, that's how they phrased it. It's not like they came out and immediately claimed that he was wrongly convicted. They are a little more subtle than that."

"Got it."

"We got a little sidetracked," Rachel said. "I was going to tell you about the murder of Grace Goodall."

"Right. Go ahead."

"Grace was killed in San Luis Obispo in 2011. I know that's a full eight years after your mother's murder, but it would be foolish to rule anything out until we know more. Grace was in her early thirties. She had no children. She was killed at home and was strangled."

Rachel didn't acknowledge that it was the same way my mother had been killed. There was no need.

"Once again, the ex-boyfriend became the main suspect. Norm Unger."

"Doesn't sound like a killer's name, does it?"

Rachel surprised me by laughing.

"So true. The name Norm conjures up some professor in a bow tie. Certainly not a vicious murderer."

"And yes, I'm not dumb. I know there have been Norms who have killed. And Cliffs. And Alfreds. And Miltons. And Ralphs."

"Is that your Hall of Fame of dorky names?"

"Hey, it was off the top of my head," I said.

We both sat silent for a few seconds. I'm not sure Rachel loved this game, but I gave myself a pass. I knew how crucial levity could be in these situations.

Rachel continued.

"So, Norm went on trial and was convicted of first-degree murder. He was sentenced to life in prison."

"Did they find his DNA under Grace Goodall's fingernails?"

"They found his DNA at the scene, but it wasn't under her fingernails. That's a fairly big difference between Jill's and Mary Jane's cases."

She continued to use their first names. I understood why, but it was still odd, considering she was the lawyer for the men convicted of their murders.

"They had been dating. Wouldn't it be natural to find his DNA?" I asked.

"It had been a few years since they'd broken up."

"Couldn't his DNA still be at her place?"

"She'd moved since they had broken up. This was a new place."

"Oh, shit."

"Yeah, oh shit. So the DNA couldn't be explained away and was probably the biggest factor in Mr. Unger's conviction."

"Did they have a rocky relationship?"

"No. From all accounts, they had gotten along famously."

"Did the defense bring that up at trial?"

"Of course, but once again, it's hard to explain away the DNA."

"Jesus," I said. "If he was actually framed, this guy is a fucking sociopath."

"But a damn smart one. Don't just think of him as some moronic psycho."

"I hear ya."

"It gets worse."

"How?"

"The shoe prints found at the scene matched the size of the shoe that Norm Unger wore. Not only that, they were able to determine it was the same brand and model of a shoe that Mr. Unger was seen wearing in the weeks leading up to the murder."

I didn't know what to think.

"Do you want to know what my initial impression is?" I said.

"Yes."

"That the guy probably did it."

"That was mine too. And then I did a little more digging."

"I'm listening."

"At the trials of Derek Tice and Derek Collier, shoe prints were a big part of the prosecution's case."

"Doesn't that make sense, though?"

"Yes and no. If you were a killer, wouldn't you do everything in your power to avoid leaving a shoe print? I mean, these women were strangled. It's not like there were pints of blood you couldn't avoid stepping in."

"So you're saying this guy is intentionally leaving clear footprints? And not only that, but he knows what the guy's shoe size is and the style of shoe he's wearing."

"Yes," she said.

"This is fucking insane," I said. "Pardon the language."

She waved me off, effectively telling me she'd heard much worse.

"Maybe I'm way off, and they are all guilty. That's what I'm trying to find out," Rachel said.

"Have you gone to the cops?"

"No. The police don't care. These guys have been convicted of murder. In the cops' eyes, these cases are over and done with. If we get the courts to overturn a conviction or two, the police will take notice."

"Makes sense," I said. "And you said you're trying to get Derek Tice a new court date?"

"Well, there's a lot of things we must accomplish first, but a new court date is the long-term objective."

"I meant a court date in general, not a new trial date."

"Yeah, hopefully, that will be coming sooner rather than later."

"Are we talking weeks or months?" I asked.

"Probably still a few months away. And that's just for Derek. Dale Collier and Norm Unger won't get their day in court for maybe another year, if ever."

"Slow moving process."

"They were all convicted of murder. The courts aren't going to do backflips to get any of them a new trial."

I nodded.

"I've read up on your mother's case," Rachel said. "And as I said earlier, I'm having difficulty finding a good link to the other murders. There was no DNA left at the crime scene, after all. No shoe print broke the case. These were both crucial in the other three."

I thought about it for a few moments.

"Maybe he hadn't mastered his craft yet," I said.

She took a few seconds to ponder what I'd said.

"It's possible," she said. "Your mother's murder did occur before any of these others. And it would make sense he'd get better over time."

"If my mother's was his first murder, maybe he knew her better than the others. Knew her longer."

"Just because your mother's murder occurred before Mary Jane's, Jill's, or Grace's doesn't mean it was his first murder."

"True," I conceded, but the seed had been planted in my head. Maybe this guy had grown up with my mother.

"So, what do you think?" Rachel asked. "Do we have a killer going around framing other people for his murders?"

"It's possible."

"I'm not sure I even believed it when I first took Derek Tice's case. Now that three of my clients claim the same thing, it's hard to discount it."

"I agree," I said.

There was another quick silence between us.

"Do you want anything to drink? I need a coffee right now."

"Coffee sounds good, thanks."

Once Rachel left the room, my mind started racing.

I'd separated my investigative wall into two separate parts. The people she knew and the serial killer angle.

What if both were true?

What if my mother was one of his first murders? Maybe even the very first. That would make it much more likely he grew up in Santa Barbara and knew my mother well.

Could this person have both known my mother and grown into a serial killer?

In *The Silence of the Lambs,* Clarice Starling is left confronting the murderer alone because she's the only focusing on his initial murder. The other murders took place in different locations, but the initial murder was close to home.

Maybe that was the case with my mother.

Rachel returned.

"Here's your coffee," she said.

I stopped thinking about old movies.

I'd had another idea that had been percolating.

"So I was thinking...," I said.

"Give it to me. What do you got?"

"Have you asked Tice, Collier, and Unger who might have wanted to frame them?"

"It was one of the first things I asked each of them."

"Did they name names?"

"Derek and Dale named several. Norm couldn't only come up with a few."

"I'm going to assume that you didn't hear Derek and Dale mention the same name."

"No. I wasn't that lucky."

"That would be highly unlikely, anyway," I said. "Only an idiot would try to frame someone for murder if they knew they might become a suspect themselves."

"Say that again."

"You wouldn't frame your archenemy because it would be too obvious. You might become a suspect."

"I'm not sure I agree. I've heard of several cases where inept killers tried to frame a rival."

"The key word is inept. If our guy is framing people and hasn't been caught, he's far from inept."

"Point taken."

"If it only happened once, maybe he just got lucky. But if he's done this twice, three times, or God forbid four times, this guy is a criminal mastermind."

"I don't disagree, but what exactly is your point?"

"That he's not framing people that he's close to. He's too smart for that. I'm contending that our killer would only frame people who'd never suspect him. He wouldn't be one of those first few names your clients mentioned."

Rachel pondered everything I'd said.

"It's an interesting take. But what kind of maniac would want to frame someone with whom he wasn't an enemy? People don't just go around framing people who stole their parking spot."

"People don't just go around framing people in general."

"True," she conceded.

It was time to bring up the idea I'd been building up to.

"I have a suggestion," I said. "You can take it or leave it."

"Let's hear it."

"Go see each of your clients in jail and ask them to write down twenty-five people they've argued with over the years. I don't care if little Johnny stole their crayon in Kindergarten. Or, as you said, some rando stole their parking spot two years ago. I don't care how trivial they sound. Shit, maybe they'll come up with fifty people who they had minor gripes with—the more the merrier. And if you can get each of these three men to make a list, we'll see if they mention the same guy twice. If so, it's time to look into that guy seriously. And if by some chance the same name is mentioned by all three men, well then, we've got a huge story on our hands."

Rachel sat back for a moment, her eyes never leaving mine.

"You're better at this than most cops I've dealt with," she said.

"Thanks."

"It's a great idea. I disagree with you on one point, though."

"What's that?"

"It won't be little Johnny or the guy who stole the parking spot. You don't go through the process of trying to frame someone unless you truly despise them."

"Maybe, maybe not. I'll concede it probably wasn't a fellow Kindergartner, but I'd be surprised if it's someone they were close with."

"I guess we'll find out. It's a great idea, regardless."

"How long do you think this would take?"

"Not as quickly as I'd like. I'll have to set up a meeting with each of the respective inmates, which isn't always easy. The prison only has certain times you can see guests, including their lawyers. And I doubt they will come up with twenty-five names off the top of their head. They'll probably have to think about it for a few days or more before getting back to me with a list."

"So...two weeks?"

"That's a good working estimate."

"And you're onboard with this? I asked.

"This is fucking crazy," she said. "You're not a cop. You're not a PI. And you're certainly not a lawyer."

"Thank God, Thank God, and Thank God."

Rachel smiled.

"And yet, I love your idea and am on board with it."

"Great. So what's next?"

"Well, let's still meet up in Santa Barbara on Friday. That will give me three days to contact my clients. Hopefully, I can meet with them next week. At least one or two of them."

"This won't officially start until you get two lists," I said. "With one, it's just a bunch of random names. We start getting suspicious if we see a repeat name on the second list. And like I said, if we get the same name on all three lists, we might have triangulation."

"There's your first miss, Bobby. Triangulation is actually a manipulation tactic where someone, usually a narcissist, brings in a third person to a situation to remain in control. He pits the other two against each other."

"Well, my version of triangulation means something different."

"Different than Webster's dictionary, I guess."

I laughed.

"Can't win them all," I said. "Not a cop. Not a PI. Not a lawyer. Not an English major."

Rachel smiled.

She seemed looser than in our previous meeting—more at ease. We'd had a better back-and-forth.

And she was undoubtedly attractive. I'd also noticed she wasn't wearing a wedding ring.

If I hadn't just had a great lunch with Ivy, maybe I'd have pulled the trigger and asked her out, but not anymore. My focus was on getting Ivy back.

"I've got an idea myself," Rachel said.

"Let's hear it."

"You said no one would have framed your father, right?"

"Right. Everyone close to him knew that he worked all day. It sounds like none of your guys had an alibi. My father's was airtight."

"But then you mentioned another name. Someone that police considered a suspect. Someone I think you said might have had a motive."

"His name was Roy Cooper, and he was a bit obsessed with my mother. I no longer think he had anything to do with it."

"That's not what I'm saying."

She stared at me again, and I realized what she was getting at.

"You want me to ask Roy to make his own list?"

"Exactly," Rachel said.

"Smart," I said. "Just a heads up, though. Roy had a great deal of enemies. His list will reach fifty before he blinks. That will probably just be the people he bullied. He was also a big drinker, and I'm sure he pissed off tons of people while on the sauce."

"That's good, right? Didn't you say the more the merrier?"

"For our investigation, yes. For those who had to deal with Roy, not so much."

"And you can get ahold of Mr. Cooper?"

"Yeah. I'm sure he'll do this for me."

"Good."

"One last thing," I said.

"What is it?"

"I won't mention to Roy why we are doing this. I won't bring up Tice or the others. Even though he doesn't live in Santa Barbara anymore, Roy still knows a lot of people there. And if the killer has his ear to the ground, I don't want to take a chance he hears about our little theory."

"Smart," Rachel said. "My situation is a little different. My clients know I'm defending them for that exact reason, so they'll immediately know why I'm asking for our list."

"That's fine. They are in jail, and I'm less worried about them gossiping."

"You kidding me? Jails are worse. It's like a sewing circle in there."

"Really?"

"Inmates won't rat on their friends, but anything else is free game. Trust me, word spreads in jail. Quickly and unmercifully."

"I'll take your word for it," I said.

"So, it looks like we both have a few things to do before Friday."

"Indeed. See you soon, Rachel."

We both stood up, knowing the meeting was ending.

"Do you remember how to get out of the office?"

"This isn't exactly Fort Knox," I said.

She started laughing as I walked toward the front.

❧ 43 ❧

CONRAD

I scoff when I read the various ways in which serial killers get caught.

That will not be.

They are often arrested after leaving DNA at the crime scene or making another glaring mistake. And then the police, slowly but surely, get their man.

Ted Bundy escaped jail twice, but that's not the norm. Once they have you, you're not getting out. You're spending the rest of your life in a tiny fucking cell. No thanks.

Since I never planned on getting caught, I'd spent years planning on how to disappear forever. Literally, years.

And it doesn't involve flying to Europe or some coastal town in South America. People who flee might enjoy a few months living the good life, but they almost inevitably are caught, extradited to the U.S., and remanded to that tiny cell.

As I said, that won't be happening to me.

I FINALIZED MY PLAN SEVERAL YEARS AGO.

A man named Jesse James Hollywood was caught in a small village near Rio De Janeiro in Brazil. He'd been a drug dealer, sanctioned the killing of

216

a teenager named Nicholas Markowitz, and then fled the country. They even made a movie about it called *Alpha Dog*.

When Jesse James Hollywood - what a name! - was caught, it only confirmed my opinion that fleeing was merely a quick fix. They'd get you in the end.

It was time to go forward with my plan.

I spent several days on the internet researching the most rural areas in the United States. I then looked at properties in those areas and made sure they were affordable, which, inevitably, they were. Rural land is always cheaper.

You could get twenty acres or more of land for as low as $15,000. I had a little more money to spend than that.

I had two non-negotiable things.

First, there couldn't be any neighbors within eyesight of the house. I'd have preferred three miles, but I knew that was stretching it. I could live with one mile.

Second, there had to be a house on the premises. I wasn't just buying land for the land itself. I needed a home to live in when the time came.

I spent several months looking for the perfect spot. For a country of over 300 million, you'd be surprised how much privacy you could buy yourself if you truly needed it.

I almost settled on a place in Maine but felt the neighbors were too close. It would be inevitable I'd run into them from time to time. That wasn't in the plan.

Some secluded places in West Texas were to my liking, but I decided I shouldn't stay in Texas because of the first part of my getaway plan. More on that later.

Vermont, Wyoming, and the Dakotas were also in the running, each being states with plenty of wide-open, rural areas where you could stay lost.

Eventually, I decided that Arkansas was the best choice for me.

I found a place I loved in Jasper, Arkansas. Population 547. That's right, 547. A couple of Santa Barbara's nightclubs could almost fit that many people on a Saturday night.

I bought up a twenty-acre plot of land. There was a run-down but livable house on the lot. There was a neighbor whose home was a half mile from the edge of my property, but my house was also a half-mile in from the start of my plot. I decided being a mile from anyone else was enough. I could avoid them easily.

I was able to buy the land and the house for a mere $32,000. That's basically a year of rent in Santa Barbara, and I had this house for life.

Only it wasn't "me" who bought it.

❧

IF I ENDED UP LIVING IN THIS HOUSE, IT WAS ONLY BECAUSE I WAS ON the run from the cops, so it couldn't be under my name. The first thing law enforcement would do is to check and see if I owned any other properties.

And I hadn't bought land in bumfuck Arkansas to have the coppers come knocking on my door someday.

So, the house would have to be under someone else's name.

I'd accumulated several different forms of ID and passports over the years. I didn't think purchasing a home in rural Arkansas would be all that tough, but I'd need more than just a stolen credit card.

Eventually, I found the guy.

His name was Wyatt Trimble. It turned out to be a perfect name for Bumfuck, Arkansas, population nothing.

Wyatt was an old acquaintance of mine. He'd always take the Amtrak up and down the central coast. At first, he seemed like a reputable guy. He said he worked as a traveling salesman, and I had no reason to doubt him.

Over time, I started to consider that Wyatt might be a drug dealer. He was always cautious with his luggage, never letting anyone else handle it. Once, he opened his bag, and there were probably twenty little brick-shaped objects, all symmetrical in size. I immediately assumed they were either stacks of drugs or money.

It was dark on the train, and he didn't realize anyone was watching, but I was in the aisle.

Wyatt looked up at me, fear covering his face.

I leaned closer and whispered, "I've got some skeletons in my closet too."

It seemed to set his mind at ease.

We became friendly after that, having the occasional drink together somewhere along the central coast. He seemed to make as many stops as the damn train did.

No one else who worked the train enjoyed Wyatt's company. They probably suspected he was up to no good, but they kept their mouths shut since they lacked any evidence. It got to the point where every employee tried to avoid Wyatt. They'd gladly have me patrolling his section.

While I never out-and-out asked Wyatt what he did for a living, I'd make jokes at his expense.

"*Not many traveling salesmen in the 21st century.*"

"*Are those Bibles you're selling door to door?*"

"*Back to Pismo Beach again? They sure must love what you're selling.*"

It became a running joke between us. Wyatt's comeback would often be him using my own words against me.

"I know you've got your own skeletons in your closet."

If he only knew.

WYATT TRIMBLE'S LIFE CHANGED IN JANUARY OF 2016 AND CONFIRMED my suspicions about his profession.

He was in a drug den when something exploded. Wyatt's face and upper body caught on fire. He tried the whole '*Stop, Drop, and Roll*' shit they taught you in grade school, but it was too late. The chemicals had already eaten up half of his upper body.

In the days and weeks that followed, I visited Wyatt in the hospital a few times. Not out of the goodness of my heart, mind you. I had ulterior motives; I always do.

I knew that even if he got out of the hospital, he'd never live an everyday life again. He was going to be disfigured permanently.

The scars on his face were extreme. You couldn't make out where his normal skin used to be.

Most people saw a freak. I saw an opportunity.

When he finally moved into a one-bedroom apartment following six months of rehab, Wyatt told me he planned on being a hermit for the rest of his life.

'*What girl will ever sleep with me? Shit, what girl would even have lunch with me? My former employer won't use me, that's for sure. I'm worthless. My life is over.*'

It would have been a sob story for some, but I'm emotionless, so it did nothing for me.

Wyatt said he'd saved enough money to pay for his apartment for a few years.

He wouldn't last that long.

Wyatt used drugs, drank all day, every day, and eventually killed himself in October of 2016.

He used a sawed-off shotgun.

Luckily, I'd already accomplished my goal.

Wyatt and I looked vaguely similar.

We were both around 5'10", skinny but muscular, and our ages were within a few years of each other.

He wore his hair longer, so after his accident at the drug den, I started growing my hair out. I'd already decided to buy a house, and I knew Wyatt was the perfect vehicle.

As I said, I'd accumulated some driver's licenses and credit cards, even a few passports over the years.

The problem was that none of them had my face on them.

That would change.

Within a month of Wyatt moving into his apartment, I noticed his driver's license would expire in a few months.

When he was hammered drunk one time, I got him to give me his social security number and a few other crucial things I might need. I also stole his birth certificate.

I went online and scheduled a meeting with the DMV for a month away. I needed a little more time to grow my hair out.

On the day in question, I parted my now long hair down the middle, just as Wyatt had it in his driver's license photo. Sure, I had his birth certificate if needed, but I wasn't taking any chances.

It turns out I didn't have a reason to worry.

The lady at the DMV took a cursory glance at me, and that was it. Five minutes later, I was taking a picture, and three weeks later, I had a new driver's license with my picture on it. For all intents and purposes, I could be Wyatt Trimble when I wanted.

The two new credit cards arrived around the same time, and I knew it was time to make my way to Jasper, Arkansas.

It was September 2016 when I walked into Northern Arkansas Bank. I had a cashier's check for $32,000 under Wyatt Trimble's name, made out to the owner of the property, Gilford Moore.

The bank was in Harrison, Arkansas, which was about twenty-five miles from Jasper. With a population of 571, it's not like Jasper was the world's banking capital, so we had to go to a "big" city like Harrison.

I also had "my" driver's license, the supporting credit cards, and "my" birth certificate. I'd called Northern Arkansas Bank ahead of time to ensure that would be enough. I'll never forget their response.

"As long as you got that cashier's check for 32k, you could be Charles freaking Manson and get that house."

He thought it was the funniest thing ever, and I'd had a good laugh too.

Well, Jasper wasn't getting Charles Manson as a resident. I didn't have to delegate people to do my murders for me. Jasper was getting someone far worse.

I was in and out of Northern Arkansas Bank in minutes. I gave Gilford Moore the check, and he gave me the keys and the deed to the house. We all shook hands.

Easy as pie.

It was a month later when Wyatt Trimble killed himself.

He had no family and had been ex-communicated by his work friends. A few nurses and I were the only ones who really knew him.

I held on to his driver's license and credit cards for my eventual move to Jasper. And if people didn't believe me, I always had his birth certificate. Tough to argue with that.

I'd visit my house in Jasper every six months or so.

I'd never stop by and introduce myself to the neighbors. I wouldn't even shop in town. I'd get my groceries thirty minutes away. I didn't want anyone to know what I looked like just in case I had to move there someday.

I kept paying for electricity and basic cable, knowing if I ever moved there, it would be to avoid the rest of humanity, and I didn't need Gerald the Cable Guy coming by my house to set everything up.

GETTING THE HOUSE WAS THE MOST ESSENTIAL PART OF MY GETAWAY plan, but I'd also thought long and hard about how I'd escape Santa Barbara.

I'd come up with a foolproof plan.

It involved a fake license plate, driving at night, Eagle Pass, Texas, and the Rio Grande River.

⚛ 44 ⚛

BOBBY

Ivy came over on Monday night, and I spent almost an hour explaining my investigative wall.

She wanted to know everything I knew about each photo on the left side of the wall. As if that wasn't enough, I had to tell her about every murder on the right side of the wall.

I'd invited Ivy over, at least partly, in hopes of rekindling the old flame, but it had been evident from the start that this night would be more about my investigation. Questions and answers had replaced the back-and-forth flirting at Joe's Restaurant.

But she was asking all the right questions. They were all ones I'd pondered myself.

If I had one critique, Ivy jumped to conclusions rather quickly.

"Look at that guy. He is a freaking wimp. He had nothing to do with your mother's murder."

"Ivy, we can't just make assumptions like that," I said.

She had the perfect response.

"Didn't this all start because someone was glancing at your mother wrong? I'm not the only one who relies on gut instinct."

"Ouch," I said.

The only time I wasn't immediately forthright with Ivy was when it came to Mary Jane Cushing and Jill Venable. I'd put them next to each other atop a corkboard, and she asked about them in unison.

"Any reason these two cases are at the top by themselves."

My pause before answering gave me away. She read me like a book, just as she always had. My poker face needed some work when it came to Ivy.

"If I tell you a crazy theory, you promise not to call me the crazy one?"

"I promise."

"I've been talking to an attorney who specializes in representing the wrongly convicted. She's currently representing the man convicted of killing Mary Jane Cushing as well as the man convicted of murdering Jill Venable."

"And she's convinced they are innocent?"

"Yes, but she'd probably use the phrase not guilty."

"I'm not talking about what they are in a court of law, Bobby. I'm asking if she actually thinks they are innocent of the charges."

"Yes, but it gets even crazier."

"Let's hear it," Ivy said.

I realized she hadn't taken a seat in an hour. My investigation had transfixed her. And now, I was going to drop a bomb on her.

"She thinks there might be a serial killer who is framing innocent men."

She didn't respond right away. Ten seconds became twenty seconds and I had to intervene.

"So, what do you think?" I asked.

"My initial impression is that it does sound a little crazy, but my opinion could be swayed. Does she have any evidence?"

I spent the next fifteen minutes talking about Rachel Tatum, Derek Tice, Dale Collier, Norm Unger, DNA under fingernails, shoe prints, shoe sizes, and my idea about having the inmates and Roy make a list.

By the end, it was apparent she was taking it seriously.

"This is nuts," she said. "But not crazy. Do you know what I mean?"

"I do."

"So, did Roy give you his list yet?" Ivy asked.

"I'm going to call him tomorrow."

"Why not now?"

"Because I can't do much with it until Rachel gets her lists."

"And when is this Rachel woman talking to her clients?"

"Hopefully sometime in the next week. Two tops. She said there's a lot of red tape involved. You can only see them on certain days. Specific visiting hours,etc. Plus, she's got a job to work around."

"I wonder if the prison knows what she's up to?"

"I'd guess not. Rachel is still trying to secure the first court date for Derek Tice. It's certainly not public record yet."

For the first time, Ivy walked away from the wall. She walked over to the couch, and I joined her.

"This is wild, Bobby."

"I know."

"Does your family know about your current theory?"

"My sister has no idea. We've only talked once since she left Santa Barbara."

"And your father?"

"My Dad knows I'm still out here investigating, but he knows nothing about this. He'd think I was losing it."

Ivy smiled.

"It is a bit much."

"It sure is."

"So, how is your father, anyway?"

"He's doing well. Just turned sixty recently," I said.

"Can we go see him one of these days?"

Ivy's visit had been all business, but maybe this was my chance to switch gears.

"I'll tell you what," I said. "If you go out to dinner with me on Sunday night, we'll swing by my Dad's after. And then we can come back here and talk more about the case."

"So, I only get to visit your father if I agree to a dinner with you?"

"Not just my father. You also get to come back here and learn more about the case you're clearly infatuated with. I'm throwing you two bones."

"That's not the only bone on your mind," Ivy said.

I laughed.

"You're not wrong. I miss you."

I leaned toward her. She did the same, but only to give me a hug.

"Alright, I'm in on Sunday, with one minor wrinkle."

"I can't wait to hear this. What is it?"

"Your father joins us for dinner."

"I can ask, but it's a long shot."

"Use me as bait," Ivy said. "Tell him I'm only going if he does."

"You can be devious when you want to."

Ivy stood up from the couch, leaned back down, and kissed me on the cheek.

I grabbed her waist and half-heartedly tried to pull her down toward me.

"Want to check out my bedroom? I have these brand new sheets."

Ivy laughed.

"Nice try, Bobby. It's not going to be that easy getting me back."

"How about Sunday?"

"We'll see," she said in a flirtatious way. She backed over to the wall. "Now, back to this Derek Tice guy. What did Rachel say he's like?"

There would be no trip to my bedroom on this night.

৩৮৩

I CALLED ROY COOPER ON MONDAY MORNING.

He seemed initially resistant to my idea.

"Do you know how many people I've had spats with?" he asked.

"I'm not going to judge you on that."

"You will when you see a list of a thousand people."

"I doubt there will be that many."

"You'd be surprised."

"Like I said, I'm not here to judge you."

"I don't know."

I was tired of dancing around the subject.

"Are you going to do it or not, Roy? It could really help our investigation."

I had mentioned nothing of Derek Tice or any of the others. I hadn't brought up the possibility that Roy himself was being framed.

Roy still had plenty of friends in Santa Barbara.

The less he knew, the better.

"You think someone was trying to get revenge on me by killing your mother?"

"I'm just trying to explore every option," I said, keeping my answer vague.

"Okay, I'll do it," he finally said. "When do you need it?"

"The sooner the better."

"If you want an exhaustive list, it would probably take a few days. Today is Monday. How about Thursday?"

"That's fine. Talk to you then. Thanks, Roy."

❧

I woke up Wednesday morning and realized we were two weeks from the 20th anniversary of my mother's murder.

I wanted to know if KEYT or the *News-Press* might have reconsidered and might now run a segment or an article. Or, was I still looked on as a wild card, a loose cannon not to do business with?

I called both and was promised a callback.

I had my doubts I'd receive any.

❧

On Thursday, I received the list from Roy Cooper.

He'd texted me, asking for my email. He said there were way too many names to text.

He wasn't kidding. At first glance at the email, it looked to have well over a hundred names. Maybe closer to two hundred. I took a superficial glance at some of the names. The first two I saw were Ty Brownstone and Ethan Drury. And these guys were supposed to be friends of Roy's.

There was no point in reviewing this many names until Rachel had her first list.

❧

I met with Rachel on Friday at a coffee shop on State Street.

I told her that Roy Cooper had come through with an exhaustive list.

"Have you looked it over?"

"I gave it a few perfunctory glances. Once you get your list, I'll review it with a fine-toothed comb. How are we doing on that front?"

"I will be visiting Derek on Monday and Dale on Tuesday. I'm going to be putting a lot of miles on my car. Derek is in Pleasant Valley State Prison in Coalinga, a city in Fresno County. Luckily, Dale is in a Los Angeles prison, so that won't be as bad. I've talked to both on the phone, and they know what I'm looking for. So I expect a list of some sort when I see them."

"Okay, now we're getting somewhere. How about I come to see you on Wednesday, and we compare lists?"

"I was going to say the same thing. Are you free early that morning?"

I wasn't sure if Rachel knew I was unemployed and dedicating every waking minute to this investigation. I felt no need to broach the subject.

"Yeah, I'm free," I said.

"Alright, how about eight on Wednesday?"

That would be October 21st, one week from the anniversary.

"I'll be there."

❧ 45 ❧

CONRAD

I'd woke up on Wednesday, October 14th with an uneasy feeling.

No, it wasn't the fact that it was exactly two weeks from the 20th anniversary of my first murder. And yes, I do keep track of things like that.

The uneasiness was caused by the silence surrounding Heather McGowan's murder.

A month ago, all anyone could talk about was Bobby McGowan and how he'd become a laughingstock. He'd made an ass of himself on the local news and then trumped that after I'd set him up with the cupcakes.

But now, I heard nothing. Nothing from Bobby, nothing from his website, nothing from KEYT, and nothing from the *News-Press*.

The lack of any news made me nervous. I know I'm usually up to no good when quiet.

The strong likelihood was that I hadn't heard anything because Bobby was no longer investigating the case. He'd tried to play hero and catch his mother's killer, but it had all been for naught..

And yet, my always suspicious mind told me that I should look into Bobby's current doings.

Just in case.

CONRAD

I KNEW WHAT I HAD TO DO.

It was effortless, yet one of the most effective things in my arsenal.

I would attach a homing device to Bobby's car, which was basically just a GPS tracker.

I wanted to know where he was going and who he was communicating with.

Was it that sad old father of his? That worthless detective, Patchett? I wasn't scared of those has-beens.

Maybe Bobby would surprise me and visit someone who would force me to take notice.

I WAS ABLE TO FIND OUT BOBBY'S ADDRESS IN A MATTER OF MINUTES.

It came with an apartment number, which made things easier. Attaching a homing device could be problematic if someone lived in a house and parked their car in a garage. Apartment complexes either had open-air parking outside or an underground parking garage. Either one was easy to navigate.

Next, I needed to find out his license plate number. Within my bag of tricks - which I often mention - I had accrued many "shortcuts" over the years. One of these was gaining access to a website where you could find anyone's license plate.

After the disaster of Roy having drinks on the day I murdered Heather McGowan, I'd started attaching a GPS tracker in every subsequent murder. In 2005, when I committed my second murder, the device was the size of my fist. Now, they were the size of the tip of my pinkie. God bless technology.

I needed to know that my mark was not on the move on the day in question. His staying home was part and parcel to me framing him. If, by some chance, I saw his car moving on the day in question, I'd have to abort.

This only happened one time. My mark's mother was admitted to the hospital within an hour of my planned murder. I watched the homing device and was shocked to see him drive to the hospital. I had to call the murder off. I found out a week later that his mother had passed away. She had unknowingly saved her son's freedom and his ex-wife's life.

At least for a few months.

I still went through with it later that year.

CHAPTER 45

BOBBY LIVED ON THE MESA, AND I DROVE BY HIS APARTMENT COMPLEX that Wednesday night. It had four units and was reminiscent of Victoria Bosco's. Don't think I'd forgotten about her. She'd be paying the piper soon.

Each apartment had one assigned spot in the parking lot directly outside of the apartments. I guess if you were a couple, one of you had to park on the street. There were also two spots for *'Visitor Parking.'*

The place was tiny, the Mom and Pop store of apartment complexes.

I decided to return later once I knew everyone would likely be asleep.

AT 2:45 A.M., I WAS BACK AT BOBBY MCGOWAN'S COMPLEX.

I knew he was in apartment #3 and found the corresponding parking spot. Bobby drove a silver Hyundai Elantra, which looked to be about three or four years old. I made sure the license plate matched with the information I'd received. It did.

GPS trackers are so advanced these days. I could attach it anywhere on the car, but I didn't want it visible for obvious reasons.

I had attached an ultra-sticky substance below the GPS tracker, which would strictly adhere to the car.

I looked around one more time and didn't see anyone. All of the apartment lights were off. I got on my knees and reached between the back tire and the bumper, looking for a spot underneath the car to place the sticky substance. I found one and started pressing it up against the aluminum. I then kept pushing the sticky substance against the car for fifteen more seconds.

Satisfied with what I'd done, I returned to my car and drove home.

Who have you been talking to, Bobby?

Where have you been going?

From now on, I'd know.

46

BOBBY

Knowing I'd see my father that night, I called my sister early on Sunday. My father was assuredly going to ask about her, and I didn't want to admit I'd only talked to her once since her visit to Santa Barbara.

I was sitting on my couch watching football when I made the call.

"Hey, Bobby,' Jen said.

"Sorry, I haven't been in touch much, Jen."

"No problem," she said. "It's my fault, too. I've been busy with the kids."

There was no guilt trip to start with. I'd caught her on a good day.

I'd often wondered if we'd have a more normal relationship if our mother were still alive. Was it her death that started causing the fissures, or was there something brewing before then? Jen and I got along great as kids, so I tended to think it was the former. And it was more than just her death. It was how I handled it and the fact I never really could let it go.

"How are they?" I asked. "They don't think Uncle Bobby is some convict on the run from the law?"

Jen laughed.

"No, they don't think that. Avery is too young to remember it, and Aaron seems to think it was some sort of performance art."

It was my turn to laugh.

"Maybe it was," I said.

"Oh, yeah? Was spending the next several hours in jail part of the performance?"

"Hey, you've got to go all out in my field."

"Well, congrats on the new job, then."

"Oh, Jen."

"So, what's up?" she asked. "Anything new on Mom? I'm assuming, despite your arrest, you haven't stopped investigating completely."

"I was back at it pretty soon thereafter," I admitted.

"I'd expect nothing less from you."

It was another prime example of Jen saying something that could be construed as either a compliment or a putdown.

"Do you want to know my latest theory?" I asked.

"Sure, why not?"

I'd vowed to keep this on the down low, but Jen was my sister and, more importantly, the daughter of the deceased. She deserved to know.

"I've been talking to an attorney, and well, I guess it's her theory, but she thinks there might be a serial killer on the Central Coast who is framing other people for the murders he's committed."

"Is this another case of performance art? That's the craziest thing I've ever heard."

I knew at that moment - and it's something I should have known going in - there was no way to win Jen over on this. Better to cut my losses.

"You nailed it—performance art," I said.

"Okay," she said, unsure of what to think now.

"On a lighter note, I've hung out with Ivy a few times lately."

"Wow, some good news to report. Tell her I said hello."

"I will. We are taking it slow to start."

"Do you mean she's taking it slow?"

I laughed.

"Oh, Jen. You are the ultimate ballbuster."

"But am I wrong?"

"No, you're not wrong. Ivy is taking it slow, but I think we are headed in the right direction."

"That's nice to hear," Jen said, and this time, I could tell she meant every word of it.

"I'm taking her and Dad out to dinner tonight."

"Where are you guys eating?"

"Lure Fish House."

"Only ate there once, but I remember it being a nice place."

"I'll have to take you next time you guys are out here."

"You won't have to wait long. I'll be out for Christmas."

Jen probably made it back about every other Christmas, so this was a pleasant surprise.

"Good to hear. I wasn't sure."

"Despite your antics on my last trip, I realized how important it is to get back. We're both young and hopefully going to live long lives, but Dad is getting older."

"He's only sixty."

"I know, but sometimes I feel like he's eighty."

"Agreed. Sometimes, when he's walking, he looks like an octogenarian. He'll be happy to see you, that's for sure. And I will, too. Tell Aaron I'll be working on my performance art leading up to your guys' visit."

"You're too much," she said.

This had gone better than expected, so I ended it on a high note.

"I'll call you soon, Jen. I promise it won't be so long this time."

"Thanks for calling, Bobby. Talk soon."

⚜

IVY LIVED ON THE MESA WITHIN A MILE OF ME, SO I WOULD PICK HER up first and then swing by and pick up my father.

She knew I was on my way and was already waiting outside her apartment complex as I arrived. She was wearing a light blue dress and looked stunning. I was in slacks and a white dress shirt. We might have been a tad overdressed, but we looked good.

"You look great," I said.

"Thanks. You too."

As we drove to my father's house, I told her about my conversation with my sister and that she'd said hello.

Ivy was pleased.

We picked up my father, who was a little more casually dressed.

"What, are you guys going to the opera afterward?"

Ivy laughed.

"Yeah, once we drop your old ass back home," I said.

"Screw that. I'm hitting up State Street till the bars close tonight. This sixty-year-old is going to act twenty-five."

It was likely only because Ivy was with us, but my father was giving off a more youthful vibe. Jen would have been impressed—no eighty-year-old in sight.

⚜

WE ARRIVED AT LURE FISH HOUSE AFTER A SHORT, FUN-FILLED DRIVE. My father had brought his A-game, that's for sure.

We got a table for three reasonably close to their Oyster Bar. It was the most vibrant part of the restaurant, and I always tried to sit near the bar when I could. The few times I'd eaten at Lure alone, I sat at the Oyster Bar but felt like getting a table was more appropriate for the three of us.

Our waiter was a man in his fifties who gave off the vibe of someone who was a lifer in the restaurant industry.

We each ordered a drink, and he brought some bread over.

"How are your parents, Ivy?" my father asked.

"They're fine. Still both in LA, and I get to see them fairly regularly."

The fact that Ivy's mother was not my biggest fan had never stopped my father from being interested in her. I think he had a crush.

"Did your mother ever get remarried?"

"No, she's still single."

"See, there's nothing wrong with being single, Bobby."

"Okay, I'll stay single then," I said.

My father laughed.

"I'm talking about me. You're young and have no excuse to be single. Plus, you've got this beautiful girl right here."

Ivy was smiling, loving this all.

"You are not winning the award for Most Subtle tonight, Dad; I can guarantee you that."

"Who wants to win that award? If you like a girl, tell her you like her."

"Hear, hear, Mr. McGowan," Ivy said.

If I had been this upfront, I'm not sure Ivy would have enjoyed it as much, but since it was my father, she was eating it up.

"See, Bobby? And Ivy, I know it's been a while, but you can call me Robert. Mr. McGowan was my father."

"You got it, Robert."

My father took a big sip of his drink.

"There's a beautiful woman over there, sitting alone," my father said. "Maybe I should go talk to her. Don't worry, she's age-appropriate for me."

"Jeez, what the hell did they put in your Gin and Tonic?" I asked.

"Gin...and tonic."

Ivy and I laughed.

"You're ridiculous," I said.

◆◆◆

THE DINNER PRETTY MUCH WENT LIKE THAT. A LOT OF LAUGHS WERE had. My father tried to play matchmaker approximately forty-eight times, but Ivy got a kick out of each one.

Ivy got the Ceviche for her entree, my father ordered Sea Bass, and I had the seared Ahi. All were excellent.

The restaurant was loud and a lot of fun.

Too fun for one guy, however.

He walked up to the Oyster Bar, obviously hammered, and started talking to some friend. Only, he wasn't talking. He was yelling. Every word sounded like he was screaming. Luckily, he left within a few minutes. People were looking around, wondering if we would have to alert management. It never came to that, and we'd forgotten about him a few minutes later.

Our table finished the meal with a dessert, and my father ordered a third drink, which he rarely did.

He was having a blast. I could tell he didn't want the dinner to end.

I was driving and already had one drink, so I just went with a coffee.

Despite the objection of the other two at the table, I picked up the tab for dinner.

For being unemployed, I sure had been generous lately.

◆◆◆

WHEN I DROPPED MY FATHER OFF AT HOME, I WALKED HIM TO THE door.

He had never been a big drinker, and three drinks was a lot for him. I just wanted to make sure he got inside safely.

"Do you think it worked?" he asked, still hovering outside his door as if willing the night to continue.

"Did what work?"

"When I said that whole thing about when you're young, you should be dating. I was hoping Ivy took that to heart so she'd get back together with you."

"I guess we'll see, Dad. But thanks for trying to push her in my direction."

"I'm your father. It's the least I can do."

"You need help getting in?"

"No, I don't need help. I had two Gin and Tonics. I'm fine."

"And you had an after-dinner drink," I said.

"Oh, that doesn't count."

I smiled.

"I'll come by and see you in a few days. Love you, Dad."

"Love you too, Bobby."

He yelled back toward the car.

"Goodnight, Ivy."

"Goodnight, Mr. McGowan."

"I said to call me Robert."

"Goodnight, Robert."

"Goodnight, Ivy," he repeated. "Take care of Bobby."

"You're insufferable," I said.

My father finally put his key in the lock.

"You better kiss that gorgeous woman tonight," he said.

"GOODBYE," I SAID SARCASTICALLY AND WALKED BACK TO THE CAR.

I DID, IN FACT, KISS THAT GORGEOUS WOMAN.

After dinner, I drove us to The Cliff Room, an old-school bar on the Mesa.

We were on our second drink at The Cliff Room - my third overall - so I'd probably leave my car there overnight.

I wanted to say something to Ivy.

We'd been flirting, and I felt the time was right.

I leaned in close.

"I've missed you," I began. "I'm sorry if I wasn't always the most attentive boyfriend. I'm sorry if I didn't ask you to move in with me. I'm sorry for all of it. I'll be better this time around. And I don't care if we have to take this slowly. I'm fine with that, but I want you in my life."

She stared back at me, and I thought - or was it hoped? - that she'd done it longingly.

And that's when I kissed her.

After a few nerve-wracking seconds, she kissed me back, and we held that kiss for several seconds.

Public Display's of Affection are nauseating if you are on the viewing end, but when you are on the receiving end, they aren't so bad.

"That was nice," Ivy said.

"Do you want to stay at my place tonight?" I asked.

She leaned in close, nibbled on my ear, and said yes.

❧ 47 ❧

CONRAD

Move over Victoria Bosco, there's a new girl in town.

Her name is Ivy.

I haven't caught her last name yet, but she's now the apple of my eye. You've got a stay of execution, Victoria.

After attaching the GPS on Wednesday, very little happened in the intervening days. I was working on Thursday and Friday but still kept watch on my new pal, Bobby.

On Thursday, his car didn't move.

On Friday, he parked his car at a Starbucks on State Street, at least according to the GPS. It's always possible he went to a neighboring business. I wasn't too worried.

Saturday was the same.

On Sunday, curiosity killed the cat. I saw that Bobby had parked on Upper State Street near a restaurant I knew well: Lure Fish House. The parking lot was also contiguous to a Macy's, but I just didn't see Bobby out shopping on a Sunday night.

Lure had a tremendous little Oyster bar where I could go undetected. It's not like I was risking anything, anyway. Bobby McGowan and I had never crossed paths, at least not to his knowledge. After I murdered his mother, sometimes I'd walk into the same grocery store as he and his sister and father. It gave me a power trip. I enjoyed knowing that I held a secret they'd never know.

If Bobby knew who I was, it would only be because I was Ethan's little brother. If he had investigated Roy Cooper thoroughly, there's a chance I might have come up, but merely as someone Roy had bullied. He'd be the asshole. I'd be the one deserving of sympathy.

For all I knew, Bobby had talked to Ethan. I wouldn't know. I'd long ago cut that asshole off.

So, no, I wasn't worried about eating at the same restaurant as him, although I'd still be my usual, vigilant self.

I arrived at Lure thirty minutes after Bobby. I made my way into the restaurant and took a seat at the Oyster Bar. I'd eaten there five or six times over the years, but not enough to where any of the servers would remember me. For the most part, I was a forgettable guy, which came in handy in my line of work.

As soon as I sat at the bar, I spotted Bobby McGowan sitting at a table on the other side of the Oyster Bar. His recent TV appearances made him easy to recognize. He was sitting with an attractive young woman, and the other man I realized was his father.

I quickly ditched my seat and moved to the other side of the Oyster Bar. I sat down at a barstool relatively close to his table. There was still one table between us, but they were in my line of sight.

I told myself to be careful and not to be caught staring.

Bobby McGowan didn't know me from Adam, but as I'll say for the thousandth time, I didn't like taking undue chances.

I swiveled my seat about forty-five degrees so I was more in the line of sight of the young woman and less of Bobby or his father.

And what a pretty face it was to look at. She looked to be in her early thirties with noticeably paler skin than the average Santa Barbarian. Her hair was dirty blonde, and it sat shoulder length. She had a quick smile that lit up her face. I don't know if she was beautiful in the traditional sense, but there was definitely something about her. My mind was already thinking evil thoughts.

With the table between me and them, I could only pick up every other sentence or so. I was able to gather that her name was Ivy. That was easy.

And I heard enough to realize that Bobby's father was pushing Ivy and Bobby to get back together. He wasn't even subtle about it.

Ivy had been Bobby's girlfriend at some point but no longer was.

She'd have been better off with a real man like me.

"CONRAD, YOU SON OF A BITCH!"

I had just started eating the crispy calamari I'd ordered when I felt a tap on my shoulder. I recognized the man's voice before I even saw his face. I was not happy to see/hear him. I never was, but this was about the worst time possible.

I turned around quickly and shook his hand.

"How are you, Harold?"

After facing him, I quickly turned around to face the Oyster Bar. Harold was always loud and, this time, quite drunk, so if Bobby or his father had heard the commotion, I didn't want them to see me.

At least he'd only said my first name and not my last. Undoubtedly, Bobby had heard the name Ethan Drury several times throughout his investigation.

And it might seem odd that his little brother was fifteen feet from him.

I decided to nip this in the bud.

I called the waitress over and asked her to close me out.

"Leaving so soon, old buddy?"

Harold was a regular at a lot of the watering holes in Santa Barbara. We'd become pseudo-friends over the years. With my lack of empathy/emotion, I don't build real bonds, but I guess I'd consider Harold a decent acquaintance. I just didn't want to see him right now.

"I'm going to see a movie in thirty minutes," I said. "Here, have some Calamari."

"Fuck, yeah. Who doesn't love Calamari?"

I knew I needed to get the hell out of there. I was imagining Bobby's table looking in our direction. If Bobby saw me, I couldn't stalk him going forward. I couldn't risk him seeing me twice.

If I could get my check and exit away from their table, I could minimize the chance he saw me.

Harold dove in and ate three Calamari rings at once.

He was a slob.

"You ever eat at Holdren's anymore?" he asked.

"Occasionally."

"Those fuckers 86'd me," Harold screamed.

I was sure even more eyes were on us now, but it was not like I could turn around to find out.

"Listen, Harold, it was good to see you. I've got to get out of here, or

I'll never make that movie. You want to sit and have the rest of these Calamari?"

"No thanks. I'm going downtown to hit up the bars. Meet me at Brew Co. after the movie is over."

"Okay, I'll do that," I said.

"Great, Conrad."

Stop saying my fucking name!

I wanted to take a pen knife to Harold's eyes.

They brought my bill, and I left cash so as not to have to spend a few extra minutes closing a credit card.

"Good seeing you, Harold."

"You too, Conrad."

Fuck.

I shuffled past Harold and walked away from Bobby McGowan's table.

I then drove home.

⚜

Forty-five minutes later, the GPS alerted me that Bobby's car was driven to The Cliff Room.

Curiosity once again got the best of me.

I changed clothes and put on a blonde wig and a baseball cap. I even threw on some glasses, which I never wore. They didn't have a prescription, and I only wore them when I didn't want people to recognize me.

I looked nothing like myself.

I didn't dare go into The Cliff Room, but I did loiter outside and saw Bobby and Ivy sitting at the bar near the entrance. I walked back and forth a few times and finally decided that despite my disguise, I was taking an undue risk.

On my last walk by, I looked over and saw Ivy kissing Bobby for several seconds.

I was incensed.

They were broken up. Bobby's father had made that much clear.

How did this fucking asshole have a pretty girl who liked him?

I couldn't let that stand.

I quickly stormed off.

Ivy was my new mark. Screw Victoria Bosco.

Shit, maybe Bobby would be my new mark too.

I'd never made one of my murders look like a murder/suicide, but it is something I thought I could pull off.

I mean, what could be better?

Twenty years ago, I'd murdered Heather McGowan. And now, I could bring this full circle and murder her son and his girlfriend.

One thing was for certain: If I pulled off this murder/suicide, Santa Barbara would be too hot for me.

Bumfuck, Arkansas, here I come.

I'll be seeing you again soon, Ivy.

You too, Bobby.

❧ 48 ❧

BOBBY

I drove down to Rachel's law firm in Ventura on Wednesday morning.

I felt some genuine excitement. I'd been investigating for right around two months, and with the possible exception of the killer's messages, this was the most fired up I'd been.

I felt like we were close to making a breakthrough.

Then again, maybe there would be no matches, and I'd have to return to square one.

For the second straight time, I found parking right out front. It didn't hurt that it wasn't even eight a.m. yet, and the streets were mostly vacant.

I said hello to the now-familiar secretary, and Rachel appeared a few seconds later. This time, she took me to her office instead of the conference room. Maybe we would be discussing things she didn't want overheard.

"Thanks for coming, Bobby."

"I wouldn't miss it. Hope we've got something good."

"Oh, we've got something good, alright."

She had my full attention.

"We have a match?"

"Yes. Technically, we have three matches, but only one is interesting."

"Why is that?"

"Two of them can easily be explained away."

"I'm listening," I said.

"One is Wade McCarthy, one of the San Luis Obispo County prosecutors. He's an Assistant District Attorney in name only. The real District Attorney doesn't try many cases, and Wade gets all the high-profile ones. And the murders of Mary Jane Cushing and Jill Venable were both high profile. Both Pismo Beach, where Mary Jane was killed and obviously, San Luis Obispo, where Jill was killed, are both in San Luis Obispo County. So Wade was the prosecuting attorney in both Derek Tice's and Dale Collier's cases. While there's a good chance that Wade McCarthy might have wrongfully prosecuted both men, I don't think he's our killer."

"Yeah, probably not. Although I do see why they might hold a grudge against him."

"Indeed," Rachel said.

"And the second one?"

"Karl Kimmers."

"What a name."

"It's probably fake. He runs a true-crime website and is known to attend most Central Coast murder trials. I'll be sure to ask my clients, but my guess is that Mr. Kimmers attended their trials. He's known for writing scathing articles online, usually with the defendant taking the brunt of it. It's probably warranted in most cases, but if you were wrongly convicted, you could imagine how Mr. Kimmers would get on your nerves. Maybe there were arguments between my clients and Mr. Kimmers in the courthouse. I'm not sure. But I highly doubt this guy had anything to do with the murders."

"Would be quite a story, though," I said. "A guy who writes true crime out there killing people to give himself more business."

"I guess it's not impossible. I'll put Karl Kimmers on the back burner, possibly to be returned to later."

"Okay," I said. "And the third?"

"I've never heard of him. He's not a prosecuting attorney or a true crime writer. I tried Googling the name, and if I've got the right guy, he works for Amtrak."

Something registered in the recesses of my mind, but I couldn't place it. Rachel could sense it.

"What is it?" she asked.

"It's nothing. What is his name?" I asked.

She paused, adding to the intrigue.

"Conrad Drury," she said.

It took a second to register. When I first heard the name, my mind quickly went to Ethan Drury.

Was Conrad his brother's name? I tried to remember my conversations with both Ethan and Rick.

I remember Rick saying he wanted to reach out to Ethan's brother, who worked at Amtrak. That's why Amtrak had registered with me. And he said his name was Conrad. I was sure of it.

I hadn't responded yet, and Rachel could tell something was up.

"You know who this guy is, don't you?"

"I've never met him, but I know the name. And I know his brother."

"Who is his brother?"

"Ethan Drury. He was drinking with Roy Cooper on the day my mother was killed, and Ethan provided Roy with his alibi."

"Is Conrad on Roy's list?"

I took out my printed set of papers. I started scrolling through the names, but I already knew Conrad would be there. Ethan and Rick had both told me that Conrad had been excessively bullied by Roy, who'd all but confirmed it when I showed him the picture with Ethan, Conrad, and the others.

I found Conrad's name at the bottom of the second page.

"He's on here," I said.

"Holy fucking shit," Rachel said.

Neither one of us said a word for several seconds.

There was no question that this was the most significant moment of my investigation. It didn't mean that Conrad Drury was the killer, but I had my first bonafide suspect.

"Let's not get ahead of ourselves," I said, even though I was doing just that.

"I agree. He's a suspect. Nothing more. I'm not planning on going on *Dateline NBC* and shouting his name from the rooftops."

Because I was afraid to get my hopes up, I decided to play devil's advocate.

"What if Conrad Drury is just the ultimate jerk? He works on Amtrak, so it makes sense that both Derek Tice and Dale Collier might have run into him at some point. Maybe Conrad was always an asshole, and he's had hundreds of these run-ins with passengers."

"That's plausible, but maybe you're just looking for a reason to discard him. Be honest, did you ever think we'd have the same name on three of the lists."

"No," I admitted.

"Shit, I don't know what to do next," Rachel said. "I guess I never really thought it would come to this, either."

"Can I make a suggestion?"

"Absolutely," Rachel said.

"As soon as possible, I'd return to see your clients. Ask them everything you can about Conrad Drury. Why did he make their list? When did they meet him? Times and dates. Things of that nature."

"I beat you to it," she said. "I called both prisons last night."

"How soon are we talking?"

"Probably a few days. I never know."

"We aren't going to the cops, correct?" I asked, even though I knew what her answer would be.

"No, of course not. I need to find out more. What would I say anyway? *'Hi, I'm defending two men convicted of murder, and they both got in an argument with the same guy, so I'm sure that guy must have framed both of them for murder.'* They'd laugh me out of their precinct."

Would Mark Patchett would have the same reaction? We'd reconciled, but he still probably thought I had a screw loose. I couldn't go to him with what we had. It wasn't enough.

"I agree," I said. "No cops yet. I can talk to some of my friends in Santa Barbara and find out more about Conrad Drury. And we could meet up again after you talk to your clients."

"Okay. Did your mother know Conrad?"

"Conrad was several years younger, but my mother knew his older brother, so she at least met him in passing. There's a picture of my mother with a few neighborhood kids and Conrad is in it."

"Do you want to see a picture of him now?" Rachel asked.

"Yes."

She had a laptop beside her and reversed the screen so it faced me.

On first impression, Conrad Drury looked a lot like his brother. They both had gaunt faces with deep-set brown eyes. He gave off an intense vibe and didn't look like someone you would want to fuck with. There was something familiar about that face.

"Is this the only picture you have?" I asked.

"Yes. It's an employee picture from Amtrak's website. I looked for a Facebook or an Instagram account but couldn't find anything."

"If he is what we fear, it would make sense that he wouldn't have a social media presence."

I looked back at the photo. Was this the guy who had strangled my mother to death? The man who'd caused me an immeasurable amount of grief over the years? The man who'd made my father half the man he used to be? The man who helped fracture the relationship I had with my sister?

I didn't know, but it was my first real suspect. Lyle Taft didn't count; he just got this all started.

Had Conrad Drury tried to frame Roy? Or, was he just trying to get back at him by killing someone he knew? Would some harsh bullying be enough to set this guy off? Did Ethan Drury have any idea what his brother was capable of?

I had so many questions.

The most important might have been, *Were we jumping the gun on Conrad Drury?*

A guy was bullied as a child and became a jerk later in life, causing him to argue with people frequently.

It didn't mean he was a killer. Far from it.

And yet, some things were fitting into place.

Mentioned on all three lists. From Santa Barbara. Knew who my mother was.

"Here, take this back," I said and pushed Rachel's laptop back to her. I was sick of looking at his squirrelly face.

"I'm fascinated by what you'll find out," Rachel said. "I shouldn't have to tell you this, but keep your distance from this guy."

"I'll be smart about it. Trust me, I'm not planning on confronting Conrad. We don't know what we have just yet."

"No, we don't," Rachel said, but her face belied her point. She was just as excited as me. Maybe she was envisioning an end game where her clients were granted new days in court, and Rachel, through adroit legal maneuvering, got her clients' convictions thrown out.

"Why don't you call me tomorrow?" I said.

"I will. And the day after that. And the day after that. I want to know anything you find out, Bobby. Maybe even the smallest thing will help one of my clients remember more about Conrad Drury."

"Okay," I said. "I'll be in touch."

I got up to go.

"Are you in a rush?" Rachel asked.

"Yeah, I guess I am.

"Who are you going to see?"

"My uncle."

Ventura was thirty minutes south of Santa Barbara, and Santa Maria was fifty minutes north of Santa Barbara, so I had a little drive ahead of me.

I got to my car and called Rick.

"Hello."

"Rick, this is Bobby. Will you be at your place in an hour and a half?"

"No. I'm leaving for a cruise with Bo Derek."

"I'll take that as a yes. See you soon."

"Okay, Bobby, looking forward to it."

I parked outside of Rick's place and headed toward the door.

The last few times, he'd waited for me outside, but the temperature on the Central Coast had taken a precipitous drop as of late, and I'm sure he was enjoying God's gift of indoor heating.

I knocked, and Rick answered.

"You know where to sit," he said.

Yes, the world's worst couch.

"When I get rich, I'm buying you a new couch," I said.

"This is a classic."

"Maybe when you were growing up. Now it's just an eyesore."

Rick smiled.

"Shit, if I knew this was why you were coming up here, I wouldn't have invited you."

"It's going to get worse," I said.

Rick could tell I was serious.

"Okay. Okay."

Rick walked to the kitchen and returned with two bottled waters, handing me one.

"Thanks."

"So, what is it?" Rick asked. "I can tell you're not kidding around."

"I just want to make this clear," I said. "You're not to talk about this conversation with anyone. I mean it."

"I won't tell Bo on our cruise."

"I'm serious, Rick."

"Jeez, you can't take a joke."

"This isn't a joking manner," I said. "It's about my mother."

Rick's facial expression changed in an instant.

"You've found something."

"Maybe. That's why I'm here."

"I'll help you in any way I can."

"Alright. I'm going to throw out a name. And I want to hear everything you know about the guy. The vibe he gives off. How dangerous you think he is. How well he knew my mother—all those things. And the last thing I'll say is that this guy is just a suspect. We have nothing concrete on him. So don't jump to any conclusions."

"What's the name?" Rick asked.

"Conrad Drury."

He pondered it for a few seconds.

"Do you know what the scariest part is?"

I didn't know what he was referring to, but I played along.

"What?"

"I wasn't all that shocked when you mentioned his name."

"Tell me everything you know about him."

"I first met Conrad when he was probably around seven or eight. That would have made me around seventeen, give or take a few years. I was a few years older than Ethan, and he had several years on Conrad. What I remember most, which I told you about on one of your visits, was that Roy Cooper was a complete asshole to Conrad. A bully, through and through. Yeah, Roy was a jerk to everyone, but he seemed to especially have it in for Conrad. I stopped him a few times when I thought he crossed the line. Remember, I was one of the few guys who was not intimidated by Roy. I think it was the other way around, and he might have been intimidated by me, so if I told him he'd gone too far, he stopped. I'm guessing Roy bullied Conrad up until Roy was about twenty or so; that would have made Conrad something like thirteen. Like I said, I don't know the exact age difference."

Rick took a sip of his water.

"Conrad was not very likable. You'd think people would have some built-in sympathy for someone who was bullied a lot, but Conrad didn't espouse any sympathy. He was cold. He had these distant eyes that felt like they were looking past you. You'd get monosyllabic, terse answers if you asked him how he was doing. So, people stopped trying to feel bad for him. He didn't have many friends and didn't seem to want any. There were a couple of kids he'd go skateboarding or biking with, but not many. He was pretty anti-social. When he was about fifteen, I heard about him beating up a guy pretty bad. The bullied had now become the bully. He and Ethan were both skinny, but they were also very strong. You know the type?"

"I do," I said.

"Well, Conrad has always been like that. Still is to this day."

"When did he start working for Amtrak?"

"I think right out of high school or soon after. You don't have to be twenty-one to work for Amtrak. You can be eighteen. You see, Conrad was smart. A shit-ton smarter than his idiot brother. But Conrad wouldn't have done too well on a college campus. I don't know how to explain it, but he wouldn't have prospered. His anti-social vibe would have turned people off. And girls found him creepy."

"Didn't you say you were friendly with him?"

"I did. I'm building to that."

"My bad."

"You know the old phrase, 'the devil you know.' Well, that's how it was with Conrad. By the time he was nineteen or twenty and working for Amtrak, I rode that thing up and down the Central Coast. I was employed by PG & E back then, and it was hard work. On the weekends, I'd need to let off some steam. I'd usually do that in SB, hitting up the bars on State Street. But occasionally, some friends and I would just hop on Amtrak and head to Ventura, Pismo, or San Luis Obispo for the night. I'd say we took Amtrak because we were responsible kids and didn't want to drink and drive, but that wasn't it. We didn't want to waste time in a car where we couldn't drink. If we rode Amtrak, we could hit the bar car until we arrived at our destination. We weren't rich kids then, so we'd always have a twelve-pack of beer in our bags. We'd order one drink from the bartender and tip him $5 or something like that. After that, he'd look the other way once we started drinking beers. Remember, this was a different time. We're talking the 1980s. You could get away with a lot more."

"Would Conrad join you and have a beer?"

"Never on the train. He knew that would get him fired. But he'd join us for a few if he was getting off at our station."

"He wouldn't just take the train back to Santa Barbara?"

"No. I never quite understood Conrad's schedule, but he'd spend nights in hotels all up and down the Central Coast. Maybe he was just a loner and preferred hotels to coming home to Santa Barbara. Maybe he'd wait till the next morning and take the Amtrak back. Shit, maybe they paid for his hotels. I don't know."

"And you said this was the 1980s?"

"Yeah, that's when it started, but I think Conrad still works there to this day."

"Did you reach out to him when I gave you Ethan's number?"

"No, I haven't yet."

Good, I told myself.

"Do you remember if you were still friendly with him around the time my mother died?" I asked.

"Hmmm. In 2003, I was working for Cox Cable in Santa Barbara. I turned forty years old that year. I wasn't taking Amtrak for drinking joy rides anymore. I'm not saying I was a saint; I just did my drinking closer to home. Plus, for Cox Cable, I had a fucked up schedule. I'd have Wednesdays and Saturdays off. They were never two days right next to each other, so I didn't have the time to go on my little two-day benders."

Rick was meandering, and I had to keep him focused.

"So, you'd lost touch with Conrad?"

"He and I were local, so we'd run into each other. It's impossible not to in this town. But no, I didn't know him as well once the 2000s hit."

"When you were friendly with Conrad in the 80s and 90s, did he ever bring up Roy?"

"He hated that guy with all his heart. I don't know if he was ever the first guy to bring him up, but Roy was a well-known guy, and his name would come up from time to time. And you could see Conrad's face turn to stone every time it did."

Rick looked over at me. Something had just registered.

"Wait, do you think Conrad killed Heather to get back at Roy? I know Roy dated Heather, but that had been over fifteen years before she died. That would be a weird way to get back at him."

"What if I told you it was more sinister than that?"

"What could be more sinister than killing your mother?"

"Trying to frame someone for her murder."

"You're fucking kidding me."

"This is just a theory, but I'm not kidding you."

"And you're saying Conrad was trying to frame Roy."

"Again, it's just a theory."

"If I was going to accept this crazy premise, why would Conrad do it when Roy was drinking with his brother?"

"My guess is that they hadn't planned on drinking that day, and it just came together at the last second. Conrad probably had no idea."

I needed to ask Roy if he could remember why they went drinking that day.

"Heather was killed in 2003," Rick said. "Conrad would have been in his late twenties. Roy bullied Conrad when he was a kid. You think he waited all those years to get back at him?"

"I don't know...maybe."

"And why your mother? Did he have something against her, or was this all to frame Roy?"

"I don't know."

"Sure sounds like there's a lot you don't know."

"I concede that. That's why I'm asking questions."

"Well, I'd be careful who you ask. I know how to keep my mouth shut, but generally, people in this town don't."

"I agree. That's why I can't bring up Conrad to Roy, Ethan, or anyone else in that circle of friends."

"So, what's next?"

"I'm not sure. I just got this information this morning."

"You'll think of something."

"Last question, Rick."

"Hit me with it."

"Would you be surprised if Conrad ended up being the killer?"

"When you first mentioned him, I said I wasn't shocked to hear his name. So my answer is no, I wouldn't be."

⊗

I DROVE STRAIGHT HOME AFTER RICK'S.

I immediately went to the wall and grabbed the photo that included Conrad Drury. I stared at his eyes. They looked to have a faraway look as if the guy was thinking about something else. Lifeless would be the best description.

But then again, I was biased. Maybe I was just reading things into the photograph now that he was a suspect. THE suspect.

I stared even longer at the photo. I seared his eyes into my brain.

Had I finally - after twenty years - found the man who'd killed my mother?

And what was I going to do about it?

49

CONRAD

On Wednesday, Bobby's car started to move.

Only this time, it wasn't to State Street or his father's house - the house where I'd committed my first murder. I'll never understand why that old man never moved.

To sit in the house where your wife was killed, day after day, year after year?

What a loser.

Bobby's car was headed south and ended up stopping in Ventura.

The address was on Main Street, and I Googled it. To my surprise, it came back as a law firm. Making matters worse, the name of the law firm, including the words, '*Wrongfully Convicted.*'

My stomach sank.

What the fuck was going on?

Rachel Tatum was the lawyer's name, and I started doing a deep dive on her. I googled her name and tried to find any cases she was currently working on. I then added Santa Barbara and, finally, Heather McGowan to the searches.

Nothing stood out right away.

But I kept at it. After a good thirty minutes, something finally caught my attention.

I'd Googled, '*Rachel Tatum Wrongfully Convicted Central Coast Murder.*'

On page two of that search, a blog referenced Rachel Tatum. The blog didn't even have its own domain address - it ended with wix.com - so I knew this was likely some decrepit little blog no one read.

I clicked on the most recent blog post - the only one - and read the first paragraph with fascination and horror.

WRONGFULLY CONVICTED?

I HAD LONG THOUGHT DEREK TICE HAD BEEN WRONGFULLY CONVICTED OF murder. He was charged, tried, and convicted of killing my niece, Mary Jane Cushing, in 2005 in Pismo Beach. My sister Evelyn, who was Mary Jane's mother, also thought that Derek didn't kill her daughter. But when he was convicted and sentenced for her murder, you start to question your sanity. It seemed unlikely that the State of California would wrongfully convict someone of murder.

AS THE YEARS PASSED, EVELYN AND I STARTED TO CONCEDE THAT MAYBE Derek had done it. But then, about a year ago, Evelyn began having second thoughts once again. She sought attorneys specializing in defending those who might have been wrongfully convicted. At the very least, Evelyn wanted it looked into. Evelyn vouched to drop it forever if the attorney said it was an open-and-shut case and that Derek was guilty.

AFTER HAVING A FIRM SPECIALIZING IN WRONGFUL CONVICTIONS CHECK OUT her case, they referred her to an attorney. They must have believed there was at least some doubt about Derek Tice's guilt. And that's when my sister met Rachel Tatum. Rachel has been a godsend, working tirelessly to get Derek Tice a new court date. It's a long process, and the odds are against us, but you never know. Rachel also seems to think Derek Tice might genuinely be innocent.

THIS IS MY FIRST BLOG POST, BUT I'LL BE UPDATING IT AS WE MOVE FORWARD.

THANKS FOR READING.
Sincerely,
Helen Nevelle

FUCK! FUCK! FUCK! FUCK!

What the hell was going on? Who the fuck was Rachel Tatum? Did she have any evidence that Derek Tice might actually be innocent? What could that evidence be? How did Bobby McGowan find Rachel Tatum? How far along are they?

And the most critical question: Do they know who the fuck I am? I highly doubt it, but this was still not the news I wanted to hear.

I'D MET DEREK TICE SOMETIME IN 2003. I THINK IT WAS SPRING. I'D yet to commit my first murder - Heather McGowan - but I was in the early planning stages. Little did I know then, but Mary Jane Cushing, Derek Tice's ex-girlfriend, would be my second victim.

I met Derek Tice when he became the new manager of an Outback Steakhouse in Pismo Beach.

Pismo was one of my favorite places to stay along the Central Coast. Most Amtrak employees would have a home base they'd disembark from and return to. Sometimes on the same day, sometimes a day later.

I was more of a rogue employee. Frequently, Amtrak would need more than one type of employee or another. Someone who roamed the train and checked tickets. A bartender. A handyman who could fix a broken seat or a flooded toilet.

There were many odd jobs on Amtrak, and I knew how to do them all. There weren't that many employees like me. So, Amtrak would pay for my hotel for a night, and if a train needed a bartender/handyman/ticket checker/anything else, I'd join that train the following morning.

Technically, the Pismo Beach stop was in Grover Beach, just two miles away, but I always stayed in Pismo Beach, so it became the Pismo Beach station to me.

And when I stayed in Pismo, I often enjoyed drinking at their Outback Steakhouse.

Until Derek Tice became their GM.

HE HAD IT IN FOR ME FROM THE BEGINNING. THE FIRST TIME HE MET me, he accused me of sitting too close to a woman. We were at the bar, and Derek came and forcibly moved my seat several feet away from hers.

I was furious, and Derek Tice was on my radar from that point forward.

I WAS BACK A FEW WEEKS LATER, AND SURE ENOUGH, THAT ASSHOLE WAS there again.

I tried to behave, but I got talking to a woman again, and Tice's eyes were on me.

She complained that I was getting too touchy with her, and Tice asked me to leave.

I came back a month later.

It turned out to be my last ever visit.

Tice was there again - didn't he ever get a fucking day off?

Like always, I sat at the bar and started flirting with any woman who sat close.

I bought this woman a few drinks and felt she might be into me. It turned out I was wrong. I saw her talking to Derek Tice and knew this would be trouble.

He approached me and started yelling.

"Don't you see the ring on this woman's finger? She's married. She doesn't want to talk to a little creep like you. This is the third time this has happened."

He nudged my chair, and I fell backward to the ground.

I got up and was tempted to rush him and settle this like men, but I knew nothing good would come of it.

"Fuck you," I yelled instead.

"Get out of here and don't ever come back. You're 86'd."

"Fuck you," I repeated.

"If you come back, I'm alerting the police."

"Fuck you," I said a third time.

I walked out and never returned to that Outback.

But I didn't forget about Derek Tice.

I STARTED GOING TO OTHER BARS WHEN I STAYED IN PISMO BEACH.

I'd try to avoid going to the same one more than once a month. I didn't want to get the same reputation around town that I had at Outback.

I would try to avoid hitting on women. That had always got me in trouble. I was just trying to find out information about Derek Tice. I'd randomly bring up the Outback Steakhouse and see what they had to say.

Sometimes, I'd say I heard they had a jerk for a General Manager and see if that would elicit any response.

Over the next several months, I learned that he was dating a woman named Mary Jane Cushing and eventually heard they had broken up.

FOR SEVERAL MONTHS, I AVOIDED PISMO BEACH.

I tried to have my schedule both start and end in Santa Barbara. I'd asked a lot of questions in that town. It was time to give it a break.

Plus, I was starting to get closer to my first murder, and that took precedence.

ABOUT NINE MONTHS AFTER DOING AWAY WITH HEATHER MCGOWAN, those little demons returned to me. I knew I wanted to kill again. My thoughts naturally returned to Derek Tice.

I'd think back to the day that he pushed me off that barstool. Everyone in the restaurant was looking at me. He was yelling at me. Fuck that motherfucker.

I started returning to Pismo Beach when the opportunity arose, subtly asking questions.

I'd never use people's names directly.

I'd say things like, *'The GM at Outback. Yeah, great guy. What was his girl-friend's name again? I think they had broken up. That sure was sad. What a cute couple.'*

And one day, using that line of questioning, I found out where Mary Jane Cushing worked.

I followed her around after work for a few days, getting her schedule straight.

I returned the following week and did the same.

Mary Jane was at her apartment alone on Mondays and Tuesdays.

On my next trip, I followed Derek Tice home from work. He got off work at six p.m. on Mondays and Tuesdays and went home both times.

I'd made several mistakes when it came to Heather McGowan, and I wasn't going to make them this time.

I knew I had to leave some DNA at the crime scene. I also needed to ensure that Derek Tice didn't decide to leave his house on the night in question. Roy Cooper having an alibi had been a terrible mistake. Of course, without the DNA, he probably never would have been convicted, anyway.

Derek Tice became the first person whose car I attached a GPS Tracker to. It was easy. I'd followed him enough times from work to know which car he drove, and I attached the GPS one night as his car sat in the Outback parking lot.

And the GPS became invaluable in the weeks leading up to the murder.

❧

Four days a week, I was getting off Amtrak in Pismo Beach at two p.m and returning on Amtrak at eight a.m. the following morning.

The other three days, I had off and was driving up to Pismo Beach. I had to make sure I got this right.

Later than I should have, I realized that I was spending too much time in Pismo Beach. If I ever became a suspect, that might be tough to explain away.

So I started camping in Avila, twelve miles north of Pismo, and pocketing the per diem I'd get from Amtrak.

Better not to leave a bunch of credit card receipts for hotel rooms.

And yet, in my heart, I knew I'd never become a suspect. It had been approaching two years since Derek Tice and I had our last argument. How would anybody ever suspect me? Who could ever hold a grudge for that long?

I could. That's who.

I'd mentioned the GPS proving invaluable. Tice left work one day at one. He didn't always take a lunch break but did on this day. I looked at the address he pulled up to, and it was a barbershop. This was my chance.

I wore a hat and sunglasses and drove to the barbershop. I walked by and peeked in to see what chair Derek Tice was sitting in. He was in the second chair on the left, close enough to the front desk for my plan to work.

I waited about fifty feet down the street, never removing my eyes from the entrance. About ten minutes later, Tice left. He headed the other way, and I briskly walked down to the barbershop. I put gloves on, not wanting to contaminate his hair with my skin.

I arrived at the barber shop and made sure my phone, keys, and wallet were all in my left pocket. I asked if I could get a haircut and the guy said the wait would be fifteen minutes.

I grabbed my phone from my pocket and intentionally dropped it near the hair below where Derek Tice had been sitting.

I leaned down and, with my gloves, picked up a small chunk of his hair and cautiously put it in my right pocket.

They had no idea what I was doing. They just figured some idiot had dropped their phone.

I returned my phone to my left pocket and told the guy I'd be back in fifteen minutes.

I never returned.

THE MURDER TOOK PLACE A MONTH LATER.

By now, I had Mary Jane Cushing's schedule down pat. She lived on the bottom floor of a small, two-unit complex and would return at seven p.m. from her job. More than enough time for Derek Tice to find his way there. He left work at six p.m. each day.

Having been a blue-collar guy since childhood, picking locks had been in my repertoire for years. It was a piece of cake. I learned a lot of "skills" growing up.

Mary Jane's upstairs neighbor's car had always been gone until after six, so I broke into Mary Jane's house at five p.m. and waited until she got home.

As with Heather McGowan, I chose strangulation.

Mary Jane Cushing fought intensely but never had a chance against someone like me.

Upon finishing, I took the hair I'd collected from the barbershop and set it between Mary Jane's fingernails.

Obviously, I was wearing gloves the entire time.

I waited until the sun went down and walked out of her apartment and down the street to my awaiting car.

I DIDN'T SET FOOT IN PISMO BEACH AGAIN FOR A LONG TIME.

But I did see Derek Tice one last time. I'd been following his trial on the local news and drove up to San Luis Obispo - where the criminal court was located - when I heard they'd have a verdict the following morning. I wore a bleached-blonde wig that made me look like I had just come from surfing. I sat in the back of the courtroom and started smiling when I heard the verdict.

GUILTY!

I'd committed my second murder. It was infinitely better than my first, and I'd accomplished my goal of framing Derek Tice.

I knew I was only going to get better at this.

BUT NOW, DEREK TICE WAS COMING BACK TO HAUNT ME.

Bobby McGowan was meeting with Rachel Tatum, an attorney who had taken Tice's case. This wasn't good.

I needed to find out more.

Was this just a fishing expedition, or did they have something?

It was time to put a bug somewhere in Bobby's apartment.

I needed to know how far along he was.

Doing this during the day was risky, but I couldn't wait any longer. I didn't want to miss any conversation he was having.

I looked down at the GPS. Bobby was still in Ventura.

I grabbed two bugging devices - I had several - and set off for Bobby's apartment.

50

BOBBY

The rest of Wednesday passed by, with me accomplishing little.

I Googled *'Conrad Drury'* with fifty other combinations but found nothing useful.

I didn't know where to start with him.

My first inclination was to contact either his brother or Roy Cooper. The problem was that both conversations would likely get back to Conrad, which I couldn't risk.

My next idea was to go down to Amtrak and ask to talk to a supervisor. It would be under the guise of looking for a job there, but I'd drop Conrad's name, say he's a friend, and see where the conversation went.

This was also risky. I couldn't exactly tell the supervisor not to say anything. That would only arouse suspicion.

No matter what, I couldn't let Conrad Drury know I was on to him. If our suspicions were true, this guy killed women and framed men for their murder. He was as dangerous as they come.

Being one step ahead of him and not letting him find out we were getting closer was our ace in the hole.

I STARTED ASKING MYSELF SOME QUESTIONS I DIDN'T WANT TO ANSWER.

If I found out beyond a reasonable doubt that Conrad Drury had killed my mother, would I want to tear his eyeballs out? Yes, obviously. Would I want to torture him with some Medieval weapons? Also, yes. But would I? Or would I turn him over to the authorities and let the legal system do its job?

I couldn't decide.

The SBPD had never caught my mother's killer, and Derek Tice and others might have been wrongfully convicted.

I wasn't confident in law enforcement or the legal system.

I LOOKED AT THE CLOCK ON MY NIGHTSTAND.

It was 8:15 on Wednesday night. I'd daydreamed most of the day away.

I'd discovered some potentially earth-shattering news regarding Conrad Drury and hadn't done anything with it; talking to Uncle Rick was the lone exception.

At this rate, maybe I should just turn this over to the cops. I hadn't accomplished shit.

I told myself tomorrow would be different.

I WOKE UP ON THURSDAY MORNING AND GOT THE KICK IN THE BUTT I needed.

The phone rang at 8:30, and it was Rachel Tatum.

"I just got off the phone with Derek Tice," she said.

"What did he have to say?"

"First, I gave him a warning. I told him not to mention a word of this to any other inmate, any friend, not even Evelyn Cushing just yet."

"Smart."

"I told him I was going to mention a name and wanted to know everything he knew about the guy."

"How did he react when he heard Conrad Drury's name?"

"With shock. *Really, that guy?* That was his response. But then, once he got talking, he told me a lot. Apparently, Conrad would often stay in Pismo Beach and frequent the bars and restaurants around town when he did. Derek had started managing an Outback Steakhouse and said he knew the guy was a creep from day one. He was always hitting on the woman near him, giving off an awful vibe. He said he and Conrad had two or three altercations before Derek forever gave him the old heave-ho. Following so far?"

"Yes."

"He told me he'd probably never have thought of him again, but a few people around town told him that Conrad was asking questions about Derek. Conrad was going to other bars and restaurants and name-dropping Derek to find out more information. Derek didn't even know his name when he kicked him out, but people would come and tell him, *'Conrad asked this, or Conrad asked that.'*"

"Sounds like someone you'd remember," I said.

"You'd think so, but this only went on for a month or two, and then silence. He never came up again. Derek said he only remembered the name because he'd met so few Conrads in his life. It stuck with him. He hadn't thought of Conrad in 15-plus years until I told him to write down his long-ago grievances. That's when his name appeared from the recesses of his mind. The dark recesses. I asked him why he'd never considered Conrad until that point. He said he hadn't heard one word about Conrad Drury in the eighteen months that preceded Mary Jane's murder."

"That makes sense. How could anyone think it was some guy avenging a disagreement from that long ago?"

"It lends support to your theory," Rachel said.

"Remind me. I've got a lot of theories."

"That the killer is getting revenge for small grievances, and he's not some archenemy."

"Ah, yes. That theory."

"Derek didn't have much more to add. It's been eighteen years since Mary Jane's murder and probably twenty years since his fight with Conrad Drury."

"Understandable," I said. "Have you talked again to Dale Collier or been able to meet with Norm Unger?"

"Not yet. Hey, what are you doing today?"

"Thinking of ways to investigate Conrad Drury without bringing it to his attention."

"I've got an idea," she said.

"I'm listening."

"How about heading up to Pismo Beach? It's a small town. There's probably only so many bars and Outback-type restaurants."

"I could say, *'It's been twenty years, and who's going to remember anything?'* but sounds like as good a lead as any."

"You'd be surprised," Rachel said. "In small towns, you'll often get bartenders and servers who are lifers."

She was right. Although not strictly a small town, Santa Barbara had its share of lifers in the hospitality business.

"It's a good point," I conceded. "I'll head up there and get back to you tonight."

"Thanks, Bobby. What did your uncle say?"

"That Conrad had always been an odd duck. And when I asked him point blank if he'd be surprised if he were the killer, he said no."

"Wow."

That was all she needed to say.

❧

I LEFT FOR PISMO BEACH AN HOUR LATER AND ARRIVED AT ELEVEN A.M.

I'd been to Pismo a handful of times over the years, but I didn't know it well.

I struck out on my first four destinations. Two were Outback-style eateries, and I checked out two bars as well.

None of the people I talked to recognized Conrad Drury. The two bars hadn't even existed in 2005, but I didn't find that out until I was leaving.

It probably didn't help that the lone picture I had of Conrad was some generic Amtrak photo. I'd also taken a picture of the photo at my house, but he was approximately ten years old. Hardly useful.

I never mentioned Conrad's name. I just showed them the picture. If they recognized him, that would be different.

Once the picture of Conrad failed, I tried to go at it from a different angle, and asked a few of the older employees if they remembered the murder of Mary Jane Cushing. A few of them had, but the ensuing conversation never lead anywhere.

❧

MY FIFTH SPOT WAS HARRY'S NIGHT CLUB AND BEACH BAR.

It was now one p.m., and Harry's had just opened.

A few people I'd talked to told me to go there because Harry's had been around since the 1950s.

I approached the bar, and the woman behind it looked to be in her mid-fifties.

You didn't just tell a woman, *'Hey, you look like you might have worked here twenty years ago.'* That would put me on her bad side right away. So, I had to find a way to ease into the conversation.

I decided to order a beer and tip her disproportionately. Get her on my good side.

I ordered a Sierra Nevada draft, which came to seven dollars. I gave her a $5 tip.

"New to Pismo Beach?" she asked.

"Do you know everyone?" I asked with a smile.

"Been doing this a long time."

She'd given me the opening I needed.

"You don't look like it."

"Are you colorblind, honey? This hair is gray."

"But your skin looks like a twenty-five-year-old's," I said.

She laughed.

"You sure know how to lay it on, honey," she said.

I smiled and said, "I try."

"So what brings you to Pismo?" she asked.

"Alright, since you brought it up, I'll bite. Were you working in Pismo around 2003-2005?"

"I sure was. I've been working here at Harry's since 1999. The place has gone through a few remodels over the years, and I've been here for all of them."

"Did you happen to know a guy named Derek Tice?"

She looked around even though I was the only one in the bar.

"I can do you one better. I knew Mary Jane Cushing."

"Really? How well?"

"Pretty darn well. We'd go to the bars a few times a week in the late 90s. We were both young and cute, and the guys loved us. I stayed friends with her once she met Derek, but for obvious reasons, we didn't go out as much after that."

"What was she like?"

I'd talked so much about Derek Tice and Conrad Drury, and not nearly enough about the victim.

"She was a sweetheart. Would give you the shirt off her back. Didn't have a bad word to say about anybody. All those cliches, but with Mary Jane, they were all true."

I felt terrible. She sounded like a great person. The victims of brutal crimes never get remembered in the way they should.

"Did you think Derek Tice murdered her?"

"No, and I still don't. Nothing you could say would convince me that he did."

I could dance around why I was there, or I could just get down to brass tacks.

"I think you may be correct," I said, deciding on the latter.

"Who are you, exactly?" she asked.

It was my turn to look around and make sure no one was watching. I was still the only one in - or at - the bar.

"I'm working for a lawyer trying to reopen Derek's case."

"Wow. I had no idea. That is great news. What new evidence do they have? Was the DNA not his after all?"

I'd avoided saying Conrad Drury's name to this point, but there was no escaping it now.

"Does the name Conrad Drury ring a bell?" I asked.

She thought about it for a good fifteen seconds.

"I'm sorry. It doesn't."

I grabbed my phone and pulled up Conrad's picture.

"Do you recognize this guy?"

She took another fifteen seconds before she answered.

"I remember that asshole. Didn't he work for Amtrak?"

"Yes."

"He used to come in here. Always creeping people out."

"Did he ever mention Derek or Mary Jane?"

Another pause.

"I know it's been a long time," I added.

"Fucking A!" she yelled. "Yes, he did mention them."

"How can you be so sure?"

"Because I found it weird, and I remember telling Derek about it."

"What did you tell him?"

"I told him some creep had asked about him and Mary Jane."

"How did he react?"

"He didn't seem too worried. He said he kicked the guy out of his bar permanently. 86'd his ass. Derek was a big guy. I'm sure he thought he could protect himself."

"Did you tell Mary Jane about this?"

"No. I didn't feel the need to involve her. Plus, it was Derek's beef, not hers."

"But you're sure that this guy," I said, pointing to the picture, "asked about Mary Jane Cushing?"

"Yes. I'm positive."

"Did he come in here a lot?"

"I'd seen him at Harry's a few times. I probably wouldn't have recognized him if it had been a one-time thing."

"Do you remember if he kept coming in?"

"That gets a little fuzzy, but I don't think so. I would have told Derek he came by again, and I don't remember ever having to do that."

"When Derek was charged with her murder, did you ever think about this guy?'

"No," she admitted. "If memory serves, that was a few years later. Derek and Mary Jane had broken up, and I hadn't thought about that guy in a long time."

When she said 'that guy,' she pointed to my phone.

"Do you think he is the real killer?" she asked.

"We are looking at several other suspects," I said.

"How very diplomatic of you."

I smiled, confirming her suspicions.

"Is there anything else you can tell me about this guy?" I asked. "There's nothing too small."

I'd never sounded more like a police officer.

"Nothing else comes to mind. Two of my old bartender friends who have quit in recent years might have served him as well. They worked in Pismo back then."

"Can I get your number?" I asked. "And name?"

"I'm Kathryn."

"I'm Bobby. Sorry it took so long to introduce myself."

We shook hands.

"Don't worry about it. Usually, if a guy asks me for my name right away, he's up to no good."

She slid me a business card with her number on it.

"I'm sure you've seen it all in this line of work," I said.

"You can get a bad opinion of men if you let it warp you, but I try to stay even-keeled about it."

I liked Kathryn a lot, and not just because she'd helped me out. She was a very engaging woman. Charming as well.

"Will I hear from you again?" she asked.

"If I can tell you anything, I'll be in touch."

"Thanks, Bobby."

"No, thank you, Kathryn. You've been very helpful. And one last thing: Please don't say a word about this to anyone. I'm sure you can understand why."

She "zipped her lips" with her right finger and thumb.

I shook her hand and left my half-finished beer on the bar.

📿

I CALLED RACHEL ON MY RIDE HOME AND RECAPPED MY CONVERSATION.

"This is moving faster than I ever could have imagined," she said.

"Agreed."

"So, what's next?"

"I'll admit, I've tried to keep most of my investigation from the cops. They never solved my mother's murder, and now we've got a bonafide suspect."

"I'm expecting a but..."

"But I think we are going to have to involve them soon. I mean, what exactly can I do with Kathryn's information?"

"I get your point. But shouldn't we dot a few more i's first? Let me at least talk to Dale. Hopefully, get a list from Norm as well."

"That's fine. It's only Thursday. How about we agree to go to the cops on Monday? That gives us the weekend."

"Sure. That's fine. You're going to have a tougher time with the cops than I," she said.

"What do you mean?"

"Well, I have a woman who can confirm that Conrad Drury had a beef with Derek Tice and was also interested in Mary Jane Cushing. All you have is this crazy idea that someone is going around murdering people while framing others."

"You're missing a few things," I said.

"Like what?"

"That Conrad lived in Santa Barbara. That he had a beef with Roy Cooper. And that he knew my mother."

"You're right," Rachel said. "There's more there than I realized."

I was about to say something when Rachel interrupted.

"Listen, I've got to run, Bobby. Heading into court for an unrelated matter. I'll call you tomorrow."

"Okay."

BOBBY

IVY CAME OVER THAT NIGHT.

She wore her work clothes and only had a small bag. I didn't think she was staying the night.

We'd kind of avoided discussing what was going on between us. We'd had sex after returning from The Cliff Room, but we hadn't talked about whether we were officially a couple again.

It was ironic. Ivy had said one of the reasons she'd ended it the first time was because I hadn't been upfront about what I really wanted. And here we were, doing the same thing again.

Maybe we both preferred leaving it as is, without putting a label on it.

We sat on the couch, the monstrous wall of cork boards impossible to ignore. I'd dedicated two months of my life to it, and for the first time, I believed something might come of it.

"How was work?" I asked.

"Boring. And you know I'm here to talk about your day. You're the one who is doing interesting things."

"It only got more interesting today," I said.

"I'd love to hear it."

Ivy's mother was in town the previous night, and they went out to dinner. Due to her mother's irrational hatred of me, I knew I wouldn't get an invite. I didn't lose any sleep over it.

"We have a potential suspect," I said.

"You're freaking kidding me."

I spent the next ten minutes reciting yesterday's meeting with Rachel, our conversation this morning, and my trip to Pismo Beach.

"I'm at a loss for words," Ivy said once I finished.

"So am I. In my wildest dreams, I'm not sure I ever thought it would come to this. I mean I hoped to catch my mother's killer, but I'm not sure I ever truly believed it was possible."

"You seem pretty confident this Conrad person is the guy."

"I've got a feeling, Ivy. A pretty strong feeling."

I'd gotten ahead of myself many times during this investigation - Lyle Taft, anybody? - but this wasn't one of those times. I knew I wasn't thinking crazy. Did that mean that there was a 90% chance that Conrad Drury killed my mother? Of course not, but I thought it might be 50%, which was pretty damn high.

"You know this case more than anyone," Ivy said. "If you believe it, then I believe you."

"I believe it."

"Then you should go to the cops."

"I talked to Rachel about that."

"And?"

"And we decided to go to the cops on Monday."

"What are you attempting to do between now and then? Why not go in tomorrow?"

"You don't understand, Ivy."

"Try me."

I felt like I'd made the same point a dozen times before, usually to myself.

"For twenty years, I've lived with the Santa Barbara PD investigating my mother's murder. Their lone suspect was Roy Cooper, and that was only because he was an ex-boyfriend who stalked her. A blind squirrel could have ID'd him as a suspect. And yet, I stood by the police. I'd even call myself friends with Mark Patchett. But they never were able to accomplish their job. And in two months, I already have the name of a suspect. So sure, I could go to them tomorrow and give them the name of Conrad Drury. And then watch them fuck things up again. Maybe they'd go to his brother or his co-workers, and all of a sudden, Conrad gets wind of this and flees to Europe. Yes, I'm just throwing things out there, but my overall point is that I have zero confidence in the SBPD. I'd like to have a few more days on this myself."

I felt like I was trying to have it both ways. To Rachel, I explained why I thought we needed to go to the cops. To Ivy, I argued against going to them.

Maybe I didn't know the correct answer, so I was arguing both sides.

Ivy gave me a quick hug.

"I understand," she said. "No one has suffered more than you and your family. And no one has put more time into this case than you. But promise me one thing?"

"What?"

"If it gets dangerous, if you think this Conrad guy might be on to you, then swallow your pride and go to the cops."

"I promise you that, Ivy. But don't worry. Conrad Drury has no idea we've identified him as a suspect. From my stupid interviews with KEYT, he probably knows I'm investigating my mother's murder, but that's all he knows."

"Okay. If you say so."

I extended Ivy the offer to spend the night, but she declined.

"I've had a long few days and need some extra sleep," she said.

I looked at her, my face probably showing how tired I was.

"You could probably use a few extra hours as well," she added.

51

CONRAD

I was floored by what I saw when I broke into Bobby's apartment on Wednesday afternoon.

A huge wall - probably twenty-five feet long - all dedicated to the murder of his mother.

I couldn't take my eyes off of it. On the left were old-school family photos, likely because my message about the killer appeared in an old photo album. On the right, there were brief summaries of dozens of murders.

I saw that at least three or four of them were my doing—maybe more.

The wall looked like two sides of the same brain arguing about who had killed his mother. Was it someone from Santa Barbara that she might have known? Or was it a serial killer?

I'll let you in on a little secret, Bobby.

It was both!

I was tempted to write something on the wall.

'You're getting closer.'

Or something similar.

But the truth was, Bobby was getting closer. And bringing attention to myself probably wasn't the best idea.

The more I looked at the wall, the more enthralled I became.

I heard a noise and looked down. I'd received an alert from the GPS that Bobby had started driving north from Ventura, and I knew I had to do my thing and get out of there.

What a shame. I could have spent hours looking at Bobby's creation. Relished in some of those old murders I'd committed.

While I'd decided against something as obvious as writing on the wall, I couldn't just do nothing.

I looked at all the photos and found the one with me, my brother, Ty, his brother, Roy, and Heather.

There were tacks in the upper right and left side of the photo. I removed the tacks and pushed them back into the photo, inserting each one into one of Heather McGowan's eyes. I didn't move the tack around and create a deeper hole. I didn't want to be that obvious.

I then removed the tacks, put them back in the upper left and right of the photo, and tacked it back on the corkboard.

I smiled at my handy work and then installed the two bugs. One, on the bottom end of the coffee table in Bobby's living room. And the second, on the backside of the dresser in his bedroom.

And then I left.

THERE WAS A BRIEF CALL FROM IVY ON WEDNESDAY NIGHT, BUT BOBBY didn't say much. Nothing else piqued my interest that night.

BOBBY WAS ON THE MOVE AGAIN ON THURSDAY MORNING.

This time to Pismo Beach.

He'd received a call from someone I had to assume was the attorney, Rachel Tatum. I could only hear what he was saying, but judging from his reactions, it sounded like Rachel had been describing a conversation with Derek Tice.

Jesus Fucking Christ. Were the walls starting to close in on me?

I was incensed, but there was nothing I could do about it. I couldn't just follow Bobby up to Pismo Beach and sideswipe his car on Highway 101, sending him careening into the Pacific Ocean.

As much as I would have loved to.

CHAPTER 51

I SPENT THE NEXT FEW HOURS THINKING ABOUT PUTTING *PROJECT: Bumfuck, Arkansas* into action.

If not now, when? The longer I stayed in Santa Barbara, the more significant risk I had of getting arrested and spending the rest of my life in some tiny cell.

And I wasn't going to let that happen.

So, the move was already on my mind before I heard Bobby and Ivy's conversation on Thursday night.

But that expedited it.

Bobby said, '*And we decided to go to the cops on Monday.*'

That's when I knew my time in Santa Barbara was coming to an end.

I COULD FLEE TO JASPER, ARKANSAS, WITHOUT KILLING BOBBY AND IVY, but what would be the fun in that?

I wanted a coup de grace, a final statement.

And the fact that it would come full circle - from Heather McGowan to her son, Bobby - just made it all the sweeter.

Sunday was going to be my last day in Santa Barbara—and Bobby and Ivy's last day on earth.

I KNEW MY PLAN TO GET TO ARKANSAS WAS FLAWLESS.

And I knew I could kill Bobby and Ivy before leaving town.

But as far as me remaining anonymous, that cat was currently being let out of the bag, never to be let back in.

Bobby and Ivy knew who I was. And yes, I planned on killing them, but there was also Rachel, Derek, the waitress in Pismo that Bobby had mentioned. Likely some of Rachel's paralegals. Maybe some of her other *Wrongfully Convicted* clients.

And as much as I would have enjoyed it, I couldn't just kill everyone.

Once Bobby and Ivy were dead, the police would hear from Rachel Tatum. My name would be brought up immediately. And then the police would realize I'd fled Santa Barbara.

The local news would pick this up, and once Rachel Tatum mentioned the name Derek Tice and that I might be a serial killer who framed people, my case would be picked up nationally.

Since it was now inevitable that my name would become a household name, I decided to embrace it. I'd resisted it for a long time, not wanting to release my journal until I died.

Screw that. I was now looking forward to the attention.

I'd leave my journal at my house.

They would be the most sought-after set of writings since Ted Kaczynski's manifesto.

THERE WOULD BE INTERVIEWS WITH MY BROTHER. WITH ROY COOPER. With people who worked at Amtrak. Probably with Bobby McGowan's sad old father.

Do you know how neighbors always say the serial killer was a good guy, and they never saw it coming?

There wouldn't be many of those.

I was pretty roundly disliked.

Shit, maybe Victoria Bosco would recognize me and grant an interview. She'd never know how close she was to becoming my next victim.

It was going to be all Conrad all day.

I couldn't wait.

I couldn't wait to be mentioned among the all-time greatest serial killers. I couldn't wait to have Reddit boards dedicated to my exploits. I couldn't wait to have documentaries made about me. I couldn't wait to see my face leading the national news. I couldn't wait to see the photos of Heather and Bobby McGowan next to each other—their own little In Memoriam.

And I couldn't wait to see this all from the comfort of my new home in Arkansas.

Never to be caught.

❧ 52 ❧

BOBBY

I called my father on Friday morning.

I feared that if I visited him, I'd cave and tell him we had a suspect. If Conrad Drury ended up being the guy, my father would be the first to know, but I didn't want to burden him if we were mistaken.

It was my father, and he'd been through too much. I had to be sure.

The less people who knew, the better.

Ivy and Uncle Rick had been the only people I'd told. Come Monday, Detective Patchett would know as well, and that would probably be a good time to tell my father and my sister.

I tried to keep the conversation light with my father. We discussed sports and how he couldn't believe 2024 was coming soon. He mentioned seeing an attractive local news anchor on State Street. I told her he should have said hi to her. Maybe in his younger days, he said. That was a recurring theme with my father. I knew why.

And obviously, he wanted to hear how Ivy and I were doing.

As I got off the phone, I told my father I'd come and visit him Monday at noon.

Ivy was working, so I didn't bother calling her.

Rachel was in and out of court. We touched base a few times, but she had yet to hear new news regarding Dale Collier or Norm Unger.

I wanted to get a better look at Conrad Drury.

I had the picture of him in his Amtrak outfit, but my guess was that picture was taken when he was in his late thirties. Conrad would now be in his late forties.

I tried Googling him for probably the fifth time since discovering his name, but I couldn't find anything useful. I checked to see if his brother Ethan had any social media - maybe get a glimpse of Conrad that way - but found nothing.

I once again considered driving down to Amtrak and walking/asking around. I decided against it. Conrad had surely seen my face, and if he saw me walking around Amtrak, he'd know something was up.

I knew a few bartenders around town. Maybe Conrad had become a barfly in Santa Barbara just as in Pismo Beach. The problem I kept running into was wanting to avoid risking this getting back to him. Going around town, dropping his name, and showing his picture was one sure way to do that.

⁂

By five p.m. in the afternoon, I realized this would be a lost weekend. It was only Friday, but I didn't see myself accomplishing that much over the next few days.

Maybe it would be better to go to the cops sooner rather than later. They had so many more tools at their disposal. They could get a warrant or ask Conrad to come in for an interview.

Assuming they had enough evidence.

It was pretty flimsy if I was being honest with myself. My gut told me Conrad Drury might well be the killer, but I needed more than that if I was to go to the police. The fact that he was mentioned on the lists of Tice, Collier, and Cooper? Interesting, but hardly indicative of a crime. The fact that he asked a bartender about Derek Tice and Mary Jane Cushing? Also interesting, and maybe the Pismo Beach Police would look into it, but it meant nothing with regards to my mother's murder.

The fact that my Uncle Rick wouldn't be surprised if Conrad turned out to be the killer? That would mean next to nothing to Detective Patchett.

Without a clue what to do next, I called my uncle.

"What's new, Bobby?"

"I've come to a standstill," I said. "I was wondering if you know any friends of Conrad's who might talk to me? You must have known some of his old co-workers. And I shouldn't have to say this, but they'd have to be someone you implicitly trust to keep their mouth shut."

"Keep your phone close. I'll have someone call you back soon. I should have thought about him when I saw you the other day."

"Who is he?'"

"Just keep your phone close. You'll find out soon enough."

TEN MINUTES LATER, I HAD A CALL FROM AN INCOMING NUMBER I didn't recognize. It was an 805 area code, that of Santa Barbara's, and I answered the phone.

"Hello."

"Is this Bobby McGowan?"

"Yes."

"This is Adam Bickford. I'm a friend of your uncle's."

"Thanks for calling. How can I help you?

"What did my uncle tell you?"

"That you might have a few questions about Conrad Drury."

"That's correct. How do you know Conrad?"

"I work at Amtrak with him."

"Is that how you know my uncle as well?"

"That's right. Rick used to ride it back in the day. I'd join him and his wild friends for drinks when I could."

"And you said you are stilll employed by Amtrak?"

"Yup. For a few more months. I retire in March after thirty years there."

"Have you worked with Conrad that entire team?"

"Probably twenty-seven of the thirty years, if I had to guess. He joined like two or three years after me."

"Is it mandatory retirement at thirty years?"

"Not mandatory, but I've been there long enough."

I hadn't asked anything too specific about Conrad. I had to ensure that Adam Bickford knew this conversation was not to be repeated.

"Did my uncle tell you this conversation isn't to be repeated to anyone?"

"Yes, he did."

"Okay, good."

"I won't say a thing. I'm not a fan of Conrad's. I think that's why your uncle called me."

I had done enough vetting - probably too much - and it was time to get to the good stuff.

"What do you have against him exactly?"

"Everything. I despise the guy."

"How did you manage to work with him for so long?"

"It wasn't always that way. We got along for probably the first twenty years. It was eight years back when I discovered his true colors."

"How so?"

"I had been dating this gal for a few months back in 2015. I'd been a lifelong bachelor and was starting to think this might be the one. Penelope Chalk was her name. I was out with her one time at a restaurant in Santa Barbara, and Conrad happened to be there on a date as well. He suggested we eat together. I didn't love the idea, but Penelope sounded game, so we became a table of four. Over the course of the next hour, my opinion forever changed on Conrad. Now, I knew that he could be a jerk to Amtrak passengers. He was brief and occasionally rude, but people in our line of work know it can be a pain to deal with passengers, so I looked the other way for the most part. But this dinner date was different. He was condescending to his date. Constantly putting her down. Interrupting her every chance he got. And saying insane things like *Women have too much independence now. Bring the 1950s back.*' Even if you believe bullshit like that, you never say it to a woman on a date. I felt like I was seeing the real Conrad that day. He was a misogynist in every respect."

"I'm assuming it didn't work out between Conrad and this girl?"

"No, it didn't. Conrad saw me on the train a few days later and told me she didn't want to see him again. I wanted to tell him to stop acting like a caveman, and maybe women would take an interest in him, but I didn't. The truth is that Conrad kind of scares me."

"Did you ever see him get physical with a woman or someone riding the train?"

"Technically, no. But I saw him give some passengers an evil stare that could boil water."

I'd never heard that phrase, but his point was obvious.

"Didn't anyone else take notice?"

"You know how every company has a wild card?"

"Sure."

"Well, Conrad was ours. It was almost like we took pride in having him as one of our own. I know that sounds weird."

"No, I get it. Would your fellow employees try to avoid working with him?"

"A few of the women."

I was sensing a trend.

"It sounds like he has a problem with women?"

"I'd say that's more than fair."

"Did you ever suspect him of anything more sinister?"

"That's a tough question. Let me answer it like this. While I never explicitly thought it myself, when your brother called and asked if I'd talk about Conrad, my mind started thinking, '*What the hell did that guy do?*' Does that make sense?"

It reminded me of Uncle Rick's answer about Conrad.

"It makes perfect sense," I said. "Does he have any actual friends at Amtrak?"

"Conrad has acquaintances. I think that's all he's ever really had."

I'd only talked to Adam Bickford for a few minutes, but I trusted him already.

But if I wanted more from him, I'd have to give a little more.

I took a deep breath.

"THERE'S A CHANCE THAT CONRAD MIGHT HAVE BEEN INVOLVED IN some serious crimes up and down the Central Coast. We have nothing concrete. I'd like to say that upfront. But we do have some circumstantial evidence."

"What type of crimes are we talking about?"

"The worst kind," I said and left it at that.

"What do you need from me?"

Mr. Bickford wanted to help. That much was obvious.

"Does Amtrak keep records of what trains and routes employees were on? The cities that Conrad would have been in? The times? The dates?"

"I'm sure it's somewhere in their database, but I wouldn't have access to it."

I decided to go a different route.

"Were there other people at Amtrak who disliked Conrad as much as you?"

"Yeah. A few. Especially Harry Covington."

"Why did Harry hate him so much?"

"He never told me exactly why; I just know that he despised him with every bone in his body. Moreso even than I."

"Is there any way I could talk to Harry?"

"Harry's a pretty private guy, but I could reach out to him."

"Would you trust him to keep quiet?"

"He wouldn't talk to Conrad if they were the last two people on earth. They'd walk right by each other on the train, not even a nod of the head to say hello."

"Point taken. Could you reach out to him for me?"

"Pretty sure he works the graveyard shift on the Pacific Surfliner train every Friday night. I'd rather not bug him while he's working. Could I call him tomorrow morning and get back to you?"

"That would be great. Thanks."

I was ready to get off the phone, but I could tell Adam Bickford wanted to know more.

"Can you be more specific about the crimes Conrad might have committed?" he asked.

"Give me a few days, Mr. Bickford. Maybe I can share more then."

"Understood. Okay, so I'll call you tomorrow after I talk to Harry."

"Thank you for all your help," I said.

"Take care."

I called Rick again and got some background information on Adam Bickford. He sounded like a solid guy I could trust. Rick had never heard of Harry Covington.

At eight, just as I'd thrown on a movie, Ivy called me and asked if she could come over. She sounded like she was in a panic.

"What is it?" I asked.

"I'll tell you when I get there."

IVY ARRIVED TWENTY MINUTES LATER.

She had a bag with her and I could tell she wanted to spend the night. Something had definitely spooked her.

"What is it?" I asked.

"Do you still have that picture of that Conrad guy?"

"What the hell happened? Did he approach you?"

"No, nothing like that."

"What, then?"

Ivy took a deep breath. She looked exhausted.

"Can we sit down?" she asked.

"Of course."

We both sat down on the couch.

"What is it, Ivy? You're scaring me."

"This only occurred to me thirty minutes ago, and I called you immediately."

"What occurred to you?"

"Do you remember our dinner the other night?"

"Of course. Why?"

"Do you remember when that drunk guy approached the other guy at the Oyster Bar?"

"How could I forget? He was loud and drunk as hell."

"What was the first thing he said?"

I tried to remember back. It took a few seconds, and then it hit me. The drunk guy's voice was as clear as day. I now knew why Ivy was in a panic.

"*Conrad, you son of a bitch,*" I said.

It sounded sinister coming from my mouth.

"Yup. That's what I remember, too," Ivy said. "And you know what? The other guy left like a minute later."

"It could have been because the guy was a drunk idiot."

"Maybe. It could also be because Conrad didn't want his name shouted in public."

I didn't say anything as Ivy's words soaked in.

"Conrad isn't a very common name," she added.

I just nodded.

"It's at least possible, isn't it, Bobby?"

"Yes. It's absolutely possible."

"So let me see that picture of Conrad Drury again. The guy at the Oyster Bar was in my line of sight."

I pulled up the picture of Conrad and showed it to her. It was about time I blew up his photo and added it to my wall.

"Well?" I asked.

"I think it might be the guy, but it's hard to know for certain. It's not like I got the greatest look, but the guy had a similar jawline, if that makes sense."

"Yes. It does."

"I know this picture was taken a while back, but I really think it's the same guy."

"This is freaking crazy," I said.

"You looked in his direction, didn't you?"

"Yeah, once the guy started making the scene. I didn't get a great look, though."

I stared at the photo of Conrad Drury for a few seconds. It was probably the tenth time I'd done so, but it was now with different eyes.

I thought back to the dinner. I looked over at the drunk guy and tried to remember the guy behind him. It was only for a few seconds, but I definitely saw him. I thought it looked a bi like the picture of Conrad Drury, but I still didn't trust myself to be the most reliable witness. I wanted it to be him.

"How could he know we'd go to Lure for dinner?" I asked.

"Maybe he found out you were investigating him," Ivy said.

"I don't know how he could have," I said, suddenly sounding less convincing.

"You were on T.V. talking about your mother's murder. If he is the killer, I'm sure he took a serious interest in that."

Fuck. Had Conrad Drury been following me this entire time? Was he the one who was actually a step ahead?

"Possibly," I said.

"What do you mean, possibly? Of course, he'd take an interest in you."

Ivy was right.

"Shit."

"You have to go to the cops, Bobby. There's no other way around it. This guy could be out there, watching your every move. For all I know, he's following me too. Maybe even your Dad."

"Stop," I yelled, a little too forcefully. "Just let me think."

Ivy was right. If Conrad was keeping tabs on us and following us to dinners, things had become too risky.

I'd been looking forward to talking to Harry Covington. Finding out more about Conrad. Maybe that would still happen. But for now, I had to be cautious. I'd brought Ivy into this; she was now potentially in the line of fire. I almost assuredly was. Being cautious was the right move.

"Why don't you stay the night? We'll go to the Santa Barbara police station first thing tomorrow morning. I can call Rachel Tatum on the way."

"Thank you, Bobby," Ivy said. "I know you're making all sorts of progress, but this is the right decision."

I just nodded.

❧ 53 ❧

CONRAD

On Friday morning, I started making final preparations.

I went to my bank and asked to close my account. I had $44,000 remaining, and I asked for it in cash.

I had to talk to a bank teller, an assistant manager, a real manager, and then the general manager, but finally, after enough huffing and puffing by me, they agreed to give me the full amount in cash.

Don't worry; $44,000 wasn't the full extent of my nest egg. I'd been withdrawing approximately $500 in cash weekly for almost a decade and keeping the money secure at my house. I already had about $200,000 stocked away, and with the $44,000, I was approaching a quarter million.

That would last me a long time.

I had always known in the back of my mind that this day was coming, and I'd been prepared.

I was going to need cash. I wasn't going to be writing checks in Bumfuck, Arkansas, that's for sure.

I TOOK THE 44K HOME.

They were given to me in four 10k bricks and one smaller brick of $4,000. I'd also assembled all my previously accumulated cash in bricks. I

286

put all the money in two medium-sized brown duffle bags. They'd be my travel companions in a few days.

❧

I DIDN'T BOTHER CALLING AMTRAK TO QUIT MY JOB. FUCK THEM.

❧

I SPENT THE NEXT FEW HOURS PAINTING MY TRUCK. IT WAS cumbersome but necessary. Sure, I would have a fake license plate on the back, but if things went awry with Bobby and Ivy and I immediately became a suspect, I didn't want law enforcement to know I drove a silver F-150.

I'd now be driving a black F-150, and they'd have no reason to pull me over.

The paint job was shitty, but what did I care? Come Tuesday, I'd never see this car again.

❧

I TOUCHED BASE WITH A GUY FROM EAGLE PASS, TEXAS, WHO HAD A beat-up old 1998 F-150 he was trying to sell. He was okay with an all-cash deal. If necessary, I'd show him one of my fake IDs and tell him I planned to register it under my name. That would never happen.

We agreed to meet on Tuesday at noon in Eagle Pass.

My plan was this.

Eagle Pass was twenty hours from Santa Barbara. I was going to drive nineteen hours, starting at around one a.m. on Sunday night, right after I'd killed Bobby and Ivy. An hour from Eagle Pass, there was a rest stop, and I hoped to arrive there around eight or nine p.m. on Monday night. I'd spend the night at that rest stop.

On Tuesday morning, I would drive into Eagle Pass, leave my truck near the Rio Grande River, and pick up my new truck at noon.

I'd then be off to Jasper, Arkansas, a thirteen-hour drive from Eagle Pass.

Meanwhile, the police would eventually find my car near the Rio Grande River and hopefully assume I'd tried to cross into Mexico.

If everything went right, I'd arrive in Jasper around three a.m. on

Wednesday morning. Perfect. I didn't want the neighbors seeing some stranger driving through their small-ass town. Let them find out who "Wyatt Trimble" was on their own. Hopefully, a few months down the line. Preferably a few years.

⁂

AT 6 P.M., JUST AS THE SUN BEGAN TO SET, I DROVE MY TRUCK OVER TO Bobby's apartment complex.

I drove around three times, deciding on the best place to park my truck in order to make a quick getaway.

There was a little alleyway mere feet from the complex. I could park right on the other side of that, run through the alleyway after I'd shot them, and then be on my way to Texas.

⁂

I RETURNED AROUND SEVEN P.M. AND TURNED ON THE BUG TO HEAR IF anything was happening at Bobby's apartment.

I heard nothing for an hour.

⁂

A LITTLE AFTER EIGHT, BOBBY ANSWERED A PHONE CALL, AND JUDGING from his reaction, I could tell something was up.

It was Ivy, and while I couldn't hear what she was saying, I knew this was bad.

⁂

TWENTY MINUTES LATER, IVY ARRIVED AT BOBBY'S.

She told him about hearing my name at Lure Fish House. I was livid at myself. Why had I decided I needed to get so close? FUCK!!

I feared they were going to call the cops right then and there. If they did, I'd have quickly packed the truck and headed toward Texas.

I prayed that wouldn't happen.

I wanted to kill Bobby and Ivy—the cherry on the Sundae. The symmetry of starting my killing with Heather McGowan and ending with Bobby McGowan appealed to me greatly.

After several stressful minutes, they agreed to wait until the following morning to go to the cops.

I knew what that meant.

Tonight was going to be the night.

My plan had been pushed up by a few days.

There was no way around it.

I PACKED MY TRUCK WITH FOUR GIANT SUITCASES OF CLOTHES, LAYING them on top of the two duffle bags full of cash.

I grabbed the Glock 9mm that I would use to kill Bobby and Ivy and put it in the truck. I also attached a sheath to my belt buckle. I'd be adding a hunter's knife right before I left.

I grabbed my journal and put it on the couch so anyone could see it.

I was looking forward to embracing my infamy.

I grabbed several fake IDs and passports I'd accumulated over the years and put them in one of the duffle bags. I also threw in two burner cell phones I ordered online with a stolen ID and credit card.

I did one last walkthrough of my house, and being satisfied I'd packed everything, I sat down and tried to clear my mind.

A busy mind was the enemy of a serial killer.

I needed some time to prepare for what was to come.

PART OF ME WAS DISAPPOINTED THE MURDERS OF BOBBY AND IVY weren't going to be works of art.

They would be the '*Wam, Bam, Thank You Ma'am*' of murders.

A few quick gunshots that any old thug could accomplish.

My murders had been different. I've painted some masterpieces over the years.

TAKE THE MURDER OF GINNY TOWERS. I KNEW HER BOYFRIEND, Cameron Edding, whom I planned on framing, was a lefty. So when I ended up strangling her, I put more pressure on her neck with my left hand.

I knew it would leave more bruising and make it obvious the killer was left-handed dominant.

Sure enough, this came up at his trial, which I attended in the back row and in disguise. It might have been the most significant factor in convicting Cameron Edding. I still remember the prosecution asking in their closing argument: "How many left-handed serial killers are out there walking around?"

I had to stop myself from laughing.

THE MURDER OF LILY SPECTOR HAD BEEN ANOTHER WORK OF ART.

Her ex-husband, Zed Bellings, smoked Marlboro Reds, so I grabbed a few butts when I followed him - in disguise as always - to a bar one night. It was a week before I was going to commit the murder. I needed cigarettes that looked like they'd been smoked relatively recently.

Zed would go outside every twenty minutes, smoke a cigarette, and then toss it on the ground. I was watching from my car in the parking lot. Once he returned inside, I'd grab the cigarette while wearing gloves.

And after I killed Lily Spector, I dropped two of the cigarettes outside her house.

At Zed Billings's trial, the cigarettes were a huge part of the prosecutor's case. Zed swore he hadn't been to his ex-wife's house in six months, but the cigarettes told a different story.

He was convicted and is now serving life in prison.

THERE WERE OTHERS.

All of my murders - with the exception of Heather McGowan - were works of art in one way or another. I mean, not to toot my own horn, but what other serial killer knows to strangle a woman left-handed or leave cigarettes at the scene of a crime?

No one.

That's why I'm one of the greatest serial killers ever.

And soon be recognized as such.

BEFORE I KNEW IT, IT WAS AFTER MIDNIGHT.

I did one last walkthrough. I'd packed everything I needed.

There was no fond farewell to my home or any bullshit like that. Reminiscing is for the birds, unless you're talking about reliving old murders. Now that's a different story.

I locked up my house and got in my truck.

It was go time.

I started driving toward Bobby McGowan's apartment.

❧ 54 ❧

BOBBY

By ten o'clock, Ivy and I were in bed.

I was asleep within minutes. The last several days had finally caught up to me.

At some point, I was awakened by Ivy leaving the bed. She returned a minute later with a glass of water.

I tried to fall back asleep, but it wouldn't come as easy this time.

I sat awake for thirty minutes.

I looked at my bedside clock. It was 12:30 in the morning. Ivy was now sound asleep.

Was I going to be able to fall back asleep?

About fifteen minutes later, I heard a barely audible noise. I figured it must have come from a neighbor, so I tried once again to fall back asleep.

But then I heard the noise again.

And this time, I knew it was coming from inside the apartment.

55

CONRAD

I circled Bobby's apartment complex two times.

I knew this was my riskiest killing yet, and if the situation wasn't perfect, I could quickly get on the road and never look back.

But the whole Heather/Bobby McGowan connection kept reverberating in the back of my brain. No serial killer had ever accomplished that feat, at least none I'd ever read about. And I'd read about them all.

It was almost one in the morning, but a few lights were still on in the surrounding neighborhoods. Probably a bunch of kids from Santa Barbara City College partying the night away. Luckily, none of the lights in Bobby's complex were on. That would have caused me to abort instantly.

This wasn't going to be like strangling a woman, which I could contain and keep relatively quiet. There were going to be gunshots involved, and despite the silencer on my Glock, people were going to hear it.

Now, if the neighbors were asleep when the shots were fired, it would take them a minute to wrestle out of bed and realize what happened. They might not discern it was a gunshot, and even if they did, they might wait a minute or two, making sure they were positive it was a gunshot they heard. Most people were reluctant to call 9-1-1 unless they knew for certain a crime had been committed.

I decided driving around a third time would look suspicious. Even if the only people awake were drunk college students.

Fuck it. It's now or never.

I chose now.

I PARKED ON THE OTHER SIDE OF THE ALLEYWAY IN THE SPOT I'D chosen the night before.

I reached down and felt my Glock. I also had the hunter's knife in a sheath on my belt buckle if it became necessary. It was certainly quieter than a gun, but it brought about its own risk.

My truck was facing the right direction. I'd have to take Carrillo Street for about a half-mile before I hit the 101 freeway, but I figured it would take the police at least five minutes to get to Bobby's apartment. And that was assuming the neighbors called within seconds of the gunshots.

I was about to leave the truck, but I told myself to take a deep breath first. I'd always said that a calm mind was the friend of a serial killer. My mind was not calm at the moment. This was as nervous as I'd ever been before a kill.

I reminded myself that I could just drive away. Avoid the risk entirely.

But I knew that wasn't going to happen. I wanted Bobby McGowan dead.

I got out of the truck and headed toward his apartment.

I MADE MY WAY TO BOBBY'S DOOR.

I was tip-toeing at this point. I couldn't risk making any noise as I entered his apartment.

And even though Bobby's murder was going to be personal - I couldn't make it more personal than it already was. I couldn't sit there and scold him for re-opening the case into his mother's murder. I couldn't gloat before I shot him. Time was of the essence, especially for this kill.

There was one minor exception to that. I wanted Bobby to see my eyes before I shot him. I wanted him to know that it was me who was ending his life.

I quietly slid my device into the lock and started fidgeting until I heard the click. After an interminable fifteen seconds, I finally heard the click. I opened the door and took a step in.

I'd seen the layout of Bobby's apartment when I broke in to plant the bug. A small set of five stairs led you to the living room on the right. That's where he'd built the shrine to his mother's murder.

On the left was a small kitchen with an adjoining, equally tiny dining room. The bedroom was in the back left of the apartment, and you could get there by walking through the kitchen and then the dining room, or you could go to the right, walk through the living room, and enter the bedroom that way.

I decided to go to the right and through the living room. It was more open, and if by some miracle chance he woke up and tried to attack me, there was plenty of empty space in which to shoot him.

Maybe the blood would splatter all over his investigative wall. Now, that would be perfect.

The kitchen and dining room were a little more claustrophobic and would give him a better chance.

I methodically took the five little stairs that led to the living room. I was wearing lightweight shoes - basically slippers - so as not to make any noise.

I arrived at the top of the stairs and slowly started making my way to the bedroom. I took the Glock out and held it by my side.

I was five feet from his bedroom door.

This would all be over soon.

56

BOBBY

I realized the noise I'd heard wasn't coming from inside the apartment but instead from a key trying to enter my apartment. Someone was trying to break in. And I knew who the fuck it was.

How the hell had it ever come to this? I should have called the police when Ivy told me about Conrad being at the restaurant.

My own stubbornness had led to this.

I rolled over and saw that Ivy was still asleep. I couldn't risk her suddenly waking up and making undue noise, unaware of the situation.

With one hand, I covered her mouth; with the other, I raised a finger to my mouth, telling her to be quiet.

She instantly woke up when I covered her mouth, and I could see the fear in her eyes when she saw my 'Shhhh' sign.

I HEARD THE DOOR OPEN, BUT ONLY BECAUSE IT NOW HAD MY FULL attention.

If I'd been asleep, there was no way I would have heard it. Conrad Drury - assuming it was him - was as quiet as possible.

I considered dialing 9-1-1, but my phone was on the nightstand, and I'd make too much noise getting to it.

THINK, BOBBY!

What could I do? I couldn't just run out of the bedroom and try to rush at him. The living room was too spacious, and he'd see me in a second. I had to assume he was armed, likely with a gun. I doubted double strangulation was his intended mode of murder.

The other route was through the dining room and then the kitchen. There were two doors via that route, so I ruled that out too.

I could take Ivy and hide in the walk-in closet, which was a mere ten feet from my bed. That wouldn't work. Conrad knew we were here. I was sure of it.

He had always been a step ahead of us. I knew that now.

I heard him gingerly walk up the stairs. He was now in the living room.

I stared down at Ivy, putting my finger to my mouth again.

I came up with a makeshift plan.

I moved the comforter to the side and got on my feet, making sure not to make a sound.

Conrad inched closer. He was moving very deliberately and was barely audible. I could tell he was about halfway down the living room wall. He'd wait until we were in sight if he had a gun. He wouldn't risk shooting through the wall.

I moved to within three feet of the bedroom door. I looked down at Ivy. I'd never seen a face more frightened in my entire life.

I couldn't let Conrad win. I'd be dead. Ivy would be dead. My father would ostensibly be dead. And despite our misgivings, my sister would never recover from my death.

My only chance was to rush the door right before he opened it. Hopefully, knock him backward and, in the process, knock any weapon out of his hand.

CONRAD GOT A FEW STEPS CLOSER.

Every second felt like a lifetime.

He was about five feet from the door. I knew I couldn't rush the door too early. If he wasn't directly in front of it, I'd storm through it and be a sitting duck.

He took a step closer.

Did he know I was waiting on the other side? Was the sick bastard enjoying this?

He took another step.

He was now only one or two more steps from the bedroom door.

I told myself to wait as long as I could. The very instant his hand hit the doorknob would be perfect.

He took one more step. I figured his next one would put him right outside the door.

My heart was beating out of my chest.

He took another step, and I heard the slightest readjustment of his feet. I knew then that he was directly outside my bedroom door. I couldn't wait any longer. I had to act now.

With all the strength I could muster, I took one step and extended my arm, slamming through the door.

I could tell instantly that the door connected with someone on the other side. I kept pushing, hoping to send Conrad ten feet back. The door banged against the nearest wall, and I looked out in front of me.

Conrad had been knocked to the ground. There was enough light radiating throughout the apartment to make out his shape.

And then my heart sank.

Even though I'd knocked him several feet back, he still had a gun in his hand.

As he remained seated, he raised his gun and fired at me.

I leaped back into my bedroom just as he fired it and could tell I hadn't been hit.

Ivy was out of bed and screaming at this point. I figured our lone chance was by making enough noise. Maybe Conrad would call it off and flee.

It was highly improbable, but we didn't have many options.

I started screaming as well.

Ivy pointed to the walk-in closet.

As she did, I heard Conrad get off the ground. He was walking back toward the door. He'd be poking his head in any second.

I had a plan, albeit a terrible one.

I grabbed Ivy and moved her toward the walk-in closet. Conrad was going to be in the room in no time, so opening the dining room door would have been futile. And as much as I wanted to rush at him again, I knew that would be signing my death certificate.

So I had to outthink him.

There were approximately three feet on the left of the walk-in closet that you couldn't see very well from outside of it. The walk-in looked long and narrow, but you could potentially hide in that tiny space. Conrad wouldn't be able to see that section in the half-darkness of my bedroom.

He walked through the door. You could see the silhouette of his gun against my bedroom wall.

I grabbed Ivy, pushed her into the walk-in closet, and jumped in myself. I shut the door behind me.

Conrad took a step toward us and then spoke.

"Do me a favor, Bobby. Say hello to that mother of yours. Tell her Conrad has been asking about her."

A split-second later, the room erupted in a chorus of bullets.

༄ 57 ༅

CONRAD

I could sense something as I moved along the living room wall. Bobby was awake. I don't know how I knew; I just did.

But I had a gun, so I had the upper hand.

I continued moving toward the bedroom door as slow and quiet as any human could. Finally, I arrived outside the door.

Maybe I'd been wrong because now I heard nothing coming from the other side.

I was about to open the door when I heard one foot hit the ground, and suddenly the door knocked me backward.

FUCK!

I had been right. That fucking asshole had been waiting for me.

He'd knocked me back probably six feet or so. I looked down. I still had the gun in my hand.

Bobby was standing in the door frame, so I raised my gun and fired at him. I missed him as he dove back into his room.

I was a little groggy. That door had connected with my nose. I felt blood starting to flow from it, but I had no time for that.

At previous crime scenes, where I always worried about leaving DNA, I would have been screwed. Not this time. People were going to find out about me, whether I left my DNA or not.

I stood up. I knew I had to get out of that apartment within seconds.

I'd fired the gun, and it's possible the cops were being called at that very moment.

But I couldn't leave Bobby and Ivy alive. This had to come full circle. Heather McGowan to Bobby McGowan.

I walked into their bedroom just as Bobby pushed Ivy into a walk-in closet. He dove in after her.

His bedroom was pretty dark, but enough light was making its way in that I could see into the walk-in. It was long and narrow. There was nowhere to hide.

Bobby shut the door.

I had to get the fuck out of there, but I couldn't leave without letting Bobby know I'd won.

So I said the most evil thing I could come up with.

"Do me a favor, Bobby. Say hello to that mother of yours. Tell her Conrad has been asking about her."

I then emptied the rest of the gun into the walk-in closet and quickly ran to the door. I didn't hear even a whimper as I left the room. Maybe the bullets had hit them in the head, and the end had been swift.

I was half-expecting the police to be waiting outside Bobby's apartment, but luck was on my side.

I ran down the alleyway, got in my truck, and drove away.

I heard sirens getting closer.

When I was a block down the road, I looked in my rear-view mirror and saw three Santa Barbara police cars - lights blazing - park on the street.

They got out of their cars and ran toward Bobby's complex.

None were headed my way.

⚜

I took Carrillo Street down to Highway 101 and started heading south.

At the third exit, Milpas Street, I exited the freeway and parked in a dark area I'd already surveilled.

Just in case some neighbor had seen me driving away and taken down my license plate number, I needed to change it.

I went to the back of the car and switched license plates. I got back on the freeway and started my long drive toward Eagle Pass and the Rio Grande River.

I was on my way to a new life, and Bobby McGowan was dead.
Life was good.

THE DRIVE TO TEXAS WAS LONG AND NERVE-WRACKING.

I'd done all I could to limit the chances of getting caught, and I think I'd done a bang 'em-up job. But you never knew, so every time a cop passed me on the freeway, I tensed up.

I'd packed one of my many disguises and was wearing a hat with the long, curly black wig flowing from the back of it. It was my go-to disguise.

I DROVE FIVE TO FIFTEEN MILES ABOVE THE SPEED LIMIT FOR THE NEXT nineteen hours. I knew that I'd never get pulled over, even at 75 mph in a 60-zone.

I can't even tell you all the freeways I was on over the course of the day.

101. 134. 210. 10. 202. 10 again. 285. 90/Texas Loop 79. A few others I'm missing.

One of my burner phones guided the way with its GPS. I assumed there was no way the police would ever be able to track down a burner phone I bought with a fake credit card, but I was still going to ditch the phone once I got to Eagle Pass.

I'D LEFT SANTA BARBARA A LITTLE AFTER 1:00 A.M. ON SATURDAY AND arrived at the rest stop an hour outside of Eagle Pass at eight p.m. on Saturday night.

In that time, I stopped three times for gas. I also called my guy in Eagle Pass to see if we could push up our meeting to Sunday. He said that was fine.

I LEFT THE REST STOP THE FOLLOWING MORNING AT EIGHT A.M.

I drove into Eagle Pass, knowing my first destination would be a gas station about two miles from the Rio Grande. I'd planned this out to the tee. I wanted the truck to be found, but I wasn't going to leave it fifty feet from the Rio Grande River. I couldn't be that obvious.

I wanted the cops to conclude that I had fled to Mexico. I just wasn't going to serve it up on a silver platter.

I approached the gas station I'd found online. It had seen better days and was perfect for what I wanted. There was a large parking lot out back where I could leave my truck, but I worried the lot was too big and my truck might never be found. On the other hand, if I left my truck in one of the three parking spots out front, it would look like I wanted it found.

I decided on the larger parking lot.

I changed out of my disguise. For my next act, I wanted to look like me, and I hoped they had a camera.

It was time to leave an impression.

"Howdy," the man said as I entered the gas station.

He was wearing a monster belt buckle that his gut protruded over. He also had on a ten-gallon hat. I'd officially arrived in Texas.

"I've got a few questions for ya," I began. "Where do those Mexicans cross that Rio Grande River?"

"You ain't going to shoot them up, are you?"

He gave me a big smile.

"No, nothing like that. Just wanted to see it with my own two eyes."

He told me the best location.

I bought a backpack, loads of food, a cowboy hat, and some toilet paper.

He looked me up and down.

"You almost look like you'd be trying to cross that river yourself. Remember, you're already on the good side."

I laughed loudly. I was trying to do everything I could to make sure this guy would remember me.

"Ain't that the truth," I said, entirely too loud.

I started walking out and was delighted to see a video camera mounted above the door.

I RETURNED TO MY TRUCK AND CHANGED CLOTHES.

I also put back on a new wig - short blond this time - and some reading-type glasses. I was conservatively dressed, and nothing stood out.

Unlike the gas station, I was not trying to bring attention to myself for what was next.

This was the riskiest part of my entire plan.

But I didn't have a choice.

I couldn't just fly to Arkansas, and taking a bus or hitchhiking carried their own risks.

This was the only way.

I WALKED A HALF-MILE AWAY TO THE HOUSE OF DELMUT REED.

No cabs. No Ubers. The only impression I wanted to leave in Eagle Pass was at the gas station.

The house was a dump, with six beaten-down cars in his dirt-filled driveway. Trash was littered everywhere.

"You must be Tim Miller," he said.

Delmut looked to be about seventy and had a thick Texas accent. Like the gas station attendant, he wore a ten-gallon hat, but Delmut's had much more wear and tear.

"I am," I said.

"You ready to do this?"

"Sure am."

We walked over toward the set of cars.

"You said you want to do a cash transaction, correct?" he asked.

"Yeah. Easier for me, thanks."

"No problem. I'm fine with that."

I just nodded.

"This truck has seen better days, I'll tell you that," he said.

"I don't care," I said. "Just need a backup car."

"You'll still have to register it, you know. And get some insurance."

"I know. I'll register it first thing in the morning. And I'll just add it to my insurance."

"Good deal. And I'll need to see your driver's license as well."

I showed him the license of Tim Miller. I didn't think I looked much like him, but Delmut Reed couldn't have given two shits.

He handed it back. I wasn't even sure he'd glanced at it.

"Just protocol, you hear."

"No problem," I said.

He pointed to the truck in question. It would be the second F-150 I drove today. Only this one was from 1998 and was approaching 200,000 miles on it.

"The blue book on this thing is $3,400, but I told you I'd give it to you for three."

"Thank you, sir," I said.

I took out my wallet, where I'd folded $3,000. I handed it over.

He counted the money and then handed me the keys.

"It's that easy," he said. "Be sure to get that registration switched over to your name, Tim."

"No problem."

"Pleasure doing business with you," he said.

We shook hands, and he walked away.

I got in the truck, started it up, and returned to the gas station.

I CIRCLED THE PARKING LOT, ENSURING THEY HAD NO CAMERAS.

I didn't see any. There was only the one inside the gas station itself.

I parked my "new" F-150 next to my "old" F-150 and transferred my duffle bags and everything else I needed.

I looked at the gas gauge, and Delmut Reed had filled her up for me.

Thanks, Delmut.

A minute later, I was on the road to Arkansas.

THAT DRIVE TOOK THIRTEEN HOURS, AND I MADE TWO MORE STOPS.

The first stop was just for gas.

For the second stop, I needed some food. I didn't plan on leaving my new house for a few weeks, so I needed to stock.

When I was an hour outside of Jasper, I found a Safeway that said it was open twenty-four hours.

I didn't want to get my groceries too close to my new city. An hour felt far enough away. I put on my long dark wig and hat back on.

There was a plump woman behind the register. I didn't see anyone else working, and I only saw two other customers in the store.

It was one in the morning at this point, so it made sense.

I picked up some frozen food, cereal, rice, pasta, and more.

I approached the check-out, and the hefty woman smiled at me.

"Nothing better than Cheerios at one in the morning," she said.

I smiled.

"The best."

"I've never seen you here before. Mostly regulars shop here."

"Just passing through," I said.

"That's too bad."

I looked at her name tag, which read Peggy. She was only about thirty but had been burdened with an old lady's name.

"I'll come back and visit, Peggy."

"What's your name?"

"Tim. Tim Miller."

"You sound like James Bond."

I didn't tell her that Bond says his last name first. I'm not sure it would have registered. I didn't think Peggy was all that bright.

She finished bagging the groceries, and I paid in cash.

"See you next time, Tim Miller," she said.

"You can count on it, Peggy."

❦

I DROVE THE REMAINING HOUR TO MY HOUSE IN JASPER.

Actually, it was now a home. It would be lived in for the first time since I bought it.

It was after two a.m. when I arrived in Jasper. Like everything else, this had been planned. I didn't want anyone to see me driving around town.

I made my way to my place.

The closest neighbor's house was pitch black. It was two in the morning, but it almost looked uninhabited. Hopefully, it was.

I parked my new/old F-150 in front of the house.

It was a time for new beginnings.

Just to be safe, I switched the license plate on the F-150 from Texas to an Arkansas one I'd acquired a few years back.

I entered my new home and put the groceries away.

Continuing to pay for cable and electricity had been a smart move. I could refrigerate the food and avoid the cable guy.

I didn't like the idea of visitors. Certainly not now, and maybe not ever.

I put the groceries away and made my way to a recliner I'd set in front of the television. I turned on the TV, eager to see if the murders of Bobby and Ivy had made the national news.

And if so, had I now become famous?

🦋 58 🦋

BOBBY

As soon as I shut the walk-in closet door, I pushed Ivy against the wall. I slid next to her and tried to curl into a ball. The less mass to be hit, the better. It was dark in there, so I wasn't sure if Ivy had followed my lead.

I could feel her next to me, and I covered her mouth. No matter what happened, we couldn't have Conrad Drury thinking we survived. We had to remain silent.

I knew he was about to shoot at us.

A split-second later, the shots rang out.

By some miracle, I wasn't hit.

My hand remained on Ivy's mouth, but I could tell she wanted to cry out. I don't think she'd been as lucky as I.

A few seconds later, I heard Conrad running across the apartment and listened to the door shut behind him.

I removed my hand from Ivy's mouth.

"Were you hit?" I asked.

"Yes."

I kicked open the door to the walk-in, and a small amount of light flooded in. I could see Ivy's blood on the ground.

"Fuck," I yelled. "Where did it hit you?"

"I think in the leg. The thigh."

I stood up and turned on the light in the walk-in. There was blood all over the floor, and Ivy was bleeding from her thigh. If it had hit her femoral artery, she could die within minutes.

"I'll be right back. I need to call 9-1-1."

I ran and grabbed my phone from the nightstand by the bed.

"9-1-1, what's your emergency?"

"My friend has been shot. Her name is Ivy Harrington. Please send someone right now."

"What's your address?"

I gave it to her.

"And who shot her?"

"His name is Conrad Drury. You should put an APB out on him right now."

"Did he drive away?"

"I don't know. I think so."

"What does he drive?"

"I have no idea. Listen, I have to get back to Ivy. Send someone right now."

I walked back over to her.

If the bullet had merely entered and exited her leg - a through-and-through - she'd almost assuredly survive. It would likely be a different story if it had hit the femoral artery.

"Do you need anything?" I asked.

"No. Just hold my hand."

I did.

"I don't think I'm cut out for this kind of work," Ivy said.

I smiled. I was shocked she was trying to crack a joke after being shot. I took it as a good sign.

"You saved our lives by pushing us into the walk-in."

I put my arm on her shoulder.

"Let's save our breath until the paramedics get here."

THEY ARRIVED THREE MINUTES LATER.

With the police in tow.

I heard them coming and met them at the front door.

"Follow me. Quick," I said.

I showed them Ivy, still lying down in the walk-in closet. I'd been afraid to try and move her.

"She was shot in the thigh. I'm worried about the femoral artery," I said.

"We've got it from here," one of them said and slightly nudged me out of the way. Three of the EMTs converged on the walk-in.

A few seconds later, as I looked on in fear, I got a tap on my shoulder. I recognized the man's face.

"I'm Colin Davidson, Santa Barbara PD. You told the dispatcher that someone named Conrad Drury shot your girlfriend."

"That's right."

"Why did he do this?"

"Because he killed my mother, and I was investigating him."

"I don't understand," he said.

"Call Detective Patchett. He will."

He ignored that.

"Do you know how Mr. Drury fled? Was he on foot or driving?"

"I have no idea," I said.

"And I'm going to assume he is still armed?"

"Yes. He took the gun with him."

"What were you saying about your mother?"

"My mother's name was Heather McGowan. I'm sure you've heard of the case."

That registered with him.

"Oh, shit. You think this Conrad Drury fella was involved?"

This officer was driving me up the wall.

"Yes," I said.

"Why do you think that?"

"It would take an hour to explain, and if you want to catch him, you don't have that kind of time."

Officer Davidson shrugged.

"Fine. How did Mr. Drury get in the apartment?"

They were starting to put Ivy on a gurney.

"He broke in. Listen, I'll answer these questions at the hospital if you want, but I'm following her to the hospital."

"Okay. We'll talk there."

"Can I go in the ambulance?" I asked.

Officer Davidson looked at me.

"We'll give you a ride."

❦

Ivy was being taken to the Santa Barbara Cottage Hospital.

I got a ride from Colin Davidson in a Santa Barbara police car.

They shuttled Ivy into an operating room, and I was not permitted in.

Davidson saw the opportunity and asked me if I'd answer more of his questions. While I didn't like the guy, catching Conrad was the most important thing, and I knew more about him than anybody.

"Sure, I'll answer any questions you've got," I said.

❦

I'd spend most of the next few hours either being interviewed by the police or checking on Ivy's status.

She'd been shot two times in the thigh, but both bullets had managed to avoid her femoral artery.

She was very lucky.

They kept telling me I'd have to wait a while longer to go in and see her.

It was like a broken record every time I asked.

❦

Detective Patchett showed up about thirty minutes after I arrived at the hospital.

It was his turn to start asking me questions. Colin Davidson faded into the background with some of the other cops.

I heard one of them mention my mother's name. If word got out that this circled back to her, this would become a huge story.

Detective Patchett looked exhausted. I'm sure he'd been woken up in the middle of the night once the SBPD heard that it might involve my mother's case.

"What the fuck happened, Bobby?" he asked.

I was tired and angry, so I wasn't very diplomatic with my answer.

"I found something you guys never could. The man who killed my mother," I said.

It came off as unnecessarily cruel.

"I'm sorry," I said. "You didn't deserve that."

Patchett waved his hand.

"This is a scary scenario. I don't blame you for being mad. Is Conrad Drury Ethan's brother?"

"Yes, he is. Have you put out an APB on him?"

"Yes."

"Anything yet?"

"No. Listen, I want to hear all you know about Conrad. Anything you got might help us catch him."

I spent the next twenty minutes updating Detective Patchett on all I'd learned. I told him about Rachel Tatum, Derek Tice, Dale Collier, and Conrad's potential for framing people.

I'm sure he was pissed I'd never given him this information, but he didn't bring it up.

As our conversation neared an end, a nurse came over and tapped me on the shoulder.

"You can see Ms. Harrington now."

⚜

IVY WAS MORE UPBEAT THAN SHE HAD ANY RIGHT TO BE.

She'd been shot two times and would surely have some permanent scars.

"It's better than the alternative," she said.

She had multiple tubes going in and out of her leg, but they'd let me into the room, so I knew it wasn't life-threatening.

I looked at the digital clock on the wall. It read 3:30 a.m. It had been about two and a half hours since she'd been shot.

"Did they catch him yet?" Ivy asked.

"You just worry about your health right now," I said.

"C'mon, Bobby. You can at least tell me that."

"No, they haven't caught him yet. At least, not that I've heard. I'm not exactly in the loop."

As I said that, I heard a voice behind me. I recognized it as Ivy's mother.

She was crying and came to Ivy's side and started hugging her. After a minute, she looked over in my direction.

"What the hell are you doing here?" she yelled at me. "I heard this lunatic was after you, but it's my daughter who got shot."

I was taken aback.

"Mom, stop," Ivy pleaded.

I wanted to be mad, but it's not like anything she said was incorrect.

Conrad Drury was after me, but it had been Ivy who had been shot.

If I were her mother, I'd be furious too.

Most importantly, me and her mother arguing was the last thing Ivy needed, so I took the high route.

"I'll leave. You guys can talk."

I walked out of the hospital room, still shaken by Ivy's mother's words.

⚜

IVY'S FATHER HAD ARRIVED, AND HE WAS NO MORE POLITE THAN IVY'S mother.

He had seen me talking to an officer and gave me a pissed-off stare.

I decided it was best to avoid them.

Ivy would understand I was only acting in her best interest.

⚜

BY THE TIME 5:30 HIT, I DESPERATELY WANTED TO GO HOME, BUT Patchett told me my apartment was still a crime scene.

"Why aren't you there?" I asked.

"I'm no longer the detective du jour. That's a young guy's gig these days."

It was just as I suspected and why I always met Patchett at the precinct. He was now, for all intents and purposes, a desk jockey.

"What time will I be able to return to my apartment?" I asked.

"I'll let you know."

⚜

MY FATHER WAS AN EARLY RISER, SO I LEFT THE HOSPITAL AND DROVE to his place.

I saw a light on, and he answered the door after my second knock.

"You're scaring me. Why the hell are you here at six a.m.?" he asked.

I went into the house and explained everything.

He was overwhelmed.

After asking all the requisite questions about Ivy and me, he brought up Conrad Drury.

"So this guy killed my wife?" he asked.

"I'm almost certain of it. He said something to me that cemented it."

"What did he say?"

"You don't want to know, Dad."

"Tell me."

"Okay, He said something like, '*Say hello to that mother of yours. Tell her Conrad Drury has been asking about her.*'"

My father bowed his head. When he looked up, all I saw was rage.

"He's lucky I wasn't there. I would have gouged his eyes out with a spoon," my father said.

I'd never heard him so incensed.

"I wish I could have," I said. "But he had a gun. I was at a slight disadvantage."

"I'm not blaming you, Bobby. You've done more than I ever thought possible."

He started to cry.

"I can't believe you found your mother's killer. I can't wait to see this guy rot in jail. I'll be at his trial, sitting in the front row. Do you think they will catch him today? I'll bet he'll be in custody by noon."

Only Conrad Drury didn't end up in custody that day.

Or that week.

Or in the month that followed.

❧ 59 ❧

CONRAD

I was getting used to my new surroundings.

I liked working in the yard and spending time outside. A five-acre lot left a lot to explore.

A few tools had been left in the garage - including an ax - and I used it to cut down some small trees.

I'd planned on building something.

A small room with sound-proofed walls.

❦

WHAT I LOVED MOST WAS WATCHING THE NEWS AT NIGHT. I HAD become a bonafide celebrity.

Infamous, to be sure, but still a celebrity.

It's not like serial killers can't be celebrities.

There are too many examples to list.

Bundy. Gacy. Rader. Drury.

❦

ON THAT FIRST MONDAY NIGHT AT MY NEW PLACE, A MERE THREE DAYS after breaking into Bobby McGowan's apartment, I led ABC's national news coverage.

Yes, I was still kicking myself that Bobby remained alive, but I couldn't do anything about it. Maybe far down the road, he'd see me again, but not now.

The incident at Bobby's apartment was not why I'd made the news, but it did kickstart it. A break-in where a woman is shot in the leg wouldn't garner the lead on your local news, much less the national.

What had propelled this case into the stratosphere were two things.

One, the journal found at my home. And two, Rachel Tatum.

I don't know how my journal was leaked to the media, but that created the shitstorm of all shitstorms.

You can understand why.

I'd outlined my nine murders, going into glorious detail on each one. I then described six cases in which I'd tried to frame someone for murder. And in five, the person had been convicted of that murder. Roy Cooper being the lone exception.

Yes, the media was repulsed by my actions, but there was some under-lying amazement at what I'd accomplished.

And that wasn't just me wanting to read that into it.

Here are a few examples I've heard.

"Yes, this Conrad Drury is clearly a monster, but you almost have to be astounded at what he accomplished. The fact that he's potentially been doing this for twenty years is unbelievable."

That anchor later had to apologize for using the word "accomplished."

"I can't believe that Conrad Drury has avoided detection this long. I hate to say it, but he's been a step ahead of the police this whole time. Assuming this is all true."

It was funny to hear them say things like, 'potentially' and "Assuming this is all true.' They had my journal. This wasn't hearsay.

So, while my journal had caused the most uproar, Rachel Tatum was also helping fan the flames. And I loved her for it. She was out there spouting to anyone who would listen. She'd mention Derek Tice and Dale Collier every time she could. At least she'd gotten those two right.

Then she mentioned a guy named Norm Unger a few times. I couldn't help but laugh because I'd never met a Norm Unger in my life and certainly hadn't framed one for murder.

MY CASE MUST HAVE HIT A NERVE WITH THE AMERICAN PEOPLE because, after my initial appearance on ABC's Nightly News, I was on

CHAPTER 59

NBC, CBS, CNN, FOX, and even the local Arkansas news in the days that followed.

The first few days' reports were rooted in the fact that I might be a serial killer. Then, it got out that I might have been framing others for my murders. So that became all anyone could talk about for a few days.

The fact I was still on the loose almost took a back seat. I was shocked. America usually loved hearing about a bad guy who hadn't been caught.

D.B. Cooper and The Zodiac came to mind

꧁꧂

I'D HEARD A FEW NICKNAMES THROWN OUT THERE, BUT NONE HAD stuck.

"The Serial Framer. Drury the Devil. The Devil Incarnate. The Amtrak Assassin. Conrad the Con."

None were good, and some were downright terrible.

I mean, *The Amtrak Assassin?* Come on.

꧁꧂

TWO WEEKS LATER, I HEARD THE FIRST MENTION OF MY TRUCK. Finally!

It was about ten minutes into the national news. I wasn't the lead story anymore, but I still appeared almost nightly. America couldn't get enough of me.

A Texas Ranger was being interviewed, and he said they'd found my truck at a gas station in Eagle Pass, Texas.

The anchor said that Eagle Pass, and specifically the Rio Grande River, were well-known places where immigrants illegally crossed into the U.S.

"Could Conrad Drury have been doing the unthinkable?" the anchor asked. "Escaping the U.S. by crossing into Mexico?"

The police and the media were falling for my plan, hook, line, and sinker. This couldn't get any better.

Only it could get better. The next interview they showed was with the gas station attendant wearing the ten-gallon hat, and it was an all-timer.

"Yeah, Mr. Drury asked me where them Mexicans cross the Rio Grande. I knew right then and there he was going across the border. He didn't fool me one bit, no sir. I even made a joke that he was already on the good side. You see, I've done some stand-up comedy in my life.."

The reporter's expression showed she didn't know how to respond.

I laughed out loud.

For a man who'd committed the ultimate atrocities, I was way too happy with my new life.

Bobby McGowan would be infuriated if he knew how great I currently had it.

THE FOLLOWING NIGHT'S NEWS REPORTED THAT THE F.B.I. WAS NOW working with Mexican authorities to try and track me down.

The anchor closed with this: "The Mexican authorities have agreed to extradite Mr. Drury back to the United States once they apprehend him."

I almost spilled the cereal I was eating.

Which reminded me that it had been almost ten days since I'd last visited that Safeway. I'd gone twice now; Peggy had closed me out both times. We had some pleasant discussions. She was the only person I'd talked to since starting my new life.

She could stand to lose thirty pounds or so, and she was not very pretty, but there was an innocence to her that I found appealing. Not for the right reasons, mind you.

IT WAS TIME TO PAY HER ANOTHER VISIT.

My demons were circling and might have to be fed soon.

And the best part was that this time, it wouldn't have to be a quick murder.

I had privacy now. I had five acres of land.

I was building a sound-proof room.

And I had a few ideas of how I could put it to good use.

I'll be seeing you soon, Peggy.

❦ 60 ❦

BOBBY

The weeks that followed were not kind to me.

Five days after the incident at my place, it was the 20th anniversary of my mother's death. I didn't even call or text my father or sister. There was still too much going on.

IVY'S PARENTS MADE IT CLEAR THAT I WAS PERSONA NON GRATA. I imagine they would have felt this way no matter what, but the fact that Conrad Drury was still out there probably only furthered their conviction.

I guess I couldn't blame them.

If my daughter had been shot by a guy who was still out there, I wouldn't want her hanging with the guy who the shooter had it in for.

They allowed me to come by Ivy's apartment and say goodbye to her. She was released from the hospital after two days and had now been recuperating at her apartment for a week, her mother never leaving her side.

"I'm going down to my mother's in Los Angeles for a few months," she said.

"Is this what you want or your mother?"

"Her for sure. And you know what, maybe me too. Conrad is still out there, Bobby. Maybe he's not in Mexico, like everyone is saying. And I mean, I hate to remind you, but he knows where you live. It's probably best we go our separate ways for a while. You don't know how scared I was that night."

I'd seen her eyes when I woke up. I knew how frightened she was.

"I understand," I said. "Do you think you'll move back?"

"If I do, it won't be until they catch that psycho. Plus, our company has a branch in Los Angeles."

That was her way of telling me she wasn't coming back.

"I don't know what to say, Ivy."

"It's not your fault, Bobby. I know that. I was the one who got interested in your investigation, and I just happened to be in the wrong place at the wrong time. I don't blame you one bit."

I heard her mother make some noise in the back. She was suggesting we wrap this up.

"What about us?" I asked.

"Let's be honest, your mind will be elsewhere until Conrad Drury is caught. It's better if we go our separate ways."

"Okay, I'll respect your decision," I said.

I could hear her mother take a step closer. I looked back and was greeted by her requisite snarl.

"We've got somewhere to be, Ivy," she said.

"Was good to see you," I said. "Don't be a stranger."

"Take care, Bobby," Ivy said.

I gave her a hug.

Were we really ending like this?

It sure seemed that way.

THE OTHER ELEPHANT IN THE ROOM WAS UNMISTAKABLE.

They hadn't caught Conrad Drury.

While my brain told me he was far from Santa Barbara, my synapses hadn't caught up yet. Whenever I heard a loud noise, or someone appeared around a corner, my heart rate went through the roof.

The common belief was that he'd fled to Mexico, at least amongst news media, which ran with the story of him leaving his car a few miles from the Rio Grande River.

Police deduced he drove from Santa Barbara to a rest area an hour outside Eagle Pass, Texas. The following day, he drove into town, and there has been no trace of him ever since. The guy at the gas station where Conrad's car was found seems to be the last person to interact with him.

That guy sure was a piece of work.

❦

KEYT AND THE NATIONAL NEWS CALLED ME SEVERAL TIMES, ASKING for interviews.

I turned them down each time.

I'd wanted to find out who killed my mother, which I had accomplished.

Now, I wanted to find out where he was.

So unless they had information on Conrad's whereabouts, I didn't have any use for them.

❦

THE *SANTA BARBARA NEWS-PRESS* WOULD NOT BE CALLING ME.

I'd found out that they went under.

They had to file for Chapter 7 Bankruptcy and hadn't even alerted their employees that their closing was imminent.

Another newspaper bites the dust.

❦

I DECIDED TO RESURRECT MY INVESTIGATION.

It had never died completely, but it had been on life support.

It was now a different investigation altogether. Initially, I was trying to find out who killed my mother. Now, I was trying to find out where that man had fled to.

Police in Santa Barbara and Texas were out there looking for Conrad Drury. So was the F.B.I.

And now, I would be too.

❦

I TALKED TO RACHEL TATUM ALMOST EVERY DAY.

She had secured new court dates for Derek Tice and Dale Collier.

She was confident that they'd be released from jail soon.

"Norm Unger wasn't in Conrad's little book, was he?" I asked.

"No, he wasn't. He's no longer a client."

"That must have been awkward."

"You don't want to know. Norm showed his true colors. Called me some names I'd never heard before."

"I'm sorry."

"Thanks," Rachel said.

"How is Evelyn taking all this?"

"She's happy about the new court date for Derek Tice and being proven right about his innocence. On the other hand, her daughter's killer is out there, running free. She doesn't like that one bit. You know what she asked me?"

"What?"

"If Conrad was now going to come after her."

"Why would she think that?"

"She said, '*Well, he went after Bobby McGowan after killing his mother. Maybe he wants to kill me since he already killed my daughter.*'"

"That's horrible, " I said. "Tell her it was an isolated incident and only happened because I was investigating him."

"I'll tell her, but I'm not sure that will set her mind at ease."

"This is so fucked up. Why can't they catch this guy?"

"He was probably meticulous in planning his escape. Just like he was with his murders."

I didn't want to give Conrad Drury any credit, so I just said, "I'll call you soon, Rachel."

◈◈◈

AFTER TWO WEEKS OF PESTERING HIM, MARK PATCHETT FINALLY GOT me a copy of the latest police reports.

I arrived at the police station, and he was waiting for me right outside the entrance.

"Here are our reports, Bobby. I shouldn't have to tell you this, but don't share these with anyone else."

"I won't."

"Do you think he's in Mexico?" Patchett asked.

It seemed to be the question on everyone's mind.

"No," I said.

"Why not?"

"If you're fleeing to Mexico, why go make an impression on some hill-billy gas station attendant so everyone now thinks you really are going to Mexico?"

Patchett nodded.

"It's a good point. Keep in touch, Bobby."

And with that, he walked away.

Had he not considered that?

With every passing day, I believed I'd be an above-average cop.

And I meant at this very moment, with no training whatsoever.

I APPROACHED ETHAN DRURY'S HOUSE ONE DAY. IT HAD BEEN THREE and a half weeks since his brother had fled Santa Barbara.

He was in the back of his house, and upon seeing him, I opened the back gate and walked in uninvited.

"No, no, no. You can't be here," Ethan said.

"I'm breaking in just like your brother did to my place. And many other women's houses who would suffer a far worse fate."

He didn't have a response to that.

"What the fuck do you want?" he asked.

"I have two questions."

"Fine. What are they?"

"Do you know where Conrad is?"

"I have no clue. That's the God's honest truth."

"I figured that was the case. Now, my second question. As I'm sure you heard, Conrad contacted me via the website I'd set up. What hasn't become public knowledge was that he referenced my family photo albums."

"That's not even a question."

"I'm not done. Pay attention. Your brother claimed that he knew he was in a photo in one of my parents' albums. How could he have known that?"

A smirk slowly appeared on Ethan's face.

"What's so fucking funny?" I asked.

"This was all Roy."

My heart sank. Had Roy Cooper been involved, after all?

"What was?"

"Your mother held a memorial at her house about two years before she got murdered. One of our classmates had been killed in a car crash. Your mother was close to him, but so was Roy, and your mother had to invite him. Roy, being the prick that he was, brought some old photos and put them in some of your family albums. A few were truly uncalled for. One was of your mother half-clothed. There was one with Roy kissing your mother from when they were dating. The other few were kind of normal. The one you are referring to was of Conrad, me, Roy, Ty, his brother, and your mother."

"And Roy told you that he inserted these photos into our old albums?"

"Yes. It became a running joke among our friends. *Do you think Heather looked through her albums today?* Roy would say shit like that."

"And you probably thought that was funny."

He didn't respond. I was sick to my stomach. I couldn't imagine my mother scrolling through her photo albums and landing on a picture of her and Roy kissing. Or worse, what if my father was with her when she saw those photographs?

"You guys are disgusting," I said. "All of you."

I had nothing more to say to Ethan Drury and walked away.

I CALLED ROY COOPER AS I DROVE BACK TO SANTA BARBARA.

"Hello."

There was no need to beat around the bush.

"This is Bobby McGowan. Did you attend a memorial at my parents' house and leave photos in my mother's albums, including one of you two kissing and one with my mother half-clothed?"

He didn't respond for a few seconds.

"Yes, I did. But you have to understand..."

"Shut the hell up," I said. "You're a disgusting pig."

I hung up the phone.

Fuck Roy Cooper.

My father had been right; I never should have forgiven him in the first place.

ALL OF A SUDDEN, WE WERE A WEEK FROM CHRISTMAS.

Conrad Drury had still not been caught.

People were in the holiday spirit, and no one wanted to talk about him anymore. He hadn't been on the national news in a while, and KEYT only mentioned him in passing.

It's like everyone had forgotten the guy who'd killed my mother was out there, roaming free.

But I hadn't forgotten.

I still had faith.

Somebody would come forward. Some small overlooked piece of evidence would be reexamined, which would end up being the key to finding Conrad.

Something had to happen.

He couldn't just go on evading the police forever.

Could he?

🏵 61 🏵

CONRAD

I t was January 30th, and more than three months had passed since I'd moved to Arkansas.

The weather fucking sucks, but besides that, it couldn't have worked out any better.

I was now a famous serial killer, and law enforcement had no idea where I was.

Santa Barbara, California, to Eagle Pass, Texas, to Jasper, Arkansas, had worked perfectly.

I had no plans on making that public. Still, when I finally do pass away (and my body gets discovered), the people fascinated by serial killers will just have another argument as to why I'm the greatest.

There's never been an escape like this that lasted.

I LOVE DOING DEEP DIVES ON THE INTERNET. THESE SERIAL KILLER lovers are everywhere. Reddit boards. 4chan. Facebook groups.

I've been amused reading all the conspiracy theories of these "amateur sleuths." That's what they call themselves.

They love to guess where I fled to. All these know-it-alls are pretending like they are God's gift to sleuthing.

Mexico still comes up a lot because of where my car was found. I get South America quite a bit. Europe. Asia. Even Antarctica.

You know what hasn't been mentioned even once? Arkansas.

Good for nothing amateur sleuths. You're as bad as the law enforcement I've evaded for decades.

Shit, at least Bobby McGowan got close.

❧

MY "DATE" WITH PEGGY WAS TWO DAYS AWAY.

Of course, she doesn't know about it yet.

I couldn't risk her telling her friends she was going on some date with a mysterious customer she'd met at Safeway.

Instead, I was going to surprise Peggy when she got off work.

That was six a.m. every Sunday, Monday, Tuesday, and Wednesday.

Peggy had been up front in giving me her schedule. We both knew why. She only wanted me to come in on her shifts. I knew she liked me. It even seemed like she'd lost a few pounds. Probably trying to impress me.

❧

I WAS ENTERING NEW TERRITORY.

Planning and executing a murder in a few short months.

Well, maybe just a kidnapping. I wasn't sure exactly what I would do to Peggy once I got her back to my house. Perhaps I'd keep her around for a little while. Hahaha.

I'd built a small, sound-proofed room in the woods near my house. No one would ever find it. I could do what I wanted.

In fact, besides going to Safeway, my lone trip out of the house was to a Home Depot to get wood, acoustic panels, and other supplies to sound-proof a room.

It wasn't quite a work of art, but it would work for what I had planned with Peggy.

❧

SO, WHILE THIS PLAN CAME TOGETHER AT BREAKNECK SPEED, I WAS still being as diligent as possible.

CHAPTER 61

I'd checked the Safeway parking lot the last time I was there. While plenty of cameras were inside, none were facing out on the parking lot.

Arkansas was just different. If this was Santa Barbara or Los Angeles, you could be damn sure they'd have cameras focused on the parking lots.

This was good for me.

I would wear a disguise and put a fake license plate on my truck regardless, but it was still advisable to avoid video cameras when you could.

I HAD A FEELING PEGGY WOULD JOIN ME OF HER OWN ACCORD.

I think she liked the mysterious guy who frequented her Safeway at odd hours.

I imagined her getting in my truck with a big smile on her face.

And if I was wrong, and she wouldn't come willingly, I had a few tricks up my sleeve.

IT WAS TEN P.M., AND I'D DAYDREAMED THE DAY AWAY.

I kept imagining all the things I could do to Peggy with no neighbors to speak of, and a sound-proofed room

I couldn't wait to get her here.

I flipped through the channels, hoping to see if anyone was discussing my case. I found nothing. The case was rarely on the news anymore.

However, *Dateline NBC* was doing a one-hour special a week from Sunday. You could be sure I'd be watching.

AS I WALKED TO THE KITCHEN, A LOUD NOISE WENT OFF.

For a second, I forgot what it was.

It was the trip wire I'd set up!

Who the fuck had set that off?

Panic set in.

Hopefully, it was just an animal.

CONRAD

I walked from the kitchen into the dining room and looked out the window. A man stood in the middle of the gravel road, staring back at me.

And I was almost certain it was Bobby McGowan.

❧ 62 ❧

BOBBY

Everything changed on a cold day in late January.

It was raining like mad outside, and I spent the morning applying for new jobs at my apartment. Yes, I still lived in the same place where a significant crime had occurred. Like father, like son.

I was getting low on cash and needed to find a new job soon.

Technically, I'd accomplished my goal of finding out who had killed my mother. There was not a doubt anymore. The journal that Conrad Drury had left had cleared that all up. Not that I needed that confirmation.

The journal also led to the release from jail of Derek Tice and Dale Collier. Those were gratifying days for Rachel Tatum. I joined her when Tice was released, and he thanked me profusely for my help. I also met Mary Jane Cushing's mother, and she was also extremely thankful.

And yet, despite having accomplished some good, there was unfinished business.

Conrad Drury had killed my mother and eight other women. He'd framed what appeared to be five innocent men. He'd shot Ivy Harrington and had tried to kill me.

And he was still out there somewhere.

I GREW TIRED OF APPLYING FOR NEW JOBS.

They all paled in comparison to my investigations. I set my computer down and vowed to return to job applications in a day or two.

I grabbed the police reports and other information I'd accumulated over the last few months.

Wyatt Trimble had always interested me. It sounded like the one acquaintance of Conrad Drury's whom Conrad treated kindly. I had talked to a few of Wyatt's nurses, and they assured me that Conrad would be there at least once a week to speak with his sick friend.

That continued when Wyatt exited the burn unit and rented a small apartment. The nurses made house calls and still reported seeing Conrad sometimes.

That starkly contradicts the man who said in his journal that he had zero empathy for anyone. Something didn't ring true with this whole Wyatt Trimble friendship.

For the 212th time in the last three months, I Googled someone from the case file. I'd often throw Conrad's name in these searches, hoping there was some cross reference that Google might pick up. I'd struck out every time.

I Googled Wyatt Trimble, something I'd surely done before.

The first link was to a very short obituary of his. It was only two sentences and sounded like it had been written using ChatGPT. I sure hope my obituary sounds like a human wrote it.

I scrolled down that first page. Nothing stood out. Some other Wyatt Trimbles had current Facebook and Instagram accounts and were still among the living. One Wyatt Trimble had just gotten drafted in the 14th round of the recent MLB baseball draft and there were a few articles on him.

I progressed through my Google search's 3rd and 4th pages, and things were getting more random. Less Wyatt Trimble's and more articles about Wyatt Earp and the character Ben Wyatt from the show *Parks and Recreation*. I guess they were the two most famous Wyatt's.

I decided to look at the fifth page of the Google search, and then I'd be done. It was diminishing returns at this point.

The fourth story on the fifth page sparked my interest.

It was a link to houses bought in Arkansas. I saw the name Wyatt Trimble among many others on the link.

After scrolling down to the T's, I clicked it and found what I was looking for.

Wyatt Trimble bought a house in Jasper, Arkansas, in September of

2016. I looked at it closer. There wasn't too much information, but what there was shocked me. It gave the name and the DOB of both the seller and the buyer of the home.

This house was sold by Gilford Moore, born on 11-2-1953. The house was bought by Wyatt Trimble, born on 7-19-1985.

I scrolled through the old police reports until I found a page on Wyatt Trimble.

His DOB was 7-19-1985.

HOLY. FUCKING. SHIT.

Now, was it possible that Wyatt Trimble bought a house in Arkansas in September of 2016?

I guess.

However, according to the police reports and nurses' testimony, Wyatt was in lousy shape in September 2016. He'd lost a lot of weight and was excessively using drugs and drinking.

And then there was the kicker.

Wyatt Trimble killed himself in October of 2016.

Did that sound like someone who would be worried about buying a house? In Arkansas?

Certainly not.

But I did know a guy who wouldn't be above stealing the identity of a "close friend."

I should have told everyone I knew.

I should have shouted it from the highest mountain.

I should have told KEYT I was ready to drop a bombshell on live TV.

But I told no one.

Once again, I had found something that law enforcement had missed.

And I wasn't going to give it to them.

This had become personal between me and Conrad Drury.

He'd killed my mother, and now I wanted to kill him.

BOBBY

I WENT ONLINE AND LOOKED AT FLIGHTS.

The easiest way to get to Jasper, Arkansas, was to fly from Santa Barbara to Dallas and from Dallas to Little Rock. I could rent a car and drive the remaining two hours from there.

I booked my flights and rental car for the following day.

⚜

WAS I BEING A HARD-HEADED IDIOT WHO SHOULD HAVE JUST GONE TO the cops instead of flying to Arkansas in hopes of confronting Conrad Drury?

Yes.

And I didn't fucking care.

⚜

I WOKE UP THE FOLLOWING MORNING AND, WITHOUT TELLING ANYONE, drove to the Santa Barbara airport and started my journey.

The layover in Dallas was less than an hour, and I landed at Little Rock at six p.m. local time. I went to Enterprise and picked up the car I had booked.

I input Jasper, Arkansas, into my GPS, and it said the trip would take two hours and twenty-one minutes.

I left the Little Rock airport, shocked this had come together so quickly.

⚜

I STOPPED AT A SPORTING GOODS STORE TWENTY MILES OUTSIDE OF Little Rock.

I grabbed a shopping cart and put a knife and a pair of handcuffs in it.

I was walking by the gun section.

Surely, a person from out of state couldn't buy a gun this easily?

It was time to find out.

The employee was happy to answer my question.

"Arkansas has no waiting period," he said. "You can buy a gun right here and now."

And so I did.

I bought a Sig Sauer p365 for $400. I'd been to the gun range enough times to know how to handle a gun, but I still asked the employee for a quick lesson on the Sig Sauer. He also sold me an inside-the-waistband holster, saying it was the best way to conceal your firearm.

I ARRIVED IN JASPER AT NINE P.M.

I'd always known it wouldn't go down this first nigh, but I still wanted to get the lay of the land. I drove around Jasper's downtown, which wasn't much. This city had a population of a mere 500, after all.

From the Google Earth searches I'd done, Wyatt Trimble's house was in a heavily wooded area on the outskirts of town.

I wasn't going to risk driving up there at this time.

If it's as rural as it looks, a pair of headlights might bring unwanted attention my way.

THEY HAD NO HOTELS IN JASPER, SO I BOOKED A ROOM AT A HAMPTON Inn in Harrison, twenty miles away.

The hotel was fine, but I had difficulty sleeping that night. It didn't help that I was still formulating a plan.

Conrad Drury had been fastidious in every aspect of his murders, sometimes waiting several years to carry them out.

I was the polar opposite.

I'd flown into Arkansas without any plan of action, flying by the seat of my pants. It was an infantile, simple-minded decision.

And yet, here I was.

And I knew I wasn't going anywhere.

I WOKE UP THE FOLLOWING DAY AND DROVE BACK TO JASPER.

I wore jeans and a long flannel shirt covering the belt and holster I used to hide the gun.

My guess was that Conrad hadn't exactly been a social butterfly since arriving in Jasper. He'd probably want to stay on the down low, considering his face has been plastered all over the television for the last three months.

Still, in a town of 500, it wouldn't be unreasonable to think you might run into someone. So I had the gun on me even though it was nine in the morning and I was walking into a grocery store.

Pru's Country Grocery Store, to be exact.

There was only one employee in the store, a woman in her thirties, and no other customers.

I approached the woman right away.

"Good morning," she said.

"Good morning to you," I replied.

"How can I help you?"

"I've got a friend who lives in town, and I was thinking about surprising him."

"Oh yeah, what's his name?"

"Wyatt Trimble."

"That don't ring a bell, mister."

I tried to remember the name of the man who previously owned it. It would look weird to check my phone to find it.

It came to me.

"He bought a piece of property from Gilford Moore a few years back."

"Can't help you there, either. I don't know everyone, though."

Damn.

"I'll bet Pru does. Prudence, get out here," she yelled. "Pru is short for Prudence."

"Ah, got it," I said.

A woman in her seventies emerged from the back of the store. She was wearing jeans and a flannel, just like yours truly.

"You know a Wyatt Tringle?" the younger woman asked.

"Trimble," I corrected.

"He lives here in Jasper?" Pru asked.

"Yes, he does," I said.

"I don't know him."

"He bought his house from Gilford Moore," I said.

"Oh sure, I know Gilford. Everyone knows Gilford. He moved to Harrison. He always was a big city boy."

Harrison was most assuredly not a big city, but I loved her perceived dichotomy between Jasper and Harrison.

"Do you know the person who lives in his old house?" I asked.

"I've heard of him. People say he keeps to himself. Never comes into town."

"That's too bad," I said. "Looks like you got a great shop here."

Pru smiled.

"I think he only moved in there about two or three months ago. It sat unused for years."

Bingo.

"What's the old Moore place like? My friend Wyatt likes his firearms, and I don't want to give him too big a surprise, if you know what I mean."

Pru laughed.

"I sure as hell know what you mean. Don't you get your ass shot off. A surprise ain't worth that."

I smiled. I liked Pru.

"So, can you tell me what the house is like?" I asked.

"Well, assuming he still has the same house as Gilford, it ain't much to look at. It's like two or three bedrooms. Nothing fancy."

"Does he have neighbors?"

"Yeah. The Duncans. They are an ancient married couple who live in the property next to the old Moore place. And I mean, they are really old, like older than me."

I smiled.

"Are they nice people?"

"Sure they are. But I wouldn't go surprising Dale, either. Dale Duncan knows how to use a firearm himself."

"Thanks. Noted."

"You want some more advice?"

"Sure," I said.

"If you're going to surprise your friend, I'd do it during the day."

"Why is that?"

"Because the house on Gilford's property is a half mile up the road from the Duncans. Your friend would see your headlights coming."

Just as I'd thought.

"Thanks for the advice, Pru."

"And what was your name?"

I feared that they might recognize me if I said my full name. My name had been plastered all over the national news a few too many times for my liking.

So I just said, "Bobby."

"Get yourself a scone while you're here, Bobby. We have the best in town. The best in all of Arkansas, if we're being honest."

"I'll buy two right now. Thank you ladies."

Before Pru turned to go, I thought of something.

"Do you have Giflord Moore's number? I just want to make sure my friend still owns his property."

"Yeah, I got Gilfrod's number."

"Can I get it? You'd be a lifesaver."

She gave it to me.

"Thanks, Pru."

"You take care now, Bobby."

As I bought the two scones, I knew there was something else I might need.

"Do you guys sell flashlights?"

They sure did.

I WENT BACK TO THE HOTEL AND CALLED GILFORD MOORE.

I was able to charm him with bullshit stories I made up about a young Wyatt Trimble and me.

"He sounds like a wild man," Gilford said. "Sure didn't seem that way in person. He was real quiet when we were at the bank finalizing it."

This was what I had been leading to.

"I sure hope I got the right Wyatt. Can I send you a picture and make sure it's him?"

"Sure. I'll call you back. I'm not so good at looking at my pictures while talking on the phone."

"Me neither," I said.

I had saved about ten pictures of Conrad Drury on my phone. Most of them had been shown on the news.

I sent Gilford the one photo I hadn't seen used; it was from one of the police reports. I didn't want him to recognize Conrad Drury.

Gilford called back a minute later.

"I'm pretty damn sure that's the same guy, but his hair was a little longer, and he had his parted in the middle."

That made sense. That's how Wyatt Trimble's hair was on his driver's license and what Conrad was likely trying to resemble.

"Thanks so much," I said.

"Let me know how the surprise goes," Gilford said.

"I will."

It was going to be the surprise of a lifetime.

AS I WAITED FOR THE SUN TO SET, I DECIDED THAT MY FATHER AND sister needed an explanation in case things didn't go as planned.

I wrote in the Notes section of my iPhone, explaining how I'd ended up in Jasper, Arkansas. I gave them the address. And I said if they didn't hear from me the following day, they should call the cops.

I saved the Note. I wasn't going to send it until I descended on Conrad Drury's new home. I didn't want to send it too early and have the Arkansas State Police waiting for me.

WAS I POSITIVE IT WAS GOING TO BE CONRAD DRURY IN THAT HOUSE?

I was almost certain that the answer was yes. I had already been 95% sure when I arrived in Jasper, and then Prudence told me that "Wyatt" had only moved in a few months ago. Then I had Gilford Moore positively ID Conrad.

That had all but confirmed it.

I USED GOOGLE EARTH TO SEE HOW CLOSE THE DUNCAN'S HOUSE WAS to Conrad's.

It was a minimum of a half mile. Looked closer to a mile.

The plan was to park my car a quarter mile from the Duncans and quietly walk by their house on my way to Conrad's.

I was going to leave for Jasper around eleven p.m. Prudence had said the Duncans were an older couple, and I assumed they'd be asleep by then.

I didn't want Dale Duncan firing his gun at me.

AT 11:29 P.M., I ARRIVED BACK IN JASPER.

I parked my car below the Duncan property.

I wore the same jeans I'd worn earlier that day, and my Sig Sauer was still at my side. I was now wearing a dark jacket. The flannel would have been easier to see. I had dark tennis shoes on as well.

I had the handcuffs and the small flashlight in my pockets, but I'd left the knife at the hotel. It was a case of less is more. I didn't want to be lugging too many things around.

I locked the rental car and started walking toward the Duncan property.

I COULDN'T REMEMBER ENCOUNTERING A DARKER NIGHT IN MY LIFE.

I knew it was different in rural areas, without the glow of the city lights. But I'd been to some pretty darn rural locations and never witnessed anything this dark.

I kept walking and passed by the Duncan residence about ten minutes later. All the lights were off, and there was no sign of human life.

A gravel road led up from the Duncans, but I chose to walk on the side of it in a light brush. Gravel could make too much noise.

I continued walking toward Wyatt Trimble's property. Toward Conrad Drury.

After walking for about twenty minutes, I saw a house in the distance.

There was a small light emanating from it.

I DECIDED TO STOP FOR A MINUTE.

It was time to send my father and sister the Note I'd saved. They deserved that.

I cut and pasted it from Notes and pressed send.

I was greeted with a red alert on the message. *'CAN'T BE DELIV-ERED AT THIS TIME.'*

Fuck. I had no cell service out here.

Should I just go back to town and find some local police department? Tell them my whole story and ask them to escort me to the Trimble property tomorrow?

Yes, of course, I should have, but I wasn't going to.

This was now mano y mano. Me vs. Conrad.

I WALKED CLOSER TO THE HOUSE.

The surrounding brush was getting so high that I had to return to the gravel road. I took every step super slowly, knowing a slight slip on gravel could be loud.

It continued to be the darkest night I could remember. The brush was surrounded by trees, which prevented any light from getting in.

The only two light sources were the stars in the sky and the small light emanating from the house ahead.

I was within a quarter mile now.

I kept walking.

The house was coming into view, which meant I might also be coming into view. The trees and brush were just too big and thick to walk in. I was stuck using the road.

Hopefully, my jeans and dark jacket made me invisible in the dark.

I got to within two hundred feet of the house when I almost tripped. I looked down, and there was something sprawled across the road.

I didn't want to use my flashlight, so I felt for what had tripped me. It was a wire.

FUCK!

Had this been a tripwire? Had this alerted Conrad that someone was close?

I looked toward the house, unable to move.

And that's when I got the biggest scare of my life.

A face suddenly appeared in one of the windows of the house.

It was staring right at me.

A shiver went down my spine.

What the fuck should I do?

The Duncans' was a twenty-minute walk. I could enter the brush and trees, but I had no idea where I was going and couldn't see anything.

Oh, God. This was really bad.

BEFORE I KNEW IT, A TRUCK PULLED OUT FROM THE HOUSE. IT quickly got on the gravel road and was traveling right toward me. And fast.

I had no choice. I had to duck in the brush.

The car slowed as it drove by me, and the driver and I made eye contact. There was no longer any doubt. It was Conrad Drury.

I turned around and saw the truck stop about two hundred yards down the road. I knew what Conrad was doing. He was boxing me in, so I had

BOBBY

no escape. I couldn't run to the Duncans now. And he knew there was no cell service up here. It truly was me vs. him.

This hadn't been what I'd envisioned.

The truck lights turned off, and I saw the distant shadow start walking toward me.

I'd only heard Conrad Drury say one thing in his life, and it was right before he attempted to kill me. But I will never forget that voice.

I heard it for the second time in my life.

"I'm so glad you found me, Bobby."

Another shiver went up my spine.

❧ 63 ❧

CONRAD

I knew what I had to do.

I had to corner Bobby. I knew this terrain. I knew this house. He could only escape by running to the Duncans or calling the police.

With no reception, the Duncans were his lone passage of escape, so I had to prevent that.

I ran and got into my truck, and sped down the road.

I slowed down to see who it was. Maybe I'd been wrong; it had just been Dale Duncan lost, but I knew that wasn't the case. I'd seen the shadow of the person standing on the gravel road. It wasn't an eighty-year-old man.

I looked across, and although he was now looking at me from the brush, there was no mistaken who it was.

Bobby McGowan.

The fucker deserved credit for finding me. I had no idea how he'd done it.

When I managed to subdue him, maybe I'd ask him a few questions. If he didn't answer, there was a pair of decrepit old garden shears I wouldn't mind using on him.

I'd been planning on Peggy being my first houseguest.

Instead, Bobby McGowan had crashed the party.

And he was going to pay for it with his life.

❊ 64 ❊

BOBBY

I walked out of the brush and returned to the gravel road.

I couldn't risk doubling back to the Duncans, and I certainly had no chance in the brush and trees. I did have a gun. That was my only chance.

Why hadn't I shot Conrad when he drove by?

My mind was racing, and this was not the time. I told myself to concentrate on the situation at hand. It was the only way I'd ever get out of this alive.

Conrad could have a house phone that worked, and I could call 9-1-1.

I now needed the police, whom I'd so readily avoided.

As I started running toward the house, I heard footsteps on the gravel road behind me.

Conrad was running after me.

❧

WHEN I WAS FIFTY FEET FROM THE HOUSE AND RUNNING AS FAST AS I could, I heard the first gunshot.

I had two choices: Turn around and fire back or get to the house first.

I ran toward the house.

One more gunshot rang out. This one whizzed by me, but I wasn't hit.

I arrived at the house and grabbed at the front door.

338

It wasn't locked.

I walked in, being sure to lock it behind me.

There was still just the lone, dimmed light emanating from a small room to the left of the front door. I walked there, crouched on the ground, and barely let my eyes rise above the windowsill. I had a clear view of the gravel road.

I took the gun out of its holster and waited for Conrad to appear on the road.

It wouldn't be an easy shot, but it wasn't impossible, either.

❧

THREE MINUTES PASSED, AND HE STILL HADN'T COME INTO VIEW.

I didn't know what to do.

He had likely entered the brush and woods and was taking a back entrance to the house. I'd have no chance fighting him out there. I had to stay in the house. And for the time being, I still thought looking at the road was the best course of action.

❧

A MINUTE LATER, I HEARD HIS VOICE.

"You're out of your element, Bobby. This isn't Santa Barbara. There isn't some walk-in closet you can hide in."

It was coming from outside of the house. I think it was from behind me, away from the gravel road. The dimmed light was no longer an advantage. I reached up and turned it off and then got back down to the ground.

"Was a good idea to turn off the light," Conrad yelled. "Only now I know where you are."

Fuck.

I hurried into the next room, continuing to stay low. I couldn't give him a clear shot at me.

He spoke again.

"How did you find me, Bobby? Pretty impressive stuff, I must say. Give me one word, and I'll figure out the rest. Was it the Duncans who ratted me out? Did you somehow find Peggy?"

I knew he was trying to get me to talk. To narrow down where I was in the house. I vowed not to say a word, no matter how personal he got.

Which he did a few seconds later.

"C'mon, tell me how you found me, and I'll tell you your mother's final words. Well, really, they were more of a gargle, but you know what I mean."

I wanted to do more than just kill him. Death wasn't enough for this vile human being.

"And thanks for making me famous," Conrad said. "I've been loving seeing myself on the TV. We're going to be linked forever, you and me. Especially when you meet your inevitable demise here."

I still thought his voice was coming from the back of the house. I slowly, quietly moved in that direction. He thought I was in the front, so I better move. And maybe, just maybe, he'd show himself through one of the windows, and I'd get a clear shot. I didn't want to shoot randomly, or he'd fire back in response. I had to be sure.

"Rachel Tatum must be happy," he said. "Getting those people out of jail."

I entered a new room. It was still really dark, but I thought I saw a bed. There was a window on the other side of the room, so I got on the ground and crawled in that direction. There was a bed and nightstand of some sort. I was in Conrad's bedroom.

"How's your sad old Dad doing?" he said. "He'll probably take his own life after you end up dead. First his wife and then his only son? He won't be able to take it. You're pretty selfish for coming here, Bobby. Maybe you should have thought this through. It shows you care more about yourself than your family. Very, very selfish of you."

I reached the window and raised my eyes above it but saw nothing. There was enough light from the stars where I would have seen a human being.

"Back to your mother," Conrad said. "She was a pretty woman. Did I ever tell you what I did to her before I killed her?"

I knew this was a lie. My mother had not been sexually assaulted, but I was still incensed. I despised Conrad Drury with every fiber of my being.

I desperately wanted to respond but knew I should remain quiet. Unless...

What if I said something and then swiftly darted out of this room? If I did it quickly enough, and he fired at me, I'd know where he was. I could then fire a few shots in that direction.

I didn't want to waste bullets, but I had ten in the clip. I would be willing to lose two or three if it gave me an outside chance of hitting him.

I made my way back to the front of the bedroom so I could run out as soon as I opened my mouth.

I wasn't sure if this was the right plan, but I had to do something. This was Conrad's house, and he knew the layout. The more time that went on, the less chance I had.

I decided to go for it.

"I have nothing to fear," I yelled. "You couldn't even kill two people stuck in a walk-in closet."

As soon as I started talking, I was already on the move. Good thing because bullets rang out in the bedroom. They were coming from outside the house and to the left of the bedroom, so I fired three times in that direction.

I heard a moan or a gasp.

Had I hit him?

Should I fire more shots in that direction?

Was he just setting me up?

A split second later, gunshots were fired into my current room. I ran out as fast as I could.

I was back in the room with a view of the gravel road. There were only three rooms, and I'd been in each. The bedroom with the window. The room I'd just run from, which was some sort of TV room. And the room I currently stood in was some sort of dining room.

"You're a pretty good shot there, Bobby. You got me."

I couldn't believe a word he said, so I just assumed I'd missed him.

"And that line about the walk-in closet? Damn funny stuff, Bobby."

He was still outside but was now on the same side of the house as me.

Do I fire outside?

How many shots?

I had seven bullets left.

The problem was that if I shot and missed, he'd know where I was.

This was like a high-stakes game of poker.

But if your bluff was called, you'd die in a hail of bullets.

"This is like an old-school duel, isn't it, Bobby? But I'm Burr, and you're Hamilton."

His voice was getting closer.

I heard nothing for thirty seconds but felt he was getting close.

Say something!

"It's really a shame you came all this way. You could have remained among the living if you'd stayed in Santa Barbara."

The voice was ever so close.

I thought he was kneeling outside of the room I was currently in.

I might not get a better chance.

Fuck it, I told myself. Life favors the bold.

I leaned down and fired three bullets in the direction of his voice.

I aimed low because he wouldn't risk being visible from the windows.

I heard him scream, so I fired three more shots.

Simultaneously, he was shooting at me.

A bullet tore through my upper chest.

I immediately fell backward onto the ground.

I grabbed my chest and felt blood.

Shit. This wasn't good.

I only had one bullet left if I'd counted correctly.

What should I do?

I heard some noises coming from outside. They weren't words; more like strained attempts to catch a breath.

Had I mortally wounded Conrad? Could I have been so lucky?

One thing I knew, I couldn't sit in this room much longer. I was losing blood, and with no cell service out here, I'd be dead before long.

I reached down to my chest again. The blood was seeping out pretty quickly. It was getting worse.

I had to find out if Conrad had been hit. If he was just faking it and had outthought me, then oh well. I was going to die anyway if I sat in this room much longer.

With great difficulty, I got to my feet. I placed my gun in my left hand and walked toward the window. I looked out, and Conrad was on the ground a few feet from it. It was obvious he was in bad shape.

I quickly ran to his bedroom and turned on the lights.

I grabbed a t-shirt and made a quick tourniquet out of it.

That would only help for so long. I needed to get to a hospital.

I opened the front door and cautiously made my way to the side of the house. Conrad was still on the ground.

His gun was five feet from him. I quickly walked over and kicked it away.

I continued to hold the gun in my left hand. My right side was writhing in pain, and there was no chance I could clutch the weapon. No problem. I was only three feet from Conrad and a regular old Annie Oakley from that distance. Even with my left hand.

I rolled Conrad over so he had to look up at me.

He was breathing, but each one was exaggerated. I knew he didn't have much time.

With all the strength he could muster, he got two sentences out.

"You did it, Bobby. You won our battle."

Blood spurted out of his mouth as he talked.

I remember him mocking me before he attempted to kill me.

Two could play that game.

"Listen, Conrad, I'd love to stay and chat. But I'm going to take your truck and get to the hospital. You see, I've got a long life ahead of me, and you've only got a few seconds left on this earth. You fucking maggot."

I could tell he was trying to say, '*Fuck you*', but he couldn't get it out.

More blood splattered up from his lips.

I stood above him, smiling.

Yes, I needed to get to a hospital, but these were the last few seconds of Conrad Drury's life. I wanted to revel in it, and more importantly, I wanted him to see me struggling.

After smiling at him for a few seconds, I reached down and felt for his keys. They were in his right pants pocket. I took them out and ensured a car key was on it.

There was.

I stood up and looked back down at Conrad Drury.

He was dead.

There was no doubt.

It was hard to describe my feelings in that moment.

It should have been exultation, but it more closely resembled regret.

Not regret that he was dead, obviously, but that he'd ever entered my family's life in the first place.

I turned to go.

Conrad Drury was a thing of the past.

And I should treat him as such.

I MADE MY WAY DOWN THE GRAVEL ROAD AND STARTED UP THE TRUCK.

I called 9-1-1 every fifteen seconds.

Finally, as I got closer to the downtown, it went through.

"9-1-1, what's your emergency?"

"I've been shot. Where is your closest hospital?"

"Are you losing blood?"

"Yes."

"Pull the car over. It's way safer if we come to you."

"Okay."

I pulled the car over. It was good timing because I was starting to get dizzy. I'd lost a lot of blood at this point.

"What's your location?" the dispatcher asked.

I looked up at the street sign. I realized I was a block from Pru's.

"I'm a block down from Pru's," I said.

"Pru's Country Grocery Store?"

"Yes."

"We're sending someone right now. Do all you can to stay awake."

"Okay, I will," I said.

<hr/>

I THINK I WENT IN AND OUT OF CONSCIOUSNESS OVER THE NEXT FEW minutes, but I was awake when the ambulance pulled up next to me.

I couldn't believe it.

I was going to get out of this alive.

❧ 65 ❧

CONRAD

I knew I wasn't going to get out of this alive.

I had raised my gun to shoot at Bobby, who I knew to be in the dining room, but he shot me before I had the chance.

I fell backward but had the strength to fire off a few bullets in his direction. It must have been all adrenaline because I was severely injured.

At the same time, more bullets came in my direction, and I was hit again.

This bullet entered me on the left side of my upper chest. I was pretty sure it had punctured some portion of my heart.

My gun had dropped from my hand and now sat several feet away.

Not that it mattered. I was going to die soon anyway.

Bobby McGowan appeared a short time later.

"You did it. You won our battle," I said, blood spurting out as I talked.

He stood above me, and I hated every second of it. I was supposed to have won. I was supposed to be standing above him.

He had been shot as well, but it looked like he was going to make it. I was not.

He stared at me with disdain. I just wanted to die. I was tired of looking at him.

This wasn't the way I was supposed to go. I wasn't supposed to see his face before I died.

He started talking, and I hated every word of it.

CHAPTER 65

"Listen, Conrad, I'd love to stay and chat. But I'm going to take your truck and get to the hospital. You see, I've got a long life ahead of me, and you've only got a few seconds left on this earth. You fucking maggot."

I tried to say 'Fuck You' back, but all that came out were spurts of blood.

I couldn't even get the last word in. Bobby's were going to be the last ones I ever heard.

I was dead a few seconds later.

✺ 66 ✺

BOBBY

The days that followed were a whirlwind.

I was taken to a hospital that night and underwent a few surgeries. The bullet had hit some bones in the lower shoulder that needed to be corrected.

I didn't wake up until seven p.m.

And by that time, my father and sister were by my bedside.

They were in tears seconds after I opened my eyes.

"What the hell?" I said.

My father tried to speak first, but he was too choked up.

My sister took over.

"You've been under the knife or sleeping for the last eighteen hours. We've actually been here for a while."

"Thanks for coming," I said.

"No, Bobby, it's us who owe you thanks. I've underestimated you from the beginning of your investigation and been rude to you throughout. I was wrong. You did it. You caught Mom's killer."

"Did they find Conrad Drury?"

"Yes, they did."

My father still couldn't talk.

He just leaned over the hospital bed and hugged me.

"How long are they going to keep me?" I asked.

"Only a few days," Jen said. "And then back to Santa Barbara, where there will be some rehabbing."

"Thanks. Is your family here, Jen?"

I was in a dream-like state, but my words didn't sound cluttered.

"The kids had school, and Justin had work, so no. But right before I flew out, I told Aaron and Avery that their uncle was a superhero."

Jen leaned in and hugged me as she broke out in tears.

"Thank you, Bobby. Thank you so much."

"Yes. Thank you, son," my father said, his first words.

A few seconds later, some police appeared by my bedside.

"Hello, Mr. McGowan? Do you feel strong enough to answer some questions?"

I pointed to my father.

"That's Mr. McGowan. I'm Bobby."

My father laughed, tears spilling down his cheek.

"Sure, officers. I can answer some questions," I said.

"We'll be close by, Bobby," Jen said.

She and my father walked away, and I spent the next hour describing what had brought me to Jasper and my one-on-one battle with Conrad Drury.

THE POLICE IN ARKANSAS HANDLED ME WITH KID GLOVES. THEY realized I would be hailed as a hero, and it would be a bad look if they treated me harshly. They seemed in awe at what I'd accomplished.

In return, I was polite and forthright with them.

Their only bone of contention was me not calling the police before I went to Conrad's house. I told them that the next time I found a serial killer, I'd be sure to do that. It got a few laughs and diffused the situation.

The F.B.I. experts were next, and while they were more thorough, they were no less appreciative of what I'd done.

After two days of interviews, they told me I could go home.

I FLEW BACK TO SANTA BARBARA AND STARTED REHAB.

Within a month, I felt like I was almost completely rehabilitated.

I'd get the rare sharp pain in my right shoulder, but I could live with that.

⊗

IVY CAME UP AND VISITED FOR A FEW HOURS.

We called ourselves the '*Bullet Twins*' a good five times. We both got a kick out of that.

She had been fully recovered for a few months and had started working again—this time, in her Los Angeles branch.

She'd moved down there permanently.

We had a pleasant visit, but it was apparent that things weren't the same and probably never would be again. I'd always remember our times fondly, but we were both moving on. That much was obvious.

Her mother was probably thrilled.

⊗

I FACETIMED JEN AND HER FAMILY AT LEAST TWICE A WEEK.

Aaron and Avery loved seeing the scar on my lower shoulder, so I had to show that every time.

I was flying out to see them at the beginning of April. I was hoping the weather would be better by then. I couldn't deal with those East Coast winters.

⊗

MY FATHER HAD SEEMED CHIPPER LATELY.

The burden of his wife's murder would never be gone, but the fact that her killer was now dead hopefully allowed him to move on in his own way.

He said he'd asked Angela out, and she'd said yes.

That was a good sign that he was moving forward.

I was elated.

⊗

I DIDN'T THINK I WOULD BE SINGLE FOR LONG, EITHER.

I met a young lady named Alexis while I was doing rehab. She'd torn her rotator cuff when she got bucked from a horse, and we were at the same rehab center.

She knows who I am now but swears she hadn't seen me on TV when she first approached me at rehab.

I'm calling bullshit.

I TURNED DOWN SEVERAL INTERVIEWS.

All the major networks had reached out; some had offered quite a bit of money. I said no; my sister and father thought I was crazy. I was still unemployed, and they thought I'd lost my marbles, turning down that kind of money.

I'd started this whole investigation to find out who killed my mother. It had never been about money or fame.

I THOUGHT ABOUT CONRAD DRURY FROM TIME TO TIME. HOW COULD I not?

He was a rotten, vile, evil human being, and I'm glad he was no longer of this world.

Another journal had been found at his latest home, and he'd been planning on kidnapping a local woman named Peggy. I was happy to be a part of that never happening.

MY FATHER INVITED ME TO GO TO COSTCO ONE DAY.

It was March 19th and the first day of spring.

He always seemed to get lost in Costco and appreciated me telling him where everything was.

There was a specific frozen pizza that he just loved. I didn't have the gall to tell him it was terrible.

We had just entered the frozen food section when a man around my father's age approached me. He was wearing a suit - which you don't often see at Costco - and some funky, green glasses. His shopping cart was filled with wine and coffee.

"Are you Bobby McGowan?" he asked.

348

"I am," I said.

My father had been facing the freezers but quickly turned around.

"My name is William Ryan. Can I tell you a thirty-second story?"

This was odd.

"Sure," I said.

"I grew up in Los Angeles and raised my family there. We had a huge, extended Irish family. Wait, is McGowan Irish or Scottish?"

"It can be either, but we are Irish."

"So you know about big families."

"Sure," I said, even though our extended family was quite small.

"Well, we'd often have fifty people over for Christmas Eve. We'd rotate among about four families. The people with smaller homes were usually exempt. You need a big place to host fifty people. Okay, I know I'm rambling. Anyway, in 1998, my niece visited our house on Christmas Eve. It was our year to host. She was my brother's daughter. Her name was Annie Ryan, and she was only twelve years old. By the time we'd all eaten our Christmas Ham and opened our presents, Annie was nowhere to be found. And she remains missing to this day."

"That's terrible," I said. "I'm so sorry."

"Thank you. It's been a drain on our family, as I'm sure your mother's death was on yours."

"Yes. It was."

My father still hadn't said a word, but he was intently listening in.

"What exactly did you want from me, Mr. Ryan?" I asked.

"I've been following your family's case for a long time. I moved to Santa Barbara in 2002, so I remember when it happened the following year. And obviously, I've been fascinated by what's happened in recent months with your discovery of Conrad Drury and his eventual demise. So, let me get to the point. I've been very impressed by your investigative skills. I heard about the wall you built in your apartment, how you originally found Drury, and how you found him again in Arkansas. I've probably put ten private investigators on Annie's case over the years, and none showed your excellence. So my offer is this: I will pay you $20,000 for one month's work. I will give you all the details, and then you can go in whatever direction your hunches take you. I will stay out of your way and not be a burden. If you think you're making progress at the end of the one month, I'll renew you for another month at $10,000, and every subsequent month you deem fit. I have enough money for five lifetimes, and if you could ever find out what happened to Annie, it would be the best money I ever spent."

I was floored and didn't know what to say.

It was a lot of money and an intriguing mystery.

But I'd been through a lot over the last five months.

I wasn't sure I was ready.

"So, what do you think?" he asked.

"Can I have a week to think about it?"

"Sure," he said.

He took out a business card and handed it to me.

"I hope to hear from you again, Bobby. Have a good day, gentleman."

And with that, he walked away.

I KNEW WHAT MY FATHER WAS GOING TO SAY BEFORE HE SAID IT.

"If you don't take this case, you've gone batty. You never really loved your previous job anyway, and now you've found something you're good at. And the pay is more than generous."

"If all I cared about were money, I'd have done all those interviews."

"Good thing you didn't," my father said.

"Why is that?"

"Because now you can still go undercover when you are out there looking for Annie Ryan. You might have to change your name, though."

My father was enjoying this. I loved seeing him so happy.

"Oh yeah, what's a good undercover name?"

"You've got to go old school. Think Humphrey or Archibald."

I laughed.

"Hard pass on those two."

"We could go brief and to the point," he said.

"Like what?"

"Ed Lee. Or Ned Sax."

"These aren't any better."

My father laughed.

"Yeah, I guess these do need some work."

I DIDN'T KNOW IF I WOULD TAKE THE CASE OF ANNIE RYAN, BUT I knew I was loving this time with my father.

We were walking up and down the aisles at Costco—something most people would consider tedious.

But I was enjoying every second of it.

"How about Dicky Roundtree?" my father asked.

"I'm not starring in a kung fu movie."

"Okay, what about Peter Parker?"

"That's Spiderman, Dad."

"Oh shit, you're right. Okay, how about Peter Peterson?"

I couldn't help but laugh.

"Why don't we go find that frozen pizza you love so much?"

"Okay, son, let's do that," he said.

We'd only walked a few feet when he stopped me in my tracks.

"I have to tell you something very important."

"What is it?" I asked.

"Your mother would be proud of you," he said.

"Thanks, Dad."

"I mean it. You've turned into a great young man, and she's smiling down on you."

If I didn't change the subject, I might start crying. And Costco wasn't the place.

"So, tell me more about this, Peter Peterson," I said. "Is he a Private Investigator?"

"Yes, but he's not just any old PI. Peter Peterson is the best there is. He wears a fedora, he smokes a pipe, and the dames love him."

"The dames?"

"This is old school, Bobby. That's what they called women back in the day."

"Whatever you say, Dad."

He put his arm on my shoulder as we meandered down an aisle of Costco, looking for some shitty frozen pizza.

Life was good.

THE END!!

Printed in Great Britain
by Amazon

43744530R00209